THE TERRACE

Born in Dublin, Maria Duffy knew from an early age that she loved writing, but she started out her career working at a bank after completing a business course. Maria went on to have four children with husband Paddy and became a stay-at-home mum, but she never stopped writing. When her youngest started school four years ago, she decided to dust off the book she'd once started and once she began to write again, she knew it was what she wanted to do for the rest of her life.

A self-confessed Twitter addict, Maria also writes a blog for *Hello!* online magazine entitled 'Stars in the Twitterverse'.

The Terrace is her second novel.

ALSO BY MARIA DUFFY
Any Dream Will Do

www.mariaduffy.ie

The Terrace

MARIA DUFFY

HACHETTE
BOOKS
IRELAND

First published in 2012 by Hachette Books Ireland
First published in paperback in 2013 by Hachette Books Ireland
Copyright © 2012 Maria Duffy

2

A CIP catalogue record for this title is available from the British Library.

ISBN 978 1 444 72609 1

Typeset in Plantin by Bookends Publishing Services.

Printed and bound in Great Britain by Clays Ltd, St Ives plc.

Hachette Books Ireland policy is to use papers that are natural,
renewable and recyclable products and made from wood grown
in sustainable forests. The logging and manufacturing processes
are expected to conform to the environmental regulations
of the country of origin.

Hachette Books Ireland
8 Castlecourt Centre
Castleknock
Dublin 15, Ireland

A division of Hachette UK Ltd
338 Euston Road
London NW1 3BH

www.hachette.ie

For Mam and Dad, with love

PROLOGUE

Saturday, 10th September

'So, now, let's play lotto. Your jackpot tonight is two million euro, so check your tickets carefully and the very best of luck to you all. The first number out this evening is twenty-nine ... and the second ball is number twenty-two ...'

Maggie grabbed the remote control from the little oak coffee table and pressed pause. 'I'm just going to grab the photocopy of our numbers, Dan. I'm sure we have those two.'

'Wishful thinking, Mags. And two is a long way from six.'

'I know, I know,' Maggie said, rooting in the drawer of the sideboard. 'But I just have a feeling in my waters.'

'You and your waters,' laughed Dan. 'Just hurry up, will you? I'm dying to see this movie.'

Maggie and Dan were enjoying a night in together. They'd just finished off a delicious steak dinner that Maggie had cooked and were now waiting for the Saturday movie to come on.

'Right, here we go,' said Maggie, sitting back down beside her husband and unfolding a sheet of paper. 'Look, look! I told you. We've got those two. Fingers crossed for the next ones.' She pressed play on the Sky remote control.

'… and the third ball in tonight's lotto is number six …'

Maggie paused the telly again. 'For feck's sake,' said Dan, getting a bit irritated. 'Will you let the bloody thing play or I won't get to see all of *The Bourne Supremacy* before I have to collect Steph?'

'But that's three, Dan. When do we ever get three numbers in a row like that? It's good to create a bit of suspense.'

'Here, give me that.' Dan tried to grab the remote control out of her hand but just at that moment, the doorbell rang.

'I'm taking this with me,' laughed Maggie, clutching the remote control as she headed out to see who was at the door.

'Hiya, Maggie,' said Lorraine, as soon as the door was opened. 'Any chance of a few teabags? I forgot to get them in the shop earlier.'

Maggie pulled her friend inside. 'Come on in, quick. Me and Dan are just looking at the lotto draw and we have three of the numbers so far. I have it paused so we can watch the others being pulled out.'

'Ooh, lovely. Is it our syndicate numbers or your own?' Lorraine followed Maggie into the sitting room. 'How's it going, Dan?'

'Howareya, Lorraine. Maggie here has me driven mad watching this bloody lotto thing.'

'Will you shut up,' said Maggie, nudging her husband, good-naturedly. 'Right, c'mon, Lorraine. It's the syndicate numbers I'm looking at, so let's see if our luck is in.' Maggie let the draw continue for the second time.

'… and the forth number this evening is thirty-three …'

'Jesus, that's four! We have four numbers.' It was Lorraine's turn to get excited.

'... followed by number two ...'

'Jesus!' exclaimed the two girls in unison.

'Bloody hell,' Dan said, eventually showing an interest. 'Five numbers? That's got to be worth a bob or two.'

The draw was paused again. This time it was Lorraine.

'Let it play, for God's sake, woman. We're one number from being millionaires!' Dan was on the edge of his seat now.

'Oh, God, let's just imagine what it would be like before our bubble is burst,' said Lorraine, clinging onto the remote control. 'Just think, if we—'

'JUST PLAY THE GOD DAMN DRAW!'

CHAPTER 1

Friday, 26th August

'Jesus, Mary and Holy Saint Joseph,' muttered Maggie, dropping the edge of the net curtain she'd been peeping through as though it was a hot coal. What the hell was she doing having thoughts like that about another man? And a gay one at that!

She'd only intended to sit down for a few minutes to mull over the bloody financial mess she and her husband were in and had been distracted by the hustle and bustle outside. She could barely believe an hour had passed and Dan would be in any minute.

She rushed into her little kitchen, wiping her sweaty palms on her well-worn apron that was pulled tightly over her expanding middle. She busied herself pulling out pots from the large pine drawer and filling the kettle with water. Thank God for Jamie Oliver and his quick and delicious recipes. As she chopped the vegetables for the casserole her husband would devour after a long day's work, she began to relax.

Maggie smiled to herself as she thought of the exciting goings-on in her beloved little street. She felt privileged to belong to such a fantastic community. St Enda's Terrace (or Enda's, as it was affectionately known) was a little cul-de-sac of two-bedroom, terraced houses, nestled just north of the River Liffey, no more than a thirty-minute walk from the city centre. Maggie loved everything about the area. She'd grown up in number one St Enda's Terrace, the youngest of seven children, and had moved Dan in when they'd wed sixteen years ago. Maggie couldn't ever imagine herself living anywhere else. Enda's represented all that was good about community and friendship and she loved being a part of it.

A loud banging on the door startled her, causing her to nick herself with the knife. 'Feck, feck, feck!' Blood dripped onto her carrots. Ah, shite! Sticking the bleeding thumb into her mouth, she went to see who was there.

'Evening, Mags,' said Marco, flashing his whiter than white teeth. 'Got a tin of beans to spare?'

'Jesus, Marco! Didn't you ever hear of doorbells? You frightened the life out of me!'

'Ah sorry about that, Mags. But my toast was in the toaster when I realised I'd no beans. And my stomach thinks my throat is cut!'

'Well come on in and I'll have a look,' Maggie said, still nursing the cut on her finger. But she had to stifle a giggle when she thought of her earlier inappropriate thoughts when she was watching him paint the railings outside. She didn't fancy Marco – far from it. He was more like her little brother. But, come on, the man had beads of sweat running down his gym-made, naked torso – what hot-blooded female wouldn't react to that?

Marco sashayed into the kitchen behind her, filling the hall with his overpowering aftershave. 'Did anyone ever tell you you're a gem? I'm very lucky to have you next door.'

'Ah, go away with you,' blushed Maggie, rooting in a corner cupboard. 'You're looking good this evening. Off out somewhere?' Maggie indicated his floral shirt, unbuttoned half way down his chest.

'Thanks, Mags. But I just had to get out of those filthy clothes. I'm having a quiet one tonight. All that outdoor work is exhausting.'

Maggie smiled to herself. Nobody else she knew would load on the aftershave and dress to impress just to sit at home watching the telly! 'Here we go. But are you telling me that you're only having beans for dinner? A big strapping lad like you?'

'Ah, Mags, sure you know what I'm like,' he smiled. 'I get stuck into a project and lose all track of time.'

'Well why don't you drop in for a bit of casserole instead. I'm making loads and Stephanie is at her friend's house so there's just me and Dan.'

'I, em, I think I just fancy the beans tonight, to be honest,' said Marco, eyeing up the bloodied carrots. 'But thanks all the same for the offer.'

'No problem. But if you change your mind, just pop in.'

That's one of the things Maggie loved about Enda's. You need never be short of a teabag or a bowl of sugar. Her mother, now passed on, had instilled in her the importance of keeping the traditional values of a neighbourhood alive and Maggie had worked hard to ensure that she did just that. Some said she was the glue that held the street together. She'd blush and wave away the suggestion, but she knew that it was true.

A born nurturer, Maggie O'Leary was the Mammy of

Enda's. Although a mere forty-six years old, she was the one who everyone turned to with their problems. Whether a sick child or a flirtatious spouse, a broken nail or a broken heart – Maggie was always on hand with a plaster, a 'there there' and a nice cup of tea.

But Maggie didn't lick her mammyishness from the ground. Agnes McKenna, Lord rest her soul, was exactly the same. Maggie grew up watching her mother be everything to the street and saw how her kindness and generosity helped people in so many ways. Those who knew Agnes would say: 'God, Maggie, you're the spit of your ma' or 'Cut from the same cloth, you two.' And it was true. The pictures displayed on the O'Learys' mantelpiece showed Agnes with the very same red frizzy hair and plump, dimpled face. It was uncanny.

With the dinner simmering in the oven, Maggie made herself a cup of tea and resumed her place in her favourite brown-corduroy armchair by the window in the front room. Although almost six o'clock, there were still a number of people out gardening, painting and cleaning the front of their houses. Maggie never really liked the silver railings that framed every little garden in Enda's and would have loved if they could replace them with white picket fences. But she knew that would never happen, so the rusted railings were all being painted in fresh silver paint to brighten them up. Some of the gardens had been replaced with cobblestones to make room for cars, but the gardens that remained here and there brightened up the street with a burst of colour. In just a couple of weeks' time, Enda's was going to be under the spotlight and each and every one of the residents was going to make sure the street lived up to its good name.

Maggie remembered back to that scorching hot day in June when it had all begun. Given the uncharacteristically high temperatures and lack of customers, the owner of the little bakery where she worked part time had decided to close early. Maggie hadn't needed to be told twice to go. Grabbing her bag from beneath the counter and a box of 'end of day' cakes, she'd raced home to enjoy the last of the evening sun. Not twenty minutes later, she'd been happily sitting on a deck chair in the back garden, a book in one hand and a cup of tea in the other. But she'd barely taken two sips from her tea when she heard the 'coo-eeeeee' from next door.

Feck! Marco certainly knew how to pick his time. He'd asked if he could come in – said he had some exciting news. Before Maggie had time to answer, he was already taking the loose panel of garden fence out and was stepping into her garden. At least she hadn't felt the need to cover up. Her nipples were clearly showing through the hanky-like bikini top she'd been wearing. But Marco was, to all intents and purposes, just one of the girls.

Apparently he'd been on that Twitter thing that everyone seemed to be raving about and had seen a tweet from a production company in New York. Now he'd tried to explain how he'd seen the tweet, how the company had tweeted it and somebody else had retweeted and in turn someone else had retweeted that – but he may as well have been talking Swahili. It wasn't that Maggie was a complete technophobe – in fact she'd even discovered how to stalk her daughter on Facebook – but she'd dipped her toe into Twitter one day with Marco's persuasion and she just hadn't got it at all.

Anyway, back to the exciting tweet from the production company. Apparently, some station in New York was planning to make a documentary about Ireland to air on St Patrick's Day. They wanted to portray Ireland as it's imagined by those Americans who haven't been here.

They didn't want to film the contemporary wine bars and nightclubs – they wanted diddly-idle-die, spit on the floor pubs! They didn't want modern spaghetti junctions – they wanted fields of cows and sheep. But, most importantly, they wanted neighbourhoods that showed the warmth of Irish people – places just like Enda's! Marco had put his beloved street forward for consideration and had been emailing back and forth with the assistant producer. He'd even managed to keep it all to himself, God love him. Usually Marco couldn't keep his mouth shut about anything. But he'd wanted to wait and see what the outcome would be. Lo and behold, they'd loved what they'd been told about Enda's and had decided to come over and do a bit of filming.

Word had spread around the street like wildfire and it hadn't been long before a plan was put into place. Marco had taken charge and had loved the attention. Being a perfectionist in every way, he'd wanted to make sure that the street was looking its very best for the cameras and that everyone would do their bit. He'd set up weekly meetings to chart progress and made sure everyone had access to power hoses to clean up their cobblelock driveways and lawn mowers to keep their grass looking neat. His attention to detail was really starting to pay off now, and Enda's was looking fantastic.

Not for the first time, Maggie wished her mother had been around to see it all. She closed her eyes tight and imagined how Agnes would have delighted in the happenings on the little street and how she'd have rolled up her sleeves and got stuck in with the rest of them. Maggie was doing her bit, of course, but she hadn't been in great form recently and had been happy for Dan to do the bulk of it. Maybe she'd get out and do a bit of painting this evening, if she could muster up the energy.

She remembered how Agnes had been pottering around in the nursing home, tending to the gardens and doing whatever bits and pieces she could, right up until the day she'd died. *If she could do it in her declining state of health*, Maggie thought, *I should be able to help out too. I'm still young and fit.* Right, that was that. She'd let Dan relax after dinner for once and she'd take herself outside and help with the clean-up. She'd make sure the O'Leary house would stand out as being the most looked after house on Enda's.

CHAPTER 2

'I'm home, love. Something smells good.'

Maggie woke with a start and realised she'd dropped off to sleep in the big comfortable chair. She found herself doing that a lot lately. Usually so full of energy, she hated the fact that she was exhausted come six o'clock every evening.

'Hiya, Dan,' she said, jumping up from the chair and wincing from a darting pain in her stomach. She followed her husband into the kitchen. 'How was your day? A long one today, wasn't it?'

'*Very* bloody long. I'm knackered. Where's Steph?'

'She's staying over at Maddie's tonight, since it's the weekend. So it's just you and me for dinner. Go on and get yourself washed – it'll be ready in half an hour.'

'Thanks, love,' he said, kissing her lightly on the forehead. Maggie watched her husband run a hand through his thick black hair as he headed for the stairs and felt sad to see how exhausted he looked. She wished things could be different and that he didn't have to work two jobs.

The bloody loans were crippling them and not for the first

time she cursed the banks that were so willing to hand out mortgages during the Celtic Tiger. Stirring the casserole, she thought back to the time, only a few years ago, when money wasn't really an issue. They were never loaded by any means, but her little bakery business had begun to take in a tidy sum and Dan's job as a forklift driver at Smithfield Markets paid reasonably well too. But then everything seemed to happen at once – an extension was needed to the house when her mam could no longer get up the stairs and then she'd had to let the business go because of mounting debts. Maggie had loved her little business and although the new owner had kept her on as a member of staff, it saddened her not to be her own boss any more.

They'd only been getting their head around that, when her mam's worsening condition had made it impossible for them to care for her at home and they'd had no choice but to put her into a nursing home. And those places certainly didn't come cheap. With the debts mounting up, Dan had been forced to get a second job in a warehouse – it was only part time but Maggie would feel sorry for him on the days where he had to do both jobs. Sometimes, he'd be up and out at 4 a.m. and wouldn't get in until after six in the evening.

But Dan never complained. She loved that about him. He just got on with it and trusted that things would get better. Everybody on the street loved Dan. He was the strong, silent type – the sort of person you could trust with your life. He didn't talk much, not that he ever got much of a chance with Maggie for a wife! She giggled to herself at the thought. The poor man. Honestly, he had such a good sense of humour and could be really funny at times but God love him, he never got a word in when she was around. He'd sometimes start a story when they were in company and he'd barely have the first words out of his mouth when Maggie would take over. 'Oh sorry, love,' she'd say, when she'd realise what she'd done, but he'd just roll his eyes in a mock annoyed gesture and let her carry on.

A sizzling from the overflowing pot on the stove startled Maggie out of her reverie. She didn't often get maudlin but, just every now and again, she wished a bit of luck would come their way. She wasn't looking for anything big – just a bit of a win on the bingo even to ease the pressure – but for now she was going to concentrate on having a nice evening with her husband. It seemed they were never alone these days so she was grateful for Steph's sleepover with her friend.

She had a bit of pastry in the fridge she'd made earlier so she'd whip up an apple tart for them to have afterwards. It was Dan's favourite and he deserved a bit of spoiling. She'd have it rolled out in a jiffy and in the oven while they were having dinner. She glanced over at the fruit bowl before cursing the lone apple that sat amongst the oranges. Feck it! Maybe Lorraine would have some. Her friend wasn't much of a cook so she tended to keep her fruit bowl filled and her cupboards stocked with packets of soup and cans, etc.

Quickly untying her apron and smoothing down her skirt, she swapped her slippers for shoes and headed to the door. With the shower already switched on, she doubted her husband would be able to hear but she shouted up the stairs anyway. 'I'll be back in a minute, Dan. Just popping to Lorraine for something.'

She blinked as her eyes adjusted to the sunlight and realised that it was the first time she'd been outside the door that day. Since she only worked part time in the bakery, she had plenty of time to spend at home. Lorraine lived at number eight so only a few steps away. She had to stifle a giggle as she passed number six. Eddie was out cleaning his driveway and the power from the blast of water was splashing muck up all over him. He looked a picture in his shorts and hiking boots, the whites of his eyes shining through the dirt.

As she headed up to Lorraine's door, she noticed that the paint on the railings looked a little dull. She knew both Barry and Lorraine had been working a lot of overtime lately and so hadn't had much time for tending to the outdoor stuff, but she made a note to gently hint that they might do a bit of touching up.

'Howareya, Lorraine,' smiled Maggie, as her friend opened the door. 'Any chance of a few apples?'

'Come in, Maggie.' Lorraine opened the door wide and headed into the little kitchen.

Maggie closed the door and followed her friend inside. 'Barry not home yet?'

'He should be in any minute now. There you go – help yourself.' She indicated the bowl that was brimming full of fruit, some of which looked as though it had seen better days.

'Ah, thanks. Just two is all I need.' Maggie looked at her friend who was looking a bit subdued. 'Are you okay, Lorraine? Are you not well or something?'

'I'm fine.' Lorraine turned away and busied herself wiping down the kitchen counter, which suggested to Maggie that she was anything *but* fine.

'Right, I've got five minutes before I have to dish up dinner so stick that kettle on.' Maggie pulled up a chair and plonked herself down without waiting for Lorraine to answer.

'Ah Maggie, it's all right really … honestly it's nothing … I don't want to be—'

'Jesus, Lorraine, will you shut up and pour me a cuppa – I'm gasping here.' It wasn't like Lorraine to be so downhearted and Maggie wanted to get to the bottom of it.

Lorraine flicked in the switch of the kettle and avoided Maggie's eye. 'It's just this baby business, Maggie. Barry talks about nothing else these days and it's making me nervous.'

'But I thought you'd come around to the idea of having a baby,' said Maggie, leaning her elbows on the table. 'What are you nervous about?'

'It's everything, Maggie. It's the pregnancy … and the baby … and would he even want a baby with me if I told him about you know what? And before you go off on one, I know I *have* to tell him!'

'Ah, Lorraine, for God's sake. Just tell him and be done with it. Barry is a good guy – I'm sure he'll understand.' Maggie rubbed her temples.

'I'm … I'm sorry, Maggie. It's just … it's just—'

'Ah, Jesus, I'm sorry, Lorraine,' said Maggie, immediately regretting her harshness at the sight of her friend's wobbly lower lip. 'I know I'm being harsh with you, but I really believe you've got to just tell him. You *need* to tell him before he finds out for himself – end of story!'

'I know, I know. It's just that … well … you know who has never put any pressure on me to tell Barry. He's happy with the way things are and he'd never say anything … myself and Barry have only been married for *one* year. Oh, God, what would he think of me if he knew?

'Well he might just surprise you, Lorraine. That man loves you – there's no doubt about that. And love can overcome a lot of things.'

'Maybe you're right,' Lorraine sighed. 'Nothing could be worse than the guilt.'

Thanks be to the Lord God, thought Maggie. 'Good girl.

Well don't leave it too much longer, eh? The sooner the better it's all out in the open – for everybody's sake.'

Barry slipped as quietly as he could back out the front door and walked until he was well out of sight of the nosy neighbours. He stopped to lean on a rusty railing, leaving a brown mark across the shoulder of his good suit jacket. He didn't care. He didn't care about anything anymore.

He never would have seen that one coming. His beloved Lorraine. God, he loved her so much. And he thought she loved him. Tears pricked his eyes and he tried to compose himself so as not to draw attention from passers-by. *How could she? How could she look at another man? It just didn't make sense*.

His head was spinning and he was finding it hard to get his thoughts together. He'd been working extra hours in the Eurospar where he was manager so that they could put some money aside for having a family. They knew having a baby would be an expensive business but they'd made the decision to try. *Bloody hell*.

Lorraine hadn't been too keen on the idea of a baby at first but he'd talked her around. He knew she was just nervous. He couldn't blame her really. It must be hard for a woman who's never been pregnant to think of her body being taken over like that – not to mention what she'd have to go through for the labour! Lorraine had said that she just didn't know if she could handle it. He'd tried to educate himself as much as possible – he'd even bought a pregnancy book so that he could allay some of her fears.

But now he couldn't quite get his head around what was happening. Maggie had said Lorraine needed to tell him and

Lorraine had indicated that there was another man involved. *Shite, shite, shite!* His worst fear was being realised. He'd always felt he wasn't worthy of Lorraine. He thanked God every day that he'd found her, but part of him still felt that he didn't deserve her. She was such a nice person – loving, kind and accepting. She constantly assured him that she loved him and didn't want or need anyone else but now he wasn't so sure.

He needed to think. He blinked away the tears and began to walk again. But he felt beaten. Was this the end for them? Could the fairy tale be over? Was he going to end up back where he was a few years ago – alone and depressed? Should he approach her about what he'd heard or just wait?

As he walked farther up the road towards the River Liffey, his shoulders became less hunched and his strides more purposeful. The shock was turning to anger. How could she betray him like that? How could she make a fool of him and, not only that, talk to the neighbours about it! Well he'd bide his time and wouldn't make any rash decisions. But one thing was for sure, he wasn't going to let himself be treated like a piece of dirt, no matter how much he loved his wife!

CHAPTER 3

Friday, 2nd September

Turning her key in the door, Lorraine prayed that Barry would be at home and dinner started. She was exhausted. Today was probably one of the hottest days of the year and they hadn't got the bloody air-conditioning sorted in the office yet.

Shite! The alarm was still on so he must be delayed again. As far as she knew, Barry was due to be finished today at four and it was already half past six. She put in the code and closed the front door. Throwing her bag over the banister, she fished out her mobile. Maybe he'd left a message to say he was running late. But no, not a peep.

She couldn't quite put her finger on it, but he'd been a bit distant this last week. Usually so upbeat and chatty, he'd been quiet and even a bit snappy with her. She hoped it was nothing other than the usual pressures of a busy life, but there was just something niggling at the back of her mind. Maggie had been going on at her to come clean with him and she'd promised her she would, but now she was feeling even more nervous than ever. How would she broach something like that with him while he was in such a foul mood? No, she'd put it off for another while – at least until this filming thing was over. The last thing she needed was a stand-off between them with a bloody television camera stuck in their faces!

Sighing, she kicked off her shoes in the little hall and headed into the kitchen she hated. The people who owned the house before her had ripped out the old pine units and replaced them with nasty, plastic-looking white ones. She opened the fridge and scanned the contents to see what she could throw together, but nothing appealed to her. Their busy lives meant that they lived on mostly convenience foods but, to be honest, Lorraine wasn't much of a cook even when she did have the time. She'd ring Barry and suggest they get a take-away. Maybe a pizza in front of a good movie might get things back on an even keel with them again. He was probably just tired because of all the overtime he'd been doing lately. Yes, that would be it. They both worked very hard and could probably do with a bit of a break. Maybe she'd even suggest a little holiday – nothing too exotic – just a couple of days down in Galway or something.

She loved Galway – it was one of her favourite places in the world. Before they'd moved to Enda's and took on a mortgage, they'd travelled down a couple of times a year, staying in the same hotel in Eyre Square right in the centre of things. They'd while away the evenings walking around the bustling town, pub hopping and eating in one of the many gorgeous seafood restaurants. During the day, they'd drive to Salthill and take a walk along the beach, no matter what the weather. Yes, they could probably do with a bit of Galway magic to bring a bit of sparkle back into their lives.

She'd have a chat with him when he got home and see what he thought.

Having tried him on the phone a couple of times with no answer, she decided to nip up and have a quick shower and change. She stripped off in the little bedroom they shared and wished, not for the first time, that they had an en-suite. These little houses on Enda's were cosy and homely but she'd give anything to have the money to jazz things up a bit. Barry reckoned that they could probably fit a tiny en-suite where the fitted wardrobes were but, like everything else, it wouldn't come cheap. She wrapped a towel around herself and padded into the bathroom.

Minutes later, she was feeling much less stressed as the warm water sluiced over her long, lean body. Lorraine knew that thousands would kill to have a figure like hers. At five foot ten and a size eight, she was the envy of many, but, in truth, she wished she was a bit curvier. She let her hand wander to her flat stomach and wondered if this month could be the one. She shivered at the thought. She'd agreed to try for a baby with Barry, but it was more for his sake than hers. It's not that she was totally against the idea, but there were just a number of things making her nervous. Barry was five years younger than her but, being thirty-nine herself, she'd sort of felt the time had passed. She'd reckoned that babies wouldn't figure in her life and that was fine by her. But Barry had grown up as an only child and dreamed of a big family. She'd tried to reason with him that at her age, it may not be easy to conceive and, even if they did, it was hardly likely they'd have more than one or two. But Barry just laughed it off, determined that she'd pop one out every year for the next few years. God, even the thought of that made her feel queasy.

Just as she was washing the shampoo from her hair, she

heard a door slam downstairs. *Good, he was home at last.* She hoped he might come up and join her in the shower – it's amazing how imaginative he'd become over the past few months when he had a mission on his mind. That was definitely the plus side of trying for a baby! And she was mid-cycle, too, so if he wanted babies, now was the time to do something about it!

'Hiya, love,' she shouted, opening the shower door a fraction so that he'd hear her. 'I'm up here in the shower.'

'Oh, right so,' came his reply. 'When you're finished, I'll hop in myself. Any dinner going?'

Well that wasn't exactly the response she'd expected. He usually wouldn't pass up on an opportunity like that. 'I thought we'd just order in some pizza. I'm not long in myself.'

'That's fine by me. I'll probably head down to the pub with Rob after, if that's okay with you. Things aren't going too well in the job for him at the moment and he needs a few pints to cheer him up.'

Lorraine sighed. So much for a romantic night in!

Stepping out of the shower and wrapping a towel around her wet body, she headed back into the bedroom. She sat down heavily on the bed and listened to her husband come up the stairs and switch the shower back on. He hadn't even come into the bedroom to strip off!

Maybe she was just letting her imagination run off on her. Maybe there was nothing to worry about. It was probably all this talk about coming clean that had her reading far too much into things. They were happy really, weren't they? Sure, they wouldn't be talking about starting a family if they weren't.

The past four years with Barry had been the happiest of Lorraine's life. She'd been independent from a very early age, getting a job in a city centre insurance company at the age of twenty and moving into her own bedsit just a few years later. She'd never really had much luck in love, flitting about from relationship to relationship – that is until she met Barry. She'd never believed in love at first sight and certainly never expected it to happen to her, but from the first moment she'd spotted him in The Duke pub, laughing with his mates, his unruly blond hair falling in curly tufts over his eyes, she'd known she was destined to be with him.

She'd felt his eyes fixed on her from the moment she'd walked into the pub. She was with a group of girls, having a few drinks before hitting the clubs on Leeson Street. She'd just broken up with a guy and her friends had been trying to cheer her up.

'Can I buy you a drink?' he'd asked, his grey eyes twinkling, oblivious to the nudging going on around them.

Lorraine had been sold on those eyes and had excused herself from her group to go and have a drink and chat with him at the bar. She'd never before felt the way she did that night. She'd been physically attracted to him, but it was more than that. He was funny and engaging and she'd felt the urge to tell him her life story. They'd just clicked and although she continued on to the clubs with her friends, she'd made sure he had her number written on his arm where he wouldn't lose it. They'd gone out together the very next night and had never looked back.

'Right, have you ordered yet or do you want me to do it?'

Lorraine jumped as Barry came into the room and she was struck by his handsomeness again. With just a small towel covering his bits and his wet hair sending drips of water down his long, lean body, she just wanted him to scoop her up and make love to her.

'Not yet,' she replied. 'I could wait another while before I eat – how about we build up an appetite?' She stood up and slowly began to peel the towel from her body – firstly exposing a hard, dark nipple and then quickly covering it up again. Barry loved it when she teased him.

'Well it's gone half seven, and I said I'd meet Rob at half eight. If we order now it'll just give me time to get ready before it comes.' He didn't even look at her as he slipped a pair of boxers on under his towel and used the towel to dry off his hair.

Lorraine's eyes stung with tears as she quickly pulled the towel back up around her body. But she didn't want to let Barry see she was upset. She hated confrontation and didn't want to start an argument. 'Right, do you want to share a pepperoni?'

'Yep, sounds good. I'll be down in a few minutes.'

Not even bothering to get dressed, Lorraine threw on her old towelling robe, her mousy blonde hair dripping down her back, and hurried downstairs. Why wouldn't he talk to her? Their relationship was built on trust and honesty – well except for the one thing that she was keeping from him and she was going to put that right very soon. She picked up the phone and dialled the number for Dominos – although she'd lost her appetite now.

Ten minutes later, Barry was downstairs, looking delicious in a pair of faded jeans and a white T-shirt. 'Pizza not here yet?' He seemed to be still avoiding her eye.

'It should be here in the next few minutes … Barry …'

He glanced at her and then quickly turned his eyes away. 'You're still all right with me going out, aren't you, Lori? I won't be late.'

'Yes, of course … it's just that … it's just …'

'What is it, love?' He came over to her and put his arms around her and it was all she could do not to burst into tears with relief. 'Is there something you want to tell me?'

'It's nothing, Barry. Just ... just tell Rob I was asking for him.' With his arms around her, everything seemed all right.

'Right, will do,' he said, pulling away from her. Was it her imagination or did he stiffen again?

'Here's the pizza now,' Lorraine said, rushing out to the hall to open the door. 'Why don't you open a bottle of wine and we'll take it into the sitting room.'

'Better not,' said Barry, taking the box off Lorraine and opening it on the kitchen table. 'I'll just grab a few slices and eat them on the way.'

'Oh! I thought we were going to sit down together for a bit. I feel we've been ships in the night these past couple of weeks.'

'Sorry, love. I don't want to leave Rob waiting.' He paused for a minute at the kitchen door and his voice softened. 'But maybe we should do something tomorrow night – maybe get a DVD and we can open some wine then. What do you think?'

God, it was like an emotional roller-coaster. 'Yes, that'd be lovely, Bar. I'll look forward to that.'

He ducked briefly back in to place a soft kiss on her lips before heading out the front door without a backward glance.

'Hiya, Sis,' said Marco, holding open the door for Lorraine to come in. 'So what can I do for you? Teabags? Milk? Biscuits?'

'I don't want to borrow anything, Marco. I just want a chat. I swear, if I don't talk to somebody, I'll go mad!' No sooner had Barry disappeared out the door than Lorraine had decided to go and pay Marco a visit. There were definitely benefits in having your family close by.

'God, what's up with you? You're looking very stressed.' He followed Lorraine into the little kitchen and pulled out two stools from under his ultra modern breakfast bar.

'It's ... it's Barry. Oh, Marco, I think we're in trouble.'

Marco grabbed a box of tissues from a shelf and quickly pulled out a handful. 'Jesus, Lori. What's happened? I thought you two were rock solid. You were only talking about planning for a baby the other day.'

'I know, I know,' sobbed Lorraine. 'I thought so too but ... but ... I can just feel there's something wrong. He's distant and moody this last week and I'm really worried.'

'Ah, for feck's sake, is that all? Sure it could be anything. You're such a bloody drama queen.'

'No, that's not all.' She stopped to blow her nose. 'He even ... he even, em, knocked me back tonight.'

'Knocked you back? For what?'

'In the bedroom, Marco! Keep up, will you?'

'Christ, Lorraine! I don't want to know – that's far too much information!'

'Well you did ask,' Lorraine sniffed. 'But have you spoken to him in the past week? Has he said anything to you?'

'I've only just passed a few words with him out on the street. He seemed fine to me. What do you think is wrong?'

'I honestly don't know, Marco. But as far as I can see, there are only two things that it could be – if it was anything else, he'd talk to me, I know he would.'

'Well, spill,' said Marco, chin in hands, leaning his two elbows on the kitchen counter.

'The first and most obvious thing is that he has another woman.' She left it for a moment to sink in with Marco and when he didn't respond, she continued. 'But I honestly don't think it's that. Sure when would he get the time? He's been working all the hours God sends and he's with me the rest of the time.'

'Right, and the other thing?' Marco loved a bit of gossip but hadn't got much patience.

'The other thing is that maybe he's gone back to his old ways. Oh God, Marco, what if he's gambling again. I couldn't bear it. It's the only thing I can think of that he might be afraid to tell me. He wouldn't even meet my eye earlier.'

'But he hasn't gambled at all since you two have been together, has he? I thought that was all behind him.'

'No, he's never gone back to it as far as I know, but you know what they say, once an addict, always an addict. Maybe he's just got sucked back in to it again.'

'Lorraine! Listen to yourself, will you! You need to talk to him about it. You could be worried over nothing but if your suspicions are true, the sooner he's confronted the better. Get it knocked on the head now, before it's too late.'

'You're right. And maybe I'm worrying over nothing. I'll have a chat with him tomorrow and see if I can get to the bottom of it.'

'Good girl. Now, are we having wine or are you just over here for a moan?'

'Oh, definitely wine,' smiled Lorraine. 'I'll just nip back down to the house and grab a bottle. I picked up a bag of those sea salt and black pepper snacks you like in Marks & Spencers at the weekend so I'll grab those too. Wine and nibbles are exactly what's called for!'

Walking the few steps back to her house, Lorraine's mind wandered to what Barry had told her about his gambling days. It had started in his early twenties when he'd been living at home with his parents. He'd started putting the odd bet on the horses, not much at first, but he'd quickly become sucked in to the whole scene and it wasn't long before he was losing his whole week's wages. His money would be paid into his account on a Friday and, by Saturday morning, it would be in the bookies' till. This had gone on for a few years until he'd really hit rock bottom. He'd found himself forging his father's signature on a bank withdrawal slip to take money from his account. Luckily, he'd copped on to himself in time and hadn't gone through with it.

He'd become depressed after that and had sunk to an all-time low, continuing to gamble away his wages. His elderly parents weren't aware of any of it; they'd just been delighted to have their only child still living at home.

It was only one day when he'd been watching one of these Jeremy Kyle-type shows on telly and saw a man who had a story similar to his that he'd begun to look at himself. It had given him a glimpse of what he could be in ten years' time if he didn't cop on and try to turn his life around. That had been the turning point for him. He'd moved out of home and into a flat with a few other lads. He'd got himself a new job in Dublin and forced himself to go to Gamblers Anonymous meetings. When Lorraine had met him, his gambling days were far behind him and he'd never looked back since.

God, she needed to shake herself out of this maudlin mood. A few drinks with Marco would cheer her up – and maybe she'd call in to Maggie, too, and bring her down to make a night of it. She thanked her lucky stars for the day that Maggie and Marco had persuaded her to buy a house in Enda's. Having grown up in Enda's, she never thought she'd find herself back there, but Maggie had rung her all excited one day to say there was a house for sale on the road.

She and Barry had been looking for somewhere to buy at a reasonable price and it just seemed to fit the bill.

Barry was easygoing and had said that he didn't care where they lived, as long as they were together, so the deal had been done, much to Maggie and Marco's excitement. It had been weird at first, living just ten doors away from the house she'd grown up in, but it was worth it to have her friends and Marco around her.

She was probably getting her knickers in a twist over nothing. She'd have a chat with Barry tomorrow and see if she could get to the bottom of what was bothering him. And when this blasted filming thing was over, she'd just have to do as Maggie said and talk to him about the more serious issue. She wasn't looking forward to that but, under the circumstances, it just had to be done.

CHAPTER 4

'Bloody hell, is that the time?' Maggie said, scrunching up her eyes to see her watch. 'Where has the night gone? And I told Dan I'd be back in twenty minutes.'

'On a promise then, Maggie,' giggled Lorraine, draining the last of her wine. 'Lucky you! Where did you get him from at all? He's definitely a keeper!'

Marco rolled his eyes. 'Come on – time you were off too, lady. I think you've had more than enough for one night!'

'Ah, but sure itsh only early yet,' Lorraine slurred, trying to squeeze another drop of red out of an empty bottle.

Maggie pulled herself up off the slouchy sofa in Marco's sitting room. 'I'll walk you down to yours, Lorraine. It's about time we let Marco go to bed.'

Marco offered up a silent prayer of thanks. He loved them both dearly, but he'd hoped to have an early night tonight and catch up with some of his friends on Twitter. Still, he'd enjoyed a good old natter with the girls – Maggie was always great with the bit of gossip.

'Marco, darling, it's been lovely,' said Lorraine, standing up unsteadily and air-kissing him. 'We should do this again soon.'

'Jesus, what are you like?' said Maggie, laughing at the theatrics of her friend. 'Come on and I'll get you home before you burst into song. Thanks for tonight, Marco. It was just the pick-me-up I needed.'

'No problem, Maggie. But why do you need a pick-me-up? Is there something up?'

'Ah no, nothing's wrong. Maybe I should have said 'perk-me-up'! I'm just a bit tired, that's all. Nothing a holiday couldn't fix!'

'Well I'm glad you enjoyed yourself. I enjoyed the natter too. But you'd better go and catch her and make sure she finds the right house!' He indicated to Lorraine who was already out the door and looking unsure about which way to turn.

'Ha! Well at least she's in better spirits now. Although I suspect she'll regret it in the morning when she has a woodpecker knocking at her brain!'

'Oh, the evil drink,' laughed Marco, waving the two girls off before shutting the door and breathing a sigh of relief!

'For God's sake, Mimi, will you hurry up,' shouted Marco from the back door. 'How many blades of grass do you have to sniff before you decide which ones are worthy of your bodily fluids?' Honestly, sometimes dogs were more trouble than they were worth! But Marco knew he'd never trade his little black cockapoo for the world. He loved her from the moment he'd set eyes on her just over a year ago and she'd become his best friend.

'Oh, so finished now, are we?' Mimi wiped her paws triumphantly in the grass before running back inside to the warmth of the house. 'And can we have a lie-in in the morning please? It's been a busy week and a long night and I don't fancy having to get up to let you out at an ungodly hour again.'

Marco yawned as he checked the locks on all the doors and set the alarm. What a funny old evening it had been. Honestly, it seemed like an age since he'd woken up that morning. Thank God tomorrow was Saturday and he could at least stay in bed for a while. He knew he still had some painting to do out front, but he could do that in his own time.

He felt a bubble of excitement growing as he thought about the imminent arrival of the film crew from New York. Imagine, his little street being featured in a television programme in the States. He'd have to tell all his relations to watch. Two of his dad's brothers lived over in New York with their families so they'd probably tune in. They said they'd record it on a disc for him too since it wouldn't be broadcast over here, so he'd be able to send that on to his parents in Spain. Maybe he'd even throw a party here one night so he could show the programme to all his friends. Oh, he'd be a celebrity for sure!

With Mimi tucked under his right arm, he grabbed his laptop from the sitting room and headed up the stairs. His head was so filled with stuff, there was no way he'd be able to sleep, so he'd have a gander at his emails and Twitter instead.

Ten minutes later, he was propped up on his John Rocha raspberry silk-covered pillow with Mimi snoring softly at his feet. Marco was very house-proud and never in a million years would have imagined he'd have a dog sleep on his bed. But Mimi was different. She was just so human-like that it seemed cruel to stick her in a basket on the floor. And, besides, he washed her at least twice a week and used some of that lovely scented doggie powder on her. He could almost see the other dogs' eyes light up when he'd take her to the Phoenix Park for a runaround at the weekends.

Switching on his computer, he cursed his financial situation that meant he couldn't afford a new one. This one was ancient and took forever to warm up. While he was waiting for a sign of life from the screen, he thought about Lorraine and Barry. He was surprised by how upset she'd seemed earlier and more than a little worried that she might be right about the gambling thing. It did sound as though he was hiding something and, for Lorraine's sake, Marco hoped to God it wasn't that.

At twenty-four, Marco was a whole lot younger than Lorraine, but felt very protective towards her. They were lucky that they got on so well and Marco had been more than happy when she'd married Barry the previous year. He was a good, decent man and, most importantly, he made Lorraine happy. She'd only just confided in him that they were trying for a baby and Marco couldn't be happier for them. So this latest development was a bolt from the blue, but hopefully they'd sort it out.

At last, the screen sprung to life and Marco stuck in his Twitter details. He was hoping Claude might be online. Claude was an assistant producer with the production company, Regal International Productions, and was the one who'd answered his email when he first made contact with them. It turned out that Claude was Irish and had been working for RIP over in New York for the past three years. They'd hit it off straight away and had connected on Facebook and Twitter so that they could chat more often.

Maggie had been fascinated at the fact that Marco knew Claude was gay without him saying anything. 'But *how* do you know?' she'd asked only the previous week when Marco was gushing about Claude. 'Did he actually *tell* you he was gay?'

Marco had laughed and told her that he just knew. Maggie had rolled her eyes and eventually given up.

@Marcofashion1: Are you there @ClaudeRIP? Just thought I'd say hello before I go asleep.

@ClaudeRIP: Hiya, Marco. Yes, I've only just popped in for a minute myself. How are you?

@Marcofashion1: I'm great, thanks. Can't believe you'll be over here so soon. I'm counting down the days.

@ClaudeRIP: I know, I can't wait. And I'll be there for ten whole days too!

@Marcofashion1: How long do you think it will take to film what you need on the street?

@ClaudeRIP: We'll probably do most of it in a day or so but we have other places to film too. But hopefully I'll have a couple of days free.

@Marcofashion1: And the nights! I'll show you all the best places here in Dublin.

@ClaudeRIP: You seem to forget I'm a Dubliner myself! But I'd love to see where you hang out. I'll be staying with my parents just off the Navan Road so I'll just be a stone's throw away.

@Marcofashion1: It's a deal! And I can't wait for you to see our little street. You'll love it – and all the people in it.

@ClaudeRIP: I'm sure I will. It sounds so different from where I grew up. We never really talked to our neighbours

unless they were complaining about balls going over the wall into their garden!

@Marcofashion1: Ha! Well nobody complains here – we're like one big happy family.

@ClaudeRIP: Right, I'm off to bed. Only ten more sleeps! Can't wait to see you. Night. x

Marco snapped his laptop shut and closed his eyes. Was it possible he was falling a teeny weeny bit in love with Claude? It seemed ridiculous since they'd never even met, but he was all Marco could think about these days.

At first, their emails had been quite official, only talking about St Enda's and the possibility of the production company using the street for their documentary. Then after a couple of weeks, Claude had asked for Marco's phone number, saying he needed to ring him about something. And that was that! After they'd chatted to each other on the phone, Marco was hooked. He didn't know what it was about Claude that excited him so much but he'd never felt like this before. Sure, he'd dated men – quite a few actually – but he'd never been in love before.

Oh, Jesus, he'd want to cop on to himself, thinking about love! Maybe it was because he hadn't had a boyfriend in a while and was latching on to anyone who showed a bit of potential. But he knew it was more than that. For whatever reason, Claude had got under his skin, and his arrival at St Enda's couldn't come quickly enough!

'Bloody hell, Mimi! Give it a rest, would you?' Marco rubbed his eyes and glanced at the bedside clock. *Six o'bloody clock!*

That damn dog must have an alarm in its brain set for six. It's the same every morning – six on the button and she's barking her little brains out. 'Right, I'm coming, I'm coming!'

Pulling on his paisley-patterned satin robe, he followed Mimi downstairs and disabled the alarm. He opened the back door to allow her to run out and do her business. He felt knackered but found it hard to go back to bed these bright mornings. He flicked in the switch of the kettle to make himself a cup of tea to bring it back up with him. Maybe he'd finish reading the latest Marian Keyes novel Maggie had given him for his birthday last month. He loved Marian Keyes – both she and Cathy Kelly were his favourite authors.

Marco never felt the need to be manly and pretend he was something that he wasn't. From about the age of thirteen, he'd known he was gay. His mam and dad said they'd always known and so had his sisters, so it hadn't come as a shock to any of them. He was never in the position of having to make an announcement or battle with himself over it. He was just gay – he knew it and so did everyone else – and it had sat comfortably with him from the very beginning. His family had all been amazing with their support, particularly Lorraine, who he'd always been close to. He was most definitely one of the lucky ones.

The kettle boiled and he poured the water into the cup just as Mimi bounded back into the house, tail wagging furiously and tongue hanging out. 'Looks like you're in need of a cuppa yourself, sweetie. But let's stick to water for now, eh?' He filled her bowl from the tap and she lapped it up gratefully before tearing up the stairs to no doubt get back to her spot on the bed while it was still warm.

Marco didn't bother setting the alarm this time, knowing

he wouldn't go back to sleep. Back up in his room, he made himself comfortable once again and settled down for a read. But his mind wouldn't let him get stuck into the book. Maybe he should think about offering to work today. His boss had offered to let him do overtime this weekend but he'd refused because of all the work that had to be done on the street. But, to be honest, he really needed the money.

All in all, Marco was happy with his life. He couldn't wish for a better family or friends, he loved where he lived and had a good job working in a boutique that sold exclusively from up-and-coming Irish designers. But it bothered him that he never had any money. Between loans and bills, his salary disappeared each month as quickly as it appeared. Maybe if he wasn't putting himself through college at night he'd have a lot more to spare, but he was determined to make it as a designer and he needed the qualification if he was to get anywhere.

He was very lucky that, despite his lack of funds, he had a wardrobe full of designer gear. The staff got a clothing allowance as they were expected to wear some of the stuff they sold as an advertisement and, on top of that, they could buy stuff at a fraction of the selling price. That said, he hated not to be able to afford to go on holidays, own a car or even to shop in somewhere other than Lidl or Aldi!

He took his last gulp of tea and realised his eyes were growing heavy again. Maybe he would be able to sleep for another hour or two after all. He'd ring his boss at around nine and offer to do a few hours in the afternoon. And his left hand had been so itchy for the past couple of days so maybe, with a bit of luck, he'd have a win on the bingo on Thursday. Fingers crossed. Even a couple of hundred would do. It had been a while since any of them had a win. The last one had been Maggie about six months ago and that was only seventy-five euro. Yes, definitely due a win. With that lovely thought he closed his eyes and joined Mimi in the land of Nod!

CHAPTER 5

Monday, 5th September

'That was brilliant,' said Lorraine, as the titles rolled on *It's a Wonderful Life*. 'You really can't beat the old ones, can you?'

Barry stretched his long, gangly limbs and yawned. 'They really don't make them like that any more. James Stewart could blow all those modern-day actors out of the water.'

'That's for sure.' Lorraine stood up and began picking up the dirty plates and glasses from the floor. 'Let's keep it on Sky+ and we can watch it again another day.'

'Right, good idea,' said Barry, standing up himself. 'I'm done in though and the thought of the early shift tomorrow is killing me. Do you want a hand with that before I go up?'

'No, you're grand. I'm just going to dump everything in the dishwasher and I'll follow you up. You can warm up my side of the bed!' Her heart soared as she watched her husband head upstairs and a wave of relief washed over her. Hopefully things were getting back on track again.

She did a quick tidy around and followed Barry upstairs.

She could hear him brushing his teeth in the little bathroom and a wave of anticipation rose inside her. Barry was a fantastic lover and she needed to be loved tonight. She'd come home from work a bit early and had showered in her Marc Jacobs shower gel. Barry loved the smell of that. She'd even dug deep in her underwear drawer and brought out a Victoria's Secret internet purchase that she'd never worn – a mauve silk camisole and panties set. That was sure to set his heart racing.

Teeth brushed and an extra spray of Marc Jacobs Daisies on her hair and neck, and she was slipping under the duvet and spooning herself into Barry. She nuzzled into his silky hair that curled in little tufts at the back of his neck. He was breathing heavily but she knew he wasn't asleep. She began to run a hand down his torso, with slow purposeful movements, just stopping at the top of his boxers and slipping a teasing finger inside.

This is where Barry would usually turn around, not being able to contain himself a moment longer. Usually. She could feel him stirring but he still made no attempt to turn to her. She wrapped one of her long, smooth legs around his thighs while thrusting her silken-clad body against his. Still nothing from him.

'Barry?' She was close to tears.

He turned around slowly and draped his arm around her, pulling her in close to him. But he didn't look her in the eye, or kiss her on the lips, as he usually would. Skilfully removing both his own and her underwear, he was inside her in seconds. It lasted for no more than a minute – a minute of confusion for Lorraine, a minute of wondering if she'd ever see the old Barry again. He'd been cold – not nasty or rough – just cold.

Blinking away the tears, she looked at her husband's beautiful face. He had chiselled features any model would be proud of. Fast asleep now and quietly snoring, she saw the man who had taken her breath away that first time she'd seen him. His skin was soft and peachy, which wasn't very masculine, but it was a beautiful frame for his exquisite blue eyes and plump lips.

She sighed heavily as she reached down to retrieve her underwear from the bottom of the bed. Barry didn't have a bad bone in his body and she knew he wouldn't be intentionally trying to hurt her but, whatever the reason, he was putting up a barrier between them. But she wasn't about to give up on him or their relationship. She loved him too much for that. One thing was for sure, she never wanted to feel as alone and unloved as she did at that minute.

Barry willed sleep to come but he had too many thoughts running around in his head. God, he was behaving like a right bastard. But he just couldn't help himself. He was aware of Lorraine softly crying beside him but he just couldn't bring himself to comfort her. They'd had a lovely evening and he'd almost managed to forget the reason he was so angry. But when she'd come to bed and wrapped her arms around him, he'd pictured her doing the same to somebody else. Who else had seen her in that silky underwear? Who else had felt her tongue teasing the nape of his neck?

He hadn't been able to resist her advances and now he felt like a disgusting human being. It was the first time he'd made love to her just for pure sex. They were so much more than that. Even at times when he'd feel frantic and about to burst, he'd always at the very least hold her afterwards. These unspoken words between them were turning him into some sort of monster and he didn't like it one bit.

Lorraine was now breathing heavily so she must have dropped off. Thank God for that. He'd make it up to her over the next few days by being less angry. But he couldn't forget what he'd overheard, much as he'd love to. He'd bide his time for the moment and have a good hard think about how he was going to deal with the whole sorry situation.

CHAPTER 6

Thursday, 8th September

'Those beautiful legs, eleven … four and five, forty-five … two fat ladies, Mary and Kate, eighty-eight … have more wine, number nine …'

'Jesus, I'm waiting on one,' whispered Marco, sending a ripple down the row of bingo-goers.

'Clickity-click, sixty-six … the cock and hen, number ten …'

'For feck's sake, call all the fives! I'm weeing myself here.'

'All the fours, forty-four …'

'Shit!'

'Still early days, Marco,' said Maggie, paying more attention to Marco's card than her own. She didn't have a hope of winning this one. The marks were dreadful tonight. She knew she should have waited until most of the queue was gone before buying her book. She had a theory that the winning books were the last ones sold.

'Top of the house, ninety … all the fives, fif—'

'CHECK!' Not content to shout it at the top of his voice, Marco jumped up, swinging his winning card in the air. 'Whoohoo! About bloody time I won something!'

'And we have a winner,' announced the bingo caller. 'Anyone else or is it just one check?'

'Jesus, Marco, you're a jammy cow,' muttered Lorraine. 'There've been two or three in on the winnings all night but looks like you've got this one on your own!'

'And the gentleman receives three hundred euro,' continued the bingo caller, causing a cheer amongst the Enda's girls. 'And now to our last game of the night. Eyes down ... the duke-box jive, number five ...'

Maggie went into autopilot to mark the numbers on the last page. Honestly, she sometimes thought she could have a little nap and still mark the right ones. Week after week of coming here with very little to show for it – it had become a Thursday night ritual on Enda's. The girls, and Marco, would catch the bingo bus from the end of their street and it would bring them to St Finbarr's Hall on the North Circular Road.

Her mother before her had gone religiously every single week and as soon as Maggie had been old enough, she'd gone along too. As the older generation of Enda's had fizzled out, Maggie had dragged a few of the young ones along and, very soon, they'd started a whole new generation of bingo-goers!

Although the few bob was nice, and she was absolutely delighted for Marco, the money wasn't the be all and end all of the bingo! To Maggie, it was much more than that. It was the one night of the week that the friends and neighbours of Enda's got together. It was to all intents and purposes like a social club. They'd spend the ten-minute bus journey gossiping on the way there and giving out about the lack of decent marks on the way back. It was an institution – a good honest night out with plenty of laughs and very often a few drinks afterwards.

She'd hoped by now that, at fourteen, Steph would have shown an interest in coming along. Of course she wouldn't be allowed mark a book until she was eighteen because of the gambling laws, but Maggie had gone along with her own mother to watch from the age of twelve. But Steph thought the bingo was 'naff' and she 'wouldn't be caught dead in a place like that'. Maggie sighed as she thought about her daughter and how challenging she'd become since she'd hit her teens. It was nothing serious like drinking or drugs, just the usual teenage attitude and the firm belief she had that the whole world was against her.

'Are you with us, Maggie?' Lorraine said, startling her. 'C'mon, would you? Fergus will be moaning again if we don't get out quick smart.' Fergus was the bus driver who brought them to and from the bingo and he was a right old grump. It annoyed Maggie that he was so hostile towards them; they were keeping him in a job after all.

At the door of the hall, they were hit by a deluge of smoke and Maggie scowled at the women who were lighting up even before they got outside.

'There's no smoking allowed inside, love,' she said to one of them as she passed. She just couldn't resist speaking up about it. It made her so mad that people smoked in the first place, never mind doing it where they shouldn't. Both her parents had died from smoking-related illnesses and it had left her with an absolute hatred of the habit.

'So what are you gonna do with your winnings, Marco?' Rita Byrne asked, as they all piled onto the bus. 'Three hundred is a nice little sum.'

'Oh, you know me, Rita, I think clothes will be the first thing on my list. After that, I don't really know.'

Rita took a seat at the window halfway down the bus. 'Oh, well I hope you enjoy it – it's nice to see somebody having a bit of luck for a change.'

'Thanks, Rita.' Marco plonked himself down in the middle seat at the back of the bus and Maggie had to laugh. He loved to be the centre of attention and he sat in that seat as though it was his throne. He was revelling in his winnings and Maggie suspected that it wasn't only the fact that he'd won but the fact that it gleaned him so much attention.

'So how are things with you, Rita?' asked Maggie, sitting down beside her friend. 'You've missed the past few weeks. How are those boys of yours?'

'They're grand thanks, Maggie. Having them both in school now makes things so much easier. I know I should've been sad to see Conor start this year since he's my baby, but, to be honest, I'm glad to have some time to myself.'

'Ah that's good. And what about their daddy? Any word from him lately?'

'Haven't seen or heard from that *pig* in ages,' spat Rita. 'And I'm happy to have it that way – the boys are much more settled when he's not around causing trouble.'

'But what about you? Is it better for you?'

'It is and it isn't, Maggie. I'm lonely – there's no point in pretending otherwise, but I honestly wouldn't want him back. The worst of it is him not paying maintenance and ...' She hesitated and Maggie saw the crushed look on her face. She'd obviously hit a nerve. Poor Rita – it must be awful for her. '... it's so hard to keep everything ticking over,' she continued. 'I even had the electric cut off last month because I was so behind on the payments.'

'Ah, no, I didn't realise things were so bad. And what did you do about getting it reconnected?'

'My ma brought the payments up to date for me, but I was mortified. It just makes me feel like such a loser. I swear, that bastard should rot in hell for what he's done to us.'

Maggie was taken aback by Rita's fury, but she understood it at the same time. 'Well, I'm sure he'll get his comeuppance, Rita. And your mother would hate it if you didn't share your troubles with her. Take it from one who knows.'

Rita fiddled with the strap of her black handbag. 'I know you're right. But I just wonder when I'm ever going to get out of this bloody financial mess. I know I'm not the only one under money pressures and at least I've still got the house, but I'm sick of having to stress every single day about whether or not I have enough to get us through the week. That's why I haven't been coming to the bingo much lately. I only came tonight because my ma came over and insisted I take the money and she'd babysit.'

Their chat was suddenly interrupted by Marco, who'd stood up and was waving his winnings in the air triumphantly. 'Right, who's coming to the pub? The drinks are on me!'

'Well, if you're buying … I suppose,' said Lorraine, grinning.

'Count me in for sure!' said Rita. 'My ma is staying over tonight, so there's no rush on me.'

'Ah, go on then,' laughed Maggie. 'Sure I'll have one with you – just to be sociable!'

Marco clapped in delight. 'We'll get Fergus to drop us down at O'Mahony's. I'll just go sort it out with him.'

Maggie smiled as Marco went to charm the grumpy Fergus into changing direction. O'Mahony's was only a stone's throw from Enda's, but Fergus didn't take too kindly to being asked to do anything. Maggie had also noticed how he seemed to be a bit intimidated by Marco, which was funny in itself because Marco was the least intimidating person she knew. She reckoned it was the gay thing – Fergus was a man's man and was probably uncomfortable around such an openly camp guy.

'Right, sorted,' said Marco. 'Now let's go and have a celebration drink before I die of dehydration!'

'So are things any better between you and Barry?' Maggie was sitting beside Lorraine at a little table in the lounge of O'Mahony's and the others were just behind them at a bigger table.

'Things aren't great, Maggie, to be honest. There's definitely something up with him and I just can't figure out what it is.' She lowered her voice to a whisper. 'We even had sex the other night but, oh Maggie, it was terrible. Not the sex, but how he was with me. He was cold and was just going through the motions.'

'I'm sure you're reading far too much into it,' said Maggie. 'I just don't understand why you don't confront him. Ask him outright what's up with him.'

'You know me, Maggie. I hate arguments. And if he is gambling again, I'm really not sure how I'd handle it.'

'Well, I suppose there's no point in asking you if you've told him about the other thing yet then.

'How can I tell him something so important while he's in such a mood?' said Lorraine, close to tears.

'Well, maybe you're right, Lorraine. But as soon as the two of you are back on track, he needs to know. No more secrets, okay?'

'Okay,' sighed Lorraine, rubbing her temples. 'No more secrets.'

'Right, I think I'm calling it a night,' said Maggie, pushing the old wooden chair back from the table so that she could stretch her legs. A wave of nausea engulfed her as she stood up and she gripped the edge of the table.

'Are you okay, Maggie?' said Lorraine, looking over in concern.

'Not a bother, Lorraine. I just jumped up too quick. All this 7Up is going to my head! So is anyone coming yet or are you all set to get sozzled tonight?'

'I'll come, Maggie,' said Rita, pulling herself up unsteadily to her feet. 'I'm such a lightweight but two drinks are quite enough for me.'

'I'm going to stay for one more,' said Marco, draining the last of his gin and tonic. 'Anyone else?'

Nobody else seemed inclined to move, so Maggie bid her goodbyes and headed out into the cool night air with Rita for the short walk home.

'So, let me guess, you didn't win again!' Dan poured boiling water into the teapot as Maggie took off her shoes and rubbed her aching feet.

'Right again!' she grinned. 'And I wouldn't mind but my left hand was tearing itchy all day. I was full sure I was going to win something tonight.'

'Ah, well, better luck the next time – or not, as the case may be!'

'But Marco had a bit of luck. Three hundred euro! It would have been nice to win that but I couldn't begrudge Marco it. He was so excited, I thought he was going to cry.'

'Good old Marco,' said Dan, affectionately. 'And I'm sure he'll use the money for outfits that Laurence Llewelyn Bowen would be proud of.'

Maggie giggled. I think that's the plan! You know Marco – he's such a fashion diva. How was Steph this evening? Was she okay?'

'Yep, she's fine. She was asking again about that disco on Saturday night, so I said I'd talk to you about it.'

'Oh, God, I know we'll probably have to let her go but I just hate the thought of it. Did she say all the friends are allowed?'

'Oh, yes, apparently *everyone* is going to this disco. It's thirteen to fifteen year olds so there won't be alcohol sold or anything.'

'But that doesn't stop kids bringing it into the place in their handbags, does it? Or the guys stashing bottles in their coats!'

'I know it's a worry, Maggie, but we really need to choose our battles carefully. Why don't you give some of the mothers a ring tomorrow and see what they have to say. If there's a few of them going and they promise to stick together, maybe we should just let her go.'

'You're right,' sighed Maggie. I really need to let her spread her wings, but it's just such a worry. I'll have a chat with Maddie's mam and maybe Sarah's too, and see what they think.'

'Good,' said Dan, dunking a biscuit into his tea and swallowing it in one. 'And don't forget I'm not working in the morning. I haven't to be at the warehouse until two, so I thought I'd paint the railings out front before I go.'

'Ah, Dan, you never get a rest. I don't think it really needs to be painted again. Why don't I give it a good scrub tomorrow and see how it comes up?'

'No, Maggie, have you not looked at it since Marco painted his? I thought ours was okay until he did his. Now ours looks old and the peeling paint is so much more noticeable.'

'Right,' sighed Maggie. 'Well, I'll give you a hand in the morning. Two pairs of hands will have it done much more quickly. The sooner that film crew are finished with us the better.'

'I thought you were looking forward to it?' Dan looked at her puzzled.

'Oh, I *am* looking forward to it, but at the same time, it's a hassle, isn't it? Sure look at all the work we've had to do over the past few weeks – painting fences, power-washing driveways, cutting hedges, washing the stone cladding on the front of the houses. And with me not feeling the best of late, it's just been a hassle at times.' The words were out of her mouth before she realised. She could have kicked herself.

'What do you mean, Maggie? I didn't know you weren't feeling well. What's up?' Dan was staring at her, his eyes crinkled up in concern.

'Nothing except a bit of exhaustion, Dan. I think I just need to get my iron checked. You know how it dips every now and again.'

'God, you had me worried there for a minute. Maybe you should go back on the iron tablets again. I know they made you feel sick last time but they worked, didn't they?'

'Yes, I might just do that,' said Maggie, glad she'd managed to get out of that one. 'When this camera crew are finished on the street, I'll get started on the tablets again.'

'I was just thinking,' said Dan, changing the subject, much to Maggie's relief. 'Could you imagine if your mother was still alive? She'd just be lapping all of this telly thing up.'

'She certainly would,' said Maggie, thinking of how her

mother loved Enda's and everything it stood for. 'She would have been so proud.'

'Well, hopefully you might get to talk about her when they're interviewing you. You can tell them how she was so important to the residents on the street and now how you seem to have taken on that role.'

'Stop it, will you.' Maggie turned a bright red. 'I'm hardly going to tell them that I'm Queen Bee on the street, am I? I don't want to come across as all saintly and wonderful.'

'Well, there'll be plenty of us to tell them what you do for this street, Maggie. Only for you, it would be like any old street, with neighbours too busy to chat and barely knowing each other's names.'

'I suppose I do like to bring us all together,' said Maggie, delighted for her husband to be saying what she was too modest to say herself. 'And I really hope the production company can see what a wonderful street it is.'

'They will, Maggie, mark my words. St Enda's is looking fabulous now with everything tidied and cleaned up and all we have to do is tell it as it is when the camera crew come on Monday.'

'You're right, Dan. It'll be wonderful. Whoever would have thought it, eh? St Enda's Terrace being broadcast throughout New York! It will certainly be one to tell the grandchildren, that's for sure.'

Maggie loaded the cups into the dishwasher and wiped down the little table. She'd told Dan to go on up and that she'd follow him in a minute. She hadn't meant to mention about not feeling well but, thank God, Dan was easily fobbed off. She knew herself it was more than iron and that she'd have to get it checked but she really didn't want to worry Dan unless it was completely necessary.

He was a good man and a fantastic husband. It did her heart good to see him getting so excited about the film crew. Just talking about it tonight made her realise that it was one of the best things that had ever happened to her. She just wished her ma was around to see it.

'Treasure Enda's,' Agnes had said to her only days before she died. 'It's a gem of a place, but it takes effort to make it what it is.' Well she hoped she could do her ma proud next week by portraying her precious little cul-de-sac in the best possible light. It shouldn't be hard though. The people on Enda's were all lovely and, as Dan said, just giving an honest account of life on the street would be enough for everyone to see how special it was.

Switching off the lights in the little kitchen, she padded out to the hall to set the house alarm. Glancing into the little sitting room, she stared at the picture of Agnes McKenna on the mantelpiece. 'Hope you're happy where you are, Ma. Keep an eye on us next week, won't you? Make sure we do your street proud.'

Maggie could have sworn she felt a breeze on her face at that moment and yet there were no windows open. She smiled to herself as she made her way upstairs and whispered the words 'Thanks, Ma' before heading in to make love to her husband.

CHAPTER 7

Friday, 9th September

'So there I was, just marking my card like any other night and, before I knew it, I was getting the numbers one after the other.' Marco was leaning his two elbows on the black granite counter, chatting to Felicity, one of the shop's regulars. 'Honestly, I couldn't believe it when she called the last number. I frightened the life out of everyone when I jumped up!'

'Oh, I could imagine,' said Felicity, her face barely moving. 'But how wonderful for you, darling.'

She'd definitely had more Botox – there was no doubt about it. It was an ongoing discussion in the shop as to what work she'd had done but nobody dared ask her. She'd come in every single Friday without fail and would spend a small fortune on outfits, some of which would probably never see the light of day.

'Honestly, Felicity, it was so exciting. It was like all my

birthdays had come at once. Can you imagine what I'd be like if I won the lotto?' Marco grinned at the very prospect.

'Well, it's all very well and good winning a few hundred, but sometimes having a lot of money can do more harm than good.' She let those words hang in the air and Marco was curious but reluctant to pursue things. She seemed to be talking from personal experience.

'So what's new this week then?' asked Felicity, changing the subject, much to Marco's relief. 'I should really be stocking up on some autumn stuff but this weather is making me think light cotton and pastels.'

'I've got just the thing, Felicity. Follow me.' Marco led the way to the back of the tastefully decorated shop and indicated a rail with an assortment of pale mauve, peach and dusky pink dresses. 'These just came in yesterday. Aren't they divine?'

'Oh, darling, they're perfect. I'll try each of these in a fourteen if you have them. A twelve would probably do but I like to have an extra bit of room.' She indicated three calf-length dresses and one knee-length one and Marco smiled to himself. Felicity was at least a fourteen, bordering on sixteen but she seemed to feel the need to say otherwise. No matter how tight anything was on her, she'd never ask for a sixteen and woe betide the shop assistant who'd suggest it. Felicity wasn't nasty or demanding by any means, but she had a regal air about her that made her seem powerful and everyone was a little bit scared of upsetting her.

Marco disappeared into the stock room and reappeared within minutes with the requested dresses. He led her to one of the large fitting rooms and hung the dresses up for her. 'Just give me a shout if you need me.'

'Thanks, Marco. I'll get you to zip me up in a minute.'

Marco reckoned he'd have about ten minutes. Felicity usually used the time in the fitting rooms to redo her make-up. He knew this because she usually came out with lipstick on her teeth and her face looking a lot less shiny. She was a good-looking woman, for her age, whatever that might be. Marco guessed she was heading for sixty, but she tried to conceal it with her sleek, bobbed auburn hair and her thick coverage of make-up.

It was almost twelve, which would make it seven over in New York, so Claude should be just about getting up for work. He'd send him a text and see. He grabbed his iPhone from under the counter and texted his friend quickly. Within seconds a text came back telling Marco to turn to Twitter. It was costly to text back and forth but, with the shop's wifi coverage, the tweets cost nothing.

@Marcofashion1: Hi, Claude. Are you just waking up? I have half a day's work done here already.

@ClaudeRIP: Hey there, Marco. Yep! Just starting my day. So what are you up to?

@Marcofashion1: In work but guess what? I had a win last night at bingo – three hundred euro!

@ClaudeRIP: Good stuff. And just in good time for your week off next week. What are you going to spend it on?

@Marcofashion1: Well I'll pick up a few bits and pieces in the shop but I was thinking maybe we could have a few good nights out with it while you're here.

@ClaudeRIP: Sounds great but I won't be sponging off you, Marco. I can pay my own way you know.

@Marcofashion1: Oh, I know you can, Claude. I wasn't suggesting you couldn't. But I'd like to treat you – even one night.

@ClaudeRIP:Well, if you insist, gorgeous. I look forward to that special night.

'Marco, can you come and do up this zip please? And I honestly don't think this is sized right. I think it's only a twelve – it's far too tight.'

@Marcofashion1: Sorry, Claude, gotta go. A customer looking for help here. Catch up later. x

'Now, Felicity, let me have a look.' Marco rushed over to the fitting room and pulled back the curtain. 'Oh, I'm not sure that's you really. Let's not bother with the zip on that one. Try the mauve one – it'll go beautifully with your hair.'

'You're probably right. I really wasn't all that gone on this one anyway. Right, give me two secs.'

Marco breathed a sigh of relief. He was very proud of the way he could handle the customers, especially the ladies. He was very honest and never tried to sell somebody something that didn't fit properly or didn't suit them and he always seemed to get his point across in a very subtle way. He knew he could sell loads more stuff to Felicity because she had the money and seemed to completely trust his opinion, but he'd never let her leave the shop with something he didn't believe looked fantastic on her.

His mind wandered back to his conversation with Claude. He'd called him gorgeous. That was the first time he'd said that. Marco flushed at the thought of Claude lying in bed having just woken up. Imagine, in just two days he'd be seeing him in the flesh. And with a bit of luck, there *would* be flesh involved!

'I think this is a much better fit. What do you think, Marco?' Felicity came out of the dressing room, looking a picture in the pale mauve, knee-length dress.

'Gorgeous, absolutely gorgeous,' gushed Marco, pulling the zip the last few inches up her back and twirling her around to get a look from all angles. This one is perfect. Does it feel comfortable?'

'Yes, there's plenty of room and I love the feel of the material.'

'Right, that's one definite. Now go and try the peach silk one. It's a bit dressier but would be gorgeous for a wedding or something.'

'Well, I have a few things coming up this month so I could do with a couple of dressy things. I'll just go and stick it on.'

'Good. I'll wait right here.' Marco never ceased to be amazed at how Felicity could 'need' more stuff. She rarely left the shop on a Friday without at least one outfit so she must have hundreds sitting at home in her wardrobes.

He wondered what it would be like to have an endless pit of money like she seemed to have. He knew that Felicity lived in a huge house in Castleknock and that she didn't work but that was about all he knew. He liked to imagine how people like that came into money – were they born into it, did they win it or did they earn it through hard graft all their lives? He reckoned Felicity married into it. She often mentioned her husband and how she had to get dressed up for another of his work dinners, so he must have a good job. Marco had tried to suss her out about it on a few occasions but she wasn't giving anything away. Today was the first time he'd ever heard her mentioning money in a negative light.

A half an hour later, he was wrapping up two dresses and a gorgeous pale blue silk cardigan for his best customer, and thanking God it was almost lunchtime. 'So are you happy with this lot then?'

Felicity beamed as he handed over the precious bags. 'Delighted as always, darling. Toodles.'

Marco giggled at her regular parting word as he watched her totter outside in her Louboutin heels. If you saw her from the back, you'd be forgiven for thinking she was in her thirties because of her immaculately sleek hair and mega high heels. The staff at the shop had varying opinions, some thinking her to be as young as forty-five while others put her at over sixty. It was really difficult to tell beneath the mask of make-up and her cosmetic work.

Anyway, someone else could serve her next week because he wouldn't be there. He'd hopefully be out enjoying himself with Claude and cherishing every minute before having to let him go again. Marco sighed at the thought. What if he and Claude got on really well and fell for each other? How would they cope with being wrenched apart again? And it wasn't as though they'd only be a couple of hours away – how on earth would they be able to sustain a relationship with thousands of miles in between them?

Jesus, he was now in danger of running a million miles ahead of himself. He hadn't even met the guy yet and he was already worrying about saying goodbye! Maybe they wouldn't get on at all face to face. He'd have to stop all this stressing about what may or may not happen and concentrate on enjoying the week ahead. Right, he'd go and get himself some lunch and have a think about how he was going to treat Claude to a nice night out next week with his bingo winnings.

It was a lovely evening, so Marco decided to take the thirty-minute walk home. Having been cooped up in the shop all day, he was relieved to step out into the warm sun and stretch his legs. At least it was Friday. He loved his job really but it was nice to have some time off too.

He crossed over a gridlocked Dame Street and weaved his way through the crowds around Temple Bar. Within minutes, he was out on the south quays at the Ha'penny Bridge. Crossing over to the northside, he looked down at the murky River Liffey and scrunched his nose up at the smell. Much as he loved the sun, they could probably do with a drop of rain to freshen up the river. It hadn't rained in well over a week which was very unusual for this time of year – or for any time of year, for that matter!

About ten minutes later, a guy texting on his mobile came rushing out of a shop and bumped right into him, almost knocking Marco to the ground. 'Jesus, watch where you're—'

'Marco!' said a grinning Barry. 'God, sorry about that. I was miles away. Are you okay?'

Marco brushed himself down, more worried about getting a mark on his white jeans than whether or not he was hurt. 'I'm grand, Barry. No harm done. Are you off home too?'

'Yep. I promised Lorraine we'd sit down and have dinner together this evening. We've been a bit like ships in the night lately.'

They fell into an easy silence as they walked the short way home and Marco wondered if he should take the opportunity to address what Lorraine had told him the other night. 'Are you two okay?'

He immediately regretted his words as Barry stopped dead and looked at him. 'Why? Did Lorraine say something to you?'

Jesus, why had he opened his big mouth? 'Eh … no, not at all. I just wondered … you know … with you both working so hard. It can't be easy.'

Thankfully, Barry resumed walking but didn't say anything for a minute or two. 'There's bound to be a strain I suppose,' he said, eventually. 'We don't get much time together these days, with me doing overtime a few evenings a week and then we're both knackered at night.'

'I can imagine,' mused Marco, wishing he hadn't started the whole conversation. He really didn't want Barry to start confiding anything in him when really his loyalties lay with Lorraine.

'And has she told you yet … about … about, you know …?'

It was Marco's turn to stop in his tracks. Oh, Jesus, what was he talking about? He wished he'd just kept his nose out. 'Em, told me about what?'

'About us trying for a baby.'

'Oh, that.' Marco breathed a sigh of relief. 'Yes, she did mention it all right. That's great news, Barry. I really hope it all works out for you.'

'Thanks, Marco. I really hope it does too. And it's great for her to have you so close by for support. You two are very close, aren't you?'

'Yes, yes we are,' said Marco, glancing at Barry, but he was looking straight ahead.

'And she talks a lot to you, doesn't she?'

Marco felt a bit uncomfortable, as though Barry was trying to suss him out about something. 'Well you know me, Barry – I love a good old chat.'

'You can't beat family, eh?' said Barry, slapping Marco on the back as they walked.

'Absolutely!'

They turned off the quays and Marco was grateful they were only minutes from home. Maybe Lorraine had been right about her suspicions that Barry had reverted to his gambling. There was definitely something not quite right. 'The old street is looking great, isn't it?' said Barry, as they turned onto Enda's.

'It's a credit to us all,' said Marco, proudly. 'And if the sun shines on Monday when the television crew arrive, it'll be perfect.'

'So, what time are they coming at? Lorraine has insisted that I take the day off, but I certainly hope we won't have to be filmed. I'd die if I had to talk in front of a camera.'

'Ha! A fine-looking fella like you, Barry? You'd be great. I can't wait to get on camera myself. It'll be great gas. I'll be talking to Claude over the weekend about the arrangements. They're hoping to get what they need here in one day but, if not, they may have to come back a second day.'

'Howareya, lads,' said Maggie, who was on her knees painting the last of the railings. 'I'm feckin' sick of this. If I never see a bit of silver paint again, it'll be too soon!'

'Well, you're doing a fine job. Isn't she, Barry?' said Marco, laughing at the amount of paint she'd managed to get into her hair.

Barry smiled faintly. 'Yes, well done, Maggie. Well, I'd better head on down to Lorraine. She's expecting me to be home on time.'

Maggie stopped what she was doing to look at Barry. 'Em, right so. Tell Lorraine I'll be down for a natter in the morning.'

'Will do. See you later.'

'Now is it my imagination or is he a bit jittery?' said Maggie, wiping the sweat off her forehead with her arm.

Marco nodded. 'No you didn't imagine it and, yes, he *is* a bit jittery. I've just had a sort of strange conversation with him on the way home.'

'Jesus, I was hoping it was all in her head. What exactly did he say to you?'

'It's not exactly what he *said*, Maggie, it was how he was behaving. He was talking about him and Lorraine trying for a baby and it felt as though he was testing me or something.'

'Oh, I don't know, Marco. Maybe we're all just looking for something that isn't there.

'Hmmmm! You might have a point there. Well, I'm not going to worry any more about it for now. I'll have a chat with Lorraine again over the weekend. I need to go and say hello to my Mimi and take a long, cool shower.'

'Right, ten more minutes and I'll be done with this too. At least Dan won't have to come home and get stuck into it. We both did a bit this morning before he headed to work and he said he'd finish it when he got home.'

'Ah, good on ya, Maggie. You're one of the good ones! Dan's a lucky man!'

'Go on with you, Marco Gallagher. Sure I'm the lucky one to have my Dan. He's a real gem.'

Marco smiled as he bid his goodbyes to Maggie. He wondered if he'd ever find the kind of love Maggie and Dan had. They were so good together and rarely had a cross word

– well, not that he'd ever heard anyway. Sixteen years they'd been together. It was a lifetime.

He pictured him and Claude, sixteen years from now. They'd both be forty. Maybe they'd have kids. There were plenty of avenues open to gay couples these days and he fully intended to explore them. He couldn't imagine living his life without kids. He wondered how Claude felt about it.

The sound of the alarm as he opened his front door startled him out of his daydream. Jesus, he'd gone off on one again! What the bloody hell was he thinking? Firstly, Claude was *not* his boyfriend, secondly, he didn't even know if they'd get on, and thirdly – sixteen years? He didn't even know if they'd last sixteen minutes! He'd have to get a grip. He was a romantic at heart. That was his trouble. He believed in happy ever afters and wanted one so badly for himself. Well he'd just take the next week as it came and keep his fingers crossed that maybe his happy ever after may not be too far away!

Barry knew he'd been a bit short with Maggie, but he really hadn't felt like having an idle chit-chat. And it had been an awkward exchange with Marco on the way home, too. God, he felt as though his life had been thrown into turmoil and he just didn't know how to handle it.

One part of him wanted to scream and shout at Lorraine; tell her that he knew her dirty little secret and let her know in no uncertain terms that he wouldn't be made a fool of. But the trouble was, every time he'd planned to say something to her, he just had to look at her to see the woman he'd fallen in love with. Did he really want to throw away what they had? Or was it too late anyway? If only he hadn't overheard her that day. He'd be none the wiser and things would be just as they were. But the reality was that he *had* heard her and it would all have to come out sooner or later.

Lorraine knew there was something up with him because he'd been avoiding her as much as possible this past week or so. He knew they needed to talk, but he just feared that if he gave her the opportunity to tell him what had been going on, it would be the end of them. He just couldn't face losing her. He sighed heavily as he turned the key in the front door. Tonight he'd try to put his worries aside and just enjoy a night with his wife. If everything came to a head soon, it may well be one of the last nights they'd enjoy together. Life always seemed to have a way of paying you back for past indiscretions. Just like the gambling, his luck was bound to run out some day.

CHAPTER 8

Saturday, 10th September

'Your dad will be outside at eleven o'clock on the button and that's that.'

'Pleeeease, Ma, just let me have until half past. I promise I won't ask to go again for another few weeks. Pleeeeease.'

'A quarter past and that's my final offer.'

'Ah, go on, Ma. I'll clean my room tomorrow and I'll even empty the dishwasher for the next week.'

Maggie sighed. Her daughter was like a dog with a bone when she got something into her head. There was no such thing as meeting halfway with Steph – she'd always manage to wear Maggie down until she got exactly what she wanted and today was no different.

'And I'll look like a real loser if I'm the first to leave,' continued Steph, obviously realising her mother was weakening. 'And it's not a school night or anything.'

'Right, half eleven then, but don't take that as the norm. Next time it'll be eleven, do you hear me?'

'Thanks, Ma, you're a legend!' Stephanie gave her mother a hug before running upstairs, probably to pick her clothes for later. And that would be another bone of contention – but at least Dan would be with Maggie on that one. He hated to see his daughter go out in skimpy clothes and although he gave in to her on a lot of things, he put his foot down when it came to skirts that were more like belts, and tops that revealed far too much.

Maggie was finding the teenage years quite difficult. She knew Dan was right and that they should choose their battles carefully with a hormone-fuelled fourteen year old, but these days everything seemed like a battle. If they weren't fighting over what time she should be home, it was over the mess in her room or her lack of help around the house. Their last big blow up had been only last week when Stephanie had come home with a plum hair colour she wanted to put into her long, sleek, black hair. Maggie just couldn't understand it. She was thankful her daughter had taken after her husband in the hair department and hadn't inherited her own frizzy red offering, so why on earth would she want to ruin it with an ugly colour?

To Maggie's further dismay, Stephanie had taken to staying awake for half the night at the weekends to text her friends. As a result, she'd emerge from the bed sometime around lunchtime and lob about watching telly while Maggie buzzed around the house cleaning, cooking and ironing. She hadn't brought Steph up to be a lazy good for nothing, and she worried that her daughter would turn out to be just that. She'd taken her phone off her at one stage in a desperate attempt to shake her up, but it had resulted in so much sulking that it really hadn't been worth it.

'She's just a teenager, Maggie,' Dan had said only last

week. 'She's just doing what teenagers do and challenging the boundaries.'

'But surely we can't just turn a blind eye to everything she does,' had been Maggie's response. 'Surely as her parents, we have a responsibility to make sure she grows up to be a decent human being and the only way we can do that is by disciplining her.'

'I know what you're saying, Maggie, but you let her away with nothing. I think we need to let her make some mistakes. How else is she supposed to learn?'

Dan had shocked her with that. How come he had such a good insight into the life of a teenager when she herself just seemed to get wound up constantly by her daughter's behaviour? Steph was a daddy's girl and always had been, and sometimes it irked Maggie that the two got on so well.

She stuck on the kettle and headed out to check on Dan's progress. As Maggie had finished the painting the previous evening, he'd taken out the power-washer to clean the cobblestones out front. Maggie smiled as she watched her husband, his black floppy fringe falling over his eyes as he concentrated on the job in hand. He was nothing if not a hard worker. He hated being idle and it sometimes frustrated Maggie that she could never get him to just slow down and relax.

'It's half twelve, Dan. Are you coming in for a bit of lunch? Will I make us a few sandwiches?'

Dan switched off the power-washer and wiped the sweat and dirt off his face with his sleeve. 'Thanks, Maggie, almost done here. I'll just fly up for a quick shower before I eat, though.'

'Right, I'll have a bite ready when you come down.' Maggie wished Dan didn't have to go off working today. Even though it was only for a few hours, she hated the fact that it put a hole in their weekend.

Still, with Stephanie out later, maybe they could have a nice romantic night in. It was getting harder to find a bit of time to themselves these days because Stephanie always seemed to be around. Only a few years ago, they could tell her to go to bed at nine o'clock but now they all seemed to go to bed at the same time. It really made it difficult to be intimate.

'Maggie, she's always been in the room next door, so what's the problem?' Dan would ask, sliding his hand inside her panties.

'But it was different when we knew she was asleep,' Maggie would retort, before brushing his hand away. It's not that they didn't make love – because they did, they'd always had a healthy sex life – but lately Maggie found herself on tenterhooks, expecting Steph to throw open their bedroom door to declare some drama or other.

Maybe tonight after Steph was gone, Maggie would cook them a nice steak and chips and they could have it in front of the telly. When Steph was a baby, they used to make a lot more use of the rug in front of the gas fire in the living room. One of them would peep into her room and make sure she was out for the count before both getting naked on the rug. She giggled at the thought. Good thing she'd been generous and given in to Steph's demands of a half eleven pick-up. That should give them plenty of time to gain a few carpet burns! As soon as Dan had gone to work, she'd go and have a nice soak and give her legs a shave. With not feeling well lately, she'd let herself go a bit but tonight she was going to change that. Despite her confrontation with Steph earlier, she suddenly felt happy.

Tonight she'd put all her worries aside and enjoy just being with her husband.

'You are absolutely *not* wearing that, missy. You can go back upstairs and put on something else.'

'For God's sake, Ma, it's what everyone is wearing these days.' She indicated her tight, lycra mini-skirt which was more like a belt in Maggie's opinion. 'Just because you're such a fuddy-duddy yourself.'

'That's enough cheek from you, young lady. Apologise to your mother *now*.' Dan was fuming and Maggie couldn't help but feel a little sense of satisfaction. All too often, she was at the receiving end of Steph's cheek and Dan, being forever the peacemaker, would try to smooth it over by suggesting that maybe Maggie had read too much into what her daughter had said.

'But she's always on my case, Da. If it's not what I'm wearing, it's what I'm saying or what I'm doing – she just never lets up!'

Maggie was torn between rage and devastation. She so badly wanted them to have a good mother-daughter relationship, but it was becoming increasingly difficult to deal with her teen. 'Steph, I'm your mother. I'm supposed to be on your case.'

'But not for, like, every hour of the day,' said a sulky Steph. 'Honestly, Ma, I just can't seem to please you these days. You're always, like, in bad form and I seem to take the brunt of it.'

'That's *it*,' said Dan. 'You can go back up to your room now for the night, Steph. I won't have that sort of talk in this house. You can forget about the disco and you only have yourself to blame.'

Steph was speechless. It wasn't often Dan raised his voice and, when he did, they knew he meant business.

'Did you hear me, Steph? Up to bed … *now*!'

Oh, this wasn't at all how Maggie had seen the night panning out. She and Dan had been relaxing over a glass of wine in the living room while the steaks cooked slowly in the oven. She'd been so looking forward to her night in with her husband and she could see it slipping through her fingers every time Steph opened her mouth. She'd have to do something. 'Look, why don't we all just calm down for a minute. I'm sure we can sort this out.'

'I'm … I'm sorry. Steph was practically whispering, obviously shocked by her dad's outburst. 'It's just … it's just …'

'I know you and me haven't been seeing eye to eye lately, Steph,' continued Maggie, 'but I wish you'd realise that I have your best interests at heart.'

'I do, Ma. And I'm sorry I was rude, but can you please just not nag me over everything?'

Dan wasn't letting anything past him tonight. 'Stephanie! You need to—'

'It's all right, Dan.' Maggie looked at her daughter and saw a vulnerable little girl instead of the confident fourteen year old that had come down the stairs only minutes before. 'I'm sorry too, Steph. I can remember being a teenager, you know, and I know it can be hard. I'll try to cut you a bit of slack if you promise to pull your head in and have less of an attitude.'

'Seems fair to me,' grinned Steph, and Maggie breathed a sigh of relief.

'But you're still not going out in that excuse for a skirt,' Maggie added.

This time Steph didn't argue. 'Right, I'll go and change and be back down in a sec. I've to be around at Maddie's at seven and her dad is bringing us. I told her you'd drop her home after, Da. Is that okay?'

'That's fine,' said Dan, looking relieved the confrontation was over. 'Be outside at half eleven, though. You know the score – if you're not out at exactly half, I'm coming in.'

Maggie couldn't help laughing when her daughter raced up the stairs to change. 'God, Dan, I always get a feeling of déjà vu when you say that. I have memories of my own da walking in to the school disco and seeing me and Colin O'Hara kissing. God only knows what you'd see in discos these days.'

'Jesus, Maggie, I don't want to even think about it. Are those steaks nearly ready? My stomach thinks my throat's been cut!'

Maggie grinned at her husband. 'As soon as Steph is gone, I'll bring us two plates in here. *The Bourne Supremacy* is on after the lotto draw at eight, so I thought we might have a look at that. What do you say?'

'Perfect, Mags. And maybe we'll even look at injecting a bit of life back into that rug later on.'

'Now why didn't I think of that?' said Maggie, hiding a smile as she tottered out to the kitchen to check on dinner.

'Do you have to go out tonight, Barry? Couldn't we just stay in and watch a movie? *The Bourne Supremacy* is on later.'

'We had a night in last night, Lorraine. I'm only going for a pint to O'Mahony's. I won't be late.' Barry didn't meet her eye as he tied the laces on his trainers.

'But what about saving our pennies? I thought we were cutting down on the nights out?'

'Well, a night at the bingo is about the same price as a few pints, so that makes us even.'

It was as though he'd just kicked her in the face. They'd never worried before about being even. 'But what about dinner? I was going to make us a nice stir-fry.'

'Don't bother on my account. I had a sandwich an hour ago and I'll probably go to the chipper on the way home.'

'I really don't begrudge you your few pints, Barry, but it's just … it's just … I just want us to talk about what's wrong.'

Barry stopped what he was doing and looked at her. 'Go ahead and talk then, Lorraine. It seems you're the one with the tales to tell.'

She was thrown for a minute by his comment, but then became angry. 'Honestly, Barry. You've been talking in riddles for weeks now. What the hell is going on?'

'I'm not saying another thing until you tell me what *you've* been up to!'

'Oh, for God's sake, Barry! You keep making these snide comments and I haven't a clue what's going on in that head of yours. If you don't want to talk about it, fine! But stop trying to turn things around so that I'm to blame for something!'

'Don't come the little miss innocent with me, Lorraine. You know well that … oh, do you know what, fuck it! I'm done here.'

Lorraine balked at the viciousness in his voice. Barry used bad language very rarely and it just seemed so out of character. But his whole demeanour had been out of character these past few weeks.

He was heading out the door so she ran down the hall and pulled him back. 'Barry, look, whatever's wrong – whatever's come between us, we can come back from it. I love you and I know you love me. Let's try to stop all this fighting and just talk to each other like we used to.'

Barry looked at her and his face softened. 'I do love you, Lori. And, yes, we do need to talk. It's just that sometimes talk can lead to us hearing things we don't want to hear. I won't be late.'

Lorraine's heart plunged as he pecked her on the cheek and was out the door without a backward glance. She leaned her back against the door and banged it with both fists. God, Barry could be so frustrating at times. She remembered reading somewhere that it was a sign of a guilty conscience – that when somebody feels guilty about something, they often try to lay some sort of blame on those closest to them.

She felt physically sick at the thought of him gambling again. She knew she'd no real reason to think he was, but she just couldn't think of another explanation for his mood. Oh, God, how would she handle it if he went back there again? She didn't know the first thing about dealing with an addiction like that. How would she make him stop?

Ten minutes later, Lorraine realised with a start that she was still standing in the hall. Right, she needed to get a grip and not allow herself to get depressed about this. God, she wished she had some company. She hated the thought of being alone with her thoughts tonight.

Maggie had said that she and Dan were having a quiet night in, so would it be a bit much to intrude? Maybe she'd call on the pretence of borrowing some teabags or something and if they weren't up to anything too intimate, maybe they'd invite her in. If she felt as though she was interrupting something, she'd head down to Marco.

It was no wonder St Enda's had been picked for this

documentary. According to Marco, they'd be here on Monday morning to chat to the residents. The street was looking fabulous and no doubt they'd be impressed by the fabulousness of the residents, too. Maybe she should just park this 'thing' with Barry until after they'd gone because it wouldn't do for those telly people to pick up on an atmosphere. She'd heard how these programmes can get edited in a certain way and words and stories can be twisted. They'd just all have to pull together for the few days the cameras were here. Let those Americans see what a wonderful place Enda's is and how fabulous, warm and friendly the Irish are.

CHAPTER 9

'JUST PLAY THE GOD DAMN DRAW,' screamed Maggie, standing up from the sofa. She, Dan and Lorraine were gaping at the paused television screen.

'Five numbers, Maggie,' said Lorraine, her voice barely audible. 'Do you realise how much our lives could change if we got the sixth?'

Dan gently prised the remote control from Lorraine's hands. 'Well, we need to know. Come on, here we go ...'

'We've only gone and *won the bloody lotto*!' Marco screamed, bursting in the door and making everybody jump.

'Jesus, Mary and Joseph,' said Maggie, clutching her hand to her chest. 'How the bloody hell did you get in? You frightened the life out of me ... hold on ... what did you say?'

'Sorry, your door was on the latch. But we won, Maggie. We won the lotto!' Marco was waving a piece of paper in the air.

'Oh ... my ... God,' said Lorraine, turning pale. 'Are you serious?'

'No way! We've actually won? Maggie indicated the screen

that showed the five numbers. 'Jesus, I don't believe it. We were watching it ourselves and just paused before the last number.'

Marco looked confused. 'Now why the bloody hell would you do that? Anyway, never mind that. Believe me, it's true all right. Woohoo! We're in the money!'

Lorraine's lip quivered. 'Is it really true? We're not just dreaming, are we?'

'It's true all right, Lori,' said Marco, who was now getting carried away and doing a can-can around the little living room.

Dan shook his head. 'I can't believe it. All that money.'

'Well, play that last bit of the draw,' said Marco, hopping over the back of the sofa to plonk himself down beside Dan. 'Seeing is believing, Dan.'

The two girls squeezed themselves in beside the boys on the sofa and everyone held their breath to hear the winning number called out.

'And the sixth ball this evening is number eleven ...'

They all jumped up from the sofa, cheering loudly. Maggie felt as if she was in a dream. God, she couldn't even win a measly hundred at the bingo and now they'd just won two million. *Two million euro!* Jesus! It was a lot to take in.

'So how many are there in this syndicate then?' asked Dan. 'It's more than just us, right?'

'It's split five ways,' said Marco. 'Us three ...'

'Four,' interrupted Maggie.

'Yes, but you and Dan together only count as one. Then there's Rita and Majella.'

Lorraine's eyes lit up. 'Oooh, let's go and tell the others now. I hope they haven't checked already. I want to see their faces when we tell them.'

'Good idea. C'mon, Mags.' Marco was already half way out the door, still kicking his legs in the air. Although how he didn't rip those skin-tight jeans in the process, Maggie would never know!

'I'm coming. Dan, come on. Let's go and break the good news.'

They trooped the few steps down to number fourteen where Majella lived with her husband, Chris. Giggling like schoolchildren, they rang the bell and waited.

'Doesn't look like anyone's home,' Dan said, after they'd waited a few seconds.

Marco wasn't giving up. 'One more try and then we'll head to Rita's.' He held his finger down on the doorbell, just to be sure.

'Oh, come to think of it,' said Lorraine, 'Majella said they were visiting her mother over in Malahide earlier. I imagine they'll probably have a few drinks and stay over.'

'Well that's that then,' said Maggie, leading the way back down the little driveway. 'Let's head in next door and give Rita the good news.' God, this was exciting. Honestly, you could make a movie out of Enda's. First the documentary, now the lotto – what next?

They didn't have to wait this time because Rita was out the door before they got up the driveway. 'Shhhhh, will you! You'll wake the boys – I've only just got them down. What's up with you all anyway?'

'We've got a bit of news,' smiled Maggie, savouring the moment.

'Well come on then, spit it out.' Rita didn't look amused.

'You might want to sit down for this,' added Dan, obviously keen to join in.

'Ah, shite. Is it something bad? I must have been a terrible person in a previous life to attract all this bad luck!'

'Rita, it's brilliant news – the best!' Marco just couldn't keep it in any longer. 'We've won the lotto, Rita. St Enda's syndicate has won the lotto! We're rich. Woohoo!'

'Wh– what? Rita said, stumbling backwards.

'Maybe we should go inside,' said Maggie, afraid her friend was going to keel over with shock. 'We'll stay quiet and won't wake the little ones.'

Rita opened the door wide and they all piled into her little kitchen. 'I … I can't take it in. Did we really win? Are you sure?' She indicated her worn oak chairs and everyone sat down while she propped herself up against the grey Formica worktop. 'I mean, who checked the numbers? Did you double check to be sure?'

Marco laughed. 'Rita, we've all checked. We won, we really won!'

'Jesus! I can't believe it. All that money! I've been so strapped for cash these past couple of years, and now I'm not going to have a worry in the world.'

'It really is a blessing,' said Maggie, realising how much it would change Rita's life – how it would change all of their lives.

Rita continued while busying herself making tea for her guests. 'And to think we were all envious of Marco's win on Thursday night. God, I thought three hundred quid was a fortune!'

'It's … it's unbelievable … I can't …' Lorraine burst into tears, much to everyone's shock.

'What is it, love? Maggie was first to jump up and put her arms around her sobbing friend.

'I … I just can't believe it. It's so much money and … and

me and Barry have been working so hard to save and … and we were fighting tonight … and he should be here with me to share the good news.'

'Did you ring him?' asked Rita, placing mugs of tea on the table in front of everyone. 'Just tell him to come home – that you have some important news to tell him.'

Lorraine blew her nose. 'I've rung him about twenty times in the past twenty minutes! He's either got his phone on silent or he's ignoring my calls.'

Maggie rubbed her friend's arm reassuringly. 'I'm sure it's just noisy in the pub. Sure, you know what O'Mahony's is like on a Saturday night.'

'Well, maybe you should lie on the bed naked with money draped all over you for when he comes back,' suggested Marco. 'Wouldn't that be a lovely way to tell him?'

Lorraine giggled although her eyes were still wet. 'Or maybe we should all go down to O'Mahony's and share the good news?'

Dan bristled at that. 'Not a good idea.'

'Why the hell not?' Maggie asked, annoyed that her husband seemed to be putting a dampener on the celebrations.

'No, Dan is right,' said Lorraine. 'We really don't want to be announcing this to the world until we have a think about it.'

Dan shot her an appreciative glance. 'Exactly! Firstly, Majella doesn't know about it so she needs to be told before anyone else and, secondly, we need to have a proper chat as to how we want to go about it. I mean, do we want to go public with it or would it be better to keep it to ourselves?'

Marco looked shocked. 'Jesus, Dan. Do you honestly expect me to keep quiet about something like this? I'm *dying* to tell everyone.'

'Oh, God, I don't want that bastard husband of mine finding out about it,' said Rita, looking panicked. 'I'd burn it before he got his hands on one single penny!'

Maggie nodded. 'And as Dan said, Majella needs to be told, but let's wait until she's back instead of phoning her. I'll be dying to see her face when we tell her.'

'Oh, me too,' said Lorraine, sipping the scalding hot tea. 'One of us should text her and arrange something for tomorrow. God, it's all so exciting!'

Dan took charge again. 'Well, why don't we agree to meet in our house at, say, three tomorrow? Hopefully Majella will be home by then and we can give her the good news together.'

'Great idea,' said Rita. 'I'll text Majella now and say we're having a meeting in your house at three about the documentary and see if she can make it.'

Maggie clapped her hands. 'Perfect. And Marco, maybe you should put the ticket somewhere safe for now.'

'What do you mean?' Marco looked confused.

'I mean you should lock it away somewhere. If you don't have somewhere suitable, Dan and I have a little safe in our bedroom. We could put it in there.'

'No, I mean I haven't got the ticket. I thought you had it.'

Maggie was taken aback. 'What? I was looking at the photocopy of the numbers tonight. I haven't got the *actual* ticket.'

'Hold on, hold on, hold on,' said Lorraine, looking panicked. 'So if you two don't have the ticket, who does? I certainly don't.'

Everyone's eyes turned to Rita. 'Don't bloody look at me. I haven't got it. Fuck! Does this mean that maybe we haven't won at all? Maybe nobody did the numbers this week. Whose turn was it?'

'Well, I think I did it last time,' said Maggie, searching her brain to remember. 'Yes, I did it on 23 July for four weeks. I remember because it was Steph's birthday and I thought it might be a lucky day to do it.'

'So it was due to be done again on 20 August.' Marco's voice was almost hysterical. 'Oh, please God, let it have been done! Can you remember who you gave the slip to?'

Maggie rubbed her forehead as she tried to remember what had transpired. 'I do remember us chatting about it on the bingo bus. Remember, Lorraine? Did you not take the slip off me that night?'

'I remember us all chatting about it all right and I do remember volunteering, but I'm sure I forgot to get it off you.'

'Well I can't remember who took the slip,' mused Maggie, 'but I think I put it on the table in O'Mahony's after the bingo. I remember throwing my thirteen euro in.' Maggie didn't actually remember anything of the sort but the thought that she might have forgotten to play the numbers had put the fear of God into her and she wanted to deflect the attention from herself.

'Me too,' said Marco, his face fixed in a grimace. 'I definitely threw my money in because I remember looking for change of a twenty so that I could put in the exact money. But I definitely wasn't the one to take the slip to play the numbers. Oh, Jesus, I hope to God somebody did play it. I couldn't bear the disappointment after all that excitement!'

'I remember somebody looking for money off us too,' chimed in Rita. 'I'm telling you, if somebody collected the money and forgot to play the numbers, there'll be hell to pay!'

Dan had been quiet during the exchange. 'Well, we'll

know tomorrow. If Dargle's sold the winning ticket, they'll be notified, so we should just wait until then.'

'But what a bloody come-down if it hasn't been done,' said Marco, close to tears. 'I already had half the winnings spent in my head.'

'Well, if it's none of us who has it, it has to be Majella.' Rita suddenly brightened up again. 'I bet that's what it is. And now that I think of it, I'm sure it was her who took the money and the lotto slip.'

'I think you're right,' Marco said, excitedly. 'I think Majella said she hadn't done it in a while so she'd do it.'

'Well I don't want to put a dampener on things, but first things first.' Dan, forever the sensible one, brought the conversation back to basics. 'We need to know if the ticket was played for sure and then, when we know that, we'll make sure we find the ticket. So let's leave it that we meet at ours at three. That okay with everyone?'

'Fine by me,' said Rita.

Marco nodded. 'And me.'

And Lorraine. 'Yep, I'll be there.' She'd stopped trying to get a hold of Barry, and Maggie could see that she was upset that he wasn't answering his phone.

'Right, I think we'll call it a night so,' said Dan, standing up from the table. 'I've got to go shortly and collect our Steph from a disco. Let's just sleep on it and maybe something will come to us overnight.'

Marco followed Dan's lead and stood up, stretching his long, lean arms over his head. 'Oh, I couldn't sleep a wink with all this going on in my head. But I will have a think and see if I can remember anything about the ticket.'

'Me too,' said Rita. 'But I'm convinced Majella took it last time. The more I think about it, the more I'm convinced.'

Lorraine looked pensive. 'Well, let's hope so.'

They all walked quietly out to the front door, conscious of Rita's boys sleeping soundly upstairs. What a mad couple of hours it had been. To think they could possibly have won the lotto and lost it all on the same night. It didn't bear thinking about. Having said goodbye to the others, Maggie took her husband's arm as they crossed the little road back to their own house.

'God, Dan, I hope to God we really have won all that money. Can you imagine what that would do for us? It would change our lives completely.'

'But is life so bad really, Maggie?'

Maggie looked at her husband to see if he was being sarcastic but he looked serious. 'Of course life isn't that bad, Dan. But you know as well as I do that a bit of money would help sort a lot of things and would certainly make things a bit easier for us.'

'I suppose you're right. I just don't want you pinning your hopes on it. Let's just wait and see if one of us has actually done the numbers first – then we'll need to find the ticket.'

'I know you're just being cautious, Dan, but couldn't we just have one night of imagining we've won? Let's just think about what we could spend the money on. Oh, and just imagine what Steph will say.'

Dan smiled as he unlocked the front door. 'Yes, Steph will have plenty to say about it, I'm sure. And she'll have a long list of things she 'needs'! But let's not tell her tonight just in case. Wait until we know more tomorrow. It would be awful to get her hopes up if it comes to nothing.'

'I suppose you're right,' sighed Maggie. 'Part of me wishes I didn't know myself until it was definite.

'Well how about we stick on that movie after all to take our minds off it. We can pause it while I go and collect Steph and maybe you can rustle us up some dessert while I'm gone. All this celebrating has made me hungry again.'

'Good idea,' smiled Maggie, plonking down on the sofa. 'I think there's a bit of apple pie left from yesterday and I could make us a bit of custard.'

Dan looked at her mischievously. 'Well there's still another half hour before I have to go so why don't we forget about the lotto, forget about the movie, forget about the food and go and get ourselves some carpet burns to take our mind off things!'

'What a great idea, Mr O'Leary. There's nothing like a good carpet burn to end a perfect night!'

CHAPTER 10

'At bloody last,' said Lorraine, jumping up from the sofa as soon as she heard her husband come in the door. 'Have you lost your phone or something? I've been trying to call you all night.'

'Bloody hell, Lorraine. Nag, nag, nag, nag!' Barry stumbled into the little sitting room looking dishevelled and red in the face. 'It's only half eleven. You were hardly expecting me back before now.'

Lorraine was taken aback by how drunk he seemed. 'Jesus, look at the state of you. You must have had a right bellyful.'

'Any more complaints? And I'll have you know I only had a few, but since I had nothing in my stomach except a measly sandwich, it seems to have hit me harder than usual!'

'Well you can't blame me for *that*,' Lorraine said, hurt at his jibe. 'You were the one who decided to go out before I had a chance to make dinner.'

Barry stumbled across the room and plonked himself down on the sofa, stretching out his legs so that there was no room for his wife to sit down. 'And what was so urgent that you were trying to ring me anyway?'

Lorraine sat down on the chair under the window. 'Oh, Barry, I've been dying to talk to you all night. You'll never guess what's happened.'

'Go on,' said Barry, suddenly looking very sober. He swung his legs back down on the floor and straightened himself up to look at his wife. 'I've been expecting this.'

Lorraine looked confused. 'Expecting what, Bar?'

'Nothing, nothing. Go on, what's happened?'

'Well …' said Lorraine, pausing for effect. 'It's very possible that tonight—'

'Jesus, spit it out, woman!'

'It may just be that tonight we've won the lotto!'

Barry just stared at her.

'Did you hear me, Bar. We may very well have won the lotto!'

'I, eh, I wasn't expecting for you to tell me *that*.'

'Well, of course you weren't you big eejit,' laughed Lorraine. 'It's come as a shock to us all.'

'What do you mean 'us all'? Who else knows? And what do you mean we "may have" won?' Barry was rubbing his head as though trying to make sense of it all.

'I'll tell you what,' said Lorraine, jumping back up off the sofa. 'You have a look at the telly for a minute and I'll go and make us some coffees and I'll tell you all about it. But God, Barry, it's so exciting.'

Ten minutes later, they were both sipping their drinks and Lorraine had filled Barry in on the evening's events. It had been such a topsy-turvy night, with her emotions going up and down like a yoyo and yet just talking to her husband like this made her feel normal – it gave her hope that everything would be okay.

'Jesus, why didn't you come down to the pub and tell me? We could have had a right celebration.'

'Three reasons,' said Lorraine, cupping her hands around her mug. 'Firstly, we're not sure if the numbers were played yet. We should know that in the morning. Secondly, we'll need to try and locate the ticket and, thirdly, we may not want to go public with it. We'll really need to take a vote on what we want to do.'

Barry nodded. 'I hadn't thought of that. I suppose we wouldn't really want everyone to know our business. It's sort of a pity we didn't win on our own though, isn't it? All that money to ourselves and nobody at all would have to know.'

Lorraine was quick to shoot him down. 'I'd *hate* to win all that money on our own, Bar. It's just so much. And, besides, it's lovely to share it with our friends and see how it'll make the others happy too.'

'Hmmmm. I suppose. Just think, no more having to work overtime, no more scrimping and saving – we'll be able to have a nice holiday, buy a new car! It'll be amazing.'

Lorraine beamed. She loved seeing Barry back to his old self again. Maybe she'd been wrong about her suspicions. But if they had actually won and were about to come into a load of money, she'd have to make sure that the gambling wasn't an issue. 'It'll be brilliant all right, Bar. And it will definitely sort out a lot of our problems.'

Barry was on a roll. 'And don't forget the baby. We'll be able to buy it everything it needs and not the cheap stuff either. It'll want for nothing.'

'*If* it happens, Bar. Don't get too ahead of yourself.'

Barry reached over and put his hand on his wife's flat stomach. 'Oh, it will, Lorraine. I just know it. And if we've won all that money, we can have as many as we want and not worry about the cost.'

Lorraine paled. 'Well it's not just the cost, Bar. There's more to think about than that. I'm not a baby machine and can't churn out one after the other on demand!'

'I know that, Lorraine. But time isn't on our side so if we're going to have a few, we should try to have them as soon as possible.'

Lorraine sighed but decided not to say any more on the subject. People always say that money comes with its problems and she could never really understand that. But they hadn't even got the money yet and there was already a problem. She'd certainly be putting Barry straight – there was no way she'd be having one baby after the other, no matter how much money they had! One was more than enough. But with the uncertainty that seemed to be hanging in the air between them at the moment, she'd just put it on the queue with the whole list of things they needed to discuss!

She saw Barry had nodded off beside her on the sofa, mouth open and a line of drool dripping out of the side of his mouth. Very attractive indeed! It didn't look like they'd be making any attempts to make babies tonight. She picked up their two mugs and went into the kitchen to tidy up before going to bed. Sticking the mugs in the dishwasher, she thought about the evening and how the excitement had turned to uncertainty.

God, it was unbelievable to think they might have won the lotto. But what a cruel twist of fate it would be if the numbers hadn't been played. And even if they definitely *were* played, they still had to find the ticket. What a palaver!

She turned off the light in the kitchen and went back into the sitting room to give her husband a gentle shake before heading upstairs. Tonight she wasn't too bothered if he slept on the sofa. All the talk of babies was putting her right off sex and, anyway, she hated it when he breathed beer fumes all over her. Let him stay down there and sleep it off. Hopefully tomorrow they'd find out about the ticket and they'd know their fate. And hopefully fate would deal her a good hand *this* time!

C'mon, Mimi, will you? I'm going to lock you outside if you don't come back in now.' Marco wanted to lock up for the night and maybe have a Twitter chat with Claude if he was online.

The little black cockapoo stopped for a minute and stared at his owner who was slowly closing over the door. Mimi didn't have to think twice! She obviously understood enough to know that sleeping on the end of a nice warm bed was far more favourable to being left outside in the cold. She shot in the door which was still open a fraction and legged it upstairs in fright.

Marco giggled to himself as he went into his eclectically styled living room. This was the room that most had his personality stamped all over it. Never one to go for boring magnolia-painted walls, he prided himself on being able to throw together any combination of colours or styles and make them work. He could mix old with new and his antique aubergine and cream striped armchair alongside his modern red chenille sofa was a typical example of that. Pink candles, green cushions, stripes mixed with spots – in theory it should have looked gaudy and tasteless, but Marco's magic touch made everything look fantastic. Switching on his laptop, he sat back on the sofa while it was warming up. He tried to remember that night in the pub after the bingo a few weeks ago when Maggie had asked who was taking the lotto slip next.

He remembered there being a flurry of people throwing their money on the table but after that, he really didn't know what had happened. He'd only agreed with Rita earlier that it was probably Majella in case he had taken the slip and money himself and forgotten to do it! God, imagine it had been him and he hadn't played the numbers!

At bloody last, he thought, as the computer finally stopped making burping noises and the welcome screen appeared. His fingers found the keys quickly and within seconds he was on Twitter.

> *@Marcofashion1: Hi @ClaudeRIP. Are you there? I'm dying to tell you some news.*
>
> *@Marcofashion1: If you're there, turn to DM and we can have a private chat.*

Ah, shite! No answer. He mustn't be online. He's probably out getting his last few bits and pieces for his trip. Marco decided to just text him instead and if he was free, maybe they'd have a chat. Marco quickly sent a text and prayed his friend would answer. He switched off the computer and decided against bringing it up to bed with him. If he was going to chat to Claude, they could do it on the phone.

He headed up the steep, narrow staircase and into his room. He loved the relaxing vibe in his bedroom. The soft blue painted walls shouldn't really have worked with the raspberry pink bedding but somehow they did. Having brushed his teeth and stripped to his boxers, he was just about to burrow under the bedclothes when his mobile rang.

'Hello ... Claude?' He knew nobody else would be ringing him at that hour.

'Hey there, Marco. Yes it's me. I just got your message. How are you?'

'I'm just great, Claude. What are you up to? I've been dying to talk to you.'

'I'm just finishing off my packing and I was actually just thinking of you when the tweet came through.'

Marco never tired of listening to his friend's Irish accent which was touched lightly with a New York twang. 'Were you? Good thoughts I hope?'

'Of course,' purred Claude, and Marco could feel himself growing hard. 'So what's this news you wanted to tell me then?'

'Oh, it's just brilliant, Claude. You won't believe it. I'm not supposed to tell anybody yet but it's possible me and a few of my friends on the road have won the lotto!'

'Are you serious? But how come you don't know for sure?'

'Well the winning numbers are ours all right, but we won't know until tomorrow whether they've been played or not. It's all very complicated but I'll fill you in more when you're over.'

'It sounds intriguing. And congratulations. That's brilliant news.'

'Well, as I said, we won't know for sure until tomorrow so I suppose we shouldn't count our chickens. But I'll tell you one thing, if we have won, I'm really going to show you a good time when you're over here!'

There was no response. 'Claude, are you still there?'

'I'm here,' said Claude, his voice low. 'But I've told you

before, you don't need to spend your money on me. It's *your* money. I'm well capable of paying my own way.'

'Ah, come on, Claude. I know you are but if I've won the lotto, I'll be rolling in it so the least I can do is splash out a bit.'

'Right, well we'll see. I'd better go here and finish this off and I'll be seeing you on Monday then.'

'Eh, right so,' Marco said, feeling he was getting the brush off. 'I can't wait.'

Marco put the phone on his locker and lay back on his feather pillow. That was the second time that Claude had bristled at the mention of money. Maybe he was just used to paying his own way. After all, he'd left home to go and live in the States when he was fairly young so perhaps he's just very independent now.

Well, whatever it was, Marco wasn't going to let it burst his bubble tonight. 'Night, Mimi,' he said to the little dog who was already softly snoring. He pulled the duvet up to his neck and curled up onto his side. Within minutes he was drifting off and dreaming dreams of money falling from the skies and him and Claude riding off into the sunset on a pair of white horses!

'Something smells good,' said Steph, arriving into the little kitchen where Maggie was heating up some apple pie for her and Dan.

'Howareya, love,' said Maggie. 'Did you have a good night?'

'It was great, Ma. Thanks for letting me stay until the end.'

Maggie shot her daughter a grateful look. It wasn't often she got a thanks from the strong-headed girl. 'Well, as I said, it won't be every night but now and again is okay. And you can take your eyes off that tart. It's for me and your dad. You can have a bowl of cereal and straight up to bed.'

'Ah, Ma!'

'Don't you "ah, Ma" your mother, Steph,' said Dan, following his daughter into the kitchen. 'It's almost midnight. Get yourself something small and up to bed.'

'All right,' said Steph, giggling. 'It was worth a try. Did you two have a nice night? How come you're only having your dessert now?'

'We just got engrossed in the movie,' said Dan quickly. 'Then before we knew it, it was time to go and get you.'

'Well, we did get distracted from the movie for a bit,' said Maggie. She couldn't help it. She was bursting to tell her daughter about the lotto. Steph would be over the moon.

Dan shot her a warning look. 'Yes, we got distracted by Lorraine. She dropped in for some teabags and we had to pause while her and your mam got nattering.'

'Oh, I see,' said Stephanie, pouring milk over a bowl of Rice Krispies. She obviously had no interest in what her parents had been up to and had only asked out of politeness. 'I'm just taking this into the sitting room to watch MTV and I'll be gone in five minutes.'

'Right, love,' said Maggie, before turning to Dan. 'Ah, Dan, can we not tell her? I'm dying to.'

'No, Maggie. Absolutely not. She doesn't need to know yet until we're sure. Imagine how she'd be gutted if we told her and it turned out that the ticket wasn't played?'

'I know, I know. But it's just so exciting. I'm bursting with the news.'

Dan came up behind his wife and slipped his hands around her waist, kissing her neck softly. 'Hopefully we'll know more tomorrow and we can tell her then.'

'Eeew, get a room you two,' said Steph, coming back into the kitchen to leave in her bowl. 'I'm off to bed. And by the way, you might want to sort out that rug in front of the fire. For some reason it's all messed up. Night.'

Maggie turned to kiss her daughter goodnight and when she was out of earshot, she burst out laughing at Dan's shocked face. 'Come on, Dan. She *is* fourteen, you know. She's no fool.'

'I suppose you're right,' he sighed, shaking his head. 'Maybe if this money happens, we should think about buying a bigger house somewhere – one that would give us more privacy.'

'Are you mad, Dan?' Maggie was shocked at the thought. 'I wouldn't leave Enda's for all the money in the world. I've no desire to live anywhere else. I'm guessing all the others feel the same. No, the money will be great for a number of things, but moving house is not one of them.'

'I suppose you're right, Maggie. I wouldn't really want to leave the street either. Let's just hope the others feel the same or it could be the end of Enda's as we know it!'

Maggie shuddered at the thought. Please God, it would all work out for the best.

CHAPTER 11

Sunday, 11th September

'Go in peace to love and serve the Lord.' The priest raised his hands to bless the congregation, which consisted of no more than twenty people.

'Thanks be to God.' Maggie blessed herself and genuflected hastily before leaving. Mass wasn't like it used to be when she was a child. When her own mother had dragged her here every Sunday, they had to be there early to find a seat. These days, there was rarely more than a scattering of people – and the earlier the mass, the fewer in attendance.

Although Maggie and Dan were both Catholic and had brought their daughter up in the faith, they'd lapsed in recent times. Most of their friends were the same – the Catholic Church had never really recovered from the abuse scandals and certainly Maggie just didn't feel the same draw to it any more.

She hadn't been able to sleep much last night between the excitement and her stomach playing up again. She hadn't felt too bad earlier on, but by the time they'd gone to bed that had changed. She wasn't sure if it was from the love-making or too much food, but her gut had felt as though it was in a knot. Dan had been tossing and turning too, but, unlike her, he seemed to have fallen into a deep sleep before the sun came up. Maggie had given up at around half six and had padded quietly downstairs to put the kettle on.

It was while she had been sitting at her kitchen table sipping tea that she'd felt the urge to go to mass. She still believed strongly in the power of prayer and it dawned on her that there were a number of things she could pray for. She knew that if she went to the eight o'clock one, she'd be well back before anybody even stirred.

Nodding at the few familiar faces, she had quickened her pace until she got out the church gates. The last thing she wanted at the moment was to enter into conversations when she'd so much going on in her own mind. She'd stuck an extra few bob in the box in front of the St Anthony statue and practically begged him to find the lost ticket – that was after she'd said a prayer to Our Lady that the numbers were done in the first place!

As she left the church, she pulled up the collar of her old grey coat to fend off the cool breeze. Then a thought struck her. Maybe Dargle's would be open. It was still early, but Mr Dargle was savvy enough to know that it would make good business sense to open and catch the Sunday mass crowd. Oooh, imagine if she could go home with the news that they actually *had* won. But the flip side of that was the thought of having to be the bearer of bad news if the little newsagents hadn't sold the winning ticket.

Her luck was in. Sure enough, Mr Dargle was putting the signs out front as she rounded the corner towards Enda's.

Now, how would she broach it with him? She didn't want to let him know about the syndicate yet, but it would probably look strange if she asked. Well, she'd go and buy one of the Sunday papers for starters and take it from there.

'Howareya, Mr Dargle,' she said, smiling at the stooped form in front of her.

'Ah, not too bad, Maggie. Sure who'd listen if I complained anyway?' He rewarded her with a toothless grin as he held open the door for his first customer of the day.

'So, you're up and about early,' Maggie said, rummaging through the selection of Sunday papers. 'Don't you ever take time off?'

'I can't afford to stay closed in this climate, Maggie. With all the bigger shops opening all hours, I wouldn't stay afloat if I closed of a Sunday.'

A young mother with a toddler came rushing in for an emergency lolly, so Maggie stepped aside to let her go.'

'No, you were before me,' said the frazzled mother, clutching the hand of the teary-eyed child.

'Not at all, you go ahead. I'm still deciding on which paper to get.' Maggie needed more time to question Mr Dargle.

'Thanks for that.' She was gone again within seconds.

'So, Mr Dargle, any news with you?'

'Not much, Maggie, to tell you the truth. The grandson is starting in Trinity next week – where does the time go? Eh?'

Damn! He either didn't sell the ticket or he doesn't know about it yet. 'I know what you mean. Steph has just started her Junior Cert year and it seems like no time since I was changing her nappy.'

'Sorry, just give me a sec,' he said, indicating the ancient phone at the end of the counter that had started ringing. 'Eh … hello … it's, eh … it's Dargle's here.'

Maggie stifled a giggle. He sounded as though he'd never answered a phone before. Honestly, he must be heading for ninety. Her mother used to say that she didn't remember a time when Mr Dargle wasn't serving behind that counter, so that's going back a right few years.

'I *what*?' he said into the receiver. 'Bloody hell, are you sure?' There was a silence when the person at the other end of the phone must have been talking. Then Mr Dargle again: '*Jayzus*!'

Maggie had never heard the old man swear before. She watched him nod his head as he listened to what the caller had to say, thanked them and then hung up.'

'Jayzus,' he said again, shaking his head.

'What's up, Mr Dargle? Are you okay?'

'You'll never guess what, Maggie. That was my local rep from the National Lottery. I've only gone and sold the winning ticket from last night's draw.' It was as though he'd won the money himself because he'd gone white as a sheet and was having to steady himself against the grey plastic counter.

Maggie could scarcely believe her ears and felt wobbly herself for a minute. 'Ooooh, wow! That's absolutely brilliant. Really brilliant.'

'Ay, it is that. You'd want to go off home and check your own numbers. You'd never know!'

'Em, I suppose,' said Maggie, reddening. She hated lying. 'So would you think it's definitely somebody from around here then?'

'You wouldn't know really. It could be someone passing through but, to be honest, it's mostly locals that come in here. I certainly hope it's one of my regulars – wouldn't that be cause to celebrate?'

'And … and, em, do you know any more details about it?'

Maggie would have loved to tell him, but she needed to get some information and get out of there fast.

'Well, apparently there were two winners last night and they shared two million. The other winner is down in Cork. Oh, God, I still can't believe it. In my little shop!'

'So a million each,' said Maggie, already making plans for her two hundred thousand share. 'That's a nice little sum, isn't it?'

'Oh, it's fantastic,' said the old man, the colour coming back to his cheeks. 'And I'll get a few bob myself for selling the ticket. I just knew this was going to be a good day when I woke up this morning.'

'Well, it's great news, Mr Dargle, but I'd better be heading off. I've promised Dan and Steph I'd do them a nice fry-up this morning.'

'Ah, you can't beat it on a Sunday morning,' he said, nodding his approval.

'Right, and congratulations again. Let us know if the winner claims the money.' Shit, now why had she gone and said that.

He did that toothless grin again. 'Well, I'm pretty sure they *will* be claiming the money, Maggie. But they might choose to stay anonymous. I hope they don't. I'll be dying to know who it is.'

Maggie handed over the correct change for the paper and turned to leave. 'Me, too, Mr Dargle. I'll be dying to see who has that winning ticket!'

Marco hadn't been able to sleep and, since Mimi was up at her usual time anyway, he'd decided to go out for a walk. His head had been pounding since last night and even a double dose of Solpadeine hadn't sorted it out. He knew it was nothing more than an overcrowded brain – there was so much going on in his head at the moment that it was difficult to get his thoughts straight.

He locked the front door and headed out through his newly painted silver railings. 'Are you warm enough, Mimi?' he whispered to his little dog, who was safely tucked up under his arm. 'Maybe I'll get you one of those little doggie coats for the winter.'

Mimi didn't look bothered about whether or not she'd get a new coat. She was busy looking around and watching the world go by. Marco had given up putting a lead on her because he'd only get looks from passers-by as he'd practically have to drag her down the street.

God, it wasn't even nine o'clock yet – another six hours before they were due to meet in Maggie and Dan's. He was bursting to find out about the lotto ticket. Just imagine, they could be millionaires and here he was, just going about his day-to-day stuff like he normally would.

Just as he got to the end of the terrace, he almost jumped out of his skin when a woman seemed to come out of nowhere. 'What the fu—? Maggie. What's up with you? You look as though you're trying to escape from somewhere.'

'Ah, Marco, I'm glad I bumped into you. I was just on my way home to tell Dan ... so that he'd know before I told everyone else ... but since you're here and he's not and I really need to tell you all anyway but you'll have to promise ...' Maggie was out of breath and tripping on her words.

'Jesus, Maggie! Just spit it out, woman, will you?' It was a bit early for his friend to be playing a guessing game!

'The lotto, Marco. We've won the lotto!'

'I seem to have a bit of déjà vu here, Maggie!'

'No, I mean I've checked. Dargle's sold the winning ticket. We've definitely played the numbers. We've *won*, Marco. We're rich!'

'Oh, Holy Mother of God,' gasped Marco, putting the palm of his hand over his forehead in a dramatic gesture. 'So we really *have* won? It's got to be us, right?'

'Of course it's us, Marco. They're our numbers and that's our local shop so unless it's the biggest coincidence of all time, it's definitely our win!' Maggie looked at Mimi, who seemed to be listening quietly to every word they said. 'And, by the way, doesn't it defeat the purpose of walking the dog when it's you walking and she's relaxing under your arm?'

'That's how she likes her walks,' said Marco, defensively. 'She doesn't like it when I let her down in the streets. The noises make her nervous so I like to keep her here under my arm where she feels safe.'

'Hmmmm!' said Maggie, obviously not convinced. 'Anyway we'd better bloody find the ticket now. Do you still think Majella has it?'

Marco hesitated. 'I, em, well, I did say that last night but, to be honest, Maggie, I'm not so sure. I remember seeing the money on the table in the pub but I didn't see who took it up!'

'Me neither,' admitted Maggie. 'The more I try to remember, the more scrambled it all seems in my brain.'

'Well hopefully it *is* Majella who has it,' he said, more confidently. 'We'll know soon enough.'

Maggie sighed. 'I really hope so, Marco. What time did she say she'd be back? I can't wait to tell her the news.'

'She told Rita she'd be back early, so it could be any time.' Mimi began to wriggle in his arms, which was a sign she was getting bored.

'And if she doesn't have the ticket, we'll all just have to go and rip our houses apart to look for it. And, of course, we'll need to get on to the National Lottery straight away if it hasn't turned up by morning.'

'Definitely. Oh, God, I'll have a nervous breakdown if it doesn't turn up. All that money …'

'I know, Marco. Well at least we know it's been played. I think we'll all be having a nervous breakdown if we don't find it quickly, but let's just make sure we do.'

Marco nodded. Right, let's think positively. We'll just *have* to find it. I'm off to finish our walk and I'll see you at yours at three.'

'Yep, it will be good to get us all together. I can't wait to go and tell Dan the news from Dargle's.'

'God, the excitement is almost too much to bear, Maggie, isn't it? Our lives are about to change massively.'

'That's for sure. Ah, feck! With all the excitement, I've only gone and forgotten to pick up the sausages and rashers for the fry.'

'Well, I think you can be forgiven under the circumstances.'

'That's true. Well, I'll head back anyway. Maybe I'll make some French toast instead.'

'You spoil that family of yours, Mags,' teased Marco. 'Well if you're looking for tasters, I'm your man.'

'Ah, go on then, I'll send you in a slice or two since you probably have nothing at all to eat in those empty cupboards. One of these days I'm going to teach you how to cook properly and then you'll never go hungry.'

'No, don't! Ignorance is bliss and all that! I'm happy as I am.'

'And you're about to be a whole lot happier with two hundred thousand euro in your pocket!' said Maggie, smiling at her friend.

'Fingers crossed,' said Marco. 'And if we do find that ticket tonight, the film crew that arrive here tomorrow are going to be delighted that Enda's is living up to the happy street I've portrayed it as. There'll certainly be plenty to smile about!

'Coo-ee! Majella! You're back early.' Marco was just coming back from his walk with Mimi when he saw his neighbour step out of her car. It amazed him that even at this early hour, her long chestnut hair was flicked back to perfection and her make-up looked as though it had been professionally applied.

'Hiya, Marco. Yes, I decided I needed an early escape. It's good to get home to the parents but sometimes it's just too stifling.'

'And where's Chris?' Marco craned his neck to see if Majella's husband had yet to get out of the car. 'Did he decide to stay for the sausages and rashers?'

'Oh, don't! The thought of my mother's greasy fry-ups is enough to make me gag. He's gone off golfing with my dad, so I told my mother I was working today.'

'Naughty, naughty,' laughed Marco, eyeing up her gorgeous dusky pink sling-backs. He had a divine dress in the shop that would go perfectly with them. 'So are you coming to this meeting today at three?'

'I'm planning on a nice quiet day at home so, yes, I'll drop down for the meeting. What's it all about though? Rita said it was about this documentary thing when she texted but what is there to talk about?'

'Eh, yes, the documentary thing. That's what it's about.' Marco was bursting to tell her but it had been agreed that they'd tell her together so he knew he couldn't say anything yet.

'But what *about* the documentary?' Majella persisted. 'They're just coming to chat to a few of us and take some shots of the street. Or have I missed something?'

'Well, just come down at three and you'll see what you've missed.' He just couldn't help himself!

'Marco! Tell me! What is it?'

'I'm sworn to secrecy. My lips are sealed.' He started walking down towards his own house. 'Mimi is starving. I'd better get her in for a feed. I'll see you at three.'

'Marco Gallagher! You're not getting away that easily!' Majella obviously wasn't going to let it go and caught up with him before he got to his own gate. 'Why the mystery? Has something bad happened?'

'Ah, Majella, don't make me tell you. I'll get into trouble. But it's nothing bad – quite the opposite actually.'

'Jesus, Marco. Will you just bloody *tell me!*'

Well how was he expected to keep quiet about it now? She'd practically bullied him into telling her. 'Shhhh, Majella, will you? Come on in and I'll tell you what's happened.'

'Oooh, if I have to be taken off the street to be told, it must be something good!'

'Trust me,' said Marco, opening the door and letting Mimi down onto the shiny, laminate floor. 'It's as good as it gets.'

Majella followed Marco in and shut the door behind them. 'No, Marco, what would be "as good as it gets" would be winning the lotto. Now that would be something worth getting excited about.'

Marco spun around to look at his neighbour, his mouth gaping open. He didn't have to say anything.

Majella caught the look. 'Jesus!'

CHAPTER 12

'Right, let's get started, will we?' Maggie placed a pot of tea in the centre of the table and took a seat beside her friends.

'Yes, can we get through this quickly,' said Rita, nervously eyeing up her two boys who were playing cowboys and indians and darting in and out of the kitchen. 'These two had Coke with their dinner and they're wired. I need to get them out into the fresh air for a while. I just want to know when I'll be getting my share of that money.'

'Well, we'll keep it brief,' said Maggie, ducking as a foam bullet shot across the room, narrowly missing her head. 'Marco has brought Majella up to speed on last night's goings on, so there's no need to go over it.' She paused to glower at Marco, who at least had the sense to look guilty.

'Mags, I said I was sorry for telling her but she practically dragged it out of me, didn't you, Majella?'

'I did sort of make him tell me.' Majella ran her fingers through her long chestnut hair. 'But why shouldn't I have? I'm as much a part of this as all of you are so why should I have been kept in the dark?'

Rita banged her hand on the table, rattling the cups and startling everyone. 'Sorry, but let's just get to the point. It doesn't matter who told who, what matters is that we find that ticket.'

'You're absolutely right, Rita,' Maggie said. 'Well let's have a look at the facts. We play the lotto four weeks in advance so by my calculation, it was three weeks ago when it was last done. As I told you all, I wasn't feeling the best on the Thursday night, but I do remember putting the lotto slip with my own thirteen euro on the table.'

Majella was quick to add her piece. 'Me, too – I definitely remember throwing in my money, but I don't remember what happened after that.'

'Well, it seems none of us does,' said Marco, shaking his head. 'But one of us must have taken it up and played the numbers in Dargle's. It seems unbelievable that whoever did it can't remember.'

'Well, in fairness, it was three weeks ago – sometimes I can't remember what I did three minutes ago,' laughed Rita, until she realised all eyes were on her. 'Oh, Jesus … I don't mean, well, you know what I mean. I might suffer from mammy-brain but I can assure you, I definitely did *not* play those numbers!'

'Well, that's what we *all* think, Rita,' said Lorraine, who'd been quiet up until that point. 'We're all full sure that we didn't play the numbers, but clearly one of us did.'

'Look, let's all just take a step back for a moment and think about it.' Maggie felt the meeting could get out of hand if she let it, so she wanted to take control. 'I honestly don't remember playing the numbers but I'm willing to admit that maybe I did and the ticket is lying around here somewhere.'

'I'm fully sure it wasn't me either,' chimed in Marco, 'but, like you, I'll take a look at home, just in case.'

'Me, too,' said Lorraine. 'Like everyone else, I don't remember doing it but I'll never say never.'

'I know it wasn't me, but I'll have a look anyway.' Rita was remaining stubborn about it but at least she was going to have a look.

'So what about you, Majella?' Maggie realised they'd all had a chance to sleep on it but Majella must be still taking it all in. 'You must have got a shock. What's your take on it?'

'It wasn't me anyway,' she said defiantly. 'I haven't done it in ages but I'm always first to hand over my money. I do remember that night at the pub when the money was on the table, but I can't remember who took it at the end of the night.'

'Well, maybe have a little look at home anyway,' Maggie said gently. 'We may as well all cover the bases by looking and it might even jog our memories in the process.'

'Of course, I'll look – but it won't be there.' Majella's face remained determined and Maggie could see that there was no point harping on about it.

'Right,' said Maggie, trying to move things on. 'It'll turn up, I'm sure it will. It just has to. So the next thing is privacy. What do we all think about going public with this? Anyone got any thoughts on the matter?'

'Yes, I've got plenty of thoughts on the subject!' Rita was first to chime in. 'There's absolutely no way I want anybody to know I've won the money. Can you imagine what would happen if my bastard husband got to hear about it? He'd have me in court in a flash and would claim half of it. There's no way he's getting his hands on a single penny.'

'I agree with Rita,' Majella said quickly. 'You know what people are like – as soon as they think you have a bit of money, they think you should be throwing it at them.'

'Exactly,' Lorraine chimed in. 'I think people look at you in a different light when you have money – not that I've ever really had any, but I know how people think!'

'Well, I think you're all killjoys to be honest.' Marco didn't look impressed. 'Half the fun in winning money is being able to spread the joy. I'd love to scream it from the rooftops!'

Maggie rolled her eyes at the dramatics of her neighbour. 'Look, I'm probably somewhere in between when it comes to going public. I can see where you're all coming from. Part of me would love to tell everyone – I'd love to go down to O'Mahony's and have drinks on me for the night. But, on the other hand, Lorraine is right. We don't want people treating us differently just because we have a bit of money. We have a good life around here with good friends. It would be a pity to spoil that.'

Marco looked as if he was going to argue the point, but then thought better of it.

Maggie continued. 'Dan, you haven't said a word yet. What do you think about keeping it to ourselves or going public?'

'To be honest, Maggie, we're losing sight of the important issue. Shouldn't we just find the blasted ticket first and then talk about the next step? Because if we don't find that ticket, there'll be no money.'

He just let that hang in the air and it was a good couple of minutes before anybody spoke. Lorraine was the first to break the silence. 'Right, I'm going to head home and have a good look for the ticket. I suggest we all do the same and see what happens.'

'Right,' said Rita, standing up. 'I'll settle these two in front of a movie and have a root around. But I'm just telling you all now, I didn't do the numbers and I'm going to swing for whoever did when we find the ticket. Imagine not—'

'Oh, for God's sake, Rita. Shut up, will you,' snapped Majella. 'What's the point in making a threat like that – you'll have the person afraid to come forward if they find it!'

Rita reddened at the rebuke. 'I'm just saying, Majella. What's wrong with you all? Why aren't you screaming and shouting about it? I mean, *two hundred thousand euro* – it's not as though someone has just lost a tenner!'

Maggie tried to bring the meeting back to order. 'Rita, we all feel the same, but let's not get ahead of ourselves. I bet it will turn up this evening – someone has just forgotten they've done it and it will be in their handbag or something.'

'And another thing,' added Dan. 'If the ticket doesn't turn up by tomorrow, one of us should ring the National Lottery and inform them of our win. We can say we want it kept quiet for now, but they should be aware that the ticket is missing. God forbid it would fall into the wrong hands but at least the lottery people would be aware of our claim to the money.'

'Oh, Jesus, I hope the ticket hasn't been dropped on the street,' Marco said, looking panicked. 'Imagine someone finding it and checking to see if they'd won anything!'

Dan nodded. 'That's why the National Lottery should be informed straight away – just in case.'

'Right, I'll do that,' said Marco, standing up from the table. 'I'll check in with everyone in the morning and if it hasn't turned up, I'll give them a call. Right, now let's leave these lovely people to their Sunday. Thanks, Mags, for the tea.'

Maggie shot him a grateful look. She could feel her eyes closing and would welcome a snooze before tea. 'You're welcome, Marco. Always a pleasure to feed you up!'

'So where's your Steph today?' asked Lorraine, walking out towards the front door. 'Does she know about this yet?'

'We haven't told her a thing,' said Maggie, opening the door for her friends. 'She's gone to the cinema with a few pals – she couldn't believe it when I offered her the money, but I just wanted her out of the way for this.'

'Aren't you going to tell her, Maggie?' Marco was looking at her as though she had ten heads. 'I can't believe you managed to keep it from her. I'd be bursting.'

'I was bursting to tell her last night, to tell you the truth, but Dan pointed out that it wouldn't be fair to tell her until we knew what's what.'

Lorraine nodded her head. 'You're right, Maggie. She's too young to build up her hopes and then shatter them. Let's just wait and see what happens.'

Maggie said her goodbyes and went back into the kitchen where Dan was cleaning the table and loading the dishwasher. 'Thanks, Dan, you're a love. I think I'll take myself onto the sofa and have a little nap.'

'You go on in Maggie. Will I bring you in a cuppa?'

'No thanks, love. I've drunk enough tea today to last me until next week. I'm going to just have a little look in the sideboard though. I'm still convinced I didn't do those numbers but I'd be happy to eat my words if I found the ticket.'

'Well nobody is going to care who was right and who was wrong if we find the ticket. And I hope Marco won't say anything to Steph. You know how he just can't keep his mouth shut.'

'Ah, he won't, Dan. He can be a real blabbermouth at times, and I know he told Majella, but he wouldn't do that to us. He'll respect the fact that we don't want Steph to know yet.'

'I suppose,' Dan said reluctantly. 'But if the word starts spreading around, we'll have a fair idea who's to blame.'

Maggie smiled at her husband's worried face. 'Well as you said yourself, Dan, let's worry about finding the ticket first and then we can iron out all the other bits.'

Dan kissed his wife lightly on the forehead. 'You look exhausted, Mags. Go on in and have a sleep. I'll have a good look for the ticket and I'll wake you up if I find it.'

'I won't argue with you there,' said Maggie, yawning. 'Just give me an hour and then wake me up. That is, unless you find the ticket in the meantime.' She plonked herself down on the sofa in the living room and before she got a chance to go over everything in her head, she was snoring softly.

Back in his house, Marco sat at his breakfast bar and fretted. Why on earth had he told Claude about the lottery win? The fact that Claude was on the other side of the world had made it seem okay at the time. He'd better warn him to say nothing about it when he arrived.

He was jolted out of his reverie by Mimi pushing her stainless steel bowl against the wall. He took her bowl and dipped it in the huge bag of dried dog food and placed it down on the floor beside the back door. Taking the other bowl, he filled it with water and watched the little black ball of fluff almost disappear into it as she lapped it with gusto.

He wondered where Claude would be at that moment. Hmmmm! Four o'clock. He'd told him he was on the 9.50 flight from JFK that night, so he was probably just about ready to leave. He'd text him and see if he had time to go on Twitter for a few minutes. Grabbing his iPhone from the counter, he headed into the sitting room to switch on his computer. Despite the computer being ancient and slow, he still preferred to tweet from that than the fiddly keys of the phone. He switched it on and sent the text while it was groaning to life.

Making himself comfortable on his sofa with the laptop balanced on his knees, he thought about what two hundred thousand euro would mean to him. *God, it was a fortune!* The first thing he'd do would be to clear his mortgage. He'd grown up in number two, St Enda's Terrace, the youngest of four kids, and when his parents decided to up sticks and move to Spain he'd decided to buy the house off them. Although he sometimes appeared scatty, Marco was similar to Lorraine in that he was very sensible with money. He'd managed to save a bit since he'd left school at sixteen and he knew he'd have been mad to let the opportunity pass by.

It had seemed like a good idea at the time. The banks had been practically throwing money at people, offering 100 per cent mortgages, even more in some cases, so he'd only needed to get the bare minimum together for fees. However, with interest rate rises over the past few years, he was finding the mortgage difficult to maintain. He never regretted holding on to number two, but he sometimes hated the fact that he was crippled with a mortgage at such a young age. On top of that, there were education loans, credit card bills – he'd got to a point where he reckoned he'd never pay off his debts. Until yesterday! God, it was unbelievable to think that they'd won the lotto – they'd actually won the lotto! That bloody ticket had better show up. His phone beeped and he quickly checked it. Claude was just getting ready to leave but was turning on Twitter for a few minutes. Brilliant!

@Marcofashion1: Hi there, Claude. So, you're all set to go?

@ClaudeRIP: Yep! All packed and waiting for a taxi to the airport. Really excited – I haven't been home since last Christmas.

@Marcofashion1: So what time are you due to arrive in the morning? I'd come to the airport but since I've no car, there wouldn't be much point.

@ClaudeRIP: Don't worry. I'll probably see you tomorrow anyway. If not, it will definitely be Tuesday.

Marco's heart sank. Tuesday? He thought the crew were coming to film on Monday. And even if they weren't, he'd thought, or maybe he'd just hoped, Claude would have wanted to see him anyway.

@Marcofashion1: So are you saying the camera crew may not be coming over to film tomorrow? I thought it was definite.

@ClaudeRIP: Sorry, Marco. It really depends on how tired we all are after travelling. I'll let you know.

@Marcofashion1: Well, even if they're not coming until Tuesday, maybe we could meet up – if you're not too busy that is.

Marco bit down on his nails when he sent that. Why, oh why, couldn't he just wait and see how things panned out instead of always jumping in head first!

@ClaudeRIP: Definitely! Dying to meet up. I'll text you when we arrive in the morning and we can firm up plans.

@Marcofashion1: Brilliant! Oh and one last thing. Turn to DM for this.

@ClaudeRIP: Okay, I'm here. What's up?

@Marcofashion1: Please don't say anything about us winning the lotto to anyone. The others don't want to go public yet.

@ClaudeRIP: Sure, no problem. I haven't said a thing to anyone.

@Marcofashion1: That's a relief. I'd hate for them to think I was telling people. You're the only one I've told.

@ClaudeRIP: So, I take it you've got it sorted now and that you've found the ticket?

@Marcofashion1: Well, we've found out that it was definitely played but we haven't found the ticket yet.

@ClaudeRIP: Well, I'm sure it will turn up. Right, I'd better go. I'll talk to you tomorrow. x

@Marcofashion1: Yes, talk to you then. Safe flight. x

Marco logged out and snapped the laptop shut. What he needed to do now was concentrate on looking for that ticket. He was full sure he hadn't played it, but his head was so full of other stuff at the moment that it was quite possible he'd forgotten. Well, thankfully, he hated clutter and everything in his drawers was well organised. It shouldn't take him long to check in the few places it could be. The thought of what the money could do for him buoyed him on and he began his meticulous search of every drawer in the house. He hoped the others were all doing the same. Either way, the ticket would turn up; it had to. And the timing of the win was perfect in that everyone would be in top form for the documentary. They'd show the Americans how warm, funny and kind the Irish are and how Enda's is the best place in the world to live!

CHAPTER 13

Monday, 12th September

Lorraine sat on the bus on her way to work and she could feel her blood boiling when she thought about the events of the past couple of days. Jesus! Here she was going to work as normal, when she actually should have two hundred grand in her pocket! Unbelievable! Whoever had that bloody ticket had a lot to answer for! She'd been shocked and upset when nobody had found it the previous evening.

It was obvious one of them had the ticket, but they'd all been so defensive in Maggie's house yesterday, each of them claiming that they definitely didn't have it! It was probably understandable that they'd all react like that. Nobody wanted to be the one who'd played the numbers and lost the ticket. She'd be mortified if it was her – but she'd had a good root around her house, just in case, and it had confirmed to her that she definitely wasn't the one.

As the bus trundled down the gridlocked quays, she thought about what life would be like with all that money if she and

Barry had a baby. Although she gave out about her job, she couldn't imagine not working. She loved having a purpose in life and more than that, she loved feeling independent. She'd left home at an early age and it had made her self-sufficient. Her job in Buckley Lawlor Insurance didn't pay a huge salary, but it was enough.

Barry was so into the whole big family thing and was actually quite old fashioned in his views. He'd hinted that he'd like her to be a stay-at-home mother and give up her job entirely. She understood some people were happy to do that, but not her. She would go scatty if she had to spend all day singing 'The Wheels on the Bus' or building Lego castles. But they'd already looked into the price of childcare and it certainly didn't come cheap.

The money would change all that. Barry would probably say that it would enable her to give up work without any financial pressures, whereas she'd look on it as an opportunity for her to continue working, knowing the baby was having the best care money could buy.

And then there were other issues she'd have to sort out with Barry before they started playing happy families. Maggie was right. There were things he needed to know. But she just needed a little more time before that particular can of worms was opened!

Maggie flicked through a magazine and tried to distract herself. She hated doctors' waiting rooms. No amount of air fresheners seemed to quell the stench of illness and the grey walls just added to the dreariness. There were four or five people before her so she reckoned she was in for a bit of a wait.

When she'd woken up that morning, she'd thought her day was going to be a lot more exciting. The camera crew had been due to arrive and she'd been up early cleaning and baking. She'd been gutted when Marco had called around first thing to say they wouldn't be coming until tomorrow. It was only one more day, but it seemed like they'd been waiting for this day for ages.

It would be a good thing to distract them all from the lotto thing too. Nobody had found the ticket and she could sense there was a bit of panic setting in amongst the residents. She was trying to keep a sense of calmness on the street, but she feared that if the ticket didn't show up soon, all hell would break loose.

Marco was going to ring the National Lottery headquarters that morning, but there was no way they'd pay them the money without the ticket. And the other thing worrying her was that the story of the missing ticket might just leak out and would be all over the press in a blink of an eye. She still hadn't told Steph, although her daughter wasn't stupid and could sense there was something going on.

'What's all the whispering about, Ma?' she'd asked the previous night when she'd come in on a conversation about the ticket. 'I know you two are hiding something.'

Maggie had been quick to reassure her. She'd told her it was a problem her dad was having in work. It had been quick thinking, but she didn't think for a minute that her daughter had believed her. She'd talk to Dan about it again tonight and maybe they'd let her in on the news. It wasn't that they wanted to keep her in the dark – they just wanted to protect her from disappointment. Imagine how excited she'd be to find out that they'd won two hundred thousand euro and then to be told that they wouldn't be getting it because they didn't have the ticket. But it was likely she'd get to hear over the coming days so it was probably best if they told her.

So with Dan gone to work and Steph in school, Maggie had decided to do what she should have done weeks ago. She'd picked up the phone and dialled her GP's number and asked for an appointment. They'd been pretty much booked out but Lilly, the receptionist who'd been there for as long as Maggie could remember, had squeezed her in with the warning of a possible wait.

It was the only way she'd ever keep an appointment these days. She'd often rung and made an appointment days in advance but when the time would come around, she'd cry off, saying she was feeling much better. The only thing to get her there was to make the appointment at the last minute and not give herself time to think.

God forbid she'd have told Dan though. She loved him to bits but she knew he'd never give her a minute's peace if he'd known she needed to pay the doctor a visit. Maggie preferred to keep things like that quiet. What was the point in worrying anyone if it turned out there was nothing to worry about?

Dr Higgins appeared in the waiting room at that moment and everyone looked at him expectantly. 'Right, let's have ...' He checked the chart in his hands. '... Mr O'Brien, please ... Frank O'Brien.'

There was a collective sigh in the room as a delighted Mr O'Brien followed the doctor into his room. Maggie shifted uncomfortably in her seat, conscious of the trickles of sweat on her upper thighs from the plastic chairs. Maybe this was a bad idea. Maybe she shouldn't bother waiting. It was already almost one and Steph would be wondering where she was when she came home for lunch.

She'd just about decided to get up and leave when the woman next to her decided to pick that moment to start a conversation.

'Bloody uncomfortable, aren't they?'

'Sorry?' Maggie looked warily at the younger woman and tried not to stare at the piercing in her tongue as she spoke.

'The seats – they're so uncomfortable.' She spoke loudly and it seemed everyone in the waiting room had turned to listen. 'Wouldn't you think they'd provide us with something a bit cushier when they keep us waiting so long?'

Maggie sighed and abandoned her plan to leave because it would have looked rude. 'I suppose. But they're usually very efficient. Hopefully we won't be here for much longer.'

'I don't know about that. I'm sick of coming here and waiting all the time. You'd think they'd have a more effective way of dealing with patients. It's not as if we're getting seen to for free!' She twisted her long, yellow hair around in her fingers and chewed loudly on gum as she spoke. Maggie felt a little intimidated by this opinionated girl and fiddled nervously with the magazine in front of her.

But the girl wasn't ready to stop. 'And then by the time they do call you in, they've run out of time and are checking their watches every thirty seconds. Fuckin' disgraceful it is.'

Maggie winced at that. She suddenly felt inexplicably annoyed at this young girl. She was probably there to check out an infection she'd got in one of her piercing sites or something equally trivial. How dare she make people with *real* illnesses feel uncomfortable! She'd have to say something.

'Well, I don't think there's any need for that,' Maggie said, sounding braver than she felt. 'The doctors here work very hard and the reason we sometimes have to wait is because they don't like to rush people.' Maggie held her breath, ready for the onslaught. But the girl didn't seem fazed by her rebuke.

'Well, I still say the wait could be made a lot easier if we were a bit more comfortable. And look at those magazines. Most of them are from last year. The state of them!'

Maggie gave up and went back to reading her magazine. The girl was obviously a bit of a troublemaker. Well she could moan away – Maggie wouldn't be listening.

'So, what are you here for?' she asked, much to Maggie's discomfort. 'You don't look very sick – I bet it's a cold or a sore throat. Right?'

How bloody dare she! 'Well, I don't really want to discuss what it is, but it's none of what you suggested.'

'Ah, go on. You tell me yours and I'll tell you mine.'

Maggie was exasperated. 'Well, if I knew what it was, I probably wouldn't be here.' That should shut her up. 'And why don't you leave if it's so much of a hassle for you? I'm sure you'd pick something up from the pharmacy for whatever it is you're complaining of.'

'I don't think so,' she laughed. 'They're a long way from doling out home remedies for cervical cancer at the pharmacy.'

Maggie paled. Had she heard right? This young, feisty girl had cervical cancer? 'So is that … is that what you have?' She lowered her voice to a whisper.

'Yep! It's fuckin' shite, isn't it? One minute you're as fit as a fiddle and the next you're being told you're probably not going to see past thirty.'

'Oh, God, I'm so sorry. I didn't think … I didn't realise—'

'Don't worry about it.' Her face softened and Maggie suddenly saw a scared young girl who was obviously putting on a brave face. How had she not seen it in her face before that? 'It just pisses me off that not only will I probably die from this, but the time I have left is being spent in these god-awful places.'

'Of course. It must be awful.' Maggie didn't know what else to say. She felt close to tears and of course she couldn't let the other girl see she was crying. What right did *she* have to cry?

'Eleanor Mullen.' The doctor was back and, this time, it was the turn of the girl with cancer.

'About bloody time,' she said, standing up and walking aggressively towards the doctor. 'Do you know how long I've been waiting?'

Maggie couldn't help smiling at that. At least she hadn't hit the old doctor with the f-word. But the exchange had rattled her. The girl couldn't have been more than twenty-five – far too young to be faced with something like that. But it happened. Sometimes life dealt some rotten cards and that poor girl had certainly been dealt the worst.

She tried to distract herself with the magazine. She opened it on a feature story, 'Kate and Will's Magical Wedding'. God, they really were old magazines! When she thought about it, the girl had probably been right about most of what she'd said. The seats *were* uncomfortable and even if you made an appointment weeks in advance for a certain time, it was likely you'd be waiting an hour or more!

She thought about the poor girl and all she must be going through. She wondered how she was told. What would it be like to be told something like that? What would it be like to know you were going to die young? It just didn't bear thinking about.

'Maggie O'Leary.' Suddenly she didn't want her name to

be called out. If she kept her head down, they might just go on to the next person and she could slip out unnoticed. This had been a mistake. She shouldn't have bothered making the appointment at all. What had she been thinking? She continued leafing through the magazine, afraid to look up and meet the eye of the doctor.

'Maggie O'Leary.' He wasn't giving up.

'Maggie, Dr Higgins is calling you. You're miles away.' It was Lilly, the receptionist. There was no getting away from it now!

'Oh, eh, sorry about that.' With a heavy heart she followed the doctor into his room. 'Our Lady, Queen of Mothers, pray for me,' she whispered to herself before closing the door behind her.

CHAPTER 14

Marco let the warm water sluice over his body as he
thought about the night ahead. He was going to make sure
everything was perfect. Appearances were very important
to him, especially tonight, when he was trying to make an
impression. He squeezed some Tommy Hilfiger shower gel
onto his hands and rubbed it into a lather all over. He was
aiming to tantalise all of Claude's senses!

He couldn't believe he was getting ready to meet his virtual
friend at last. Claude had rung that morning to cancel the
filming because the crew were exhausted from travelling. It
had probably been too much to expect that they'd start work
straight away.

Marco had said he understood, but he'd been gutted. He
hadn't slept a wink with thoughts of Claude going around in
his head and the thought of having to wait another day felt
like forever. He'd moped around the house for most of the
morning and afternoon until Claude had rung back just after
three.

'Hi there, Marco,' he'd crooned. 'What are you up to?'

'Oh, I'm just sorting out some paperwork at the moment. Nothing very exciting.' God, he was such a liar. The phone had actually woken him up from a deep sleep. He'd been curled up on the sofa feeling sorry for himself. 'What about you? Did you get some sleep?'

'I had a nice few hours. But I'm heading into the Westbury shortly to meet the other lads.'

Marco had been devastated at that. He'd hoped that when Claude had had some sleep he'd want to meet up. 'Well, that's lovely … I hope you have a good night.'

'Well, that's why I'm ringing really. I wondered if you'd like to come in and meet me for a drink later. We should be finished our meal by around nine so, if you like, I could meet you in the bar any time after that? And we could move on to Café en Seine or somewhere with a bit of atmosphere after.'

Marco had almost jumped for joy. It couldn't have worked out better. He'd really wanted to meet Claude for the first time on his own, rather than in full view of the street. Both Maggie and Lorraine knew how he felt, so they'd only be watching for his reactions. How embarrassing would it be to come face to face with Claude with half the street watching? He wouldn't know whether to hug him, kiss him or shake his hand. At least this way, they could get to know each other and they'd be more relaxed tomorrow during filming.

Although relaxed wasn't the word he'd use to describe the atmosphere on St Enda's at the moment. He'd felt the tempers rising that morning when everyone had realised the ticket still hadn't been found. He'd felt like screaming about it himself, but he'd convinced everyone to stay calm until the cameras had come and gone. He'd hate for the production company to get wind of the unrest on the street.

He'd rung the National Lottery headquarters earlier to tell

them about the situation and had spoken to a lovely girl called Concepta. She'd asked him details such as the name and address of the shop where the numbers had been played and also asked for the other numbers that were on the same ticket as the winning numbers. Thankfully, he'd had his photocopy to hand so he'd been able to recite them off no problem. There were more questions and then she'd told him that a note had been made of the situation. Unfortunately, though, no matter how much detail he'd been able to give her, they would not be in a position to pay out the money without the ticket. She'd been very kind and had sympathised with their dilemma and had said that if the ticket hadn't been found by the end of the week, they should get in touch again.

Marco switched off the shower and stepped out onto the black furry mat. He dried himself quickly and went to have another look at the clothes he'd laid carefully out on the bed earlier. He'd agonised over his choices – a suit; it would look as though he was trying too hard, jeans and T-shirt; it would look as though he wasn't trying at all – so in the end he'd settled for a pair of cream combat trousers with zips down the leg and a crisp white linen shirt. Both were from a very promising young Irish designer. They'd only just got a few of each into the shop on trial last week and they'd sold almost immediately.

When he'd tried them on earlier, he'd been happy except for the shirt being a little tight and accentuating his slightly protruding stomach. Marco was in good shape overall, but his stomach was the bane of his life. No matter how many sit-ups he did, he couldn't seem to get rid of that little flap of fat that slightly hung over the belt of his trousers. He put it down to having been a little overweight in his teens and losing a few stone very quickly. He knew it was more in his own head and not very noticeable to others but he was a perfectionist and hated for things not to be just right.

He checked the time and was pleased to see it was only seven o'clock so there was loads of time to spare. He threw the towel on the floor and wrapped his white towelling robe around him. He squeezed some gel into the palm of his hands and sculpted it through his blond hair until he was completely happy with the result. All that remained was for him to get dressed. He eyed the linen shirt again. Being a perfectionist, he knew that if he was going to wear it, he'd have to call in the big guns! After a few minutes of dithering, he decided what to do.

He opened his underwear drawer and reached into the back. After a few seconds and a bit of rummaging, he pulled out something he thought he'd never wear – a pair of men's Spanx! He'd picked up the body-sculpting underwear on a whim a few months previously when he'd been browsing in Brown Thomas. Almost as soon as he'd bought the matching top and bottoms, he'd regretted it, and vowed never to put them near his body. But he had to admit that they did the job they were supposed to do wonderfully and if it was good enough for Bridget Jones, it would be good enough for him!

Just before nine o'clock, Marco stepped off the bus on the north quays and crossed the road to go over O'Connell Bridge. The city wasn't buzzing the way it usually was at the weekends, but it was busy enough. He walked down Westmoreland Street and crossed in front of Trinity College. Within minutes, he was strolling down Grafton Street, his favourite place for shopping, and heading for the hotel where he'd meet Claude.

At the entrance, a helpful doorman opened the door to let him in and nodded his head. Marco loved the Westbury with its opulent décor and friendly staff. It was a fantastic place to eat – not that he ate there often, but he did sometimes go there with friends to have a drink after work.

He tried to compose himself as he walked up the carpeted stairs towards the bar. His palms were sweating and he had butterflies in his stomach. He hadn't thought to ask Claude if he'd be alone or with the crew. He hoped it would be just him because he'd be mortified if the crew were there, watching their every move. His prayers were answered a minute later as he spotted Claude sitting on his own in the large open area just outside the bar. He was leaning back on his chair, watching the world go by through the huge windows looking out onto the streets below.

Oh, God, he was even more gorgeous than his photos. His stubble coupled with his messy black hair gave him the rough look, softened only by his deep brown eyes. Marco was rooted to the spot until Claude spotted him. 'Marco, over here.'

Marco thought his legs would give way underneath him as he walked over to his friend. 'Hiya, Claude, lovely to see you.'

Claude was on his feet – all six foot of him. 'Fabulous to see you too, Marco, after all this time.'

They hugged briefly before sitting down and ordering Marco a drink from the barman who'd been hovering nearby.

'So where are your colleagues?' Marco asked, twiddling with a coaster. 'Aren't they going to join us?' *Please don't, please don't, please don't.* He wanted to drink in Claude's deliciousness without the distraction of having to talk to other people.

'They've headed out to explore the city. I've given them

a few pointers of places to go, so they'll probably see the inside of plenty of pubs tonight.' Claude looked relaxed and comfortable as he sat back and casually rested a foot on the edge of the table. He was the picture of cool and Marco wished he could be more like him.

'So … here we are…' *Oh fuck*, thought Marco. *Here we bloody are!*

'Yeah, hard to believe, isn't it? You know, you look just like yourself, if you know what I mean!' Claude certainly had no trouble chatting and Marco was happy to let him do most of the talking for the moment. 'I've found that a lot of people either use old pictures for their avatars or they just don't look like the picture when you meet them in person.'

'I haven't actually met anyone from Twitter in real life. Have you met many?'

'Oh, God, yeah,' said Claude, his left foot joining his right on the table. 'We're always having Twitter meet-ups over in New York. I've met a lot of great people that way.'

'Ooh, I'll have to try to arrange something over here.' Marco was beginning to relax, helped by the gin and tonic he'd already finished. 'So, Claude, are you coming to our little street tomorrow then? Everyone is really excited.'

'Yep! That's the plan. We're thinking that we'll be with you at around twelve. It shouldn't take more than a couple of hours to get what we need.'

'Brilliant. You're going to love St Enda's. Honestly, it's full of the best people you'll ever meet.'

'And speaking of your street, what's the story with the lotto ticket. I presume you've found it by now?'

'We haven't, actually,' said Marco, idly shaking the ice in the bottom of his glass. 'I really don't know what we're going to do. Everyone's been looking for it and it just seems to have vanished into thin air. I can't believe there's a ticket with a million euro on it just floating around somewhere. We'd better find it soon or we'll have a war on our hands.'

Claude laid further back on the velvet-covered chair – another few inches and he'd be completely horizontal. 'And who do you think is the most likely culprit?'

'Culprit? Do you mean who do I think played the numbers?'

'Whatever,' Claude said, already looking bored with the conversation.

Marco wasn't letting it go. 'What are you saying, Claude?'

'I'm just wondering who stands to gain the most by holding on to the ticket themselves.'

Marco paused to consider this. 'Ah, no, Claude. You've got it wrong. We just can't remember which of us played the numbers. Whoever it was probably has the ticket tucked away in some drawer or other and has forgotten all about it.'

'Hmmmmm! Don't you think you're being a little naïve, Marco? I mean, do you honestly think somebody has just *lost* the ticket?'

'That's exactly what I think.' Marco wasn't sure he liked where this conversation was going.

'Well, if you ask me,' said Claude, pulling his left foot up onto his right knee, 'somebody has pocketed that ticket to claim the prize for themselves.'

Marco was torn between trying to concentrate on what Claude was saying and being mesmerised by his hunky, denim-clad legs. 'No, Claude, no way. We're all very good friends; I'm absolutely sure nobody would do that. And, anyway, it wouldn't be much good to them because the National Lottery know of our situation so they wouldn't pay out.'

'Think about it, Marco. Money can do funny things to people. Maybe somebody thought about the fact that they could have all the money to themselves instead of splitting it. And what's to stop them saying that nobody paid for their share so they did the numbers themselves?'

'Nobody is going to do that, Claude. Even by dividing the money five ways, there'd still by loads for each of us.' Marco refused to believe that any of his friends would stoop so low. 'Two hundred thousand euro would change each of our lives.'

'Ah, yes,' continued Claude, a twinkle in his eye. 'But wouldn't a million change those lives even more?'

'Well, yes, but I'm telling you, I know each one of these people really well. You're wrong.'

'Okay, okay.' Claude held up his hand in defeat. 'Believe what you want. But just think about this – is there any one of the syndicate that would benefit from an extra injection of cash? Who's short of a few bob these days? And, on that note, I'm going to shut up about it because it's none of my business anyway.'

'It's fine,' said Marco, feeling a bit subdued by the conversation. 'But let's talk about other stuff. I'm sick to death of that bloody missing ticket!'

'Well, we could talk about me,' said Claude with a mischievous grin. 'I'm always a good topic of conversation.'

'Oh, go on then, tell me something about yourself that I don't already know.' Marco dared to move in a little closer as the conversation began to flow.

'Well, I was only joking really, but I suppose there really is a lot you don't know about me. But, then again, there's a lot about *you* that *I* don't know!'

'True,' said Marco, signalling the barman for another couple of drinks. 'So do you miss Ireland? I've always heard that people who leave Ireland to live abroad spend their time pining for their homeland.'

Claude laughed, a big guffaw that showed his perfect mouth of teeth. Surely they were veneers. Nobody had teeth that perfect. 'Well that's most definitely a myth,' he said, still laughing. 'Most of the Irish I know over there love New York. They like to come back here for a holiday and to see family, but not many of them would want to be back here, living and working.'

Marco felt inexplicably disappointed to hear that. It was probably stupid or just wishful thinking on his part but he'd hoped that Claude might have said that he'd love to come home if he was given the chance. 'So, you'd never consider coming back then?'

'Well, I didn't say that either. If I could get a bit of work, I'd definitely consider it. My parents aren't getting any younger and I'm an only child so I really wish I could see a bit more of them.'

'So it's something you'd consider if you got a job here? I ... I mean, if the circumstances were right, you wouldn't rule out coming home?' Marco had to resist his imagination running wild. He tried to banish thoughts from his head of the two of them living in a very stylish townhouse, decorated in sleek, modern furniture, wardrobes full of the latest designer gear. How everyone would envy their relationship when they'd be seen at all the best Dublin venues.

'Are you okay, Marco? Am I boring you?'

'God, sorry Claude. I was off in another world there. Just give me two minutes – I need the loo.' Marco jumped up from his seat and headed to the gents. What he needed was to compose himself. He was getting far too carried away with everything. This was his first time meeting Claude and he already had them almost married off in his head. That was the trouble with him – he always jumped in head first.

He splashed some cold water over his face and washed his hands with the Gilchrist and Soames hand soap. He loved the opulence of the toilets in the Westbury. There were always fresh flowers on the cream granite counters and the individual hand towels were a nice touch. He glanced at himself in the big arched mirror and dabbed his face dry. Right, he'd go back out there and act a little less enthusiastic and a bit more composed.

'So, what were you saying?' he asked, plonking himself back down on the chair beside Claude. 'We were talking about your life in New York versus here.'

'I was just saying that I'd definitely consider moving back here if there was something to move for.' He let that comment hang in the air and Marco's composure was ready to slip again. *Oh, God, was there a little innuendo in those words?*

'So, anyway,' continued Claude, changing the subject after a painful silence. 'I love your choice of clothes. You'd know just by looking at you that you were in the fashion business.'

'Really?' said Marco, thrilled at the compliment. 'I just threw these on at the last minute.'

Claude giggled at that. 'I bet you didn't! Now this,' he said, indicating his own torn denims and white T-shirt, 'is what you call thrown on at the last minute.'

'Ah, now, you see you can't fool me,' said Marco, enjoying the banter. 'It takes time and effort to achieve that thrown-together look. There's a real art in it and I never could achieve it myself.'

Claude's eyes twinkled. 'Ha! Well maybe we should go shopping one day and we'll swap tips. You can dress me up and I'll dress you down. What do you say?'

Oh, God! Marco could feel the heat rising inside him as trickles of sweat formed on the back of his neck. Claude was absolutely gorgeous and the sexiest man he'd ever met in his life. Just sitting here in the hotel bar with him seemed like the most exciting thing that had happened in years. He wished they could just check into a room right now. He'd love his friend to peel the clothes off him bit by bit until ... oh, God ... the Spanx! What a sobering thought.

He looked across at Claude then and saw he was yawning. 'You must be exhausted. It's been a long day.'

Claude nodded. 'I'm pretty tired all right. Would you mind if we headed off? I know I said we might go on somewhere after here but, to be honest, I'd probably only fall asleep. I'll be seeing you again in the morning anyway.'

'That's fine by me.' Marco felt disappointed that the night had been so short but hopefully once Claude had got over his jetlag, they'd have other nights out during the week.

'Well, why don't we share a taxi? I can drop you off at Enda's and head on home. I'll be going in that direction anyway.'

'Brilliant,' Marco said, buoyed at the thought of spending another half hour at least in this gorgeous man's company. 'There'll be loads outside and, if not, the doorman will call one for us.'

Claude stood up and stretched his long limbs and Marco tried not to ogle at the rippled muscles on his stomach which were clearly showing through his starched white T-shirt. As they walked outside, neither said a word and Marco wondered if Claude was having similar thoughts. There had definitely been a connection between them tonight – there was no doubt about it. He hoped to God things would develop further during the week but, for now, he'd just enjoy the last bit of time they had together before saying goodbye for the night.

CHAPTER 15

'So he was everything you expected him to be then, was he?' Maggie placed a mug of tea in front of Marco and stirred some sugar into her own hot chocolate.

'Oh, Maggie, he certainly was. I mean, I knew we were going to get on well because we've chatted so much these past few months, but I'd been worried that there wouldn't be any ... you know ... between us.'

'Any what, Marco?'

'Jesus, Maggie. Do I have to spell it out?' Sometimes Marco didn't know whether his friend was just teasing him or if she was actually that naïve!

'Oh!' Maggie pretended to be shocked. 'Do you mean things of a *sexual* nature?'

'Feck off, Maggie O'Leary. You know full well what I mean. And don't say it like that. You make it sound sordid.'

'Ah, I'm only joking with you, Marco. Go on, tell me what happened.'

Marco didn't need much encouragement. He'd said his goodbyes to Claude in the taxi and had been about to go home when he'd seen the lights still on in Maggie's and couldn't resist popping in for a gossip. 'Well, my eyes almost popped out of my head when I saw him. You know those pictures I showed you from Facebook? Well in the flesh, he was a hundred times better looking.'

'Bloody hell,' exclaimed Maggie, cupping her hands around her warm drink. 'I didn't think it would be possible. Ooooh, I can't wait to meet him tomorrow.'

'Anyway,' continued Marco, 'there were a few awkward moments at first where we were kind of sizing each other up, and then we just relaxed.'

'And did you confirm with him … I mean did you check … you know …' Maggie trailed off and Marco was confused.

'Check what?'

Maggie blushed. 'You know … the gay thing.'

'Jesus, Maggie. I told you he was gay. How long do you know me and you're still skirting around the whole gay issue. For feck's sake!'

'Hold on to your knickers, will you, Marco. I was only asking. You've never met this guy face to face, and I just wanted to be sure you wouldn't be disappointed if he turned out to be straight.'

Marco rolled his eyes. He loved Maggie dearly and he knew that she didn't have any hang-ups about his sexuality but sometimes she still couldn't quite get her head around the whole thing. 'He most definitely *is* gay, Maggie. I have no doubt!'

'Ooh, so did something happen then?' Maggie's eyes were out on stalks at the thought of a bit of juicy gossip.

'Ha! If only. No, we just had a lovely chat about lots of stuff and then shared a taxi home. Claude was a bit jet-lagged so he was heading home for a good night's sleep.'

'And the crew will be here tomorrow for definite this time?' asked Maggie, who'd been probably the most disappointed of them all when they'd cancelled that morning.

'Yes, Maggie. They'll definitely be here. I don't suppose there's been any news on the ticket tonight?'

Maggie sighed. 'Not a word. Sure, wouldn't it have been the first thing I'd have said to you if there was? I honestly don't know what's going to happen about it. I'm trying to stay calm but I swear, every time I think of that ticket floating around somewhere, I want to scream!'

Marco drained the last of his tea and wondered if he should tell Maggie what Claude had said about the ticket. It had shocked him when he'd come out with it because he honestly hadn't thought for a minute that somebody could be trying to pull a fast one. Part of him wanted to discuss it with Maggie but the other part of him didn't even want to acknowledge that it might be a possibility.

'Are you okay, Marco? You're miles away.'

He just couldn't say anything, not to Maggie. She loved this street and the people on it. She was annoyed about the ticket now but only because she thought it was lost. If she thought for a minute that somebody had stolen it, it would really upset her. He stood up quickly. 'I'm fine, Mags. I think it's just the few gin and tonics catching up with me. That's all it is. Nothing else. I'd better get back and leave you to go to bed.'

'Marco Gallagher. Sit back down there and tell me what's wrong.'

'I ... I don't know what you mean, Maggie?' Marco shuffled from foot to foot, nervously.

Maggie indicated his chair and Marco obediently sat back down. 'I can read you like a book, Marco. It's like the time when you were six and I was babysitting for you. You came running in from playing outside to announce that you most definitely had *not* punched Lee Lennon in the face.'

'What's Lee Lennon got to do with this?' Marco asked, completely confused. Either he was seriously drunk or Maggie was losing the plot!

'Forget Lee Lennon,' said Maggie, an exasperated look on her face. 'I just mean that I can tell when you're trying to hide something. What are you not telling me?'

Marco sighed and leaned his elbows on the table. It would probably be a good thing to get a second opinion anyhow. 'It's just something Claude said tonight. It may be nothing but ... but it's just got me thinking and, oh, God, I hate even saying it or thinking it—'

'Jesus, spit it out, will you!'

'Okay, okay! Claude said something tonight about the missing lotto ticket and it's got me thinking.'

'*Marco*! You weren't supposed to tell anybody. I can't believe you've done it again.'

Shit! The fact that he shouldn't have told Claude in the first place had completely slipped Marco's mind. 'I know, I know, Mags. But forget about that for the moment and listen to what he said.'

'Go on then,' said Maggie, folding her arms and not looking at all pleased.

'Claude thought that maybe the ticket isn't lost at all.'

Maggie looked puzzled. 'Well, of course it's lost, Marco. What a strange thing for him to say.'

'But maybe not,' said Marco, carefully. 'Claude reckons that maybe one of us has *taken* the ticket.' He left that to sink in with Maggie.

'Taken ... as in robbed? By one of us? No way, Marco. Who'd do a thing like that? Claude definitely has it wrong.'

'Well, that's exactly what I said, Mags. But then I got to thinking … is it possible that somebody has just got greedy and wants the whole thing for themselves? I mean, a million euro is a hell of a lot more than two hundred thousand!'

'I refuse to believe it,' said Maggie, standing up, defiantly. 'Yes, we could all do with that money but there's no way any of the five of us would turn on our friends.'

'I hope so, Maggie, I really do.' Marco took his cue and got up to leave. 'But there's no harm in thinking it through. Maybe we should sleep on it and chat about it again in the morning.'

Maggie shook her head. 'I'm not even going to think about it. I trust my friends completely and we're going to find that ticket very soon and prove you wrong.'

'Whoooa, Mags! You don't have to prove *me* wrong. I wasn't the one to suggest it. I was just telling you what Claude said.'

'Well maybe Claude is a bit of a trouble-maker then. What right does he have to put ideas like that into your head?' Maggie looked furious.

'Come on, that's not fair.' Marco was hurt by Maggie's unnecessary jibe. 'Claude wasn't trying to stir anything up – it was a completely innocent remark on his part. I probably should have just ignored him in the first place.'

'Right, let's forget all about it, shall we?' Maggie put the empty cups in the sink and walked with Marco out to the hall door.

'Are you off, Marco?' Dan spoke from the sitting room.

'I am, Dan. Sorry for intruding on your night. I was just dying for a bit of a chat.'

'You didn't intrude at all,' said Dan. 'I was glad of being able to watch a bit of decent telly instead of that reality rubbish Maggie likes.'

'Don't pretend you don't like it, Dan,' said Maggie, shaking her finger at her husband. 'Do you think I don't see you peeping up from behind your newspaper when I'm watching *Big Brother*?'

'You two crack me up,' laughed Marco, glad of the bit of banter to lighten the mood. He kissed Maggie on the cheek. 'Right, the crew will be here at twelve in the morning so maybe we'll all catch up again before then. We want to show them what Enda's is made of.'

'Definitely,' said Maggie, looking more relaxed. 'Let's show them Enda's in the best possible light. I can't wait!'

Marco let himself in his front door and was immediately welcomed by Mimi's high-pitched yapping. She'd cheer anyone up, he thought. She was like a little ball of soot with endless energy.

'Missed me then, have you, Mimi? Or are you just buttering me up so that I'll give you a treat?'

The little dog barked her approval and twirled around and around in circles at her owner's feet. 'Oh, go on then,' laughed Marco, opening the cupboard under the sink where he kept the doggie treats. 'But just one now – I'm not getting up in the middle of the night so you can do your business again.'

He gave the dog her treat and opened the back door for her to go out. He filled the kettle with water while he was waiting and took out a cup. He had a splitting headache and he couldn't decide if it was from the gin and tonics or from too many things going around and around in his head. He reckoned it was probably more the latter.

He just couldn't get what Claude had said out of his head.

He hated to think it, but maybe Claude was right. Maybe somebody *was* hiding the ticket.

He'd tried all evening to blot it out of his mind but it just kept coming back to haunt him. Claude had asked if there was any one of them in particular who could do with a few extra bob. The truth was that all of them had money worries and would benefit from the full winnings.

He knew it wouldn't be Lorraine but, having said that, she and Barry had been working themselves to a frazzle trying to earn an extra bit to put away to start a family. Then there was Rita who never had a penny and was struggling to bring up two boys on her own.

He popped a teabag in a cup and poured boiling water on. Stirring and squeezing the bag to get the most out of it, his thoughts wandered to Maggie. Now there's another woman who could do with a bit of money. She and Dan had been trying to get back on their feet for the past couple of years since Maggie's business had folded.

Jesus! He needed to get those thoughts out of his head straight away! He abandoned the tea and went out to join Mimi in the back garden. He needed some air. Imagine even considering Maggie as a possible culprit. It was complete madness. She was the most honest person alive – there was no way she'd ever do anything like that.

He gulped in big lungfuls of the cool night air while Mimi danced around his feet in delight. It wasn't often she had company out in the back garden, so she was making the most of it. He sat down on one of the plastic patio chairs to think.

Majella was another one to consider. Of them all, she was possibly the one who would most love to get her hands on a million euro. She'd always thought of herself as a bit of a cut above everyone else. She and her husband, Chris, owned two houses on Enda's and rumour had it that they were up to their eyeballs with mortgages that they didn't have a hope of paying back.

And, of course, there was himself! If anyone else was having similar thoughts about the lost ticket, would they be considering him as the culprit? He reckoned he'd definitely be in the running. With his taste for the finer things in life and his salary being swallowed up every month by debts, he could definitely see how the finger might be pointed at him.

He closed his eyes and thought about what two hundred thousand euro could do for him. God, it would change his life. He'd be able to pay off the damn mortgage that was a noose around his neck. The repayments crippled him every month and even just to get rid of that would be amazing. Then there'd still be plenty left over to pay off his college loan and leave him comfortable for a lot of years to come. He'd never really had a lot of money. His job paid okay, but it really just got him by. Imagine having money in the bank to enable him to go on foreign holidays whenever he wanted and to buy the clothes in Brown Thomas that made him drool every time he passed the window. If Claude was right and someone was responsible for taking the ticket, he wouldn't be responsible for his actions when he found out who it was!

'Come on, Mimi,' he said, blowing on his hands. It had turned really cold tonight and he just hoped the rain would hold off until after the filming tomorrow. The little dog ran inside and almost lost her head in the bowl of water as she lapped it up noisily.

He wondered if there was any chance Claude would be online. It was hardly likely since he'd been so exhausted. He'd said he was going to go home and just fall into bed.

Marco had savoured that comment, fully sure he'd said it in a suggestive manner. He'd probably just imagined it but, nonetheless, what harm would it do to dream?

He couldn't be bothered waiting for the laptop to warm up so he grabbed his iPhone off the kitchen counter and followed Mimi up the stairs. Within five minutes, he was in bed with Mimi snoring at his feet. He decided he'd just have a peep into Twitter anyway, on the off-chance that Claude hadn't been able to sleep and was tweeting. The familiar Twitter screen popped up within seconds.

> @ClaudeRIP: Hi, Marco. I'm just about to crash. Exhausted. But wanted to say how lovely it was to see you tonight. Sweet dreams, lovely, and I'll see you tomorrow. x

Oh how wonderful! It was like having the sweetest kiss before he went to sleep. Claude was such a darling. Marco didn't want to think about the fact that he was only here for just ten days. He couldn't stand the thought of waving him off as he was getting to know him properly.

But he wouldn't allow himself to think beyond the next day. He had so much to look forward to over the next week and he was going to make damn sure that he made the most of the time they had together. He left his phone down on the locker and curled into his warm bed to remember every last moment of their time together earlier; Claude's welcome hug, his gorgeous face and the ever-so-light feather kiss he'd placed on Marco's lips as he got out of the taxi. He drifted off to sleep with a great big smile on his face.

CHAPTER 16

Tuesday, 13th September

'Lorraine, can I come over for a cuppa or is it too early?' Maggie had been up since Dan had left at 6 a.m. and had been dying to talk to her friend. She'd tossed and turned all night, partly because of the pain but mainly because of what Marco had told her last night. Dan had even commented on her restlessness and he was usually oblivious to everything after his head hit the pillow.

'No, it's not too early at all,' said Lorraine, sounding tired. 'I know I'm off work today, but I couldn't get to sleep after Barry left. It's mad, I could cry most mornings at having to get up for work and now when I've the chance to stay in bed, I'm up with the larks!'

Maggie was impatient to get off the phone and go down and chat to her friend face to face. 'Right then, stick the kettle on and I'll be down in five minutes. I'll bring down some of those scones I made yesterday and we can have a good old chat.'

'Sounds good, Maggie. See you in a few minutes.'

Maggie hadn't wanted to admit it to Marco last night but what he'd said about the lost ticket had really unsettled her. She couldn't stop thinking about the possibility that one of her friends would do something like that. She hadn't even said anything to Dan because she hadn't wanted to upset him. Dan was everyone's friend and she knew that, like her, he'd be shocked at the very thought.

But the more she'd thought about it, the angrier she'd got. She probably shouldn't jump to any conclusions and she certainly didn't want to start any idle gossip but she had a few thoughts on the subject. She knew that Lorraine was quite level headed and would probably tell her she was mad to entertain the idea.

She took two of the delicious scones out of the air-tight container and wrapped them in tinfoil. She was well known on the street for her scones. If you were invited to Maggie O'Leary's for a cuppa, the first thing that would spring to mind would be her melt-in-the-mouth, fluffy scones. Well, so she'd been told! Her secret was that she used double cream in the recipe instead of milk. She'd learned that from her mother and refused to divulge the secret ingredient to anyone!

Setting the alarm and locking the door, she headed down the road. It had been such a blessing, the day that Lorraine and Barry had bought number eight. Mrs Bean, the old lady who'd lived there, had died a year before and it had seemed that nothing was being done with the house. And then, just as Lorraine had told Maggie that she and Barry were looking for somewhere to buy, it had come on the market. What a bit of luck! Maggie hadn't thought Lorraine would go for it. She'd thought that her friend would think it was a step backwards, since she'd grown up there, but she'd been all for it. It hadn't taken much to convince Barry either so the deal had been done quickly and they'd moved in soon after.

'Howareya, Maggie,' said Lorraine, opening the door just as Maggie was walking up the path. 'Come on in – I've made a pot of tea.'

'Lovely. I'm parched.' Maggie followed Lorraine into the kitchen and took a seat at the little oak table.

Lorraine poured two mugs of steaming hot tea and put the scones Maggie had given her on a couple of plates. 'So how come you're out and about so early? I'd have thought you'd be at home baking for the film crew again.'

'Well they can feck off if they think I'm baking anything for them today. Sure, they mightn't even turn up again. They can have yesterday's cakes and be grateful!'

'You're gas, Maggie. You didn't answer, though, what has you out and about? Am I sensing something's up?'

'Well, I couldn't get back to sleep this morning,' said Maggie, buttering her scone. 'So as soon as Steph left for school, I just felt like a bit of company.'

'I was the same last night,' sighed Lorraine. 'I barely slept a wink.'

'I take it things are no better between you and Barry?'

'Oh, Maggie I just don't know what's wrong. He's blowing hot and cold all the time. One minute, he's making snide comments and acting all distant and the next he's hugging me and telling me everything will be all right. I just don't know anymore.'

'Ah, Lorraine, you poor thing.'

'I just wish I could be brave enough to sit him down and ask him directly what's up. I still think he could be gambling again and I'm terrified that maybe it's out of control. I'm just not sure of the best way to deal with it.'

'Well, if you want my opinion, you should approach it head on. Just ask him what the problem is, why he's acting the way he is. If that doesn't work, maybe you should ask him directly about the gambling. You'll probably know from his reaction whether or not it's an issue.'

'You're right, Maggie. As soon as the filming is finished, I'm going to be more direct with him and hopefully get some answers. But you didn't come here to hear my moans. So what's the story with you?'

Maggie held back for a moment. She wondered if it was the right thing to do to burden Lorraine with yet another problem when she already had so many of her own. But maybe it would take her mind off things and give her something else to think about.

'Well, come on then,' said Lorraine, playfully kicking Maggie under the table. 'So what's the gossip with you?'

Maggie relented and launched into the whole ticket-stealing scenario. She told her what Claude had said to Marco, and how Marco had related the whole thing to her last night. She admitted that it was that very thing that had kept her awake and that her emotions were a jumble of worry and anger.

'God, Maggie,' exclaimed Lorraine, pushing her almost empty plate away from her. 'Are we just naïve not to have thought of that before now? How on earth did we think the ticket had just been lost?'

Maggie gasped. 'So you honestly think there's something in it, do you? I didn't at first, but the more I think about it—'

'Well it makes sense, doesn't it? Surely whoever did the numbers would remember doing them. And, secondly, surely they would have put the ticket in a safe place. No, I think this Claude guy might be right.'

'Oh, Lorraine, it's awful, isn't it? On one hand, I feel upset that one of our friends might be doing this to us; and on the other, I could kill whoever's done it. That money would be the making of us all.' She pushed her scone away, hoping Lorraine wouldn't notice that she'd barely touched it. She just didn't have an appetite.

'Well, I don't feel in the least bit upset, Maggie. I just feel angry. How dare they! How bloody dare they!'

Maggie was beginning to feel panicky at having riled her friend so much. 'Lorraine, we don't know anything for sure yet so let's not jump to conclusions. There's a lot to think about.'

'So, who do you think might be responsible then?' asked Lorraine, leaning her elbows on the table. 'You must have someone in mind.'

'Well … something did cross my mind … but honestly, Lorraine, I don't want to say anything yet.'

'Come on, Maggie. This is me you're talking to. Tell me who you think it might be.'

'It's only a thought,' said Maggie, not meeting her friend's eye. 'But Rita was chatting to me at the bingo the other night about how strapped for cash she is. That bloody husband of hers doesn't pay a penny in maintenance and she sometimes doesn't even have enough to pay for a bit of shopping.'

'Jesus!' gasped Lorraine, sitting back in her chair. 'You think it's Rita? Do you think she'd be so calculating as to hide the ticket in the hopes of cashing in on it herself?'

'I honestly don't know, Lorraine. I hope she isn't. I really don't want to think she's done it but it's just that it sticks in my mind how much she was talking about money the other day. Wouldn't a million euro solve so many of her problems?'

'But it would solve a lot of problems for all of us, Maggie. I don't know. Somehow I'm not sure that Rita would have the time or presence of mind to even think of something like that. She seems so frazzled all the time.'

'I just don't know what to think any more,' sighed Maggie. 'I wish these bloody thoughts had never been implanted in my head! I just want to go back to thinking the ticket is lost and trusting that it will turn up soon.'

'I know what you mean, Maggie. But even *you* will have to admit that it's not likely. I think we have a thief on our hands but the question is, who is it?'

'And what do you think yourself, Lorraine?'

'I'm at a loss, to be honest, Maggie. It could be anyone – except me of course!'

'And me,' said Maggie, quickly. 'You can rule me out for sure. As I said on Saturday night, I did it the last time so somebody else must have taken it off me.'

Lorraine drained the last of her tea from her mug. 'Well then, leaving Rita out of it, that only leaves Marco and Majella, and there's no way on this earth that Marco is involved. My money would be on Majella.'

Maggie looked thoughtful. 'Well, she does have a lot of debts. I bumped into Martha Carolan last week and she said that Joe O'Brien had told her that Majella and Chris have a number of houses around the place that they bought before the property crash.'

'You see,' said Lorraine, excitedly. 'If she's up to her eyes in mortgages, she'd need a hell of a lot more than a measly two hundred thousand euro to sort her out. I bet it's her.'

'Oh, God, what have I started here?' sighed Maggie. 'Majella's and Rita's ears must be burning like mad at the moment!'

'Well, it needs to be talked about, Maggie.' Lorraine's face was red with anger. 'Maybe we should call another meeting and this time we shouldn't be so relaxed about it. Maybe if we said what we really think, it might shame whoever has the ticket to own up.'

Maggie was beginning to panic at the thought of the disruption she may just have caused. 'I'm not sure it would work like that, Lorraine. Let's just keep our thoughts to ourselves for now. We don't want to cause too much of a stir while this filming is going on and risk making a laughing stock of ourselves.'

'I suppose,' said Lorraine, rubbing her temples. 'But as soon as those cameras go, I want answers.'

'Don't worry, Lorraine. We'll all be gunning for answers. Now, I'd better get back and get cleaning. The crew will be here in a few hours and I've nothing done.' She stood up and brought her cup and plate over to the sink, discreetly tipping the scone into the bin on the way.

'Right so,' said Lorraine, walking out to the door with her friend. I'll probably see you when they're here at lunchtime. Do you know what the plan is?'

'I think Marco is going to talk to them first and see how they want to do things. They want to chat to a few of us anyway, so I'm all ready for my screen debut!'

'Oh, you're very brave, Maggie. I think I'd die if I had to talk in front of the camera. I suppose I'd give it a go if they ask me but I'm not sure I'd be any use.'

'You'd be great, Lorraine. And it's a lovely story how you grew up here and then moved back and are hoping to bring your own children up here.'

Lorraine's face darkened. 'Well, I'd be reluctant to mention children when there aren't any at the moment. I think we should just stick to facts.'

'Okay, Lorraine.' Maggie was surprised at Lorraine's jibe.

'I was only making a suggestion about what you could talk about if they want to interview you. But talk about whatever you like. It doesn't matter to me.'

'Ah, I'm sorry, Maggie. I'm just a bit touchy because of all this stuff between me and Ba—' Lorraine suddenly paled and it looked as though she was going to be sick.

'What's wrong?' asked Maggie, holding out a hand to steady her friend. 'You look like you've seen a ghost.'

Lorraine composed herself quickly. 'Sorry, Maggie. I, em, was just feeling a bit sick there for a minute. I'm fine now. I think it's just all the goings on these past few days.'

'I know what you mean. I've been feeling off colour myself. Well, let's look forward to an exciting day today to take our minds off things.'

'Y… yes,' Lorraine said, still looking pale. 'I'll see you later on when the cameras are here.'

'Oh you will for sure,' said Maggie, stepping outside into the warm air.

Thankfully, the sky was blue and it didn't look as though the rain was going to put in an appearance. The street was looking fantastic with the sun shining on it – the perfect way to show it off for the cameras.

But, Jesus, this ticket business was making her head spin. She kept trying to tell herself that money wasn't the be all and end all, but, in truth, that money could do a lot of things for her little family. It would certainly give them a better quality of life. At the moment, Dan was working himself to the bone to earn a decent crust but two hundred thousand euro would mean he wouldn't have to keep two jobs going any more. They could pay off their loans and more of their income would be freed up. And it wouldn't be long until Steph would be going to college. That would cost a bob or two. Wouldn't it be lovely to be able to put the money aside for that and not have to worry about affording it when the time came?

She suddenly felt exhausted. All this thinking and trying to figure things out was killing her. Maybe she'd have a little nap on the sofa while it was all quiet. It was only half nine so it would be hours before the activity would start on the street. That's what she'd do. If she had a good-quality hour without being disturbed, she'd be fresh and bright for the cameras when they'd come. And she certainly wanted to look her best to represent the street she loved.

CHAPTER 17

Lorraine kept the smile plastered on her face as she watched Maggie head back to her own house.

'Nice day for it, isn't it?' shouted Eddie from number six, who was out power-washing his driveway for about the tenth time in the past week. His yellow teeth beaming through his mud-splattered face.

'Em, yes, it's lovely. You're doing a fine job there.' Lorraine didn't want to be rude but all she wanted to do was get back inside.

'It's looking good all right. Let's hope this crew come today. Will Barry be here for it?'

Lorraine sighed. 'No, Eddie. He had the day off yesterday because they were supposed to come and he couldn't swap for today at such short notice.'

'Ah, pity, that. Well I'm sure we'll all—'

'Sorry, Eddie, I have to fly. I have something in the oven. See you later.' Lorraine closed the door before her neighbour could say another word. She realised she'd cut him off and he probably thought she was a right bitch, but she couldn't worry about that now.

She leaned back against the yellow-painted wall in the hall and shut her eyes tight. Her head was beginning to thump and she couldn't think straight. Slowly, she let herself slide to the floor and hugged her knees in close to her.

For what seemed like ages, she just sat there, letting things run round and round in her head. Could there be some truth in what Maggie had said? What if she was right?

It was hard to believe that only a short few weeks ago, life had been good. Now, it felt everything was spiralling out of control. Maggie's revelations about her suspicions had set alarm bells ringing in her head.

She wiped her eyes with the sleeve of her top and tried to think straight. Right, she wasn't going to sit here and feel sorry for herself when she could be doing something about it. Life had dealt her some knocks in the past and she'd always been able to fight her way back so she wasn't going to let this beat her. Standing up, she wiped the dust off her skinny jeans and strode purposefully upstairs.

Her tears of despair turned to tears of anger and frustration as she began to tear her bedroom apart. She left no stone unturned as she searched through drawers, under the mattress, between books – she even took each item of her husband's clothing out of the wardrobe and searched in every last pocket. If the lotto ticket was here, she was damn well going to find it!

But it wasn't long before her resolve faltered and she flopped back down heavily on the bed. What was she doing? Wouldn't it be so much easier to just talk to Barry rather than acting like a madwoman? He was her husband, after all. She'd always been able to talk to him in the past so why was it so difficult to do it this time? Ever since Maggie had started nagging her to come clean with Barry, she'd become terrified of losing him. In the past, she would have just confronted him about something like this, but the Barry she knew and loved would never dream of stealing from his friends. She also knew that gambling is an addiction and addictions can take control of you. Oh, God, what was she going to do?

Jesus, she'd really want to get a grip of herself! She was putting two and two together and coming up with five! But the niggles were still there when she remembered back to the night in the pub after the bingo, when somebody must have taken the money and the numbers to play. He'd come down and met them for a drink so he'd had just as much access to the ticket as everyone else.

She glanced at her bedside clock and realised an hour had passed since Maggie had left. She'd want to get herself together and get organised for the cameras arriving. She'd hop into the shower and give her hair a nice wash and condition. Then maybe she'd find something nice and red in her wardrobe. She remembered somebody telling her that red was a great colour for telly – not that she was planning to get herself on camera. But there was no harm being prepared, just in case.

Feeling slightly more upbeat, she quickly tidied the mess she'd created in the bedroom before switching on the shower in the little bathroom. Letting her clothes fall to the floor, she stepped in and allowed the warm water to wash over her body. As she slathered coconut shower gel all over, she began to relax. What had she been thinking, pointing the finger at Barry? It was a bit of a moment of madness. There was no way her husband was responsible for the missing ticket.

She thought back to her conversation with Maggie earlier and how they were thinking Majella might have something to do with it. That seemed like a far more credible scenario.

She'd let her mind flit to the possibility that it could be Marco, but only briefly. Marco was far too honest and wore his heart on his sleeve. There was no way he'd be so deceitful and, besides, wasn't he the one who'd had the conversation with Maggie in the first place?

She could feel her anger rise again, thinking that somebody was causing all this heartache. Surely whoever had the ticket must realise the knock-on effect it would have throughout the community. Suddenly, St Enda's didn't feel like the warm and friendly street they all loved. As she stepped out of the shower and wrapped a big, fluffy towel around her body, her mood grew dark. Maybe moving back to Enda's hadn't been such a good idea after all. Maybe she and Barry should have made a fresh start somewhere completely new and not come back to a place where memories of the past could so easily come back to haunt her.

Drying herself quickly, she padded into the bedroom and slipped under the duvet. Another few minutes wouldn't hurt. Her mind was in turmoil. She was a teenager again. She was crying. Her mam was crying. Even her dad had tears in his eyes. What were they going to do? She wished she was dead. She hated to see her parents arguing like that. More than anything, she hated herself for causing it. She let her tears spill out onto the pillow as thoughts of the past haunted her.

Marco checked himself in the floor-to-ceiling mirror he'd had installed in his ultra-chic bedroom. He was looking good. He'd had his highlights done only last week and Majella had done him a spray tan at the weekend. It was handy having a neighbour who was a beautician – Marco liked to look after himself and was partial to the odd facial and manicure.

He opened an extra button at the neck of his brown and cream Burberry shirt and admired his athletic frame. The shirt was one of his most expensive purchases but had been well worth it. The slim-fit accentuated his muscles and the beautiful stitching at the bottom fell nicely over his brown denims. The cotton and silk mix of the fabric felt delicious on his skin and made him feel sexy.

Checking his watch, he saw it was eleven o'clock – just one hour until the cameras arrived. How exciting! Maybe he'd just go out and give the street the once over and make sure it looked good. He felt proud at how everyone had rallied together over the past couple of months to get the little cul-de-sac looking fantastic. Leaving the front door on the latch, he headed outside to take a peep.

'Morning, Rita,' he chirped, on seeing his neighbour out on the road, kicking a ball around with her two boys. 'Lovely day for it.'

Rita stepped up on the path and leaned against her railings. 'Howareya, Marco. I'm just trying to tire these two out so that I can plonk them in front of a DVD when the camera crew arrive.'

'Good idea,' said Marco, smiling at the two boys, who were concentrating intently on kicking the ball. 'I spoke to the assistant producer this morning and they'll be here in about an hour.'

'Great. I'm looking forward to it. And any more news on that ticket? I can't stop thinking about it. I have half the money spent already in my head!'

Marco hesitated for a moment. He knew he shouldn't say anything to Rita about what Claude had said. He'd agreed with Maggie that they'd forget all about it. There was no point in stirring up trouble when there was probably nothing to it.

'Marco, did you hear me?' Rita was waving her hands in front of his face and he realised he'd gone into a trance-like state. 'I was asking if there was any word on the ticket. Has anyone found it yet?'

'Em, no, …. I don't think so. Well, I mean, not that I've heard.'

Rita was staring at him. 'What is it, Marco? If you know something, then spill! You can't keep it to yourself.'

'Ah, it's nothing, honestly. The ticket hasn't been found but … have you considered that maybe the ticket isn't lost at all?'

'I don't follow?'

'Well,' said Marco, carefully, fully realising that he shouldn't be saying anything, but not being able to help himself. 'There's always a possibility that somebody has taken the ticket and is hoping to claim the prize for themselves.'

'Jesus Christ,' said Rita, letting her mouth fall open. 'It never even crossed my mind that somebody would do that. Do you really think that's what's happened?'

Marco began to panic slightly at spreading such a vicious rumour and tried to backtrack. 'Ah, probably not, Rita. It was just a thought. I'm sure the ticket is just missing and will turn up before long.'

But Rita was having none of it. 'No, no, you're probably right about somebody nicking the ticket. I don't know why I hadn't thought of that. I bet somebody has it. Bloody cheek. If I get my hands on the person responsible, I'll feckin' kill them!'

Oh, God, this was getting out of hand now. Why the bloody hell had he opened his mouth? He just couldn't help it! He'd always been the same – he could never keep anything to himself. He didn't mean to cause trouble or upset people, but sometimes he was just a bit too honest for his own good! And Rita was looking as though she was ready to strangle somebody. He'd better try to talk her down before things got out of hand.

'Look, Rita, we don't know anything yet so there's no point getting your knickers in a twist.'

Uh, oh! Maybe he shouldn't have said that. Rita looked ready to explode! 'Marco Gallagher! It's okay for you. You're a young, single man with a good job and only yourself to look after. Maybe two hundred thousand euro doesn't mean much to you, but it means *everything* to me!'

'Well, of course it means something to me,' said Marco, stung by Rita's harsh words. 'I could do with that money as much as the rest of you. And I'm just as upset about the whole thing as you are, but I'm also aware that the cameras will be here shortly and I want to put the ticket saga aside until they're gone.'

'Come on, boys,' Rita said, gesturing to her sons to head back into the house. 'Marco, at the moment, I couldn't care less about these bloody cameras. I just want to know what's happened to that ticket. How can you expect us to be all smiles for the camera while all this is going on?'

'Look, Rita, just do your best, okay? I promise we'll have a better chat about all this during the week when the filming is finished. We'll get to the bottom of it, don't worry.' But Marco *was* worried. Not only was his head melted from thinking about the ticket, he was now worried that he may have ruffled a few feathers on the street and maybe the film crew wouldn't be seeing Enda's at its best!

He watched Rita usher the two boys into the house and could see she was still upset. Maybe she wouldn't come out when the cameras were here. It would probably be for the best.

If she was in that sort of a mood, God only knows what she'd say. Hopefully, Claude would only want comments from a few of them so he'd steer him towards Maggie, Lorraine and, of course, himself. Having grown up in Enda's, the three of them had plenty of stories about the street and its residents throughout the years to make some good telly. Thank God at least Maggie hadn't taken what he said last night seriously. Imagine if she'd taken it to heart like Rita had? He'd really be in trouble then!

Satisfied that the street looked its very best, Marco headed back inside. Thank God the sun was shining too – everything always looked better in the sunshine. Mimi danced around excitedly at his feet as usual when he opened the door, her newly washed black hair gleaming and curling up in little tufts around her ears. To her delight, he picked her up, earning him a flurry of licks all over his face. He could always rely on his little cockapoo to put him in good form. It was going to be a great day – he just knew it. And if everything worked out as he hoped, he'd have a night out on the town with Claude to look forward to as well. But as he opened the back door for Mimi to go out, he couldn't get rid of the niggling feeling in the back of his head that something bad was going to occur. He hoped he was wrong!

CHAPTER 18

'Right, we're just going to have a look around first and then we'll have a chat with a couple of you. Is that okay with you, Marco?' Claude was looking very official with his clipboard in hand and pen behind his ear.

Marco beamed. 'That's fine by me. Do you want me to give you the lowdown on who lives where or do you just want a general look?'

'Let's just get the feel of the street first,' said Claude, gesturing to the other two of the crew who were busy taking equipment out of the van. 'Guys, leave that for the moment and let's have a walk through.'

Maggie leaned against her railings and watched in amusement as Marco hung on Claude's every word. Marco had been right. Claude certainly was a looker. She could see how her friend had fallen for him. And if her instincts were right, the feeling was mutual. She'd noticed how Claude was busying himself getting everything organised but how he'd sneak the odd glance at Marco when he wasn't looking. How exciting to have a budding romance happening right on their doorsteps.

Groups of people were gathering here and there as the three-man crew, led by Marco, walked around the little street, making notes about God only knows what. It was hard to believe they were actually here after all the waiting.

But despite her previous enthusiasm, Maggie didn't feel a bit in the humour for the filming. She didn't know why she hadn't thought about it before but it really seemed unlikely that somebody had just *forgotten* they played the numbers and conveniently lost the ticket too. No, the only plausible scenario was that somebody – one of her neighbours and friends – had taken the ticket with a view to claiming the whole prize for themselves. God, it made her want to weep to think somebody on her beloved street was behaving so thoughtlessly with no regard for anybody else.

'So what's happening then?' The voice came from just beside Maggie, jolting her out of her reverie. 'Have they started filming?'

'Jesus, you frightened the life out of me, Lorraine,' said Maggie, clutching her heart as though she was going to keel over. 'They're just having a look around and I think they're going to have a word with me then.'

'Oh, God, are you not nervous? Marco said they might talk to me, too, and I'm absolutely terrified at the thought.'

'Sure, why would you be nervous?' asked Maggie, looking at her friend admiringly. 'Look at you – you're gorgeous. If I looked like that, I'd be jumping in front of the camera.'

Lorraine blushed but was clearly delighted at the compliment. 'Ah, go away with you, Maggie. I just blow-dried my hair differently. I've had this old top for years.

'Well, you look lovely. And before they come over, I'm sorry for landing all that on you this morning. I just wanted to get it off my chest.'

'I'm glad you spoke to me, Maggie. It's really got me thinking.'

Maggie sighed. 'Oh, God. I should never have opened my mouth. So what are you thinking?'

'My head is all over the place, to be honest with you,' sighed Lorraine, leaning up against the railings beside Maggie. 'I even got to thinking that … that—'

'Jesus, what?' Maggie saw that her friend was close to tears.

'It doesn't matter now, Maggie. I was wrong. Let's not think any more about it until the cameras are gone.'

'You're right,' said Maggie. 'Let's get this over and done with and then we can have another meeting to see where we're at.'

The two fell silent, lost in their own thoughts as they watched Marco taking centre stage. He was pointing knowledgeably up to the sky, as though he had the power to even organise the sun. The crew were all nodding and Claude was scribbling something down on his clipboard.

Apparently Claude had asked Marco to give a few names of people who might talk to them about the street and Maggie's had been top of the list. He'd said that there was nobody better equipped to show the street in the best possible light. She'd been chuffed at that and had intended to put a lot of effort into getting ready, but she'd only woken up from her sleep just before they arrived. A quick lick and spit and a change into a fresh peach-coloured blouse and she'd been ready.

But looking at her gorgeous friend beside her, she just felt dowdy in her middle-aged black skirt and fussy blouse. Lorraine's red top was stunning and looked amazing over her white skinny jeans. The girl didn't even know how pretty she was. Her straight, blonde, shoulder-length hair never seemed out of place and her figure was to die for. Maggie had been a size ten herself up to the age of forty and had looked pretty good, but the past few years hadn't been kind to her. She never bothered much now with fashionable clothes, always planning to lose a few pounds so that she could fit into something nice. What was the point in spending money on clothes if she was going to drop a few sizes anyway? Unfortunately, of late, she'd been putting it on instead of losing it. Even though her appetite hadn't been great and she was eating far less than usual, her stomach seemed to be expanding. Well, hopefully, they'd only be getting head shots today, and she wasn't looking too bad from the shoulders up!

'Keep it short and simple,' Marco had said, following a phone call from Claude that morning. He'd been told to brief the residents on what was going to happen. Enda's wasn't the only place they were planning to film, so they just wanted to get some footage and get out of there. 'Just tell them about the warmth of the street and the people in it. Tell them how wonderful it is to live in a place where everyone looks out for each other.' That shouldn't be too difficult. She'd dealt with a lot worse, so telling it like it is should be a cinch!

'Cut ... cut,' shouted Claude, throwing his two hands up in the air in despair. 'We just need you to put a bit more welly into it, Maggie. Say it like you mean it.'

Oh, God, this wasn't going well. Maggie had thought it would be the easiest thing in the world to say her piece about Enda's and that would be that. But her mood was affecting what she was saying, and even though her mouth was saying all the right things, her tone was saying something else. 'I'm sorry, maybe it's just stage fright. I'll try that again.'

'Come on, Maggie,' said Marco, cheering his friend on. 'It's nothing you haven't said a hundred times before. Tell us why Enda's is so wonderful.'

'Right, quiet everyone,' said Claude. 'Take five.'

'So tell us a little bit about why St Enda's Terrace is so special,' said the presenter, a golden-haired boy who couldn't have been more than twenty.

Maggie cleared her throat. 'It's the people. They're always there for each other. We're not just neighbours – we're friends. Everyone looks out for everyone else and there's a real sense of community.'

Maggie could see out of the corner of her eye that Marco was giving her the thumbs up. She began to relax and feel comfortable with speaking. 'The world is always in a hurry these days but, on Enda's, we always take time. Everyone who lives here knows that they'll never be short of a bit of bread or a few teabags – all they have to do is knock on their neighbour's door.'

Maggie paused and the interviewer nodded his blond head. 'It sounds fantastic. And I believe you've lived here all your life?'

'Yes I have,' said Maggie, really getting into her stride. 'My mother grew up here, too, and I've never wanted to live anywhere else. My mother was a wonderful woman and did a lot for this community. She'd be proud to see how even in today's busy world, we still uphold the old-fashioned values here on the street.'

'Ha, values my arse!' A loud voice came from nearby.

'Cut, cut, cut!' Claude stared at Rita, who'd just arrived on scene and had pushed her way to the front of a gathering crowd. 'And you are?'

'Rita Byrne – number thirteen. I just think you might need

a more balanced view of the street and not the gushy love-fest being offered to you here!'

'Jesus, Rita!' said Marco, grabbing her by the arm and pulling her aside. 'What on earth are you playing at?'

'I'm not *playing* at anything, Marco,' she spat, making sure everyone could hear. 'I just think it's silly to have a one-sided opinion when clearly the street isn't all you're making it out to be.'

Maggie shuffled nervously from foot to foot, as everyone watched and waited to hear what Rita would say next. She could have strangled Marco when he'd told her that he'd spoken to Rita about their suspicions. He ought to have known how she'd react. He'd said that she'd seemed really angry about it and he was hoping she wouldn't show her face. Oh, God, this didn't look good!

'Okay then, Rita number thirteen,' said Claude, attempting to lighten the mood. 'Do you want to tell us what's on your mind?'

'I, em, well, I just think, em ...'

'Don't mind her, Claude,' said Marco, shooting Rita a vicious look. 'She's only having you on. She loves it here as much as the rest of us.'

'Well let the lady have her say,' said Claude, smiling sweetly at Rita. 'And then maybe we can get the cameras rolling again and finish off Maggie's interview.'

'Well what's the point in me having my say *off* camera?' Rita asked, finding her tongue again. 'Why can't you let the cameras roll for *me*?'

Maggie had had enough. 'Because, Rita, this is a programme about the St Enda's we all know and love. They want us to show them all that's good about it. They don't want us to air our dirty laundry – they just want us to tell them why we all love living here.'

Maggie's outburst seemed to have had the desired effect on Rita because she suddenly looked uncomfortable. 'I'm sorry, Maggie. I honestly don't know what came over me. It's just … you know … the ticket and everything.'

'What ticket?' asked the presenter, who'd been listening to the exchange.

'Nothing for you to worry about,' said Maggie, quickly. 'I think Rita is just having a bad day.'

'Look, why don't we take a break for ten minutes or so and we'll take up where we left off after that.' Claude didn't have to tell his cameraman or presenter twice. They immediately headed off towards the van, probably glad to get away from the mad people! He turned to Marco, who was looking very embarrassed about the whole thing. 'Have a word with her, will you? We'll never get anything done here if she's going to keep interrupting. We're already way over time.'

Marco blushed furiously. 'Don't worry, Claude. Give us a few minutes and I'll sort it out.'

'I'm sure you will,' Claude said, giving Marco a wink before heading off to join his two colleagues.

'I'm sorry, Marco,' whispered Rita, who now seemed conscious of the people who had gathered to watch the show. 'It's just after we had that chat about the ticket earlier, I just got more and more angry. I mean, how could somebody do something like that?'

'I know, I know,' said Marco, patting her on the back. 'It's awful to think maybe one of our friends is doing this on purpose.'

Rita sniffed. 'And that money could really change my life.

Does anyone realise the poverty I've been living in these past couple of years? Myself and the kids sometimes don't have enough money to buy bread and milk, and that's the honest truth. My mother has had to come to our rescue more times that I'd care to think about.'

'I know it's been tough for you, Rita,' said Maggie. 'But now isn't the time to bring it up. The production company don't want to hear about whatever dramas are going on here. They just want footage of a nice street with lovely people who get on like the Waltons, so let's give them what they're looking for and they can get out of here. Okay?'

'Couldn't have put it better myself!' Marco kept his voice to a whisper so as the scattering of people standing around couldn't hear. 'Lorraine, you're very quiet. Are you okay?'

Marco, Maggie, Rita and Lorraine had moved inside the gate of Marco's house and were huddled in a circle. Lorraine hadn't said a word during the whole exchange and all three were looking at her now.

'Lorraine?' Maggie was looking at her friend, concerned that she still looked pale and drawn.

'It's just that, well, I'm just finding it hard to think that one of us is responsible for taking the ticket. I mean, it could still just be lost.'

'Oh, for God's sake,' spat Rita, her tears gone and the anger kicking in again. 'Don't be so naïve. Somebody knows something about that ticket and I won't rest until we find out who it is. Am I honestly the only one who cares about this? Are you all secretly rich or something that you're not jumping up and down about it. Jesus!'

'Come on now, Rita,' said Maggie. 'We're all just as concerned about finding the ticket as you are. We're just not all as, em, vocal about it!'

'Oh, God, this is a nightmare,' Marco said, close to tears. 'Can't you all just smile and—'

'Right, are we ready to go again?' Claude appeared at the garden gate with the cameraman and presenter in tow. 'Can we just come back out to where we were a few minutes ago.'

Maggie looked at her friends in a panic. There was no way she could continue her gushing after what they'd just said. She didn't know what to do, so turned pleading eyes to Marco. After all, he was the one who'd set this whole thing up.

'Em, Claude,' said Marco, pulling the object of his affection slightly away from his two colleagues. 'Didn't you say you had other places to film as well?'

Claude looked at him in confusion. 'Well, yes, we do, but—'

'Great!' Marco clapped his hands. 'Would it matter very much to you if you did those other places first and come back to us another day? I know it's asking a lot, but I don't think you'll get much good out of us here today.'

'Well, I don't know, Marco. We're on a pretty tight schedule. The lads are only here until the end of the week and we have a lot to do.'

'I'm really sorry, Claude. I think other, em, *circumstances* are impacting on what we say so if we could just have another night to get ourselves together, we should be fine by tomorrow.' He winked and emphasised the word 'circumstances' and if Maggie hadn't known already, she would have been in no doubt that Marco had blabbed to Claude about the ticket.

Claude sighed and didn't look too pleased. 'Right, then. We'll call it a day. At least we've got some good footage of the street and we have a bit of Maggie talking, too. Another hour or two and we should be done. I'll let you know whether we'll get back tomorrow or the next day.'

'Ah, thanks, Claude,' said Marco. 'You're a gem.' It looked for a minute as though Marco was going to hug him and then thought better of it. Despite the embarrassment of the whole situation, Maggie had to stifle a giggle.

'Only for you, Marco,' said Claude, winking, as he headed towards the van. 'Talk to you later.'

'He's a fine thing, Marco,' said Lorraine, watching as Claude hopped into the van. 'And so lovely too.'

'He is, isn't he? And so sexy when he takes charge.'

'Jesus, will you two forget about Claude the Sex God and concentrate on what's going on here.' Rita was looking from one to the other and looked as though she was ready to hit them. 'I've left the boys watching a DVD so I have to get back, but what are we going to do about this ticket? I want to know who has it.'

Lorraine piped up again. 'I'm sure it will turn up. And we'll all have a good laugh about it when it does.'

Maggie was tired and fed up with it all. It had been such a waste of a day. 'Look, forget about the bloody ticket until those cameras have been and gone. Otherwise, we run the risk of us looking like complete eejits altogether.'

'Maggie's right,' said Marco. 'We need to just get over this filming thing and then we can concentrate on the ticket. And, anyway, each member of the syndicate should be party to any debates we're having about the ticket and there's no sign of Majella today. So are we all agreed then? Give the telly people what they want and then we'll get to the bottom of the lotto thing.'

'I suppose,' Rita said, reluctantly, and the others nodded their agreement. But the atmosphere was subdued and there were so many unspoken words hanging in the air.

'Right then, ladies,' said Marco, heading to his front door.

'I have a cockapoo to look after and hopefully a date to get ready for, so I'm heading in. I'll let you all know whether they're coming back tomorrow or the next day.'

Maggie headed out the gate and into her own, next door. 'Thanks, Marco. Keep us up to date. I hope your date goes well tonight and we'll make sure when they come again, we'll give them what they want.' But even as she said the words, Maggie realised that it was possible that Enda's may never recover from the saga of the missing ticket!

CHAPTER 19

Marco sat back and watched Claude order the drinks at the bar, glad to have this time on his own with him. After the crew had left earlier, he'd worried that Claude was fed up with him and wouldn't bother getting in touch or taking his calls, but he needn't have concerned himself.

Claude had rung him around six to say that they'd done a bit more filming in a few other locations so the day hadn't been lost. He was knackered after such a busy day though and had asked if Marco would maybe meet him somewhere closer to home – somewhere they could have a quiet drink and not bother having to get too dressed up.

Marco hadn't hesitated. He'd have travelled the country for a date with Claude – he didn't give a damn where, if he got to see him. So they'd agreed on a little pub in Cabra, which was halfway between St Enda's and Claude's family house. Being a Tuesday night, it was quiet and they'd had no trouble nabbing a nice couple of seats in the corner beside an open fire.

'Here we go; gin and tonic for you and a pint of Guinness for me.' Claude placed the drinks on a couple of beer mats on the old dark-wood table and scooted up beside Marco on the worn red-velvet seat. 'So, did you all manage to sort yourselves out after we left today?'

'Oh, God, Claude, I'm mortified about all that. Imagine Rita interrupting the filming like that. And it had all been going so well.'

'Well, in a way I can't blame her,' said Cláude, watching Marco's reaction. 'If that lotto ticket still hasn't turned up, how can you all pretend the street is such a lovey-dovey place to live?'

Marco was taken aback. 'But it *is* a lovey-dovey place to live! Honestly, Claude. Everything I told you about the street is true. If this lotto thing hadn't happened, you'd be seeing the street in its best possible light.'

'I believe you, but thousands wouldn't!'

'But where does that leave us then? Are you still going to do the piece on the street? We've been preparing for this for months now – you can't just decide not to do it at this stage because of one person's silly rant.'

'Hold your horses, Marco!' Claude looked amused at Marco's concerns. 'Of course we're going to continue filming. I just meant that if people were to watch what unfolded today, they wouldn't think Enda's was the all-singing, all-dancing street you made it out to be.'

Marco sighed. 'I know what you mean. I think we may have to lock Rita up tomorrow – that is if you're planning to come again tomorrow?'

'We've a few things to do tomorrow so I was thinking maybe we'll get to you first thing in the morning for an hour and we should be able to wrap things up. Is that okay?'

'That's perfect,' said Marco, taking a big gulp of his drink. 'It was good to see you doing your thing today.'

'Ha! My *things* would be more appropriate! I swear, I enjoy the job but it's certainly not the life of glamour that a lot of people seem to think it is. They definitely get their pound of flesh from me!'

'Now that you mention it,' said Marco, twisting his body around and leaning an elbow on the back of the seat. 'I thought there'd be a lot more of you involved in the filming. I can't believe only three of you came over.'

'That's just it, Marco. There's no getting away from the cutbacks. They let a lot of people in our production company go a few months ago, which means that most of us who are left have to double or triple up on jobs. For this programme, I'm assistant producer, I'm sound man, I'm director – I'm even a bloody tour guide for the other two!'

Marco laughed at that. 'Well you're the best-looking tour guide I've ever seen!'

Claude sighed. 'Seriously, Marco. I wouldn't mind if they gave me the responsibility and the wages to match, but I'm just a puppet and they pull the strings. Everything I do over here has to be run past the producer over in New York. Sometimes I just get sick of it.'

'Sounds a right pain, all right,' said Marco. 'Would it make you think any more seriously about coming back to Ireland?' Oh, God, why had he said that? He'd been thinking it non-stop since they'd met, but hadn't intended pushing it any further with him – well not for another few days anyway!

'To be honest, I actually have been thinking about it. Part of me thinks I'd be mad to give up a decent job over in the States with nothing definite to come back to here, but, on the other hand, I think I'd be a lot happier freelancing in Ireland.'

Marco couldn't believe his ears. So it was possible that Claude might come back to Ireland. It was the best news he could have heard. 'Well, it's important to do what makes you happy, Claude. If you're not happy over there, why waste your life like that?' He knew he was gushing but he just couldn't help it. The thought of Claude moving back to Ireland was making him excited beyond belief!

'It's not that I'm not happy over there really,' said Claude, pensively. New York is a great place, but it's not home. I miss my family too.' His eyes glazed over and Marco couldn't help taking his hand.

'Claude, you've never really said much about your family. You obviously get on with them if you miss them?'

'It's just Mam and Dad, Marco, but they're great.' He seemed quite happy for his hand to be held and, to Marco's delight, he even shuffled in a bit closer. 'As an only child, I used to feel quite stifled. I was the centre of their universe and since they had plenty of money, they wanted to give me everything I wanted.'

'Oh, I didn't realise you came from a wealthy family,' said Marco, enjoying getting to know him. 'So were you spoiled then?'

'Yes, I suppose I was. But I didn't like it. When I was little, of course it was great to always have the latest toy before everyone else or the latest gadget when I was in my teens. But I grew tired of that and when I first left school, they sort of used the money to control me.'

'In what way?' Marco dared to move in closer again.

'Well they wanted me to go to university and said they'd pay for whatever I wanted to do. They said they'd give me an allowance so I could concentrate on my studies and wouldn't have to work.'

'That sounds generous.'

'That's just it, Marco. All I wanted to *do* was work! I never liked studying and couldn't think of anything worse than spending years with my head in books after I'd left school. I wanted to get out and see the world – to do an honest day's work and come home with a salary at the end of the month. I didn't want to live off them.'

'Well that's very noble of you, Claude, but surely they only wanted what was best for you.'

Claude took a big gulp of his Guinness, smacking his lips. 'You're right. All they ever wanted was for me to do well in life and be happy, but I couldn't see that while I lived here. It's only in the past few years while I've been away that I've been able to see it.'

'So is that why you've been so funny about the lotto thing?' asked Marco, the penny finally dropping. 'You grew up with money and could see how it can affect people and not always in a good way.'

'I suppose,' sighed Claude. 'I just think that if you're happy with your life in general – if you have a good job that you love and plenty of good people around you – you don't need money like that to improve your lot.'

'I see where you're coming from, Claude, I really do, but I don't necessarily agree with you. Each one of us who's part of the syndicate could really do with a bit of extra cash. We're all hard workers, but we struggle on a day-to-day basis with the money we bring in. Maybe you've just never seen that side of things. If you've always lived a privileged life, you wouldn't know what it's like trying to make ends meet.'

Claude was shaking his head vigorously. 'I've been over in New York for the past few years, Marco. I didn't accept any handouts from my parents while I was there so all I had to live on was my own salary. So don't tell me I don't know what it's like.'

'Ah sorry, Claude. I didn't really think. But at the end of the day, the money would solve a lot of problems for all of us. It's not enough to retire to the Bahamas for the rest of our lives but it is enough to pay a mortgage and make the day-to-day, week-to-week money worries a little less.'

'I suppose,' said Claude, reluctantly. 'And speaking of which, has there been any news on it yet?'

'Well, nothing yet, but I did get to thinking about what you said the other night. I know I didn't want to believe it, but it makes sense really. I do think somebody has taken the ticket and that's what has us all in bad form on the street.'

'I'm not surprised. I just hope you can show me the street that you've been raving on about – the one that seems to defy what's normal these days.'

Marco looked at Claude, unsure as to whether he was being sarcastic or not. 'What do you mean "defies normal"?'

'I just mean that if everything you've told me about the street and its residents is true, it's definitely one in a million and certainly not typical of the Ireland I grew up in.'

'Of course it's true, Claude. Do you think I'd make up something like that? Why would I bother? I've lived there all my life and I honestly can't speak highly enough of it and of the people who live there.'

'I know, I know,' said Claude, squeezing Marco's hand slightly, which sent a shiver of anticipation down Marco's spine. 'It's just that in the Ireland I grew up in, nobody really knew their neighbours that well, never mind borrowing stuff off them and having them in for tea. As well as that, you describe the street as such a relaxing, easygoing place, so out of sync with the madness of modern life. It's as though time has stood still on Enda's and people aren't caught up with the worries of the modern world.'

'Well it's not quite as antiquated as that,' said Marco, noting the edge in Claude's voice. 'But it certainly does have some old-world charm about it. Honestly, if you could only live with us on the street for a while instead of just coming to film, you'd see what I'm talking about.'

'Oooh, is that an invitation then?' asked Claude, smiling. 'You know, I may even take you up on that sometime.'

Marco blushed right to the roots of his bleached hair and felt a burning heat rising up inside him. 'Claude, I'd love you to come over and stay sometime. I think you know that by now.'

'I know,' said Claude, rewarding Marco with another squeeze of his hand as he shuffled in closer again. Their shoulders were practically pressed together at this stage and Marco was finding it hard to think of anything other than Claude's proximity. They sat in comfortable silence, staring at the telly behind the bar. There was some football match on, but Marco had absolutely no interest in it and he suspected Claude's mind was elsewhere too.

Maybe he should take the opportunity to ask him back to the house now. Maybe it was the perfect opening for him to put his cards on the table and let Claude know how he felt. After all, this wasn't a normal situation. It wasn't like your average relationship where you could take things slowly and see where it led. Claude was due to go back to New York next week, so if things were going to progress between them, it would have to be soon.

And what about Claude saying he'd consider coming back to Ireland? That had been more than Marco had expected to hear. Maybe he needed an incentive. Maybe the pull of his family just wasn't enough to entice him back, whereas if he had a love interest ... Oh, God, Marco could feel the little beads of sweat forming on his forehead at the thought of taking Claude home.

Even from those first tweets, Marco had been able to tell there was a vibe between them. And it wouldn't really be like hopping into bed with him on a second date. Their relationship had progressed from tweets to emails and then eventually to phone calls, so although he'd only seen him in the flesh a couple of times, he reckoned he knew him pretty well.

'So, what do you think, Marco? Will we have another one or call it a night?' Claude startled him out of his reverie and he knew he should just go for it.

'Well ... I was thinking ... it's been a long day. I'm not really interested in another drink. I think we'll head off.'

'Yep, I'm fine with that,' said Claude, grabbing his denim jacket from the corner and sliding out from the long seat. Marco followed, throwing his own cream cotton jacket over his shoulders.

The air outside was warm and muggy and Marco felt as though he could barely breathe. He'd never brought anyone home before. He'd had a few casual boyfriends but, even though he lived alone, he'd just never thought enough of any of them to take them back to his house. Claude was different and he'd never wanted anyone as much as he wanted him at that moment.

'Here comes a taxi,' said Claude, sticking out his hand to stop the oncoming car. 'You take this one. There should be another one along in a minute.'

Marco's heart dropped down to his toes. 'But I, em, I thought—'

'I insist, Marco. I don't mind waiting. And look, here's another one anyway.' He waved again as another taxi pulled up behind the first one.

'So, we're saying goodnight then,' said Marco. *Come with me, come with me!* But the words just wouldn't come out.

'Yep, but I'll be seeing you in the morning anyway.' Claude paused for a moment. For Marco, it felt as though time had stood still. Then Claude cupped Marco's face in his hands and kissed him tenderly on the lips – a long, sweet, lingering kiss; a kiss that Marco would remember every second of when he was in bed later.

'Night, Claude. See you tomorrow.' Marco watched as Claude hopped into the taxi.

'So am I taking you home or what?' said the agitated taxi driver, who'd been waiting for the past few minutes.

'Looks like it – unfortunately,' said Marco, hopping into the taxi. As the car sped off, he cursed himself for not speaking up. What would have happened if he'd just asked Claude to come home with him? Well, he'd never know. But nothing was going to take away from that wonderful kiss. Running his tongue along his lips, he could still taste the bitter ale from Claude's breath. It was like a drug that he was high on. He wondered was Claude feeling the same. Well, he had another week to make sure of it!

CHAPTER 20

Wednesday, 14th September

'Seriously, Mam. I can't believe you didn't tell me! Imagine how I felt when I got all those Facebook messages last night.' Stephanie was in a strop. After the fiasco on the street the previous day, the word about the lotto win and the missing ticket had filtered around and Steph had found out about it through Facebook.

'Ah, Steph,' said Maggie, raging she hadn't got to her daughter before all the gossipmongers. 'It was for your own good that we said nothing. Your dad and I thought it was for the best.'

Stephanie, who was buttering a piece of toast, stopped dead and looked at her mother. 'You thought it was for the best? Jesus, Ma, how could hiding all that money from your own daughter be for the best?'

'Watch your mouth, young lady! And we didn't hide any money from you. There isn't any money to hide at the moment.' Maggie sipped her tea and cursed the decision she and Dan had made to keep something so big from their only daughter.

'But were you *ever* going to tell me?' asked Stephanie, angrily. 'Or did you hope I wouldn't find out and you wouldn't feel obliged to share your winnings?'

'Stephanie Louise O'Leary! How dare you suggest that about your father and me! We've never had much, as you well know, but we've always given you everything we could.'

Stephanie at least had the grace to look sheepish. 'I know, Ma, but look at it from my point of view. Everyone is talking about this – and I mean *everyone*! I had to pretend that I knew about it so that I wouldn't look stupid!'

'Well, as I've said already, Steph, I'm sorry you've been embarrassed by the whole affair but can we move on now please!'

Maggie was sick of it. It had started late last night when they'd allowed Stephanie twenty minutes on Facebook before she went to bed. She'd seen the messages from her friends and had gone ballistic. She'd shouted at her and Dan and hadn't wanted to hear an explanation. They'd sent her up to bed, promising to discuss it in the morning. But since Dan was on an early shift again, she was the one trying to placate her angry daughter.

'I don't think I can go to school today,' Stephanie sighed, pulling her pink fluffy dressing gown tighter around her neck. 'I just can't face all the questions.'

'Nice try,' said Maggie, pouring herself another cup of tea. 'But it's an important year. You have your Junior Cert this year and you can't afford to be missing days for no reason.'

'But, *Mam*! It's not for "*no* reason". You just don't understand what it's like. Everyone will be talking about it and they'll think I'm loaded and will be expecting me to flash the cash.'

'But there isn't any cash, Steph. Just tell them that.'

'God, Ma, you're so naïve. Nobody will really want to know any details of a missing ticket or anything – they'll just hear we've won the lotto and I'll be branded a rich girl.'

Maggie sighed. She really didn't need to be dealing with this now when she had so many other more pressing things on her mind. 'Right, Steph. Just one day! You can take yourself back to bed, but tomorrow you go to school. Deal?'

'Thanks, Ma. You're the best.' Before Maggie could change her mind, Stephanie had planted a kiss on her forehead and was heading back upstairs. But she hesitated midway. 'That money, Ma … can we go to Barbados? Portia Graham was there in the summer and she said it was like a paradise. And I should really be learning to drive soon so—'

'Stephanie! Need I remind you that we don't have any money yet and if and when we do, there'll be a lot of things to be sorted before we start thinking of luxury holidays and the likes!'

'I know, Ma, but it's just—'

'Bed, Stephanie, unless you want me to change my mind!' God, these teenage years were difficult. She thought life had been hard when Steph was a baby – the sleepless nights, the colic, the nappies – but she'd give anything to have those years back again. Steph was at that complex age where she was up one minute and down the next. There was no telling what sort of mood she'd be in from day to day.

From what she'd read, it was just her hormones kicking in and you just had to ignore the attitude. Maggie always found that almost impossible to do. When Steph would tut and roll her eyes when she was asked to do anything around the house, Maggie would always bite back, telling her how ungrateful she was. But then it would always lead to an argument and a stand-off for days. Sometimes, they wouldn't even remember what the argument was about in the first place.

And then there were those stories that you didn't want to listen to but seemed to be more and more frequent these days; stories about young girls harming themselves or, God forbid, even worse. Stories like that always made Maggie cry. She'd look at her daughter and hope and pray that she was doing right by her and that Steph would get through her teenage years and come out the other end as a well-rounded and happy girl.

Glancing at the kitchen wall clock, Maggie saw it was just gone eight so she had an hour and a half before the crew were back for take two of the filming. God, she'd been mortified yesterday with all the goings on. She'd been in such a dark mood, what with everything else that was happening, and it had obviously shown in how she was coming across. And then when she'd finally nailed it, she'd been unceremoniously interrupted. Bloody hell, she'd nearly died when Rita said what she did about the street. Thank God they'd stopped the cameras rolling or it would have been a real embarrassment.

At least they'd salvaged some of what Maggie had said. They might want her for another short piece and then they were going to talk to a few others. Lorraine had pretended she was relieved not to be interviewed yesterday but Maggie knew her friend had been secretly disappointed. She'd looked absolutely beautiful and despite her protests about appearing on camera, nobody got dressed up like that if they didn't want to be seen. And she'd even told her boss she'd be late into work this morning so she must be hoping to be interviewed.

Right, time was ticking on and she'd need to put on her glad rags. Maggie would have loved to wear something a bit more glam today, but Claude had asked her to wear the same as yesterday so it would look like a continuation of filming. When things settled down over the next few weeks, she promised herself that a shopping spree was on the cards. She'd only planned a dash around Penneys to update her wardrobe but now with that money almost within her grasp, she hoped it would be a visit to all the best shops in Grafton Street! She wanted to ignite her love of fashion again. She was growing old beyond her years and she wanted to fix that before it was too late.

Her doctor's visit the other day had given her a bit of a shake up. It had made her realise that she needed to embrace life. She didn't want to be this frumpy, middle-aged mammy figure. She wanted to be more than that. She wanted her daughter to be proud to introduce her to her friends. She wanted to turn heads the way she used to, and maybe even attract a few wolf-whistles along the way. She wasn't ignoring the more pressing matter that the doctor had discussed with her – well, not really. She needed to talk to Dan about it but not yet. She needed to get things straight in her own mind before worrying her husband.

'This is perfect, Lorraine,' said Claude, busy moving chairs into different positions around the kitchen table and removing a large vase which was proving a bit of a distraction. 'We'll just get the two of you sitting beside each other over here, and Yasper will have a chat with you while the camera is rolling.'

Lorraine had to stifle a giggle. She'd laughed when the blond-haired presenter had been introduced to them yesterday. Apparently his parents were Dutch, hence the name, but it was all Lorraine could do not to call him Casper, as in the friendly ghost! He was certainly pale enough to earn the name.

Claude and the others had arrived just after nine on the street and were anxious to get a bit of filming done before moving on to their next stop. On Marco's recommendation, they'd decided to chat to Lorraine, but when Barry had shown his face, Claude had thought it would make a nice piece to interview both of them together. Barry had been reluctant, saying he had to be in work in an hour, but before he'd realised what was happening, both himself and Lorraine had been shuffled into their kitchen and the crew were scurrying around setting everything up.

Lorraine cast a sideways glance at her husband as they made themselves comfortable at the table. 'Are you okay, Barry? You're not nervous, are you?'

'Of course not,' said Barry, nervously eyeing up the camera on the kitchen table. 'I'm just conscious of the time. I've really got to get going in the next half hour.'

'Don't worry, Barry,' said Claude. 'We're almost ready to start. We'll have you out of here in twenty minutes tops.'

Barry let out a long sigh and Lorraine suddenly felt inexplicably nervous. This was supposed to be a 'good feeling' interview. They were supposed to be showing how wonderful Enda's was and how happy they were to be living there. Judging by Barry's face, he wanted to be anywhere else! Well fingers crossed there'd be no interruptions like there was yesterday and they could breathe a sigh of relief when it was all over. Thank God at least they were inside and nobody else was there to watch except Maggie and Marco.

'Okay,' said Yasper, pulling a chair up at the table and making himself comfortable. 'I'm just going to lead in by asking you why you came back to the street. Just forget about the camera and tell me as if you were talking to a friend.'

Lorraine twisted a strand of her hair around and around in her fingers. 'Right so. Let's get started.'

Claude's voice boomed out through the little kitchen as Maggie and Marco looked on. 'And action!'

'I'm here with Lorraine and Barry McGrath,' crooned Yasper into the camera. 'Lorraine grew up here on Enda's. She moved away in her twenties, only to come back with her husband Barry a few years ago. So what brought you back, Lorraine?'

Lorraine took a deep breath and smiled enthusiastically. 'I know it sounds like an obvious thing to say, but I love it here. It was a fantastic place to grow up in and, to be honest, I missed it when I left. When Barry and I were looking for a house, one came up here and I didn't have to think twice.'

'And what's so different about this street, Lorraine?'

'It's the people mainly. We're like one big happy family. I know that might sound naïve and hard to believe, but it's true. We all look out for each other. We go out socially together and are always popping into each other's houses. It just feels safe and like a little haven outside of the busy world that's around us.'

Yasper was nodding. 'That's really cool, Lorraine. It sounds wonderful. And how about you, Barry? You didn't grow up here, so is St Enda's Terrace just as special to you?'

'Well ... I, em, well, obviously it's not as special to me because I've only been here a few years. It's, eh, okay, I suppose.'

'It's understandable you don't have the same connection with the street as Lorraine, but you must love the fact that the people are so warm and welcoming?' Yasper was clearly trying to put words into his mouth.

Barry opened his mouth and then closed it again. All eyes were on him and Lorraine suddenly felt anxious about what he was going to say. She prayed for Claude to shout 'cut' but he kept the cameras rolling.

'People are the same the world over really,' said Barry, rubbing his chin. 'None of us live in a perfect world – even though we might think it for a while. Nobody is perfect, and put temptation in their way and even the purest of the pure will take the opportunity to grab it!'

There was an audible gasp in the room and Claude almost fell over a chair in his anxiety to stop the camera rolling. 'Cut, cut, cut! What was that all about, Barry? I hope this is not going to be like yesterday all over again!'

'Can we have a minute, please?' asked Lorraine, mortified by what Barry had said. 'We just need a quick chat.'

Claude sighed. 'Fine, fine. We'll take five minutes outside. Come on, lads.'

'Jesus, Mary and Joseph,' said Maggie, coming over to sit at the table with her two friends. 'What were you thinking about, Barry? This is supposed to be a documentary about the positive side of the street. They don't want to hear your gripes!'

Barry at least had the grace to blush. 'I know, I know. I just saw red for a moment. All this talk about a fabulous neighbourhood—'

'It's the bloody ticket again, isn't it?' said Marco, pulling up a chair. 'It's really getting to everyone.'

'Well, yes, there's that, too—'

'What do you mean "there's that, *too*"?' asked Lorraine, realising that it wasn't the perfect place to air their dirty laundry but she just had to know. 'What else is up with you? Why are you behaving like this?'

'Lorraine,' said Barry, turning to look her straight in the eye. 'I think you know why. And I've been waiting for the past couple of weeks for you to tell me about it.'

Marco and Maggie shuffled on their chairs, clearly embarrassed to be party to one of Lorraine and Barry's marital tiffs. 'Em, come on Marco,' said Maggie, standing up suddenly. 'Let's give these two a few minutes.'

With just the two of them left, Lorraine squared up to Barry. 'To tell you about *what*, Barry? You've been a nightmare these past couple of weeks. I don't know what's wrong with you but I think it's about time you told me.'

Barry stiffened. 'Lorraine, I know there's something going on that you're not telling me about.'

'Jesus, Barry, there you go again, turning things around. What the hell are you talking about? You're talking in riddles again and to be honest, I'm sick of it!'

Barry took a deep breath. 'Are you having an affair?'

Lorraine sat back heavily in her chair as though she'd been slapped in the face. 'For fuck's sake, Barry. Where did that come from? Why would you say something like that?'

'But you haven't answered me, Lorraine. Why would you not answer me – unless, of course, there's some truth in it?' Barry's look was a mixture of anguish and anger. Lorraine had never seen him like this before.

But suddenly *she* became angry. How dare he accuse her

of something like that. How bloody dare he! The cheek of him to even think it, let alone say it. So that's why he'd been in a mood these past few weeks.

'To be honest, Barry, I don't think it deserves an answer.'

'Well maybe that in itself answers the question!' Barry stood up and stormed out of the room, leaving Lorraine staring after him in shock.

Maggie and Marco rushed inside. 'Lorraine, are you okay?' asked Maggie, putting an arm around her friend. 'Barry's just gone tearing down the street. What happened?'

'What's happening?' asked Claude, appearing back in the little kitchen. 'Is Barry gone? Please don't tell me another interview has been ruined.'

Marco pulled Claude aside. 'There seems to have been a bit of a domestic. I don't think you'll be getting any more out of these today.'

'Oh, God, this street is turning out to be a bit of a nightmare!' said Claude, rubbing his forehead. 'Right, Marco. Can we at least get you outside for an interview and then we'll be out of here.'

'No problem,' said Marco, obviously delighted that his time had come. 'Just let me pop back inside to my own house for a quick brush up. Give me two minutes.'

As soon as the front door closed, Lorraine broke down in sobs. 'Oh, Maggie, how has it come to this? What the hell is going on with Barry? He asked me if I was having an affair!'

'Oh, Jesus, Mary and Joseph!' said Maggie, pulling her chair closer to her friend and patting her hand. 'What on earth is making him think that?'

'I honestly don't know, Maggie. My head is about to burst. What the hell is going on in his head?' Lorraine put her head in her hands and sobbed.

'You just let it all out, love. This has been brewing for a few weeks so maybe it's as well it's come to a head. What you need to do when you've both calmed down is have a proper chat about things. Nothing is going to be achieved or sorted until you talk to each other.'

'You're right,' sniffed Lorraine, wiping her streaming nose in her sleeve. 'We'll just have to get to the bottom of it all. Do you know I've even been suspecting Barry of taking the ticket?'

'Ah, no, Lorraine. You don't really think that, do you?'

'I don't know, Maggie. It's just with the gambling thing and everything, I thought maybe he'd taken it because he had debts.'

'I'm sure you're wrong,' said Maggie. 'Barry wouldn't do something like that. Sure, isn't he the one who's been pushing to have a family? Why would he jeopardise that for money?'

Lorraine blew her nose and managed a little smile. 'Marriage, eh? I suppose the ups and downs are all part of it.'

Maggie nodded. 'Look, love, why don't you go and have a rest for a while. You look exhausted. 'I'll head out and see how Marco's interview is going.'

'Em, sorry … sorry to interrupt,' the red-faced cameraman said, peeping his head around the kitchen door. Can I just grab that camera please?'

'Go on ahead,' said Lorraine, pausing the conversation until he grabbed his equipment off the kitchen table and was back out the door. 'Maggie, thanks for everything. You're a brilliant friend.'

'Ah, go away with you, Lorraine. What are friends for?'

Lorraine walked Maggie out to the hall and waved her off.

She was never as glad as when she closed the front door and
was finally alone. What a morning! Between Barry thinking
she was having an affair and her thinking he was gambling,
there was certainly a lot they needed to sort out. Jesus! Why
was life always so complicated? And why was it that the
universe always seemed to have a way of paying you back
for past indiscretions?

CHAPTER 21

'You're looking very smart, Marco,' said Majella, who was hauling a number of Marks & Spencer's grocery bags out of her car. 'Loving that shirt.'

Another person would look frazzled after trawling around the supermarket but Majella's long chestnut hair was flicked back in a Charlie's Angels fashion and her make-up was impeccable, accentuating her huge brown eyes.

'What, this old thing? I just threw it on this morning in a hurry before the crew arrived. I barely had time to brush my hair!' In actual fact, Marco had been up hours before they'd arrived and had tried on about ten outfits before he'd decided on the burgundy John Rocha shirt over beige chinos. His hair had also been a work of art, as he'd gelled, sculpted, teased and spiked until he'd got it just right!

'Speaking of the crew, how did filming go today? I heard about the ructions yesterday!'

Marco tied Mimi's lead to the railings so he could help his neighbour with the bags. 'Oh yesterday was a disaster. Rita made a right show of herself, not to mention embarrassing the life out of us.'

Majella giggled. 'I would have loved to see it though. Sounds like it would make a good documentary in itself!'

'Oh, Jesus, I'd die if any of that stuff was caught on camera. It made us all look like right eejits. To be honest, today wasn't much better! How come you haven't been around for any of the filming?'

'I had hoped to be but they're a bit shorthanded in work and there's a run on spray tans and gel nails, what with all the Debs at the moment.'

'It's mad, isn't it?' said Marco, closing the boot after he'd taken the last bag out. 'Debs are more like weddings these days. I know mine wasn't too long ago, but I think it's getting crazier by the year.'

'Well, the boys don't need any of the pampering that the girls do. Maybe you just didn't see what went on.'

'Oh, believe me, Majella, if I was doing the Debs thing all over again, I'd be worse than the ladies! I'd need my spray tan, highlights, the works!'

'Oh, I suppose,' laughed Majella. 'I'd forgotten how high maintenance you are. Do you want to come in for a cuppa? You can tell me all the news and I might even tell you mine.'

'Well, if you didn't mind, that would be lovely thanks. I'll just take Mimi home first.'

'Don't be silly. She can come in – or she can go out the back if she wants. She's only a little dot of a thing.'

'Oh, right, thanks,' said Marco, untying his little cockapoo from the railings and carrying her inside. It was a very rare occasion to be asked into Majella's house. Even though she and her husband had lived on Enda's for a number of years, Marco could count on one hand the number of times he'd got his nose through the door. Majella and Chris were nice enough people, but they seemed to consider themselves a bit above everyone else and, as a result, they kept their distance. Majella had begun to embrace life on Enda's a little more of late, sometimes coming to the bingo on a Thursday and stopping for chats on the street, but Marco still felt a bit uneasy with her.

'Right, tea or coffee?' Majella was filling the kettle with water, ignoring the shopping bags that were taking over half the kitchen. Marco half expected to see a maid appear to put everything away.

'I'll have a tea please if you're making one – two sugars and a good dash of milk.' He opened Majella's back door to let Mimi run outside. 'Can I help you put that stuff away?'

'Not at all, Marco. I'll just stick the freezer stuff away – everything else can wait until we've had a cuppa. Sit down there, it won't be a minute.'

Just like Marco, Chris and Majella had installed a breakfast bar in the kitchen. Theirs looked a lot more expensive than his, but he wasn't too keen on the starkness of the black marble in contrast to the cream-painted wood kitchen. The high chairs were wine-coloured leather – very comfortable but, again, not in keeping with the look of the kitchen. They were clearly people who had money but no taste.

'Here we go.' Majella placed two steaming mugs on the counter and settled into the chair beside Marco. 'So go on, tell me everything.'

This took Marco a little by surprise. 'About …?'

'About the filming, Marco! Keep up, would you?'

'Well, you wouldn't believe the goings on, Majella. I think today was even *worse* than yesterday!' Marco cupped his hands around the mug, revelling in sharing the gossip.

Majella's face lit up. 'Really? What happened? God, I'm really raging now I wasn't around either day.'

'Well, Claude, that's my, em, that's the assistant producer—'

'Come on, Marco, I think we all know by now he's more than that. Sure you haven't stopped talking about him for the past few months. So have the two of you, em, you know …'

'*Majella*! No we have not! Anyway, back to my story. So Claude decided that there should be an interview with Lorraine and Barry inside their house. Because Lorraine grew up here and then came back after a number of years, he thought it would be a nice angle.'

'And?' Majella was on the edge of her seat, waiting to hear what had happened.

'So, Lorraine said her piece and it was fine. She gushed about Enda's like Maggie had done yesterday and it sounded great.'

'Well, what's bad about that then?' Majella was growing impatient but Marco loved to drag a story out.

'Nothing bad about *that* – but then Barry spoke! Honestly, Majella. I nearly died. He started saying things about people not being perfect the world over and how people will always give in to temptation, given half the chance.'

'Oh, Jesus, that's mental.'

'Honestly,' said Marco, enjoying his neighbour's reaction, 'nobody had a clue what he was going on about except that he obviously thought he was making some sort of point.'

'So did they stop filming at that stage?'

'They stopped for a while and the crew went outside. Myself and Maggie began to talk to Lorraine and Barry about it, but we were clearly in the way so we followed the others outside. Next thing, Barry was out of there like a bat out of hell, storming down the street with a look of thunder on his face.'

'Are you serious? I always thought those two had a perfect

marriage. They seem so well suited. I wonder what it was all about. You're her brother, you must know what's behind it all.'

At the mention of the word 'brother', Marco felt suddenly ashamed that he was gossiping about Lorraine. She really didn't deserve that. He wasn't a malicious gossiper, he just liked a good meaty chat. But of all people, he should be protecting Lorraine from idle gossip – not creating it.

'Well, Marco? C'mon, tell me more. Are Lorraine and Barry having marriage problems? And I thought you told me they were trying for a baby?'

Oh, God, there's another piece of gossip he should have kept to himself. 'No, Majella. I don't think they're having problems – well nothing more than the average couple. I think they might just have had a little tiff this morning and Barry was still in bad form.'

'Come on, Marco. There has to be more to it than that. I know you're dying to tell me. I'd never know anything that goes on here in the street if you didn't keep me informed.'

'Honestly,' said Marco, draining the last of his tea and standing up. He was feeling rotten now about stirring. 'There's nothing more to tell. It all turned out okay in the end – just about. Anyway, what was your news you were going to tell me about?'

'Ah nothing really, Marco. I can't compete with all that.'

'I suppose it *is* very dramatic really, when you think about it,' grinned Marco, opening the back door and scooping Mimi up into his arms.

Majella walked out to the door with him. 'It will be worth it in the end though. I can't wait to see it when it's all finished.'

'Well, it will be some time yet so you'll *have* to wait! And Claude said that sometimes these things don't even make it onto telly. So, we'll just have to keep our fingers crossed. It was an experience anyway.'

'At least things can get back to normal around here,' said Majella, indicating the pristine street. 'I'm even beginning to miss the scattering of crisp bags and the leaves blowing all over the place!'

'Ha, well I think we've benefited hugely from the big clean up,' said Marco. 'Enda's has never looked so good. Thanks for the tea, Majella. Chat to you soon.'

Marco opened his own front door and felt uneasy about something. He couldn't figure out what it was but there was definitely something bugging him. It had been nice to sit and chat with Majella. She was always the one who was a bit removed from the group of neighbours and he used to think it was because she was snooty. He'd changed his mind about it over the past year or so because the fact that she hankered after the finer things in life didn't make her snooty. Sure, didn't he like the finer things himself?

It felt as though it should be evening time and yet it was still only just after three. He'd been up at the crack of dawn beautifying himself and was now feeling exhausted. He headed into the sitting room and sprawled himself out on the sofa with Mimi happily snuggling in under his arm. He'd love a chat with Claude but he'd still be out working so he'd leave it until a bit later.

When Majella had first come to Enda's she'd made no secret of the fact that she and Chris had no intention of staying. They were after a big house in Malahide by the sea and Enda's was just a stop gap until they'd made enough money from their properties to live the life of luxury they dreamed of.

Then things had gone belly up in the property market.

They didn't speak about it much, but it didn't take a genius to know that they must have taken a hit. Marco didn't know how heavily they'd invested in property but he guessed it was pretty serious. Majella had been constantly boasting about the type of house they were planning to buy and saying that she couldn't be bothered doing any work to their little house on Enda's because they wouldn't be staying. Then all of a sudden, the boasting had stopped and they'd decided to do up the house after all.

Some people still saw Majella as the girl who'd arrived on the street initially, all superior and with ideas above her station. And in a way, there was still a bit of that Majella there. But Marco saw more than that. He saw somebody who was beginning to embrace life on Enda's, albeit reluctantly. He liked her and he really hoped that she'd given up on the idea of being a millionaire and—

That was it! That's what had been niggling him. Majella hadn't even asked about the ticket! It was the one thing that had been on the tip of everyone's tongue all week, yet not a word from Majella about it. She was a member of the syndicate and due two hundred thousand euro from the ticket, yet she hadn't seemed bothered that there was still no news about it. She hadn't asked if it had been found or if they'd had any more ideas about it. She hadn't wanted to know what the plan was or indeed if they had one.

Oh, God, there was only one reason he could think of that she wouldn't talk about it. Could she really be the one who'd taken the ticket? He had thought it at one stage, but he was still finding it difficult to believe that any of his friends would be so mean and cunning. And there he'd been, thinking about how she'd changed and how she was becoming more down to earth and less materialistic.

He grabbed the remote control from behind the cushion at his back and flicked on the telly. His mind was running away with him. Surely Majella wouldn't have sat with him, drinking tea and having a laugh, when all the time she was doing him and the others over? But she had indicated she wanted to tell him something and then shied away from it. Could it possibly have been that? He honestly didn't know what to think.

A vibration from the phone in his pocked alerted him to a message. He must have forgotten to take it off silent since this morning. Rolling onto his side, he pulled the phone out of his pocket and looked at the message on the screen. It was from Claude.

Hi, sexy. You were great this morning – the only decent interview out of the lot. And you were looking hot. Sorry we didn't get to chat more. I'm stuck down in Wicklow at the moment doing a bit of filming and I don't know how long I'll be. I'll give you a call when we're finished here and maybe if you're free, we can hook up later. Better run. They're calling me. Later. C. xxx

Oh, God, that man could make him turn to jelly even with his texts. He could imagine Claude's dulcet tones whispering that in his ear. He quickly tapped his reply.

Hi, your sexy self! Thanks for that. I enjoyed doing my bit. Well, I've no work this week and I've nothing planned for the rest of the day, so I'll wait for your call later. I hope you get finished up there soon. Would love to meet up tonight. Marco x

It gave him a little thrill that Claude had sent that text. Sometimes he felt that it was more him and not Claude that was the driving force in the relationship, if you could even call it that. He seemed to be the one who would instigate the conversations on Twitter and he definitely sent more emails and made more calls. But it was probably that he was a natural chatterbox and wasn't all that keen on his own company. Claude seemed to be more the strong, silent type. He'd told him he loved to chill out for hours at home on his own with just his music for company. Although Marco lived on his own, he liked to fill any alone time with phone calls or visitors – even at that, he was never really alone because he always had Mimi there for company.

He really hoped Claude would get back in touch and arrange to meet him later. Marco didn't care where they went or what they did, he just wanted some time with him. The days were passing by so quickly and, before long, Claude would be on that plane, heading back to his home in New York. He shuddered at the thought.

However, despite the welcome text and the thought of meeting up with Claude later, Marco still couldn't help his mind wandering back to his chat with Majella. The whole thing was such a bloody mystery. He idly flicked around the television channels, looking for something to take his mind off things. He settled on the RTÉ News but couldn't really take in what was being said.

All he could think about was the bloody ticket and the fact that one of his neighbours and friends had played those winning numbers. The ticket had to be out there somewhere. A ticket worth a million euro! Bloody hell, it was a lot of money. One thing was for sure, he wasn't going to let his share of a million euro just disappear without a fight!

CHAPTER 22

Marco was plucking a few stray hairs from his eyebrows when his phone pinged. Oh, God, if it was Claude cancelling, he'd die. They'd had a lovely intimate phone call a couple of hours before and Marco had been tingling all over in anticipation ever since.

Claude hadn't been able to give him a definite time for them to meet because he said filming was so unpredictable. Marco had wondered if that had been a jibe, considering the fiasco on the street earlier, but Claude didn't seem the sort to stick the boot in. He grabbed his phone and held his breath while he checked the message.

> Hi, Marco. Just wanted to let you know I'm getting a lift over to yours. Dad said he'd bring me so we're going to leave shortly. I should be with you in about twenty minutes. Looking forward to it. C x

Oh, thank God for that. Marco had taken advantage of the fact that Claude hadn't been able to commit to time and had asked him over to his place for the evening. He'd suggested that it was the best solution because then it didn't matter whether he was late or not. Claude had readily agreed and Marco had been over the moon.

He did one last check in the mirror and when he was satisfied his eyebrows were tidy and his hair coiffed to perfection, he liberally splashed aftershave not only on his face, but sprinkled some down his shirt and dabbed it on the back of his neck. He loved his bottle of Very Sexy by Victoria's Secret. He'd smelled it on a customer in work one day and it had really turned him on. He'd managed to get the name of it off the guy without appearing like he was hitting on him and had ordered it online that very evening.

He glanced around at his bedroom, satisfied that everything was looking just right. When Claude had phoned earlier, he'd quickly stripped his raspberry and black bedclothes from the bed and stuck them in for a quick wash. He'd only washed them at the weekend but he wanted everything to be perfect and he couldn't go wrong with a fresh lavender smell from the bed.

He loved his bedroom. Although raspberry was the dominant colour in the room, it wasn't a girlie room. The walls were painted a pale, eggshell blue except the wall behind his bed, which was covered by a very striking raspberry and black patterned wallpaper. He'd picked up his bedclothes in the Debenhams sale and the John Rocha raspberry silk fitted in beautifully with his colour scheme. He'd had a radiator shelf painted the same colour as the walls and on it he had a variety of pink and black candles. He loved candlelight. There was nothing more relaxing than the flicker of the naked flame and if things worked out as he hoped they would tonight, they'd make for a perfect romantic setting.

He checked himself in his full-length mirror one last time and was satisfied with how he looked. He'd been tempted to dress up in one of his latest purchases from the shop – a pair of front-pleat, grey tweed trousers with a gorgeous purple shawl-neck jumper, but he'd decided against it. He didn't want to look like too much of a try hard. If they'd been going out somewhere nice, he may have worn those but it seemed a bit much for a night in. In the end he'd settled on a G Star granddad long-sleeve top in a lovely shade of pale blue, over a pair of faded grey, drop-crotch jeans. He knew he looked great and he hoped Claude would think so too.

Back downstairs, he checked on Mimi, who was snoring softly in her basket in the kitchen. She'd probably come to life when Claude arrived. Thankfully he'd introduced them to each other yesterday and they'd got along brilliantly so he didn't have to bother locking her outside. No matter how much Marco adored Claude, he didn't think he could be with somebody who didn't like his little cockapoo.

Claude had said that his mother had cooked him up a feast for dinner earlier so he wasn't hungry. Marco was thankful for that as he would have hated to have to cook and get himself all smelly and frazzled. He'd been in Marks & Spencer in the Jervis Centre last week and had stocked up on finger foods for the freezer so there was plenty there if they fancied a nibble later. He hadn't been able to eat a thing himself because he'd been so nervous at the thought of entertaining Claude at home. The fridge was well stocked, too, with wine and beer and Marco had even rushed to the off-licence earlier to buy some Guinness in case Claude fancied it.

Right, he couldn't do any more. He was all ready and waiting. All he needed was his guest so that the night could begin. He glanced at the kitchen clock on the wall and saw it was ten past nine – fifteen minutes since Claude had texted. He should be here any moment now. Marco sat down heavily on one of his cream bar-stools and closed his eyes and prayed that things would go to plan.

Oh, God, he so badly wanted tonight to go well. He'd been really worried that Claude might have been put off by the goings on in the street the past couple of days. He'd wondered if maybe he thought it was more hassle than it was worth. But, thankfully, that wasn't the case. Claude seemed just as keen as he was for something to happen between them. There had definitely been sexual tension in the air and even their texts back and forth seemed to drip with suggestion.

They'd chatted the other night about Claude's discontent with his job and Marco wanted to bring that up again tonight. The thought of having to say goodbye to him next week was already killing Marco, so he hoped he could get him thinking about coming home again. It was probably a long shot but maybe if he had something to come home to, there'd be a chance. Well tonight he was going to forget about that damn ticket and concentrate on his personal life for a change.

A ring at the door almost frightened the life out of him and he jumped off the stool to go and answer it. It had woken up Mimi, too, and she was yapping happily at the realisation that they were going to have company. Marco got to the front door and could make out Claude's frame through the glass. He took a deep breath and pulled open the door.

Lorraine checked her watch and saw it was already gone nine. She flipped over the two steaks that were browning on the pan and began to set the table. Barry would be home soon and she wanted to make everything nice for him. She'd had an awful day, her emotions veering between anger and despair, and she hadn't wanted to speak to anyone.

Maggie had been very concerned about her after the crew had left the street and had come back in to see how she was. She'd assured her she was fine and that she'd talk to her when she was ready, but she explained that she just wanted to be left alone for the moment. Marco had also called in and she'd been tempted to talk to him about things, but sometimes she hated that they all lived in each other's pockets on the street. It wasn't always easy to have your private business up for public discussion.

She'd planned to go into work when the filming was over but after the big hullabaloo, she'd just rung in sick. She had a great work ethic and would normally frown upon people who cried off sick when really they weren't, but, in this case, she honestly felt like the heart was being ripped out of her. It didn't come much sicker than that!

After she'd assured everyone she'd be fine, she'd taken to the bed for hours, mulling things over and trying to figure out what it was she'd done to make Barry think she'd been unfaithful. Had he heard something about Rory Anderson in work? Rory was a right laugh and a compulsive flirt. He and Lorraine got on really well but that was as far as it went. Maybe he'd heard something and had put two and two together and made ten. It really didn't seem likely because Barry had met Rory at various work nights out and had got on well with him too. But there was really nothing else she could think of.

She'd often felt that she didn't deserve a man as good and lovely as Barry. For the first time in her adult life, she'd felt secure and looked after. Maybe it had all been a bit too good to be true.

So, she'd decided that tonight would be the night she'd talk to him. No more excuses and no more shying away from it. Suddenly, she didn't feel afraid any more. Things were so bad between them that she couldn't make them any worse, no matter what she said. Maybe if they both opened up and spoke their mind like they used to do, they might even be able to come out of this intact.

One thing was for sure, she loved Barry. She loved him like she'd never loved anyone before. The thought of losing him was absolutely killing her. She idly placed a protective hand on her tummy. Wouldn't it be poetic justice if she was to lose her husband just when she was coming around to the idea of having a baby? Today she'd realised she was ready – she'd been scared and worried before, but a lot of things had fallen into place for her earlier and she knew that, more than anything, she wanted to have a baby with her husband. She'd just have to believe it would all work out.

With everything that had been going on over the past week, she'd completely lost track of her dates and had been shocked to realise earlier that her period had been due two days ago. She was never late. And she always got crampy pains in the few days leading up to it and there'd been nothing this month.

At five o'clock, she'd tidied herself up and had rushed down to the local Centra. She'd picked up a couple of steaks and some ready-to-roast potatoes. She'd bought an apple tart and a carton of cream, some strawberries and even a box of Barry's favourite Lily O'Brien mint chocolates. Then she'd slipped into the pharmacy and bought a pregnancy test.

She stood back and surveyed the table and was happy with how it looked. They rarely sat at the table, preferring to balance their plates on their laps while watching something on telly. So she'd really made the effort and got out the Christmas tablecloth and napkins. She'd even snipped off one of the lovely yellow rambling roses that was growing over the wall from next door's garden and placed it in a little vase in the centre of the table.

With the steak almost done and the potatoes crisping nicely in the oven, she lit the hob under the carrots and broccoli. Surely Barry would see the effort she'd made and finally sit down and talk to her. She was going to make sure that they forgot about the happenings on the street tonight and just concentrated on them.

She *was* feeling a bit nervous about seeing him, given that he'd stormed out earlier in a terrible mood having accused her of some awful things. But she was hoping that she'd created a nice calming atmosphere and that she'd be able to get him to sit down and they could have some nice food and wine and just talk about what was upsetting him and she'd finally tell him her secret.

She hadn't done the test. It was such a big thing and would be a defining moment in both their lives if it was positive. She wanted them to have that moment together. She planned to produce the test after dinner and tell him she was late. She hoped that everything else would pale into insignificance and they could move on to what was important.

It was half nine now, he'd be here any minute. She ran upstairs to touch up her make-up and run the brush through her hair. She slipped out of her tracksuit and slipped on a black jersey dress and a pair of black pumps. *Right, Lorraine McGrath. Tonight is the start of the rest of your life. Don't mess this up!* She smiled at herself in the mirror and headed back downstairs to wait for her husband.

'So you'd really give up all the glitz of New York for dirty old Dublin?' Marco was opening the second bottle of red wine, the two glasses from the first having gone completely to his head on account of his empty stomach. It had been two hours since Claude had arrived and the evening had been amazing – and it wasn't over yet.

'If I could even get a bit of freelance work, I'd definitely consider it,' mused Claude, sinking down further into the sofa and popping his shoeless feet up onto the coffee table. 'I mean, I'd be able to stay with my parents and I have some savings to keep me going but I just worry about what would happen when the money runs out and I can't find a permanent job.'

'But I'm sure your parents would help you out and you wouldn't have many expenses if you're living at home.' The wine was loosening Marco's tongue and he was saying all the things he wouldn't dare to if he'd been sober. He was also having a hard time tearing his eyes away from Claude's denim-clad legs. Again, he'd arrived in jeans and a T-shirt but the jeans were Dolce & Gabbana and the T-shirt Marco recognised as Alexander McQueen from the trademark 'MCQ' on the front. He found himself drooling at both the clothes and the body!

'As I've told you before, Marco, I hate living off my parents. I know they'd support me and they'd be delighted to have me home, but I really want to be self-sufficient. At least in New York, I can pay for my own place and have enough to feed and clothe myself.'

'But surely being happy is the most important thing,' Marco said, daring to sink further into the sofa himself and sidle up to his guest. 'If you're not happy over there, what's the point in wasting your life?'

'I know you're right, but it's just such a big step. I have a life over there now that I've built up over the past five years. I have friends and a social life as well as a decent job.'

Marco moved in even closer and put his hand on Claude's knee. 'You could have a life here too, Claude. I … I think we have something really special here. I know we only met a few days ago but I feel I've known you all my life.' Jesus wept! Why on earth did he say that? He couldn't have been cornier if he'd tried!

But Claude didn't seem to mind. All of a sudden he adjusted his position on the sofa so that their faces almost touched. He held Marco's eye for a moment and then pressed his lips on his. Softly at first, then more urgently. Before Marco knew it, he was lying back on the sofa with Claude's body draped on top of him. He felt like he was in heaven as their tongues pushed and probed and their hands began to explore. All the pent-up passion that had been lying beneath the surface as they'd flirted these past few months was more than ready to explode.

Marco had no idea how long they were there but when they finally came up for breath, all he knew was he didn't want Claude to leave – ever. 'Come on,' he said, standing up on wobbly legs and holding out his hand. 'Let's go and get more comfortable.'

'Are you sure?' asked Claude, as he took Marco's hand and stood up. 'I mean, you know …'

Marco looked into his eyes. 'I know. And I'm sure.'

Lorraine threw her phone down onto the sofa beside her and tried not to cry. She'd spent enough of the day in tears. She'd been waiting and waiting for Barry to come home and when there was no sign of him by ten, she'd rung – but there still hadn't been an answer. The steaks were pretty much charred and the vegetables were soggy.

It was a quarter to eleven now and she'd rung and texted regularly since, to no avail. She'd been worried sick at first and had been tempted to go down to Maggie and see what she thought, but something told her to ride out this particular storm on her own. She was too used to using her friend as a crutch – maybe she should learn to make important decisions like this alone. She'd gone in and flicked on the telly instead, trying to take her mind off the awful possibilities that had been running through her mind.

Maybe she should have given more consideration to the fact that he'd been so annoyed and upset when he'd left that morning. Maybe she should have just gone down to the shop and demanded that they talk, instead of wallowing in her own self-pity all day. What if something terrible had happened? What if he'd been in such a state that he'd done something stupid? There was no stopping the tears this time.

Suddenly her phone gave a beep and she grabbed it up to have a look. Oh, thank God! It was Barry. But when she read the message, she began to cry all over again.

Sorry I missed your calls. In pub with the lads for a few pints. Don't wait up.

That was it. No 'love Barry' or kisses at the end – just cold, hard facts. So he'd been out drinking while she'd been here planning how they'd move forward with the rest of their lives. How could he?

She wiped her eyes with the sleeve of her dress and jumped up from the sofa. Striding purposefully into the kitchen, she took the two plates of food that were keeping warm in the oven and chucked the contents in the bin. She didn't even bother to clean up but instead turned off the lights, set the alarm and headed up to bed.

With her dress still on and her make-up intact, she curled into a ball under the covers and closed her eyes tight. She just wanted to sleep. Today had been one of the worst days of her life and she just needed it to be over. Maybe she and Barry could talk tomorrow – or maybe not. She just didn't know any more. She was going to give up trying to work it all out. Maybe it was time that her husband tried to sort things out because the way she was feeling at the moment, she just couldn't be bothered!

CHAPTER 23

Thursday, 15th September

'So you must be going mad over that ticket, Maggie,' said Doris O'Riordan, rooting for change in her purse to pay for the one scone she'd just bought.

'I've every faith it will work out, Doris. It's just a temporary glitch.' Maggie was fed up. She'd only been in work for two hours and had already had about twenty customers in just to try to squeeze a bit of gossip out of her. She knew that was the only reason they'd come in because they'd either just bought one measly item or had spent half an hour rooting for the money to pay. Doris O'Riordan was doing both!

'But imagine there's a ticket floating around worth a million euro, Maggie. I'd imagine whoever played those numbers has a lot to answer for. So, who was it that did them again?'

God, these people were so bloody predictable. 'As I'm sure you've heard, Doris, we don't know who was last to play the numbers. But there's no drama about it. We all want to find that ticket so we'll be leaving no stone unturned.'

'Oooh, it's all excitement around here at the moment, isn't it?' Doris still seemed to be having trouble locating the right change for the scone and Maggie was tempted to tell her just to have it on the house. 'I mean, between the lotto win and those cameras filming on your street, you're the talk of the terrace.'

'Listen, don't worry about the money,' said Maggie, knowing where this was leading. 'You can fix up the next time you're in.'

'I wouldn't dream of it. I just like to use up my coppers, that's all. So what were we saying – oh yes, the filming. I heard there was a big drama with that too. Apparently two of the people who were interviewed yesterday are getting a divorce. The rumour is that she's been having an affair.'

Maggie had had enough. 'Listen, Doris. Stop spreading vicious rumours. Those people you're referring to are friends of mine and I can assure you that, firstly, they are *not* getting a divorce and, secondly, there's been no affair. So stick that into your gossip pipe and smoke it!'

'Well, now … I think … I just … there's no need to be so horrible, Maggie. I was just saying what I'd heard.' Doris took a tissue out of her bag and blew her nose loudly, as if to convince Maggie she'd been hurt by her jibe. 'And here you go. I think you'll find that it's exactly right.' She finally handed over her coppers before leaving with a hard-done-by sniff.

Maggie was left staring after her neighbour as she shuffled out of the shop; no doubt off to find her cronies to tell them that Maggie O'Leary was losing it. But she didn't care. Usually so calm and in control, Maggie was feeling anything but at the moment.

She was so used to being able to solve people's problems. A

cuppa and a scone at Maggie's and they'd put the problems of the world to rights.

But she didn't feel in control of anything any more. Maybe it was because she was so bloody exhausted all the time or maybe she was just losing her touch. And the lost ticket certainly hadn't helped. She was probably more worried about the effect it was having on the street than the fact that it was lost in the first place. She knew that the money would be a fantastic bit of luck for them but if the past week had taught her anything, it was that your health is your wealth.

She was jolted out of her reverie by the sound of the bell on the shop door. 'Five of those jam donuts, please,' said an old lady with a stooped back and a blue rinse in her hair, indicating the freshly baked cakes. 'The grandkids are coming over this afternoon and they're their favourites. I hope there's plenty of jam in them.'

'Ah, we always load them with the best strawberry jam. You can't beat our donuts.' Thank God for at least one customer who wasn't there to have a nosy about the events on Enda's. If one more person came into the shop to look for a bit of gossip, she'd be tempted to shut the shop altogether!

'That's lovely, thanks,' said the little old lady, who promptly paid for her purchases. She turned to leave and then, as though having second thoughts, turned back around. 'I'm sure you must be sick of people asking, love, but are you one of the people who won the lotto? It's just Monica Duggan was telling me that it was the woman who worked in here. And did you find the ticket yet?'

For feck's sake! 'Yes, I *am* one of those people, no, we *haven't* found the ticket and, yes, I'm bloody well *sick to death* of people asking!'

The woman didn't even have the decency to look

embarrassed but just nodded her head understandingly and shuffled out the door. *I may as well be running an information centre*, thought Maggie. She was really beginning to hate nosy, busybody people!

For the first time that morning, the shop was quiet. Maggie plonked herself down on the little stool behind the counter and let out a sigh. How had life become so complicated? Only last month there was no lotto win and nobody was the worse for it. Last month she'd had no worries about the state of Barry and Lorraine's marriage – they had seemed like such a strong couple and she'd have bet they'd last the course. Last month she'd believed she was healthy.

Part of her was regretting having gone to the doctor on Monday. What she didn't know wouldn't hurt her – at least that's what her ma used to say. But the sensible side of her was thankful that she had gone. Her condition wasn't going to just disappear if she ignored it. It was just so hard for her to face up to being sick when she was so used to being the carer.

And then there was Dan. The doctor had been very firm with her about what she needed to do – and that included sharing the burden with her husband. But that was easier said than done. Poor Dan had been working all the hours God sends and he didn't say much, but she knew he was very stressed. He certainly didn't need to be taking on her problems as well. But she'd have to tell him soon – just not yet. She'd know when the time was right.

'Why didn't you wake me?' asked Claude, wandering into the kitchen, his hair dishevelled and wearing nothing but his boxer shorts. 'I can't believe I slept for that long.'

Marco let out a big guffaw. 'Well, Claude. It's not as though you actually *slept* for long at all! And I was just about to call you. Breakfast is ready.'

'Oh, wow! Pancakes! I adore pancakes and I'm absolutely starving.' He didn't wait to be asked twice and sat himself down on a chair and began liberally squeezing syrup all over the freshly made pancakes.

'Well, I just wanted to show you that we can do them as well as they do in the States. You can have your little bit of New York over here any time you like.' Marco looked at Claude to see his reaction.

'I've been thinking about that, Marco. You know, I only have to put in an hour or two of work today. I was going to suggest that we spend some time together but I think I might chase up some contacts instead.'

Marco was disappointed that they wouldn't be spending the day together but if it was something that was going to keep Claude here, he was all for it. 'And what are the chances, do you think? I mean, is there any chance you'd get a job so quickly? And wouldn't you have to work out your notice in RIP? Oh, Claude, this is so exciting. I can't believe you're actually thinking of staying after all.'

'Well, there's a lot to sort out but, to be honest, the more I think about it, the more I want to stay. I'm sure RIP will live without me. I got my workload cleared before I came over so it's not as though I'd be leaving a mess behind. But don't say a word for the moment. I'll need to look into a few things first.'

'I'll keep it zipped,' said Marco, making a zipping motion across his mouth with his fingers. 'I can be the soul of discretion when I want to be.'

'Well, the lads are coming here to pick me up in an hour

and we have to head off to do some work so, remember, not a word.'

'In an hour? That soon?' Marco hated having to let Claude go after such a fantastic night. 'I hope you'll be back later?'

'Of course I will.' Claude looked at him with those melting chocolate eyes. 'How could I stay away after, well, after you know.'

Marco did know. And he thanked God for it. It had been a fantastic night. Claude had been an extremely generous lover and had been more than Marco could have wished for. He knew now that they were perfect for each other and it seemed that Claude was feeling the same way. Fingers crossed everything would work out.

'Right,' said Claude, stuffing a last piece of pancake into his mouth and standing up from the table. 'I'd better go and have a shower and get dressed if I'm to be ready when the lads come. Thanks for breakfast. Delicious!'

'No problem, Claude. There are plenty of towels in the hotpress and you can use the shower in the en-suite. It's an electric one so no fear of the water running cold.'

Claude bent across and cupped Marco's face in his hands. He kissed him softly on the lips. Marco could taste the sweet syrup from his tongue. He was delicious. 'You really are a gorgeous man, Marco, do you know that? I certainly owe a lot to Twitter for bringing you to me.'

Marco blinked away the tears as he watched Claude head out the kitchen door. He daren't believe this was really happening. He'd found the man of his dreams and he was perfect. The only glitch was the New York thing and all going well, that would be sorted soon. At least he hoped and prayed that it would be – because if Claude wasn't going to stay in Ireland, Marco would have to think about packing up his life and moving to New York. There were no two ways about it. This time last week he'd never even met Claude and now he couldn't imagine his life without him. Life could be really funny sometimes.

But one thing was for sure, Marco was in love. He didn't just love Claude, he was deeply and passionately in love with him. Some people would say it was ridiculous – that he couldn't feel like that when he'd only known him such a short time – but he knew his own mind. He could see a future spread out in front of him. He could see children and grandchildren. He'd never, ever felt so strongly about anything in his life. Even the whole lotto debacle faded into insignificance when he thought about Claude. There was just no comparison.

He opened the dishwasher and began to load the dishes. But maybe he *should* be thinking more about the lotto money. Claude was a proud person and would never live on handouts. But what if they went into business together? What if Marco bought himself a clothes shop like he'd always dreamed of and he and Claude could manage it together? How perfect would that be?

Setting up his own shop was an amazing idea and two hundred thousand euro would certainly set him on his way. He knew enough about the business to be able to make a good job of it and maybe he could even start to sell some of his own designs if things worked out.

But first they had to find that bloody, bloody ticket. He'd told Maggie he was going to give the National Lottery headquarters a buzz again and have another chat with them. He'd do that as soon as Claude had left. He'd need to call another meeting of the syndicate, too, so that they could get a better idea of what was what. It had been a few days since the last meeting and it would be interesting to hear people's thoughts at this stage. He suspected it would be a much fierier meeting. Temperatures were definitely rising now and people were demanding answers – and rightly so!

He switched on the dishwasher and sprayed the table with a lemon spray before wiping it down. He was dying to tell Maggie all about last night and about his own ideas for the money. She was in work this morning, so maybe he'd drop down to the bakery and have a word if it was quiet. He'd tell Lorraine about things, too, but it was always a little more awkward telling her stuff of an intimate nature. They had a very close relationship, but still. He hoped she'd managed to sort things out with Barry last night. Those two were perfect for each other – just like him and Claude.

The shower went on upstairs and the thought of Claude standing naked, with the water sluicing over his toned and tanned body, was enough to make Marco break out into a sweat. Maybe he would welcome some company. Usually so indecisive, this time Marco didn't wait to think twice. He took the stairs two at a time with Mimi right behind him, wagging her little tail. 'Not this time, Mimi,' he said. 'Sometimes Daddy wants his own playtime.' He ran back downstairs with his little dog and promptly locked her outside. For once, he didn't feel a bit guilty at her pathetic howls. Daddy was finally getting a life!

CHAPTER 24

'What's up, babe? It's not like you to look so glum.'

Lorraine almost jumped out of her skin when she saw Rory Anderson hovering over her desk. 'What? I'm not, I'm fine. I'm just tired, that's all.'

'Well you look like you need some cheering up. Lunch?'

'I don't think so, Rory. I have loads to catch up on here with being out yesterday.' She liked Rory, she really did. He was great fun and they always had a laugh together, but after what Barry had said, she just didn't feel like company.

'So what was up with you anyway? Were you really sick or were you just throwing one of those diva strops, now that you've become a TV star?'

Lorraine glanced around to make sure the boss wasn't watching. She was a hopeless liar and had felt bad saying she'd been sick yesterday but she was finding it difficult to concentrate on anything. 'Yes, I *was* sick, for your information. And, to be honest, I really shouldn't be back today.'

Rory shoved aside some paperwork and perched his bum on the edge of her desk. 'You do look a bit peaky all right. What was it? Tummy bug?'

'Yep. Coming out of me from every orifice!'

'Oh, well, em, maybe it's best I leave you to it for now. Let me know if you're feeling better by lunchtime and we can grab a bite somewhere.' He scuttled off to his own desk at the other end of the office and Lorraine had to stifle a giggle.

Thankfully it was quiet enough in the office and she didn't feel under too much pressure. There were twelve people working at Buckley Lawlor Insurance, most of whom worked in the large, open-plan main office. It was a good-sized room and everyone had their own desk and workspace with partitions dividing them, so at least there was some semblance of privacy. Lorraine liked working there because the staff were nice and they had a good boss but, today, nothing could make her happy.

Last night, Barry had eventually come home after midnight, smelling of booze, and fish and chips. He'd hopped into bed and curled himself into her back, his cold hands looking for the warmth of her body. She'd had to fight back the tears. Normally she'd love when they'd spoon in bed. She'd love it when Barry would try to warm his cold hands on her breasts and pin her down by extending his long leg over her body. It would usually end with her turning to face him for a long, smooching session and inevitably they'd make love.

But not last night. She'd cried for a whole hour after she'd binned the dinners and gone to bed. How dare Barry treat her that way. Fair enough that he'd been in work for most of the day after they'd argued and probably couldn't have rung her, but to go off to the pub afterwards and not even bother letting her know until almost eleven o'clock! That had been completely unforgivable. Now she was just feeling angry again and she honestly didn't know what to do for the best.

Then there was the possible pregnancy. The test was in her

handbag, unopened. She hadn't been able to face doing it on her own. It had seemed like such a good idea last night, when she'd pictured Barry's ecstatic face if the test was positive. At that moment, she'd wanted it to be positive. But now she just didn't know. All her fears about having a baby were rising to the surface again at the prospect of possibly facing it on her own. She couldn't believe she was in this situation. It was all such a mess.

Lorraine looked down at the paperwork on her desk and decided she'd better make a start. At least the phone was quiet. She couldn't face talking to anyone at the moment. She was starving again so maybe she'd take herself out for a bit of fresh air at lunchtime and pop in somewhere for a pub lunch. Yes, that's what she'd do. It would save her having to cook later on – Barry could just fend for himself.

And maybe she'd even take Rory up on his offer. If Barry was thinking she was having an affair with somebody, maybe she should really give him something to think about! Rory was gorgeous and single and always flirting with her. Maybe she should flirt a bit back for once. Rory would probably die if she did though. They were good friends and the flirting was all in good fun but the way she was feeling at the moment, she just wanted to hurt Barry.

She pushed her chair back from her desk and stood up, smoothing down her knee-length black pencil skirt. She strode over to Rory's desk and leaned across to him. The top of her chiffon blouse fell down, exposing her cleavage and a portion of her white lace bra. Rory's face reddened and he looked shocked.

'So, Rory,' she said, trying to add an edge of suggestion to her voice. 'Are we having that lunch or what?'

'Well, I … yes, of course, if you're feeling up to it.'

'I'm perfectly fine now and dying to tuck into something delicious.' Even to her own ears, her seduction voice needed some work. Oh, God, this was so not her.

'Great,' said Rory, trying to avert his eyes from the exposed flesh. 'Will we head to Shandon's at one then?'

'Perfect. Looking forward to it.' Lorraine stuck her finger in her mouth and pulled it back out again as a last-ditch attempt to be seductive before turning on her heel and heading back to her desk. Jesus Christ almighty! What was that? She could feel Rory's quizzical eyes boring into her back. When Sharon Stone sticks her finger in her mouth in movies, she manages to look hot and sexy – Lorraine had just made herself look dribbly and silly.

Tears stung her eyes again as she sat back down at her desk. Her head was all over the place. Part of her wanted to do something to hurt Barry the way he was hurting her, but the other part of her wanted to rush home to him and hug him until they sorted everything out. She took a tissue from her bag under the desk and wiped her eyes. She could do with a distraction though, and Rory was always good for a laugh. Roll on one o'clock!

'I'll just have a Diet Coke, please,' said Lorraine, sliding into one of the long wooden benches in the pub. 'I honestly don't think my stomach could take any alcohol at the moment.' It was a quarter to six and they'd just come across to the pub for a drink. Lorraine had cried off lunch earlier because she'd thrown up again and had been feeling miserable but, having perked up in the afternoon, had suggested a drink or two.

Rory winked at her cheekily. 'So there's no chance of

getting you sozzled then and having my wicked way with you?'

'Well, sozzled – no. But wicked way? We'll just have to wait and see!' *Oh Jesus, shut up and stop embarrassing yourself, Lorraine.* She watched Rory's back disappear to the bar to get their drinks. He was so handsome and she wondered, not for the first time, how he was still single. At thirty-five, Rory was a great catch. Although he was only around five foot ten, he had a wonderful muscular build and a face to die for. His smooth chestnut hair hung to his shoulders and his unusual green eyes lit up his pale face.

Despite his attractiveness, Lorraine had never seen him as anything but a friend. They got on brilliantly and he really made her laugh. He flirted with her tirelessly but that was just the way he was. He did the same with all the girls. They probably got on best out of everyone in the office because the others were either under twenty-five or over fifty-five. But Rory knew the score with her and Barry. He knew she was off limits but it didn't stop him having a bit of fun with her.

Well, tonight, she was going to have some fun herself. Bloody Barry could sit at home and stew for a change. She was sick of being the one crying her eyes out at home while Barry was off with his mates in the pub.

'Here we go,' said Rory, placing her Diet Coke and his own pint of Guinness down on the table and sliding in beside her. 'So tell me what's up with you.'

Lorraine had no intention of talking about her problems. She was sick to death of them! 'There's nothing up with me, Rory. I just felt like a change. You get sick of the same old same old, don't you?'

'Tell me about it. At least you have someone to go home

to. I'm still heading home to an empty house and eating microwave meals for one every night.'

'Yes, what's that all about, Rory? How come you haven't found Ms Right yet? Surely you could have your pick of the ladies.'

'I'm too fussy, Lorraine. I can do the one-night-stand thing, but when it comes to relationships, I have very high standards.'

'So are you saying that there's nobody out there who meets those standards?'

Rory looked down at his drink and began to tear pieces off the beer mat. 'Oh, there's somebody all right. But unfortunately, she's taken.'

'Ah Rory, that's awful. And when you say she's taken, is there any chance for you at all?'

He wouldn't meet her eye. 'Just leave it Lorraine.'

'But sometimes you just have to—'

'I said, *leave it!*'

Lorraine was taken aback by his tone. But, Jesus, was he saying what she thought he was saying? If he was, would she have the nerve to do something about it? Did she want to? 'Rory, look at me.'

He lifted his head and stared right into her eyes. That's when she knew. Rory was in love with her. How had she never seen that before? All the time they spent together, all the flirting – she'd honestly thought it had just been harmless fun but all this time, he'd been harbouring much deeper feelings for her.

'Don't worry, Lorraine,' he said, nervously. 'I'm not going to do anything about it. I've lived with these feelings for a while now and I know nothing has changed. Barry is a good guy and I wouldn't want to come between the two of you.'

'Jesus, Rory. Why did you never say? I always thought … I just thought that … oh, God.' She was having trouble taking it all in. She'd planned on having a bit of fun tonight, maybe a bit of innocent flirting because she was so angry with Barry – she hadn't banked on this.

'How *could* I say, Lorraine?' His beautiful face looked strained and her heart melted. 'I hadn't planned on ever letting you know how I feel but now that you know, I actually feel relieved.'

'Well,' said Lorraine, desperately trying to decide how to handle the situation, 'I'm glad I know now. Let's just see what happens.' Oh, fuckity fuck! Why had she said that? It had come out wrong. But, in truth, she was aching to be held. The fact that Rory wanted her made her want him too. She wanted somebody to hold her close. She wanted to be told everything was going to be all right. She was desperately in need of a bit of love.

'Lorraine, what about Barry? I mean, you can't … we can't—'

'You let me worry about Barry, Rory. There's a lot you don't know about and, to be honest, right now, I don't feel like talking.' She stood up, every movement buying her time to think. She honestly didn't know what she was doing.

Rory was on his feet straight away, his face alight with anticipation. They walked out of the pub in silence, each lost in thought. He took her hand gently as they walked towards the taxi rank. The touch of his hand sent a shiver of longing through her and she felt both nervous and excited.

Oh, God, was she honestly contemplating being unfaithful to her husband? Was she really going to be that person? It would serve Barry right. He needed to be punished for how he'd been treating her. But as they got closer to the waiting taxis, her resolve began to falter. What was she thinking? There'd be no coming back from something like this. If she slept with Rory, it would be the end of her and Barry. What sort of a slut was she? What on earth had she been thinking?

She cast a sideways glance at Rory's gorgeous face and began to panic. He was a good friend and she didn't want to let him down. How was she going to tell him that she'd changed her mind – that she'd only been doing it to hurt Barry? Oh, God, how did she get herself into these situations?

Just as they got to the taxi rank, Rory pulled her into him and stared at her for a moment. She braced herself for his kiss. She wanted him to kiss her. She didn't want him to kiss her. She didn't know what she wanted. But what she did know was that she loved her husband. Yes, she wanted to feel loved and protected, but Barry was the one she wanted.

Rory wrapped his two arms around her and hugged her tightly, his head resting on her shoulder. 'Go home to your husband, Lorraine,' he whispered. 'You and I are friends and I don't want that to ever change. Whatever is going on between you and Barry, you were meant for each other. Go and sort it out.'

Lorraine was stunned for a moment. 'But you said ... I thought—'

'I love you, Lorraine. I've probably always loved you. But you love Barry and I'll never come between the two of you. If tonight had happened, it would have been the end of our friendship and probably the end of your marriage. I'll find my princess some day, don't you worry.'

Tears streamed down Lorraine's face as she realised what she'd almost done and she'd be forever grateful to Rory for helping her to see things more clearly. 'You're one hell of a friend, Rory. I hope we'll stay friends after this.'

'You bet,' he said, his own eyes moist. 'I can't wait to get back to a bit of innocent flirting tomorrow. You'd better watch yourself.'

'Ha! Bring it on,' Lorraine laughed. 'And thanks, Rory.'

'Right, enough of the soppiness. Off you go home to your husband and don't make me regret this. Whatever's going on between the two of you, get it sorted. Life is too short.' He gave her a friendly pat on the bum as she got into the taxi.

As the taxi drove off, she slumped back into the seat, her head brimming with a myriad of emotions. Glancing back, she saw that Rory was still standing, hands in pockets, staring after them. He was a lovely guy but, thanks be to God, she'd come to her senses!

'I'm home, love,' Lorraine shouted, as she stepped in the front door. It was nine o'clock and she knew Barry had finished work at seven so was probably home. She'd texted him to say she was having a few drinks with the girls but he hadn't replied.

She threw her coat and bag on the banister and stuck her head in the door of the little sitting room. 'There you are – did you not hear me coming in?'

Barry's gaze didn't leave the telly. 'Yep, I heard you all right.'

'So what are you watching? Have you eaten yet?'

'The News and yes.'

Oh, God, he was in a right mood, but she wasn't going to let that faze her. 'Well I'm just going to make a cuppa. Do you fancy one?'

'Actually, I think I'll just grab a cold drink and head up to bed,' he said, hauling himself up into a sitting position. 'I could do with an early night.'

'Well, just hang on there for a minute and I'll bring you in one,' said Lorraine, beginning to panic. She was determined to have that chat with him. 'Do you want Coke? I'll be just a minute and maybe we can have a chat and both have an early night.'

'Look, Lorraine,' Barry said, standing up and stretching. 'Maybe if you'd been home earlier we could have talked but I've had a long day and I'm only fit for bed.' He pushed past her and headed into the kitchen.

'But, Barry,' she said, following him and willing herself not to cry. 'You know we need to talk. Why do you keep avoiding it?'

Barry poured himself a glass of water from the tap and took a big gulp. 'Talking is overrated, Lorraine. Sometimes things are better left unsaid.'

'Well go on, feck off to bed then,' said Lorraine, the emotion of the past few days suddenly gripping her. 'You're a typical bloody man – bury your head in the sand and think things are going to work out if you ignore them. Well I'm fed up trying to sort things out!'

Barry looked at her coldly. 'Right, if you'll excuse me, I'll just feck off to bed then. Night.'

'Barry, I didn't mean … I just want …' But he was gone. She gripped onto the kitchen counter as her body trembled with a mixture of anger and sadness. Ghosts of the past floated through her mind as she sat down heavily on a chair and wondered if life had its own ideas for her.

CHAPTER 25

Friday, 16th September

'Marco, hold on a minute,' called Maggie, sticking her head halfway out the sitting-room window. 'I just want a word.'

'Hiya, Mags. It'll have to be a quick one because I'm due in work at ten.'

Maggie stuck the front door on the latch and hurried outside. 'But I thought you had the week off. How come you're going in today?'

'Stella just rang this morning and asked me to fill in for a few hours. Apparently she's broken a tooth and needs to get to the dentist as soon as possible.'

'You're too good, Marco – interrupting your holidays like that. And what about Claude? Aren't you spending the day with him today?' Marco had confided in her about his intimate night with Claude and she couldn't have been happier for him.

'Hopefully I'll see him later. He's been getting grief from his mother about not spending enough time at home so he's trying to keep everyone happy. He took her and his dad for a meal last night and was planning to relax at home this morning.' Marco leaned against the railing, giving it a wipe with a tissue first so as not to get a spec of dust on his cream linen jacket.

'Ah, good for him, Marco. My mother used to say that a boy that's good to his mammy is a keeper. So things are going well with you two then?'

'Oh, Maggie, it's wonderful. Honestly, Claude is the best thing that's ever happened to me. He's everything I want in a man. God, that sounds corny, doesn't it? But you know what I mean. He's just perfect.'

'Well I'm delighted for you,' said Maggie, noting how Marco's face lit up when he spoke about his new love. 'You really deserve a bit of happiness.'

'Thanks, Mags. Let's just hope the happiness isn't short lived. He's chasing up a few leads and if any of them work out, he could be quitting his New York job and staying on here in Ireland.'

'No way! Are you serious? That's amazing, Marco. He must really be into you then.'

Marco blushed. 'We're really into each other, Maggie. Keep your fingers crossed it all works out. I'll be gutted if he goes back to New York. I think I'd have to consider following him.'

'Now, don't you go making any rash decisions,' said Maggie, alarmed that Marco would be already thinking like that. 'When will he know if he's staying?'

'Well he's hoping to hear back about a couple of jobs today but there are other factors too. He's coming over later and we're going to have a good long chat about it.'

'Well I really hope it all works out for you both.' Maggie

loved a bit of romance and if she was honest, she was a little bit intrigued by Marco and Claude's blossoming affair. Marco was the only gay person she knew and she'd never really seen him with anyone before. Of course she'd seen gay kisses and stuff on the telly, but never in real life. Maybe they'd even get married. Well that would certainly be one to look forward to.

'So what is it then, Mags?'

Maggie had been lost in her own thoughts. 'What's what, Marco?'

'What is it you wanted to have a word about?'

'Oh, yes, sorry, I've a head like a sieve. I was wondering if you'd spoken to the National Lottery people again. We can't be just sitting around, you know. We don't want them to think we're taking all this in our stride.'

'It's my priority today, Mags. I can't believe it's been almost a week since the win and still no ticket. I'll have another chat with them today and see where we go from here.'

'Well, that's good,' said Maggie, delighted that at least they were moving things forward. 'We need to organise another meeting at the weekend like we did last week. Let us know what the lottery people say.'

'Will do,' said Marco, straightening himself up and brushing at the sleeve of his jacket. 'But I'd better fly. Don't want to be late.'

'Right so, Marco. Call in later on and we'll organise a time for that meeting.' Maggie headed back inside. Marco was right – it really was hard to believe that almost a week had passed and that bloody ticket hadn't turned up yet. Sometimes she wished they'd never won it at all. Life was a daily struggle for most of them on Enda's, but they were happy. Whatever happened with the ticket, it was hard to imagine life going back to what it had been before those numbers were called out.

It was only half nine and she felt knackered already. That bloody heartburn was back and her tummy felt like it was in knots. She tried to push away the niggling feeling that she should be talking to Dan sooner rather than later. She just couldn't face telling him anything yet.

She walked into the kitchen and sighed at the mess. She could really do with giving the whole house a good clean but she didn't feel up to it. She hated how she'd been letting things go. She prided herself in having floors that you could eat your dinner off, but glancing at the tea stains on the tiles, she doubted very much if that would be a good idea at the moment! She filled the kettle and popped a teabag into a cup. Maybe she'd just have a cuppa and catch up on a bit of Corrie before getting stuck in. The cleaning could wait – she had all the time in the world. *Let's hope I really do have all the time in the world,* she thought, crossing her fingers tightly!

Marco was feeling happier than he ever could have imagined. Not even the missing ticket or having to interrupt his holiday to spend a few hours in work could dampen his spirits.

And the shop was quiet, so he had some time to think about recent events. Fridays could be hectic sometimes, with people rushing to find the perfect outfit for a night on the town, but there'd only been a handful of customers browsing so far. Stella had left things in pretty good shape, so all Marco had to do was stand around and look pretty.

A glance at the glass clock on the wall told him it was half eleven so, with a bit of luck, he'd be out of there within the hour. He hoped Claude was on for meeting up in the afternoon. He hadn't seen him since yesterday morning and he was already missing him. Maybe he'd have a peep on Twitter and see if he was around. Poor Claude. His mam had been giving him a really hard time because she wasn't seeing enough of him.

Marco waited until the two women who were browsing left the shop and quickly tapped into Twitter on his phone.

@Marcofashion1: Are you here @ClaudeRIP? Bored out of my mind here and dying for a chat.

No answer. He was probably tucking into a big Irish breakfast, cooked by his mammy. That was something Marco missed about not having his parents around – his mammy's cooking. His mother wasn't exactly a Gordon Ramsay, but she knew how to do big and hearty with lots of flavours and different tastes. He was hopeless in the kitchen himself and, besides, there was hardly any point in cooking for one.

His parents were another reason that he badly wanted his share of the winning ticket. With them living over in Spain, he didn't get to see nearly enough of them. With a bit of money in his pocket, he could take more holidays over there and even pay for them to come back to Ireland now and again. He was dying to have another chat with the National Lottery about the ticket. Concepta, the girl he'd spoken to in the claims department, had said that they'd look into it again at the end of the week. He was pretty sure they still wouldn't pay out without the actual ticket, but it would be interesting to hear what she had to say.

He checked his phone again to see if Claude had come online and felt a little flutter when he saw the tweet.

@ClaudeRIP: Morning, lovely. Turn to DM.

@Marcofashion1: Right, I'm here. What are you up to?

@ClaudeRIP: Have just had a gorgeous full Irish breakfast – I'm in danger of bursting. But it made my mother happy to do it.

@Marcofashion1: I knew it! I was just imagining you lording it, with your mammy flapping around you. Am I going to see you today?

@ClaudeRIP: You bet. I can't wait. I was lying in bed thinking of you last night.

@Marcofashion1: All good thoughts, I hope?

@ClaudeRIP: The best! I was thinking of the other night. It was wonderful, Marco, just wonderful.

@Marcofashion1: It was, wasn't it? Just think, if you stay here, we could have that on a regular basis.

@ClaudeRIP: I'm working on it! My mam is just heading into town so how about I take a lift with her and meet you?

@Marcofashion1: Oh, that would be lovely. Maybe we'll have a bit of lunch in town and head home to mine after.

@ClaudeRIP: Sounds good to me. We'll be leaving here shortly so I should be in there in twenty minutes or so.

@Marcofashion1: Well, I won't be finished for about another hour, so why don't you head to Brown Thomas and we'll have lunch there.

@ClaudeRIP: Perfect. I'll have a wander around and you just text me when you're on your way.

@Marcofashion1: Brilliant. See you in a while.

Ooh, lunch with scrumptious Claude – this day was getting better and better. He was glad now that he'd worn his gorgeous new cream linen jacket. It wasn't that he felt he had to dress up for Claude, but he did like to look his best and when he *looked* sexy, he *felt* sexy.

It was good to get away from the street too at the moment. It was a bit depressing with all the talk of the missing ticket. He wanted to find it as much as anyone else, but sometimes he just wanted to forget they'd won at all. It had caused so much hassle that he wondered if Claude had been right about money bringing so many problems with it.

For the first time in years, nobody had even gone to the bingo last night. Maggie had said she wasn't feeling well, Rita didn't have a babysitter, Lorraine had wanted to stay in and talk to Barry, and Majella tended to blow hot and cold with the whole thing anyway. When he'd found out he wasn't going to see Claude, Marco had thought about going himself, but in the end he just didn't feel in the humour. He knew that people on the bus would have heard about the missing ticket and, for once, he hadn't felt like being the centre of attention.

With the shop still quiet, Marco headed into the small kitchenette in the back and filled the kettle. He'd bring a cup of tea and a biscuit out to the shop and have a read of the magazine he'd picked up earlier. There was still no word from Stella but, all going well, she'd be back shortly. He usually loved the banter with the customers but today he was quite content with his own company.

But it had been wishful thinking. The bell of the door tinkled just as he was settling down with his cup of tea and a customer breezed in.

'Felicity! Lovely to see you. I'd forgotten it was Friday.'

'Hi Marco. I forgot myself up until half an hour ago. I've been busy with family stuff all week and the time has just flown by.' Felicity rarely spoke about her family and Marco noted how her eyes lit up at the mention. He didn't even know if she had children. He'd often tried to get her talking about her home life, but she'd usually just change the subject.

'So what can I do for you today then?' Marco asked, taking a quick sip of his tea and coming around to the other side of the counter. 'We really don't have a lot of new stuff in since last week.'

Felicity sighed. 'You must think I'm a bit mad, coming in here every week and buying something new. It just gets a bit lonely at home and I enjoy my trip to town on Fridays.'

'Of course I don't think you're mad, Felicity. We need more customers like you. And, to be honest, it brightens up my Fridays to see you come in.'

'Ah, go on out of that, Marco. An old girl like me?'

'Honestly, only for regulars like you, I wouldn't love my job nearly as much.' It was only half true but Marco knew how to keep the customers happy. A customer leaving the shop with a smile on their face was more likely to come back again. He was tempted to pry a little more into her personal life, but, at the same time, Felicity scared him a little bit. Maybe he'd just test the waters. 'You said you get lonely – don't you have anyone to keep you company at home?'

'Not really. There's just me and my husband and he works long hours. But I'm not complaining – it's a good life. And I've had a bit of good family news this week so things are definitely looking up.'

'Oh, good news?' said Marco, dying to know more. Felicity was certainly looking chirpier than normal. The harsh lines on her face seemed to have softened since last week and she appeared a lot more relaxed. 'There's nothing like a bit of good news to lift the spirits.'

'That's very true,' she said. 'But on another note, I thought you weren't meant to be working this week.'

Typical Felicity, changing the subject when it was looking like she might share a little nugget of her personal life. He clearly wasn't going to get any more out of her. 'I was … I am. I just popped in to cover for a few hours. Actually, I'm due to finish shortly when Stella comes back.'

'Well, I'd better choose something quickly then. Stella is lovely and all that but I'd prefer to deal with you.'

Ten minutes later, Marco was wrapping up a gorgeous, cream silk knitted jumper and handing it over to his satisfied customer.

'Thanks, Marco. That's going to be gorgeous over those red linen trousers I bought last month. I might even wear it on Sunday. We're having a bit of a family thing.'

Marco didn't even bother asking what it was. Felicity clearly wasn't one for sharing her personal life and, although he was curious, he respected that. 'Well, enjoy it and I'll probably see you again next week.'

'I'm sure you will. Toodles.' Throwing her pale olive shawl loosely over her left shoulder, she sashayed out the door, leaving the distinct scent of Poison perfume in her wake.

A flashing red light on his phone alerted him to a text message. Damn! And two missed calls from the National Lottery. He'd rang them earlier but there'd been nobody to take his call. He shouldn't have left his phone on silent. Still, the text message was from Stella to say she'd be there in ten minutes. Thank God for that. He was dying to see Claude. It had barely been more than twenty-four hours but he was already missing him like crazy.

He still had so many things going through his head and was dying to talk to Claude about them. The biggest thing was his business idea. Of course nothing could happen if the damn lotto ticket didn't turn up but, if it did, they could be about to go into partnership in more ways than one!

He brought his cup into the little kitchenette and rinsed it out in the sink. The more he thought about it, the more it made sense to start a business and get Claude involved. How exciting would that be? But it made the whole lotto thing even more urgent. He just had to get his hands on that ticket. He'd give the lottery people a call back now and they'd have to have a serious meeting at the weekend. If he had to search every square inch of Enda's himself to find the ticket, he would. Nothing was going to stand in the way of a secure future for him and the new love of his life!

CHAPTER 26

'So how have you been since … you know …?' asked Marco, making himself comfortable at Lorraine's kitchen table. 'I'm sorry I haven't been down to chat to you – it's just been hectic between one thing and another.'

'Don't worry, Marco. I don't expect you to keep running down to check on me all the time. You have your own life to live.' Even to her own ears, she sounded a bit sarcastic, but she was feeling a bit sorry for herself and was envious of Marco's chirpy mood.

'Come on then. Tell me what's up.'

'Oh, nothing more than usual,' said Lorraine, placing two steaming mugs of tea on the table and plonking herself down on a chair. 'And, anyway, what are you doing here on a Friday evening? I thought you'd be enjoying your last few days with Claude.'

'I will be later on,' said Marco, dunking a custard cream into his tea. 'We've been out together for most of the day but Claude had a few things to do at home so he'll be back over later.'

'Ah, that's good, Marco. I'm delighted for you, I really am. Maggie tells me that he might even be staying on here in Ireland.'

'Well, hopefully that might be the case. He's due to fly back to New York on Wednesday but he's making a few enquiries.'

Lorraine noticed how Marco's eyes lit up when he spoke about Claude. She'd never seen him so animated about anyone in her life. 'And what about his job? Would they let him quit just like that?'

'That's all part of what he's trying to find out. He thinks they won't really have a problem because they've been letting staff go anyway. But he doesn't want to leave with a cloud hanging over him. He'll need to get a good reference and the money he's owed.'

'And what are the chances of him getting another job here?'

'Well,' said Marco, 'we're looking into a few things.'

'That sounds very cryptic,' Lorraine said. She could read Marco like a book, and it was obvious he was bursting to tell her something. 'Go on then, tell me more.'

Marco didn't need to be asked twice. He pushed his tea aside and leaned on the table with his arms folded. 'Well, Claude has been asking around to see if there's any work going. He's been checking with pals to see if anyone could offer him even a bit of freelance work. But he's not set on staying in the filming industry. His mind is open to anything really.'

'Gosh, Marco, you must have really made an impression on him if he's willing to consider working at anything just so that he can stay here.'

Marco blushed. 'We have been getting on really well, Lorraine. I think he's a bit fed up with the job and with his life in New York, but hopefully I'm a big factor in his plans.'

'Of course you are,' said Lorraine. 'It's obvious he thinks a lot of you. So what else is he considering doing?'

'I've had a bit of an idea, Lorraine. But I haven't said anything to him about it yet.'

'Go on then. Don't keep me in suspense.'

Marco continued. 'You know how I love my fashion and I've been trying to break into the design side of things? If … *when* we get our two hundred thousand euro, I was thinking I could use it to set up my own business. What do you think?'

'I think that's a fantastic idea, Marco. Do you mean a shop or a studio, or what?'

'I'm not completely sure yet, but I think I'd love a shop – something like the one I work in. And I could look into having some of my own designs made up and sell them in the shop.'

'Oh, wow! That would be amazing,' said Lorraine, getting up to hug Marco. 'I'd be so proud of you. Imagine, we could be seeing people around town wearing Marco originals. But where exactly does Claude fit in to all this?'

'Well, it takes more than one person to run a business. I was thinking that he could either help front the shop or get involved in the business side of things – whatever way he wanted to get involved.'

'Sounds good, Marco. But you'll need to talk to him and see how he feels about it. It seems like a drastic change of career – from film producer to clothes shop worker.'

'I know,' giggled Marco. 'He might hate the idea but, either way, it's something I'd love to do for myself. But nothing will happen if that bloody ticket doesn't turn up!'

Lorraine cringed inwardly. She wanted to scream and

shout about it as much as everyone else but what if it was Barry who'd taken the ticket?

'Earth calling Lorraine! Are you okay?' Marco was looking at her quizzically.

'Sorry, Marco. I was just thinking about the ticket. Do you still think somebody has taken it?'

'I honestly don't know, Lorraine. It's such a bloody mess. I had another chat with the claims department of the National Lottery today. They were very helpful, but they still can't give us the money without a ticket.'

Lorraine sighed. 'And did they say anything else? Or is it just a case of no ticket, no money?'

'I'm going to organise a syndicate meeting for tomorrow to fill you all in with the details, but, basically, we have to get a solicitor to write a letter for us, outlining our claim. Since it's almost the weekend, we won't be able to do anything until Monday, but we can discuss it tomorrow.'

'God, what a hullaballoo! Maybe if somebody's taken the ticket, they'll think twice when they hear we'll be getting solicitors involved. With a bit of luck, the ticket might even magically turn up before Monday!' That was it! They could say that whoever had the ticket needn't even own up – they could just leave it somewhere for the others to find. Surely that would get Barry out of a hole if it was really him who'd taken it.

'That's what I was thinking, Lorraine. Let's call a meeting for tomorrow and make the whole thing sound really serious. We'll say that a solicitor will be looking into everything and he'll be helping us to get to the bottom of things. That should be enough to frighten anyone who might be thinking of pocketing the full win.'

'Good idea, Marco.' Lorraine sighed and flopped back

into her chair, rubbing her temples. 'If only I could get you to organise the rest of my life, it might not be such a mess.'

'Oh, God, Lorraine. I'm sorry. Here's me going on about myself and what I really came down here for was to see how you were doing. So what's happening with you and Barry then? Have you two sorted things out?'

Tears pricked Lorraine's eyes at the mention of her husband and what she'd almost done the previous night. He'd been up and out early for another long shift in work so she hadn't even spoken to him yet today. It seemed like they weren't destined to sit down and chat any time soon. It was ironic that the very reason they weren't seeing much of each other was the fact that Barry had taken on so many extra shifts with a view to saving for a baby! God, what a mess.

'Lorraine, are you okay? Did you hear what I said?'

Startled out of her thoughts, she looked at Marco. 'No, we haven't sorted anything out. It's ... it's just so hard, Marco. I ... I ...' She really hadn't wanted to cry in front of Marco but she just couldn't help it.

Marco was quick to jump up and put his arm around her. 'Lori, you'll sort it out, I know you will. I hate seeing you like this.'

'I'm sorry,' she sniffed, blowing her nose. 'I'm just tired and emotional but, yes, I'm sure it will work out. We'll just have to stop dancing around each other and face up to what's going on.'

Marco took his empty cup over to the sink. 'Well, you know I'm here if you need me, you can talk to me about anything. You know that, don't you?'

'Of course I do,' said Lorraine, walking to the door with him. 'You're a great listener and I'm very lucky to have you.'

Marco kissed her lightly on the cheek and embraced her in a bear hug. 'That's what families are for, Lorraine. I'll agree a time for the meeting tomorrow with Maggie and the others and let you know. And good luck with Barry – just make him sit down and listen to you tonight.'

'I will, Marco, and enjoy your night with Claude.' Lorraine waved as Marco walked the few steps down to his house, envious of the lovely night he was facing with his new lover.

She remembered when she used to look forward to nights like that. And it hadn't been too long ago either. Sighing, she loaded the cups into the dishwasher. She'd had a busy day in work and hadn't even had the chance to change before Marco had come down. Barry was working the late shift so wouldn't be home until after eleven, so, once again, she probably wouldn't have a chance to talk to him.

Grabbing an apple from the fruit bowl, she headed into the sitting room to put her feet up before having a shower. She hadn't had dinner yet but she wasn't in the mood. Barry always got dinner out when he was on the late shift and she couldn't really be bothered making it just for herself, but things would have to change if they were going to have a baby. The thought of it sent a thrill through her.

She knew that people always said that it was wrong to think that a baby could bring a couple together; that nobody should use a baby as a tool to fix their relationship. She sort of agreed with that, but she also felt that knowing they were having a baby would finally make both her and Barry face up to what was wrong in their relationship and just talk. She had faith in them.

Lorraine sighed loudly. How had her life become so complicated? Although she felt exhausted and was tempted not to bother having a shower, she knew she'd feel much better after it. She pulled herself up from the sofa to head upstairs.

As she was passing the window, she noticed somebody coming out of Rita's house across the road. She couldn't resist having a closer look. Maybe it was the hubby. According to Maggie, Rita's husband was a bad egg. He didn't pay her any maintenance and didn't even bother coming to see his own children. Lorraine was keen to see what a man like that looked like.

She pressed her nose to the window, ready to pull back if she was noticed. From the back, the guy looked pretty hot and not the sort of guy she would have put with Rita. His hair was longish and had that designer messy look. He was quite tall and wearing ripped jeans and a leather jacket. Lorraine couldn't see his face yet but she'd have guessed him to only be in his twenties. Maggie hadn't mentioned the fact that Rita's husband was a lot younger than her.

Or maybe it wasn't the husband at all. Maybe Rita had found herself a new man. Good on her if she had. She'd had a tough few years being on her own and deserved a bit of fun in her life. It couldn't be easy bringing up two kids on your own. She'd have a chat with Maggie later and see if she knew anything, or maybe she'd even call over to Rita herself. She could always pretend she wanted to borrow some milk or something.

The man bent over and kissed her on the cheek, and turned to leave. Lorraine pulled back from the window slightly, in case she was spotted being nosy. As he walked down the path, a bag slung over his shoulders, Lorraine froze. What the hell? Now *that* was a bit of a surprise. She tried to imagine why he'd be visiting Rita but couldn't think of a single reason. And, more importantly, should she say anything about it or not? She needed to think. What reason in the world, other than the age-old reason, would Claude have for paying home visits to a woman?

Barry stared at the peeling paint on the wall of the little kitchen at the back of his shop. He automatically heaped two teaspoons of sugar into the Styrofoam cup and stirred his coffee. They did have proper mugs, but they were either stained brown on the inside or had the marks of lipstick on the edge. It was enough to turn his stomach. He usually went to a local coffee shop for his breaks but today he just couldn't be bothered.

He couldn't be bothered about anything any more. It was as though his whole world was falling apart. Lorraine had been the only thing in his life that made sense and now it seemed they were drifting further and further apart. But who was to blame for that? Was it possible it could be him?

Today was the first day that he'd taken time to sit back and look at the situation. So he'd overheard a conversation between his wife and Maggie. So it looked like she was in a relationship with another man. But why hadn't she said anything? He'd given her plenty of opportunity to say something. And why was it that she was acting as though she still loved him?

He'd really lost it last night when she'd come home late. He'd been feeling a bit guilty about how he'd been treating her and had planned to talk to her. But as the time had ticked away and there had been no sign of her, he'd just become more and more agitated, imagining all sorts of things. As he'd sat on the sofa watching telly, he'd imagined her with her lover. Pictures of her being intimate with another man kept creeping into his mind and by the time she had come home, he could barely look at her. He'd seen the hurt in her eyes when he rebuffed her when she tried to talk to him. He'd been way too angry at that stage.

But now, in the cold light of day, he was wondering if he'd been letting his anger cloud his judgement, making him do things he probably should have thought twice about! What's that they say about a woman scorned? Well it seems that a man scorned can breathe just as much fury!

He sipped his coffee and thought about the fact that only a few weeks ago, they'd been happy – or so he'd thought. No, they definitely had been happy. There'd been no signs of anything amiss, except for the usual money worries and stuff. Maybe he'd got the wrong end of the stick about Lorraine's secret and had jumped to conclusions. Still, there was definitely something going on and he needed to find out what it was.

At least today was Friday and Lorraine would be home for the next two days. He'd just make sure they found some time together to talk and get things out into the open. Even if it was bad news, nothing could be worse than the way they were at the moment. They couldn't go on like this; that was for sure. Yes, he'd try to swallow his anger and talk to his wife as calmly as possible. He realised it could be the making or the breaking of them. He certainly hoped it would be the former because he also now realised without a shadow of a doubt that he loved Lorraine more than life itself and he couldn't imagine his life without her.

CHAPTER 27

Saturday, 17th September

'So I'm guessing you think he's a keeper too,' said Marco to his little dog as she strained her head out the window to see Claude disappearing around the corner. 'Well, it's good to have your approval!'

Marco pulled Mimi down off the windowsill and flopped down on the sofa. He laid the little dog on his stomach and proceeded to scratch her behind the ears, much to her delight. It had been another wonderful night and Marco was feeling more and more hopeful that things were going to work out.

Claude had come over again last night and they hadn't bothered going out, opting instead to rent a couple of DVDs and order a Chinese. It had felt good to imagine they were going steady. It had been wonderful to just watch the movie with Claude by his side, knowing that they'd go to bed together afterwards. And it wasn't just about sex. Marco loved having Claude in his bed, holding him close and feeling loved.

Claude had been excited when he'd arrived yesterday

evening. He'd told Marco that he'd had a good day of networking and was pretty sure that he wouldn't remain jobless for long if he stayed in Ireland. He'd said that he wasn't after a high-flying career – all he wanted was to have a bit of money coming in to keep him going. He wouldn't need much because he was planning to live at home but he'd draw the line at taking pocket money from his parents at his age.

They'd enjoyed a leisurely breakfast together and Marco had marvelled at how quickly he'd taken to the whole relationship thing. Claude had seemed comfortable with it too. Please God it would work out that they'd get the opportunity to continue things after next week.

Mimi's snores were making Marco sleepy. He wanted to organise a meeting of the lotto syndicate today, but maybe he'd grab twenty minutes shut-eye beforehand. He closed his eyes, picturing Claude lying beside him on the sofa.

When they'd finished their Chinese, they'd sat at the kitchen table chatting for hours. With Claude so enthusiastic about staying in Ireland, Marco had thought the time was right to make the suggestion about his new business. He'd approached it tentatively, knowing how Claude felt about money. He hadn't wanted him to think he was trying to use money to influence him in any way.

But he'd been pleasantly surprised. Claude had said that Marco's talents were wasted just working in a shop. He'd said that he'd fully support him in starting his new business. The only thing was that he hadn't been overly keen on coming into the business with him. As Marco had suspected, he'd balked at the idea of being included in a business that he hadn't put any money into, but he'd also said that he'd be happy to work for him.

But it was a week since they'd won the lotto and the longer

it went on, the less likely it was that the ticket would turn up. With every passing day, it was more likely that it would end up in somebody's bin with other rubbish. And who knew what would happen if somebody had taken it. Would they ever own up?

Marco couldn't settle with all that going through his mind, so he decided to go and organise the meeting. A glance at his watch told him it was almost one, so maybe he'd try to get everyone together at around three. Pulling himself up off the sofa, he lifted his sleeping dog off his chest and carried her carefully into her basket in the kitchen. He'd call to Maggie first and see what time suited her. It was always hard to suit everybody so the others could just fall in with whatever time they picked.

Locking the door behind him, he hopped across the railings and knocked on his neighbour's door. There was no answer, which was unusual for a Saturday afternoon. Maggie usually did her cleaning on a Saturday. She was a woman of habit and he'd always see her out washing her doorstep and the downstairs front window at the same time every week. He rang the bell this time. Maybe if they were at the back of the house, they hadn't heard the knock.

The door was swung open suddenly and Dan was there, his finger on his lip in a shushing gesture. 'Maggie's just having a bit of a sleep, Marco,' he whispered. 'Do you want to come in?'

'Ah, no, Dan, it's fine. I hope I didn't wake her. Is she okay?'

'Well, to be honest, I'm not sure. She hasn't been herself lately. She says she's fine and I'm not to worry but something doesn't seem right. She's been falling asleep a lot during the day and she's not eating nearly as much as she should be.'

'Oh, that doesn't sound like Mags at all,' said Marco, alarmed to hear his friend had been so poorly and he hadn't even noticed.

Dan's expression was pained and Marco could see he was clearly worried about his wife. 'When I mentioned to her last week that I'd noticed she wasn't eating, she said that she'd a bit of a tummy bug. I believed her at the time, but now I'm not so sure.'

'Right, come on then. Stick that kettle on and we'll have a bit of a chat. I'm not interrupting anything, am I?' Marco didn't wait for an answer. He stepped inside and headed straight into the kitchen.

'I'd be glad of the chat, to be honest,' said Dan. 'Steph is gone into town with her friends and I've been working in the back garden, worrying myself sick over Maggie.'

'Well, why don't you sit down and I'll make the tea,' said Marco, seeing how upset Dan was. Dan didn't take much persuasion and Marco busied himself filling the kettle and taking two mugs out of the cupboard. When he had the tea made, he sat down at the table and questioned his friend further. 'So what makes you think it's something other than a tummy bug, Dan? I mean, something like that can wipe you out for ages.'

'I know it can, Marco, and I can't say exactly what it is, but I just have a feeling that all isn't right. She says she thinks she's low in iron too so that would explain the exhaustion but, I don't know, I think she looks really unwell. Have you not noticed anything?'

Again, Marco felt ashamed that he hadn't noticed anything amiss with his friend. 'I can't say I have, Dan. Maybe I've been too involved with what's going on in my own life to notice what's going on with her.'

'Don't be silly,' said Dan, generously. 'It's only because I'm living with her and see her every day that I can see things aren't right.'

'Maybe it's just worry,' offered Marco. 'She's had a lot on her mind lately. I know she's been worried about Barry and Lorraine, and then there's the whole lotto thing.'

Dan sighed. 'That's true. She's been trying to keep the peace on the street about that ticket, but I know she's very angry about it herself. We both are.'

Marco nodded his head in agreement. 'It's no wonder she's not been well. Stress can really play havoc with your body.'

'And another thing,' added Dan. 'Maggie is always the one to try to solve everyone else's problems. She'll be the first one to help someone out if they're in trouble, but she's reluctant to pay attention to her own problems.'

'Well, I'll make sure I keep an eye on her,' said Marco, sipping his tea. 'And I'll have a word with her, too, and see if I can find out what's up with her.'

'What's up with who?' Maggie had just appeared at the kitchen door, almost causing both Dan and Marco to jump out of their skins.

'Oh, em, nothing, love,' said Dan, jumping up from his chair. 'Come on and sit down and I'll make you a cuppa. Marco just called for a chat and I told him you were sleeping.'

'Howareya, Marco,' she said, sitting down heavily on a chair. 'But who were you talking about just then?'

Marco was quick to answer. 'We were just saying that Lorraine has really had a rough couple of weeks with all the Barry stuff and everything.'

'Oh, I see,' said Maggie, eyeing them suspiciously. 'So, Marco, why aren't you out somewhere gallivanting with your new love?'

'I'm seeing him later, Maggie. I actually came over to see if we could organise a meeting of the syndicate this afternoon. I got a bit of information from the National Lottery yesterday and I think we need to make a few decisions.'

'Here you go, love,' said Dan, placing a steaming mug down in front of his wife. 'Can I get you anything to eat?'

'Thanks, Dan. I couldn't eat a thing. I had a big breakfast this morning.'

Dan shot Marco a look and Marco gathered that she hadn't had anything of the sort. He really must make a better effort to know what's going on in his friends' lives. 'So, anyway,' Marco continued, 'I was thinking if you'd all like to come to mine at, say, three o'clock. We can have a chat about it all then.'

'That sounds fine by me,' said Maggie, gratefully sipping her tea. 'We'll definitely be there. Will you let the others know or will I?'

'No, you stay where you are, Maggie. I'll drop into them all now and hopefully they'll be able to make it. Let's try and find this ticket once and for all.'

'And are we still thinking that maybe somebody has taken it?' asked Dan. 'Someone would want to have nerves of steel to have the ticket and still be able to sit with us all and deny it.'

Maggie nodded. 'It's hard to believe somebody would do it, but greed is an awful thing.'

'It certainly is, Maggie,' said Marco. 'But something happened the other day that got me thinking.'

'Go on,' said Maggie, leaning forward on her elbows. 'Tell us.'

'Well, I was in Majella's house on Wednesday after the filming for a cup of tea and we had a long chat about a lot of things.'

'And?' said Dan, impatiently.

'Well, not once during our chat did she mention the missing ticket. I mean, the rest of us are going mad over the whole thing, but she never said one word about it. It was only when I got home that I thought it was a bit strange.'

'Oooh, that *is* strange,' said Maggie, her eyes lighting up at the nugget. 'And she never referred to it at all?'

'No, not a mention. I know it's probably wrong of me to suspect her on the grounds of her not asking about it, but this whole bloody thing makes you suspicious of everything.'

'I know what you mean, Marco. I found myself suspecting Rita because of her circumstances, until Lorraine convinced me that it didn't sound like something she'd do. And apparently, Lorraine was even suspecting Barry at one point.'

'Oh, God, it's really all getting out of hand, isn't it,' said Dan, a worried look on his face. 'It needs to be sorted as soon as possible.'

'Right, well I'll leave you two to it,' said Marco, standing up and bringing his cup over and putting it into the dishwasher. 'I'll see you down at my house at three and we'll try and suss everyone out.'

'Hang on, I'll come out with you,' said Maggie, pushing her chair back from the table.

'Stay where you are, Mags. I know my way by now. See you later.' He let himself out the front door and headed down towards Lorraine's house. God, Maggie *had* looked awful. He couldn't believe he hadn't noticed that she seemed to have lost weight and her face looked grey and sunken. Would he have noticed if Dan hadn't said something about it? He felt like such a bad friend. Well, he'd make it up to her soon. When things settled down for him and Claude and hopefully the lotto ticket showed up, he'd have more time to concentrate on Maggie.

Ten minutes later, he was heading into Majella's, having informed both Lorraine and Rita about the meeting. Before he got to ring the bell, the front door opened and Majella appeared, wheeling a suitcase behind her.

'Jesus, Marco, you frightened the life out of me. What are you doing standing there?'

'Hiya, Majella. I was just about to call into you. Are you off somewhere?' Marco eyed the bulging suitcase.

'I, em, myself and Chris are just off for a few days. It's all sort of last minute so if you don't mind, we're in a bit of a rush.'

Alarm bells started to go off in Marco's mind. 'So where are you off to then? Somewhere nice?'

Majella continued down the path in silence. She opened the boot but just left the case by the car, no doubt for Chris to lift in. God forbid she'd ruin one of those manicured nails! Although, Marco noted, she was looking a bit rough. It wasn't like her not to have her full make-up on and her hair immaculate.

'So, you didn't answer me, Majella,' Marco persisted, following her back to the door. 'Where are you off to?'

Majella sighed and turned to face him. 'We're, em, we're just heading off for, em, for a mini-break.'

'A mini-break?' he said, not content to be fobbed off with that snippet. 'So where *exactly* are you going then?'

'Jesus, you're so bloody nosy, Marco. Do you need to know *everything* that goes on around here?'

'Just making friendly conversation, Majella.' It was more than that and it seemed Majella knew it too. He was now feeling more than suspicious at his neighbour's sudden departure.

'Well, if you must know, Chris and I are heading down to Kilkenny for a spa break. We've both been working so hard lately that we thought we should take a bit of time out.'

'Ooh, a spa break,' said Marco, leaning on the newly painted railings. 'How swanky. And how come it's such a last-minute decision?'

Majella sighed. 'Marco, sometimes you've just got to be spontaneous. We don't have any ties and we're both due time off work so why not treat ourselves every now and then.'

Marco couldn't really say anything to that. She was right – they were entitled to do what they wanted and he felt a little bit bad questioning her like that. 'Sorry, Majella. You're right. It's just I was trying to organise a meeting today for the lotto syndicate. We really need to get our hands on that ticket.'

'I know, Marco. But we'll be out of here in the next half hour so count us out. You can update me on everything when we're back on Tuesday.' The conversation was over as far as she was concerned, as she tried to close the door on Marco.

'Well, just before you go, have you anything you'd like me to bring up at the meeting? Any further thoughts on the ticket?'

'Can't think of anything,' said Majella, clearly getting irritated. 'Look, Chris is anxious to get on the road so I'd better go. Talk to you next week.'

'Bye then,' said Marco, but he was talking to a closed door. Majella hadn't waited to be subjected to any more of his questions.

He walked back to his house in a bit of a daze. That was all very bizarre. The sudden holiday, Majella's reluctance to speak to him, not meeting his eye – it could only mean one thing. Majella *must* have been the one to take the ticket. It seemed like the only explanation. He'd suspected her already, but now he felt sure.

Did she honestly not realise she'd give the game away by acting like that? Everyone knew that they were struggling for money so surely heading off on a spa weekend was just asking to be found out. Those things didn't come cheap. Of course, she wouldn't be able to claim any money without the rest of the syndicate being notified but maybe she was concocting a story that she was the only one who'd paid and therefore the win was hers. The National Lottery people would have to sit up and listen to her if she had the ticket. He couldn't prove anything but he'd talk to the others at the meeting today and see what they thought. If they were all agreed, they'd just have to approach Majella when she came back on Tuesday. If they put a bit of pressure on, surely she'd admit it. The main thing was that they'd get the ticket back and be able to claim the money once and for all.

Marco let himself back into the house and closed the door behind him. On hearing him come in, his little cockapoo launched herself at him, yapping happily and chasing her tail around in circles. Marco lifted her up and hugged her. 'Why can't humans be as uncomplicated as dogs, Mimi? If only we could all be happy with a treat a day and a scratch behind the ears.'

Heading into the kitchen, he glanced at his watch. Two o'clock. In an hour, his friends would be coming here for the meeting – everyone except Majella. It was going to be an interesting one. Wait until they all heard what he had to say. He felt outraged at the thought that Majella was trying to get one over on them. He also knew he was probably one of the calmest of the group, so God only knew how the others would feel. They'd have to put their thinking caps on and form a plan. They couldn't prove anything so they'd have to figure out the best way to get her to admit it and hand over the ticket. There was always a chance that he was wrong, of course, but he didn't think so.

CHAPTER 28

'Right,' said Marco, placing pots of tea and freshly brewed coffee in the centre of his glass kitchen table. 'Now that we're all here, let's get started.'

'I can't stay long,' said Rita, helping herself to a mug of tea. 'My ma is watching the boys but she has to head off soon.'

Marco nodded. 'Well, what I have to say won't take long. You'll probably all want to go off and mull over it for a while.'

'Let's just get on with it then,' said Lorraine, impatiently. Marco glanced at her. It was very unlike her to be so tetchy.

Marco took his seat at the top of the table and cleared his throat. 'Okay, so you all know what the National Lottery said at the start of the week – that they'd put a hold on the win because we've queried it. They said that—'

'For feck's sake, Marco, get on with it, will you? We know this already.' Rita was getting impatient.

Marco glared at her. 'Well it's important to go over the facts, just to make sure we know what's what. I just want to make sure that—'

'*Marco!*' It was Lorraine's turn.

'Okay, okay! So anyway, I rang them again yesterday morning and someone was to ring me back. But then I was in work so I put my phone on silent. When I checked it, there were two missed calls from the lottery offices.

'Jesus, Marco, I'm going to slap you in a minute,' said Rita. Lorraine glared at her. 'Don't speak to him like that, Rita. He's the one trying to do something *positive* around here!'

Marco felt surprised at the venom in Lorraine's words but continued. 'Eventually, I got speaking to Concepta in the claims department again – you know, the girl who I spoke to on Monday.'

'And any progress?' asked Maggie, her voice barely audible. Marco noted how the dark circles under her eyes seemed to reach way down into her cheekbones and even her make-up couldn't hide her pallor. 'Are they any more willing to pay out the money?'

Marco shook his head. 'Unfortunately not, Mags. They still won't pay out the money unless we have a ticket. What we're trying to do in the meantime is to make sure there's an investigation if anyone tries to claim the money.'

Lorraine shifted uncomfortably in her chair and Marco couldn't help thinking she looked almost as sick as Maggie. Maybe there *was* some bug doing the rounds. 'So what else did she say, Marco?'

'Well, it's getting more serious. What we have to do now is contact a solicitor.'

'Oh, Jesus, don't get me started on solicitors,' said Rita, raising her voice. 'I've feckin' had enough of them to last me a lifetime. They're all just out to make money and don't really give a damn about their clients.'

'I know you've had bad experiences in the family court, Rita, but this is different.' Marco threw a glance in her direction. 'We just need a solicitor to write to the National Lottery on our behalf.'

'So what's supposed to be in this letter?' asked Lorraine. 'And is it just one solicitor for the whole syndicate or do we need to get our own?'

'Well, for the moment, we just need a solicitor to write a letter on behalf of the syndicate to stake our claim on the winning ticket. He also needs to request the National Lottery not to pay out on the ticket until ownership is established.'

Rita looked pensive at that piece of information. 'Oh, so would that mean that nobody would be able to claim the money for themselves, even if they presented the ticket?'

All eyes suddenly turned to Rita and she reddened. 'I don't mean … I'm not asking because … Jesus! That's the second time I've made myself look guilty. I hope nobody thinks I have the ticket. I was just asking the question.'

'Of course not, love,' soothed Maggie, although Rita's question had obviously set alarm bells ringing. Lorraine looked as though she was about to pounce on Rita, but thought better of it.

'It will probably take a while to get everything in place,' continued Marco, 'but it means that if someone tries to claim the money, they'll be notified by the National Lottery that there's an issue over the ownership of the ticket and that no prize money will be paid out until ownership is established.'

'So, it would probably be a good time for whoever has the ticket to give it up,' said Lorraine, quietly. 'There'd be no point in hanging on to it any more.'

Marco nodded. 'Exactly! And with solicitors involved, it would only get nasty if someone tried to claim on their own.'

'So what's the story with Majella, Marco? You said you'd fill us in. Did she not want to be here for the meeting?' Maggie's usual booming voice seemed to have shrunk to an almost inaudible whisper. It alarmed Marco to see his friend like this. It also surprised him that nobody else seemed to have noticed.

'Well, let me tell you the story about Majella,' he said, pausing for effect. 'And then you can tell me what you all think!'

'Go on then, it sounds intriguing.' Lorraine leaned forward with her elbows on the table and rested her chin in her two palms.

'When I went to tell Majella about the meeting today, she and Chris were loading up the car to go off on a mini-break.'

'She never said anything when I was talking to her yesterday,' said Rita. 'I popped into her for a dishwasher tablet after tea and we chatted for a few minutes. She never said a word, although I did feel she was rushing me out.'

'Well, according to her, it was all very last minute.' Marco left that to sink in with the others. He hoped they'd come to the same conclusion as he had.

'So where has she gone then?' Maggie was speaking again.

'They're gone to Kilkenny on a *spa* break until Tuesday.'

'It's well for some,' said Maggie. 'There's nothing I'd like more at the moment. And they certainly don't come cheap.'

'*Exactly*!' said Marco. 'Aren't Majella and Chris supposed to be in debt? Didn't we hear that they owe money everywhere?'

'Oh, my God! It's Majella, isn't it? It's Majella who's taken the ticket.' Rita stood up suddenly from her chair, almost sending her cup flying off the table. 'The bloody bitch! And here's me living next door to her, chatting to her almost every day, and there she is robbing me blind. She's not going to get away with it!'

Marco was alarmed at Rita's fury, but quite delighted that somebody else had the same thoughts as he had. 'Calm down, Rita. We can't say for certain yet.'

'But it's what you're thinking too, isn't it, Marco?' she

continued. 'That's why you're telling us about it. You think it's her too.'

Lorraine, who had initially been shocked by Rita's outburst, joined in. 'Do you, Marco? Do you think it's Majella?'

'I have to admit that when I came away from talking to her earlier, that had been my first thought. She seemed nervous and jumpy. She wouldn't look at me when I was asking her questions and she couldn't get away from me quickly enough.'

'Well it does sound suspicious,' said Maggie. 'But we don't want to go around accusing her without any evidence.'

Rita was furious. 'But how on earth are we supposed to get evidence, Maggie? What we need to do is shame her into admitting it was her.'

'Yes,' said Marco. 'That's what I was thinking. Maybe we should play it tactically; let her know there's now a solicitor involved and see how she reacts.'

Maggie was nodding. 'Good idea. Surely that would be enough to rattle her if she's the one.'

Marco nodded. 'Exactly. We'll have another meeting when she comes home on Tuesday, and maybe exaggerate things a little. Hopefully, it will be enough to get her to own up.'

'And I think we shouldn't jump down her neck when she comes back,' said Maggie. 'If she thinks we're all against her, we might never see that ticket. If we take the softly, softly approach, we might get more out of her.'

'Good idea,' said Rita. 'Although it will be hard not to try and strangle her when I see her.'

'So are we all agreed then?' asked Marco, standing up to let Mimi out the back door. 'We approach things gently with Majella on Tuesday, and tell her we're having another meeting that night. We'll make sure she knows that it's not an option for anyone to claim the money on their own.'

'Agreed,' everyone said in unison.

'Although,' said Maggie, looking thoughtful, 'we still don't know for sure that she's taken it. We've sort of jumped to a very big conclusion here.'

'Oh, she's taken it all right,' said Rita, who looked ready to kill. 'I think we've all had our suspicions about her from the beginning.'

'Well, I certainly have,' conceded Marco. 'I think she's been acting very strangely recently and now we know why.'

'Right, I'm going to head off,' said Rita, standing up and heading towards the door. 'Let me know if there's any more news.'

Maggie stood up too, and Marco noticed she winced as she did so. 'I'm going to head off myself, Marco. Thanks for organising all this. What would we do without you?'

'Ah, go away out of that,' said Marco, blushing. 'But would you not stay for another cup of tea?' Marco had promised Dan he'd keep an eye on her and had hoped they could have a chat on their own.

'I'd better not, Marco. Dan is expecting me back.'

'I'll walk out with you, Maggie,' said Lorraine. 'Barry is due home from work shortly and we're going to have that chat.'

Marco hugged her tightly. 'Best of luck with that, Lori. Let me know how you get on. It will be fine, I know it will.'

He waved to them both and rolled his eyes when they stopped at the end of the path to have a chat. 'And *you* tell *me* I'm a talker! Enjoy your gossip, ladies. If you're looking for me, I'll be inside … on my own … talking to my little cockapoo!'

When Lorraine was sure Marco had closed the door completely, she pulled Maggie aside. 'I don't want Marco to know what I'm talking about but I need to get your opinion on something.'

'Go on then,' said Maggie, her eyes open wide at the prospect of a bit of gossip.

'Well, you know how Marco and Claude have been getting on so well and Claude has even been thinking of staying on in Ireland?'

Maggie nodded. 'Yes, and they make such a perfect couple. It does my heart good to see Marco so happy.'

'Well, that's what I thought too. But yesterday evening, Marco came over for a cuppa and was telling me Claude had gone home for a few hours to do a bit of work.'

Maggie was beginning to look impatient now. 'And what's wrong with that? He's staying with his parents so I'm sure they want to see him sometimes, and he has a job to do as well.'

'It's not that, Maggie. After Marco went home, I was in the sitting room and just happened to see a man coming out of Rita's house. They both glanced around as though checking to see who was looking and then hugged each other.'

'Really?' Maggie was looking a lot more interested now. 'And do you know who it was? Maybe that husband of hers got wind of the lotto win and has come back to look for his share.'

'No, it definitely wasn't her husband. It was the least person you'd expect to be paying Rita a visit!'

'Go on then – I'm intrigued. Who was it?'

'It was Claude, Maggie.'

Maggie looked confused. 'Claude? Marco's Claude?'

'Do you know another Claude?'

'Well, it's just that it doesn't make sense. What would Claude want with Rita? Sure he doesn't even know her.'

'Exactly!' said Lorraine. There's definitely something fishy going on.'

'There could be an innocent explanation, Lorraine. Let's not jump to conclusions yet.'

Lorraine persisted. 'But how come Marco didn't seem to know about this visit? He seemed to think Claude was back at his parents' house tying up loose ends on the video footage they took.'

'I really don't know,' said Maggie, looking very tired and fed up. 'Why don't I have a word with Rita and see if I can find out what's going on. There's no point in us worrying Marco if there's nothing to worry about, and besides, you have enough going on in your own relationship without getting caught up in somebody else's.'

'Okay, Mags, thanks for that. I would do it myself but I think you've got a better relationship with Rita. She tends to open up to you more.'

'I'll see what I can do, Lorraine. But you don't think … it would hardly be …'

'What Maggie? Spit it out!'

'No, honestly, Lorraine, it's just my mind working overtime. For just one second, I imagined Rita with the elusive lotto ticket and Claude helping her for a share of the winnings!'

'Jesus Christ Almighty, Maggie. You're imagination is even more vivid than mine. I was thinking more on the lines of an affair!'

'Well you're definitely barking up the wrong tree there, Lorraine. From what Marco has told me, Claude definitely swings in his direction.'

Lorraine didn't look convinced. 'Well, there are plenty who swing both ways, Maggie. Maybe he's one of those.'

'Well let's not speculate any more. My head is pounding

with everything that's happening. As I said, I'll have a word with Rita later and see what I can find out.'

Lorraine looked at her friend and noticed for the first time that she had deep circles under her eyes and her face looked dull and tired. 'Are you okay, Maggie? You just don't seem yourself.'

'Don't worry about me, Lorraine, there's not a bother on me. It's *me* who should be asking *you* how you're doing! Any progress with Barry yet?'

'Not yet, Maggie, but I'll keep you posted. Go on, you go in. You look like you could do with a rest.' Lorraine didn't want to get into another conversation about her and Barry. She was sick to death of talking about it.

'All right, Lorraine. And I'll let you know if I have any joy with Rita. Talk to you later.'

Lorraine watched her friend turn the key in her door and head inside. She looked frail. It shocked Lorraine to see her that way. Maggie was always so strong and larger than life that it was strange to see her looking tired and old. She headed down to her own house, lost in thought. It was as though the worries of the world were on her shoulders. There were so many unanswered questions – the lotto ticket, Barry's behaviour, her possible pregnancy, the Marco/Claude/Rita triangle and now Maggie. She felt her head was about to burst.

God, she was exhausted. She just wanted to sleep and forget about everything for a while. But Barry would be home from work shortly and she was determined to sort things out with him, once and for all. Just as she reached the door, she felt something rise up in her throat. Oh, God, not again! She turned the key quickly in the door and just reached the downstairs toilet in time to throw up into the sink!

CHAPTER 29

Lorraine lay on the bed, her head spinning and her stomach churning. She'd never felt so sick in her life. It was twenty minutes since she'd come in from Marco's and she'd thrown up about ten times. There'd been nothing there to throw up really, just a vile-smelling yellow substance, but it had taken its toll on her and she was feeling like death.

The rattle of keys in the front door meant Barry was home. She wouldn't have time to sort herself out, so she'd just have to tell him she was sick.

'Are you home, Lorraine?' his voice echoed up the stairs.

At least he sounded a bit chirpier than he had been of late. 'I'm up here, Barry. I'll be down in a second.' She splashed some cold water on her face and dried it with the hand towel. She pulled a brush through her hair and grabbed a bobbin to tie it back in a ponytail. The result wasn't fantastic, but she looked marginally better than she had five minutes before.

Still feeling a little unsteady on her feet, she took the stairs slowly, holding on to the banister. Barry looked up as she came into the little kitchen. 'Hiya, love. What have you been up to?'

It had been a while since he'd called her love and her heart lifted a little at the sound of the word. 'I'm just back from Marco's. We had a meeting about the lotto ticket.'

'And any developments there?' asked Barry, loosening his tie and filling the kettle with water. 'Surely the ticket will have to turn up soon.'

Lorraine tried to read something into what he was saying but he seemed genuine enough. She spent the next five minutes filling him in on what was said at the meeting and what they were all thinking. It felt good to be chatting to him like that. It felt normal. And God knows, she really felt the need for a bit of normality in her life. Maybe she should just take the opportunity to talk to him about the other stuff while he was in good form.

'Jesus,' said Barry, having listened to all the goings on. 'There's never a dull moment around here, is there? And Lorraine, I was thinking …'

Lorraine looked at him with a mixture of fear and worry. She'd given up trying to predict what was going to come out of his mouth next. 'What is it, Barry?'

'I think we need to talk.' His voice was soft but not without an edge. 'There's been a lot going on this past few weeks and I think it's about time we laid our cards on the table and had a proper chat about it.'

'Oh, Barry, that's what I've been *trying* to do! We really need to get to the bottom of what's happened to us. I want *us* back.'

'Don't you think I hate all this, too, Lorraine? I thought we were happy—'

'We were,' said Lorraine, panicking slightly at where this might lead. 'We *are!*'

'Well, there's stuff we need to discuss and clear up before we can say we're happy again. Because *I* certainly don't feel happy at the moment!'

'Well, it hasn't exactly been a laugh a minute for me either, you know. I've been—' Oh God, no! She willed the bile to stay down.

'What is it, Lorraine? You've gone white as a ghost.' Barry watched her, concern all over his face.

'I think I'm going to be … sorry … have to go.' She rushed into the downstairs toilet where she retched pitifully again and again.

'Are you okay, love?' Barry was tapping gently on the toilet door. 'Can I get you anything?'

Lorraine emerged, tears streaming down her face from the force of the retching. 'I think I just need to go to bed, Barry. I– I'll be all right after a rest.'

'Come on, let's get you upstairs then. What do you think is wrong? Do you want me to call a doctor or something?'

Although she felt rotten, Lorraine was sort of enjoying seeing glimpses of the old Barry. 'No, no, I'm okay. It's just a bit of a bug. Maggie was complaining of the same thing earlier this week. A couple of hours' sleep and I'll be as good as new.'

Barry helped her into the bedroom and put her to bed. He swept the wisps of hair from her forehead with his fingers and kissed her lightly on the cheek. 'Just give me a yell if you want anything, Lori. I'll be just downstairs.'

'Thanks,' Lorraine whispered, already half asleep. As she drifted off, her heart felt a little lighter. Whatever was going on between her and Barry, it was clear there was still a lot of love there. It seemed they were destined not to have that chat but she'd persevere. Love always won out in the end, didn't it?

'Hiya, Rita. Have you time for a cuppa?' Maggie was feeling rotten and it was the last thing she felt like doing, but she had promised Lorraine she'd have a chat with Rita.

'Well this is a nice surprise,' said Rita, holding open the door for her neighbour. 'The boys are busy playing with their

Lego and I've just made a pot of tea. I'd love the company. Sometimes it gets a bit lonely here in the evenings.'

'Ah, you poor thing,' said Maggie, following Rita into the little kitchen and sitting herself down on one of the wooden chairs. 'I suppose I take it for granted that Dan will always be there – I couldn't imagine what it would be like without him.'

'You sort of get used to it, Maggie. To be honest, I'd prefer to have my own company than have that good-for-nothing pig around the place, but sometimes I wish there was someone special in my life, you know, someone just to share the day-to-day stuff with.'

Maggie cupped her hands around the mug of steaming tea that Rita had just put down in front of her and looked at her friend's strained face. 'And is there nobody, Rita? I mean, I know you're not going steady with anyone but is there nobody to even drop by and keep you company the odd time?'

'Only my ma, Maggie. But if you're talking about male company, it's been a long time since I've had any of that. Between you and me, I'm not sure I'd know what to do with it any more!'

'Ah, go on out of that, Rita. You'd never forget something like that. It's like riding a bike.'

Rita giggled at that. 'I suppose you're right – a ride is a ride!'

'Well, that wasn't exactly what I meant,' laughed Maggie, 'but you get the gist. But I want to ask you something, Rita, and I don't want you to think I'm being nosy or anything.'

'Go on then, what is it?' Rita shuffled in her chair and began to look uncomfortable. So maybe she *did* have something to hide!

Maggie pushed her cup aside and leaned forward on the table. 'Rita, we were wondering ... I was wondering ... it's just that somebody saw you—'

'Oh, spit it out, Maggie, would you!'

'Sorry,' said Maggie, looking down at the table. She felt a bit foolish asking the question. It was hardly incriminating evidence, having a man in your house in broad daylight. 'Is there something going on with you and Claude?'

Rita reddened. 'Well, it depends what you mean by "something going on".'

'Look, Rita, Claude was seen coming out of your house yesterday when Marco thought he was home at his parents' house. 'We just thought it was a bit strange, that's all.'

'Well, there's certainly nothing going on of a *sexual* nature, if that's what you're getting at, Maggie. I can assure you, he's most definitely *not* into women.'

The way she'd emphasised 'not' threw Maggie a little. Did that mean that she'd tried it on with him? 'Well, then what was he doing here, Rita? I know you'll probably tell me to mind my own business but it's just that Marco is a friend and I wouldn't like to see him getting hurt.'

Rita sighed heavily and leaned back in her chair. 'I suppose I might as well tell you, Maggie. It's bound to get out at some stage.'

Maggie was alarmed. That didn't sound good. 'Tell me what, Rita? What's happened?'

'Well, you know all the filming earlier in the week?' began Rita, slowly. 'When Claude was trying to get a decent interview and there were so many interruptions?'

'Yes, I do seem to remember a certain angry somebody interrupting my interview and making a scene!' She shot Rita a disapproving look but added a little smile, to show her there were no hard feelings.

'I am sorry about that, Maggie, but I just couldn't help feeling angry about the whole thing. I still am, to be honest.

I know you think we have a fabulous street and everyone is everyone's friend, but it's clearly not as fantastic as you make it out to be.'

'Well, I don't think you can say that just because of one incident, Rita, or because of one person. And anyway, we're getting off the subject. What's this about Claude you were going to tell me?'

Rita began shifting nervously in her chair again. 'I'll tell you, Maggie. But please don't judge me. You'd probably have done the same if you were in my position. It's just not right that—'

'Oh, God, you're worrying me now, Rita. Just tell me.'

'On Wednesday,' she began, 'when they were filming in Lorraine's house, do you remember when Barry started mouthing off?'

'How could I forget,' said Maggie. 'They had to stop the camera rolling and it ended up in a big row between Lorraine and Barry.'

'That's just it, Maggie. They didn't stop the camera rolling. The crew went outside but all the time the camera was on the kitchen table, catching everything that was said.'

Maggie gasped. 'Jesus, Mary and Joseph! There were a lot of private things discussed that day. We talked about the missing ticket and then myself and Marco left Lorraine and Barry to chat about things. God only knows what *they* said!'

'Quite a lot, apparently,' said Rita, nervously twirling a spoon around and around in her hand. 'And it was all captured perfectly on film!'

'Bloody hell!' said Maggie. 'But I don't understand – what's that got to do with Claude being in your house?'

'Think about it, Maggie. Do you think a boring interview about how lovely the street is could compare to a lovely, juicy bit of film about a street torn apart by a lotto win, a missing ticket, secrets, lies ... need I go on?'

Maggie paled. 'You're not saying ... you don't mean ... Jesus!'

'Yes, Maggie. RIP have no intentions now of including St Enda's in their documentary about the wonderful people of Ireland. They're hoping to do a piece on the lotto win and how the missing ticket has affected the community in such a negative way.'

'Oh, God. And Claude? He's heading up this new documentary?'

'It seems that way, Maggie. He said his boss in New York had sent him specific instructions to get some good interviews about the missing ticket and how it's affecting everyone. He remembered how angry I was on Tuesday and thought I'd be a good one to chat to.'

'And did you, Rita? Did you give him the interview?' Maggie stared at her neighbour, willing her to say she didn't.

Rita bowed her head. 'I did chat to him, Maggie. It wasn't on camera or anything but he did record me. What was I to do? I was in an impossible situation.'

'Rubbish,' said Maggie, disgusted that Rita would have allowed their little street to be ridiculed like that. 'You could have just refused to talk to him.'

'I know, Maggie. I should have just said nothing.' Tears began to stream down Rita's face. 'It's just that Claude was so nice. I actually didn't fully think about what I was saying. It was like he was just having a chat with me. He said he just wanted to be sure he had his facts straight and before I knew it, I was telling him everything.'

Maggie sighed. She'd usually rush to someone's side if they were upset but she was still too annoyed with Rita to console her. 'Well, it sounds a bit like he conned you, Rita. You should have known better, but that Claude should never have put you in that position.'

Rita was sobbing now and Maggie began to soften. She was more than surprised that Claude would be so underhand. She didn't know him at all really, but Marco was completely besotted by him. 'Come on, Rita, don't cry. What's done is done. We'll just have to see what we can do about damage limitation.'

'I'm ... I'm sorry, Maggie,' Rita said, blowing her nose. 'He has me on tape now, so I'm not sure what I can do about it.'

'Well, I'm thinking more about Marco, to be honest. I'd really hate to see him hurt. He's really fallen for Claude and it seems that maybe Claude has just been using him all the time.'

'Poor Marco. Should we tell him, do you think?'

'He'll definitely need to be told, Rita. The longer it goes on, the more he's going to get involved with Claude. I'm not saying Claude doesn't have any feelings for him, but he certainly can't respect him too much if he's willing to go behind his back like that.'

'Well, it's probably best coming from you, Maggie. Or Lorraine even – I'm not sure he'd listen to me.'

'Oh, God – *Lorraine*! What's she going to think when she hears that her private conversation with Barry is on camera? She'll be gutted. I'll have to go and tell her first and we can decide what we're going to say to Marco.' Maggie stood up and for a moment thought she was going to fall back down again. Her head was spinning and she was seeing spots in front of her eyes.

'Jesus, are you okay, Maggie? You look like death.' Rita looked alarmed and ran to her friend's side.

'I'm fine,' said Maggie, gripping the edge of the table. 'I just got up too fast. I'll be okay in a minute.'

'Do you want me to go and get Dan?'

'*No!* I said I'm fine.' Maggie wasn't usually so sharp but the last thing she wanted was for Rita to rush across and start worrying Dan. 'Sorry, Rita. It's just Dan has been going on about me taking better care of myself so I could do without another lecture from him. I'm grand, honestly.'

'Okay then,' said Rita, walking out to the door with Maggie. 'And I'm really sorry again for opening my mouth to Claude at all. Let me know how you get on with Lorraine and Marco. And … Maggie?'

Maggie turned to her friend and noticed the strained look on her face. 'What is it, Rita?'

'I know I don't deserve it, but can you please not make me out to be the bad guy to the others? I love living here and it would be awful if people hated me for talking to Claude.'

'Nobody is going to hate you,' said Maggie, giving Rita a brief hug. 'If there's anyone we need to direct our anger towards, it's Claude for misleading us and being underhand. Go on back in to your boys. I'll keep you posted.'

Maggie walked back across the road to her house, but she knew all wasn't well. She felt dizzy and disorientated and was having trouble putting one foot in front of the other. She hadn't eaten all day and yet she couldn't face the thought of food. Maybe it was about time she told her husband about what the doctor had said. She'd thought she could ignore it but, clearly, she couldn't.

Dan was right. She needed to look after herself. She always liked to think she was doing a good deed by putting herself at the bottom of her own list but, in hindsight, that was silly. She had a family to think of. What would Dan and Steph do without her? She knew they needed her. She'd just have to put her silly pride aside for once and turn to her family for a bit of help and support.

CHAPTER 30

Sunday, 18th September

Marco turned onto his left side and watched the rise and fall of Claude's glorious chest as he snored softly. He couldn't believe how lucky he was. The pair had grown very close, so much so that Marco couldn't imagine his life without Claude.

If somebody had told Marco last year that he'd meet someone online and end up falling head over heels in love with him, he'd have thought they were crazy. He would have said that only losers met people that way. How wrong he'd been.

Marco's feelings for Claude were stronger than any he'd ever had for anyone before, and last night, while they were chatting and laughing, he'd had an overwhelming sense of belonging. Claude was the perfect fit for him and he was going to do everything in his power to keep him with him in Dublin.

Mimi had been banished to the kitchen for the duration of Claude's stay, much to her bewilderment, so it was no surprise that she'd made herself heard at a very early hour. It had only been 5.30 a.m. when Marco had been forced to peel himself from the bed and go down to quieten her barks. He'd let her outside and had come straight back to bed but he hadn't been able to sleep since. It was gone eight now, and he was willing Claude to wake up.

They'd talked for ages last night about Claude staying in Ireland and it seemed he'd almost made up his mind. Marco was hoping that he'd have slept on it and would make his decision today. He just *had* to stay – Marco couldn't stand the thoughts of the alternative.

He continued to watch Claude and smiled as a few stray strands of his shiny, black hair covered his left eye. Although quite camp himself, Marco wasn't attracted to that sort of man. He liked his men to be masculine and rugged and that's exactly what he got with Claude. A Colin Farrell lookalike, he oozed sexiness and although he always looked scruffy, he smelled of Dove soap and Fahrenheit aftershave.

He reached out to push the stray hairs behind Claude's ear and woke him up in the process.

'Morning,' Claude said, through half-opened eyes. 'What time is it?'

'Hi, gorgeous. It's only a quarter past eight. Sorry if I woke you.'

'Don't be sorry, Marco. I'm glad you did.' He pulled Marco close to him and pressed his lips gently on his. 'What a lovely way to wake up.'

'I could get used to this,' said Marco, pulling the duvet up to his chin and snuggling in closer. 'So what's on the agenda for today then? Will we go out for lunch or something?'

'Ah sorry, Marco. I thought I told you. My parents are throwing a bit of a party for me this afternoon. Apparently all the relations are coming and everything. My mam arranged it ages ago – it was her way of getting everyone to see me before I went back to New York.'

'Oh! I didn't realise.' Marco was deflated. He'd thought he was going to spend the day with Claude as it was a Sunday but now this! And it didn't look as though he was going to get an invite either!

'And I would invite you,' said Claude, 'but I'd prefer to introduce you to Mam and Dad on their own before subjecting you to the whole family! You don't mind do you?'

'Of course not.' He did mind! He knew it was selfish but he just wanted to be with Claude all the time. 'I can't expect to monopolise your time. You have to think of your parents too.'

Claude reached over and cupped Marco's face in his hands. 'But I've made a decision, Marco. I've thought about nothing else this past week, and I've finally made my mind up.'

Marco began to sweat. He wasn't sure he wanted to hear it. Sometimes ignorance was bliss. If Claude told him now that he was going back to New York, he'd be devastated. For now, he could imagine what it would be like if Claude stayed, but if he told him otherwise, the spell would be broken.

'Marco,' said Claude, softly. 'Did you hear me? I've made a decision.'

'Go on then, Claude. Put me out of my misery.' Marco realised he was shaking and his mouth had gone dry.

'Well let me put it this way ...' Still holding Marco's face, he again pressed his lips on his, more urgently this time, until Marco was forced to pull away gasping for air.

'So you mean ... are you staying?' Marco barely dared to believe.

'Yes, Marco. I'm not going anywhere. How could I, after ... you know?'

'Oh, God, I can't believe it,' said Marco, flopping back onto his pillow and placing his palms over his face. 'I know I've been encouraging you to stay, but I kept thinking that when it came to the crunch, you'd go back to New York.'

'Well, believe it,' said Claude, pulling Marco's hands away from his face and gently wiping away a tear that was streaking down his cheek. 'I've just got to finish up on a few things for work over the coming days and then I'll be telling them I'm leaving.'

'And won't they mind? I mean, will they just let you go like that?'

'I'm sure they'll be fine, Marco. To be honest, my job probably wasn't very secure anyway as they've been letting people go for the past six months. I just want to make sure I tie up all the loose ends and that they're really happy with the job I've done over here. I want to, at the very least, get a good reference.'

'Well, after watching how you handled all the drama on the street, I think you're a star. I'm sure your reference will be glowing.'

'Let's hope so. And speaking of drama, any word on the ticket? I meant to ask you last night but there just seemed to be so many other things to, em, *talk* about!'

'Ha!' giggled Marco. 'The ticket was the last thing on my mind last night! But we have a suspect now. We don't know anything for sure but we think that Majella has taken the ticket.' Marco spent the next ten minutes telling Claude about the meeting, his chat with Majella and their suspicions. Claude listened attentively, right elbow on the pillow, leaning his cheek in the palm of his hand.

'God, that's certainly a story and a half, Marco. So will you question her about it when she comes back?'

Marco sighed at the thought. 'We're planning on having another meeting to include her but, to be honest, if I see her first, I don't know if I'll be able to contain myself from saying something. Sometimes the best way to get a result is the shock factor. If I put it to her straight that we think she has the ticket, she might just cave in.'

'That might be the best thing to do all right,' Claude said, resting his head back down on the pillow. 'I'd love to be there to see her face though. God, this little street is so full of drama, isn't it?'

'It never used to be. But this lost ticket has certainly stirred things up.'

'Right,' said Claude, pushing the bedclothes back. 'Much as I'd love to lie here chatting, I'd better get up and have a shower. My mother will be on my back if I'm not home well before the guests start to arrive.'

'I'll go down and make some tea and toast. Only the finest of breakfasts in this house!'

'Ha! Tea and toast is just fine, thanks. I'll be made eat my own bodyweight in sausage rolls and mini quiches this afternoon, so best I save myself for that.'

Marco watched as Claude rolled out of the bed and headed for the en-suite. How lucky was he? He couldn't believe that this perfect specimen of a man with his Calvin Klein boxers clinging to his tight bum was his. He wished they could spend the day together but, under the circumstances, it didn't really matter. Claude was staying in Ireland and they could spend every Sunday together from now on!

'Come on, Maggie. That's not like you. You love your Sunday roasts.' Dan was dishing up dinner for himself, Maggie and

Stephanie, having cooked it all himself because Maggie hadn't been feeling well.

'It's gorgeous, Dan, honestly,' said Maggie, cutting her roast beef into small pieces and moving her stuffing around on the plate. 'I just had too much toast for breakfast, that's all. I'll eat a small portion and make a beef sandwich later on. How's that?'

'Mam, you're *always* saying that lately,' said Stephanie, digging into her own dinner with gusto. 'Are you on one of those faddy diets or something?'

Dan looked alarmed. 'You're not, are you, Maggie? I know you said you were hoping to lose a few pounds before Christmas, but starving yourself isn't the way to go about it.'

'Will you two listen to yourselves? I'm *not* on a diet. I told you, I just don't feel hungry after only having breakfast a couple of hours ago.'

'Ooooh, touchy!' said Stephanie, earning herself a glare from her father.

'Stephanie Louise O'Leary! Mind your manners. Your mother is right – if she's not hungry, she's not hungry. End of!'

Maggie shot her husband a grateful look. She hated lying to her family – not that she was lying as such, but she was pretending everything was all right when, clearly, it wasn't.

'Right, I'm done. Can I go and watch telly now?' It never ceased to amaze Maggie how her daughter could wolf down a dinner at breakneck speed and still maintain her stick-thin figure. She only had to look at food herself and she'd blow up. Still, she'd been thin like that herself once, until middle age had crept up on her and brought with it cellulite and lots of unwanted extra inches!

'Go on then, Steph,' said Dan, sighing. 'I suppose there's no point in asking you to clean up, is there?'

'I'll do it. I haven't lifted a finger all day – it's the least I can do.' Maggie was on her feet as Steph slipped away into the sitting room.

'You will not, Maggie.' Dan was adamant. 'You'll go in and watch telly with Steph and put your feet up or go on up to bed for a rest. You work too hard, that's your trouble. Me and Steph are going to have a little chat during the week and work out a way we can help you more around the house.'

'There's really no need, Dan,' said Maggie, scraping the plates and piling them up. 'I'm just having an off day. I'll be fine in a bit.'

Dan took the plates from her. 'Go, Maggie! I'll bring you a cuppa when I get this lot cleared. I'm not arguing with you!' He stood and stared at Maggie until she was forced to do what he said.

'Thanks, Dan. Maybe I *will* head up for an hour. I'll be as right as rain when I have a little sleep.' Maggie had never felt so bad in her life. It was though her chest was going to burst from indigestion and even the small piece of roast beef she'd managed to eat was threatening to make a reappearance. Her head was throbbing and she felt weak and dizzy.

The double bed with the new winter duvet looked inviting. Not even bothering to strip off, she kicked off her slippers and buried herself in the warmth. She immediately felt better, not having to put on a show for anyone. She knew Dan would be really annoyed at her if he thought she was pretending to be fine when she wasn't, but she couldn't worry about that now.

She'd been putting off telling her husband about her visit to the doctor. There'd been only a limited amount the doctor could tell from a quick checkup, but he'd been concerned enough to make an appointment for her at the hospital the next day. But in typical Maggie fashion, she'd cancelled it almost immediately, claiming she couldn't make it and that she'd ring back for another appointment. She knew she should have gone ahead with it, but she just couldn't face it.

She didn't want to admit it, but she was scared to death. By keeping it to herself for now, she could pretend it wasn't happening. As soon as she told Dan, things would change. He'd treat her differently and would insist on her resting all the time. And then there were her friends. She knew Dan would want them to know she wasn't well, so they could keep an eye on her. She'd hate that. They all had far too many things going on in their own lives to have to spend time looking after her!

But despite her reservations, she knew she'd have to have that chat with her husband. She'd planned it a few times already and then chickened out. She was a bit of a hypocrite really – there she was, lecturing Lorraine on being open and honest with Barry, when she was keeping things from her own husband!

She'd definitely have a chat with him tonight. She'd just allow herself an hour or two's rest and then talk to Dan later. She felt as though her insides were being ripped apart as she tried to get comfortable. Eventually, the pain eased a little and she began to drift off. She heard the rattle of a cup being left on her bedside locker and felt her husband's light touch as he pulled a strand of hair from her face and swept it behind her ear. She was too exhausted to stir and finally fell into a restless sleep where she dreamed of her mother.

Maggie was in her school uniform and Agnes was trying to get her to wear a coat that was too small for her. 'Ma, it's far too tight. I can't wear that.'

'*Maggie, you don't have a choice. It's freezing out there
and right now, it's the only coat you have.*'

'*But, Ma …*'

'"*But, Ma" nothing,*' *said Agnes, buttoning up the coat so
that Maggie could barely breathe.* '*When I get my wages on
Friday, I'll see about getting you a new one.*'

Maggie twisted and turned in the bed, trying to free herself
from the coat in her dream. It was hurting her chest. It was
far too tight. Why had her mother made her wear it? It was
squeezing the life out of her and making her feel light-headed
and weak. Tighter and tighter and tighter!

CHAPTER 31

'Come on in, Barry. This is ready.' Lorraine felt her stomach lurch and, for a moment, she thought she was going to be sick again. But she soon realised it was just nerves. This conversation needed to happen, but she really wasn't looking forward to it. It could go either way. She still didn't know if Barry was gambling again but one thing was for sure, he certainly wouldn't be expecting to hear what she was about to tell him!

'It smells delicious, love,' said Barry, sitting down and immediately tucking into his plate of pasta. 'So you're feeling better today then?'

'I'm feeling fine, Bar. It must have just been a twenty-four-hour thing.' She wasn't just saying it, she really was feeling fine again, other than the nerves. She'd woken up ravenously hungry and had demolished four slices of toast in quick succession and was more than ready to tuck into her dinner now. In a funny sort of way, her being sick yesterday had been a godsend. It had brought on a bit of a thaw between her and Barry and she was hoping things would go to plan today.

'I'm glad you're okay,' said Barry, through a mouthful of creamy chicken. He reached his hand across the table and took Lorraine's. 'These past few weeks have been terrible, Lorraine. Let's just try and sort it out. I've been so angry about it all, but seeing you sick yesterday just reminded me of how much I love you and how I couldn't bear to be without you.'

Lorraine was relieved to hear those words, but she still needed to get to the bottom of what had been going on between them. 'Barry, I don't get it. What's been going on in your head? What in God's name made you say what you did the other day?'

Barry put down his knife and fork and pushed his plate away. 'You mean about you having an affair? Are you telling me now that you're completely innocent and it's all in my head?'

'Jesus, Barry, of course it's in your head. I don't know where on earth you got a harebrained idea like that from. There's nobody else.'

'You see, now I *know* you're lying to me, Lorraine.'

Lorraine looked at her husband, trying to make sense of it all. 'You know nothing, Barry! You've obviously built something up in your head that just doesn't exist. Tell me why you think there's someone else.'

Barry bristled. 'Well, maybe you should tell me what you think is going on here. Why do you think things are falling apart – why are *we* falling apart?'

'Do you really want to know what I think?' said Lorraine, her voice a little louder than necessary. 'Will I tell you what I think is going on?'

Barry sat back in his chair and folded his arms. 'Please do.'

Although she was feeling a little less certain now, she

continued. 'Are you gambling again? Is this what this is all about? Are you trying to push the blame onto me for things falling apart when really your own life is out of control?'

'*Gambling*? You thought I was *gambling*? Is that what you think all this has been about? For fuck's sake, Lorraine! I haven't gambled a penny in years. You know that. What on earth made you think I'd gone back to it?' He banged his fist on the table, causing Lorraine to jump.

'I'm sorry, Barry,' she pleaded. 'I ... I just can't think of any other explanation for how you've been behaving. I hadn't ever given you reason to think I was having an affair so I thought that ... I thought you were just ... oh, I don't know.'

'I promised you I'd never go back to that,' he said, his eyes cold. 'And I meant every word of it. I never want to go back to how things were when I was gambling. I'm a different person now and I've moved on with my life.'

Lorraine took a moment to digest what he was saying. She should have felt relief but all she was feeling was fear. 'Barry, I really am sorry. I should have trusted you. But what about what you've accused me of. Surely that's worse. Why would you think I'd want to be with anyone but you?'

Barry looked at her, his eyes glistening with tears. 'I *heard* you, Lorraine. I heard you talking to Maggie.'

Lorraine slumped back in her chair and her stomach gave a little lurch as she tried to remember what he could have possibly heard. She talked to Maggie about all sorts of stuff. Oh, God, maybe he heard her talking about Rory. She searched her brain to remember how much of the incident from the other night she'd shared with her friend. But Barry had been angry long before then so it couldn't be that.

'Did you hear me, Lorraine?' asked Barry, breaking into

her thoughts. 'Your little secret – I heard you discussing it with Maggie.'

'My ... my secret? What did you? W– what did I ...?'

'Lorraine, I *know* there is, or at least there *was*, another man. I know you haven't been honest with me. I've given you so many opportunities to tell me about it. I kept hoping you'd come to me and tell me about it yourself so that we could at least deal with it, but you seem to have decided to keep it a secret!'

Oh, God, she needed to get her head together. So he'd overheard one of her conversations with Maggie and had jumped to the wrong conclusion. But she wasn't sure the truth was any better. She had to tell him now but she was terrified about how he might react.

'So can you understand my anger now?' he continued. 'You've been keeping a secret about another man and all this time I'd thought we were happy. I thought we were rock solid and maybe even soon to become a real family.'

'Oh, so you listened in on my *private* conversation with Maggie, and then decided you knew what it was all about!' She was just playing for time now. 'So you have so much faith in me that you thought I was having an affair!'

'Well, that's what it sounded like to me, Lorraine. Are you saying you're not? Or you weren't?'

Lorraine was suddenly gripped with a rush of bile to her throat and jumped up from the table. 'That's exactly what I'm saying, Barry. Sorry ... I've got to ... I'm going to be ...' She rushed out of the room and into the downstairs toilet where she retched up the small bit of dinner she'd eaten.

'Are you all right, Lorraine?' asked Barry, from outside the toilet door. 'Do you want me to get you anything?'

'Just leave me for a bit, will you? I'll be back out in a few minutes.' She looked at herself in the mirror and noticed how her face had become thin and gaunt. She'd always had a long, narrow face but it now seemed even thinner than usual.

She took a handful of water from the tap and rinsed her mouth. Wiping her mouth with a piece of toilet paper, she took a deep breath and knew she'd have to go and face her husband. She needed to just say what she should have said years ago. He needed to know the truth.

'Are you okay?' asked Barry. He was hovering halfway between the kitchen and the toilet. 'That's a nasty bug you've got. Maybe we should get you to hospital. You don't look at all well.'

'No, Barry, I'm fine. Sit down. We need to talk.'

'We don't have to talk now, Lorraine. You're not well enough. Maybe we can do it tomorrow if you're feeling better.'

'*Barry*! Sit *down*!' She sounded more confident than she felt. But one thing was for sure, if she didn't tell him now, she never would.

'Okay, okay,' Barry said, sitting down and looking as though he might cry. 'It's just that ... it's just that ... if you don't tell me, I won't know. Lorraine, I love you so much and I'm really scared of what you're going to tell me.'

'Barry, it's not what you think.'

'Lorraine, if we're going to have this conversation, much as it kills me to think about it, you'll have to be honest with me. If you've been unfaithful, I need to know. If there's another man, I need to know. Even if it's over now – you need to tell me what happened. I really don't want to hear you saying the words, but I *need* to!'

Lorraine felt her anger rise again. He'd jumped to a pretty

major conclusion from hearing a bit of a conversation and had put her through hell as a result. 'Jesus, Barry. You don't half think the worse of me, do you? Three whole weeks this has been going on. Three weeks where you've been treating me like shit and making me feel awful. Why could you not have just come to me straight away and asked me what I'd been talking about?'

'Oh, yes, because it would have been so easy for me to approach you and ask you if you were having an affair. Cop on, Lorraine. It was a shock and it's just been sinking in.' It was his turn to be angry.

'But that's just it, Barry. What's been sinking in? You jumped to a conclusion – the wrong one, I may add – and you've let that fester for the past few weeks until things between us have become unbearable.'

He banged his fist on the table again. 'Don't you turn this around onto *me*, Lorraine. Don't you *dare*! I *heard* the conversation. I heard you saying to Maggie that you were scared of telling me. You asked how you were going to tell me about him.'

Lorraine paled. Oh, God! So *that's* what he'd heard. She had to admit that hearing that out of context could have certainly sounded suspicious. She *had* to tell him now. But it was difficult to get the words out.

Barry was watching her carefully. 'Go on then, Lorraine. Deny it. Tell me there isn't another man in your life. Go on, *tell me!*'

Lorraine looked down at the table, willing the words to come out but Barry wasn't letting her away with it.

'*Tell me!*'

'Barry, I ... I can't ...'

'So you're admitting it then?' Barry looked at her

incredulously. 'So you're telling me now that there *is* someone else?'

'There is – but it's not what you think.'

'Just bloody well tell me who it is, Lorraine. I can't take this anymore. Just spit it—'

'It's *Marco*,' Lorraine shouted, tears streaming down her face. Then her voice quietened to a whisper. 'Marco is the other man.'

Barry looked at her as though she was mad. 'Marco? I don't understand.'

Lorraine was sobbing now as she looked at her husband and gulped out the words through her tears. 'Can't you guess, Barry? Marco is my son.'

CHAPTER 32

Lorraine watched her husband as he tried to take in what she'd just told him. Tears streamed down her cheeks as she watched his face turn from confusion to realisation. Oh, God! What had she done? Wouldn't he have been better living in ignorance? How would it affect him, knowing that he wouldn't be the first man to give her a child? She wished he'd say something. This was torture.

'Wh–What are you saying, Lorraine? Marco … your son? How … I mean, why didn't you …? God, I can't take it in.' He placed his palms on his cheeks and rubbed his eyes.

'Barry, I'm so sorry for not telling you before now, really I am. It just wasn't something I've ever spoken about to anyone. It happened and we dealt with it and vowed we wouldn't speak about it again.' She blew her nose, determined to hold it together until she could make him understand. There was no point in her being a snivelling wreck.

Barry took his hands away from his face and looked at her. She expected to see anger but all she could see was hurt. 'Lorraine, but I'm your husband. I'm the man you vowed to be with for the rest of your life. Didn't you think I deserved to know something so huge and important?'

Tears pricked her eyes again but she blinked them away.

'Yes you did, Barry. You deserved the truth and that's why I'm telling you now. It just didn't seem relevant before.'

'Jesus, Lorraine. It's like I don't even know you. Marco! Fuck! Your *son*! Barry shook his head and sat back into his chair, arms folded. He just looked at her for what seemed like ages. He opened his mouth to speak but nothing came out.

'Say something, Barry. I need to know how you feel. I want you to understand.' Lorraine wanted to run to him. She wanted to throw her arms around him and hold him close. She wanted to feel his love. But she was scared. She was scared that this would be just too much for him to take. She was scared that it would be the end of them.

'I want to understand too, Lorraine. Maybe you should start from the beginning.'

His eyes seemed to soften a little and she clung on to that glimmer of hope. 'Do you really want to hear it all, Barry? Do you want to hear about the pain? Is it not better left in the past?'

'I'm sorry if it's painful for you, Lorraine, but I *need* to know.'

'Right then, if you're sure you want to—'

'Just tell me, Lorraine!'

She took a deep breath, knowing it was a story that had to be told. 'I was just fourteen, Barry and, like all teenagers, had become interested in boys. Unfortunately, I wasn't blessed with the looks of my two sisters. At sixteen, Ruth looked like a model, and even though just eleven, Janet was already a stunner. I was the one with the mousy, limp hair and the bony figure. The other girls used to say they envied me for being so tall and thin but I was just gangly, to be honest, and I obviously didn't have what it took to attract the boys. I was always the one left sitting on my own at the school disco when my friends were asked up to dance.'

Lorraine could see from Barry's eyes that he was getting impatient. It was probably better to get straight to the point.

'Anyway, you get the idea. One Hallowe'en when I was almost fifteen, I was allowed out to a *real* disco in town. It was the first time I'd gone to a disco that wasn't supervised by parents. I loved it. I loved how it was packed and dark and loved the fact that I was finally getting some male attention.' Lorraine paused, worried about how this was making her husband feel, but he nodded at her to continue. 'There was this boy, Sean Moloney, who lived close to here, who I'd fancied for ages. He was there and, somehow, amongst the madness of the hundreds of teenagers dancing as if their lives depended on it, we managed to hook up. We slipped out of the disco and got a taxi back to his house. His parents were out so we … you know … that's where it happened.'

Barry shifted uncomfortably on his chair. 'So this boy,' he said, tactically avoiding any finer details. 'Where is he now? Does he know he has a son?'

'I'll get to that in a sec, Barry. Just let me fill you in on the whole story.'

Barry nodded silently and she continued. 'After that night – the night it happened – things went back to normal. We didn't exchange phone numbers and even when we saw each other out on the street, we pretended like nothing had happened. I was hurt, of course, because it had been a big deal for me, but Sean obviously hadn't thought so. Life went on as normal until six weeks later, I realised I'd missed a period.'

Barry was shaking his head. 'I still can't believe it, Lorraine. I can't believe you never told me any of this. All the personal things I've told you – all the stories about my gambling – and not once did you give me any indication that you had such a big secret.'

'I'm so sorry, Barry,' said Lorraine, tears spilling down her cheeks. 'I really am. As I said, it was just something I didn't want to think about. It was an awful time in my life and I suppose I sort of blanked it out.'

'So what happened when you discovered you were pregnant?'

'Oh, God, I was terrified. I couldn't think straight. I didn't know whether to go and tell Sean or to tell my parents first. I kept it to myself for a few weeks but I felt like I was going to die from the stress of it all. I eventually told my parents because, to be honest, I just didn't know what to do and I wanted them to tell me. I was just a child.'

Barry reached across the table and touched her hand. It was far from a reassuring embrace but a pat on the hand was a start.

'They were gutted,' she continued. 'They didn't freak out or shout and roar but they left me in no doubt that they were so disappointed with me. That was nearly worse. I remember thinking afterwards that it would have been better if they'd roared and shouted at me, if they'd gone ballistic and screamed the place down! Anything would have been better than my father's cold gaze and my mother's obvious disgust. Anyway, I told them about Sean and I was marched around to his house to talk to him and his parents. It was awful. Sean immediately denied he'd been with me at all. He said, in front of his parents and mine, that I'd tried it on with him and he'd knocked me back. He said that I'd earned a reputation for being the school bike that night because I'd done it with so many of the boys. God, it was mortifying. He said I was only trying to pin it on him because of the fact he'd knocked me back and because I just didn't have a clue who the father was.'

'That must have been awful,' said Barry, in a much softer

tone than he'd been using before. 'Did your parents believe him?'

'Luckily they didn't. I'll always be grateful to them for completely believing me and standing by me. His parents, however, were a different story. They were disgusted by the claims and completely believed their darling son. Within a few weeks, their house was up for sale and they'd moved off down the country somewhere. I was gutted. I'd been holding out a hope that, despite what he'd said in the heat of the moment, Sean would have come good and taken responsibility. But it wasn't to be.'

Barry stood up suddenly, scaring Lorraine into thinking that he was going to storm out. He was going to leave her just like Sean had. It was history repeating itself. She was possibly carrying his baby and he was going to leave her. She couldn't bear it. But to her surprise, he got down on his hunkers beside her and took her hands.

'Lorraine, I'm mad as hell with you for not telling me. I could scream at the fact you kept this a secret for so long and I want to shake you for letting me believe that there was something more sinister going on. But, Jesus Christ, I can't bear the thought of what you went through. I want to kill this Sean guy and slap his parents hard for doing what they did.'

Barry rested his head on her lap and Lorraine put her head on top of his and let her tears fall onto his hair. 'It was a long time ago, Barry, and I'm well over it all now. What's important is that we can move on from here. Do you think we can?'

'Well, you'd better just fill me in on what happened next before we talk about moving on.' He sat back up on his chair but kept a firm hold of her hands. 'When was it decided that Marco would be brought up by your parents?'

'Well, my mother had been a bit clucky for a while and

she and my dad had been discussing having another baby anyway. It was Mam who suggested it, and it just felt right. I was way too young to be a mother, so it was decided that I was going to be a big sister again instead. I don't know how we managed to keep it all under wraps, but we did. I didn't show until close to the end of my pregnancy and, after I'd started to show, I went down to Mam's sister in Galway until the end. It couldn't have worked out better. It was the summer holidays at that stage, so it wasn't as though I was missing school or anything. Mam made sure to wear a lot of baggy clothes to get the rumour mills going so it was no surprise to anyone when Marco was born. Mam and Dad took him as their own and nobody batted an eyelid. It's funny, I didn't feel any real bond with him. I sort of felt a bit cold, to be honest. So within a few weeks, things were back to normal except for the fact that we girls had a new brother.'

'And Marco?' Barry asked, watching her intently. 'Does he know about all this? Or does he still think you're his sister?'

'Oh, God, he knows. Of course he does. We wouldn't keep something like that from him. Mam and Dad told him when he was about twelve and at an age where he understood the importance of keeping it quiet. Funnily enough, he wasn't overly put out by it. He did feel he should have been told before then, but overall, he was okay. Thankfully, he was a well-adjusted and confident child and was able to get on with things without it affecting him.'

'That's just unbelievable.' Barry seemed to be struggling to take it all in. 'What a story, Lorraine. And does nobody know about this?'

'Very few people,' said Lorraine, quickly. She didn't want

Barry to think he was the last to know. 'Maggie knows, but that's only because my mam told her at the time. She was just next door and helped Mam out by minding us sometimes.'

'But Marco still refers to you as his sister.'

Lorraine smiled at the thought of her so-called brother. 'I know, Barry. To be honest, we'll always really be brother and sister. We know what happened all those years ago, but Marco was brought up as my brother and that's the way we like it.'

Barry shook his head. 'God, I still can't believe I didn't know any of this. And has this Sean guy ever made an appearance since?'

'Nope,' said Lorraine, her mouth fixed in a grimace. 'And, to be honest, we were happy about it. Marco didn't need him or his snooty parents sticking their noses into his upbringing. We were all happy with how things were.'

Barry opened his mouth to say something and then stopped and just stared at Lorraine. She couldn't make out his expression – was it anger or shock?

'Are you okay, Bar?' she asked, concerned. 'I know you must have had a shock but …'

He clasped his hands together suddenly. 'So that's the reason why, Lorraine! That's why you've been so scared of having babies!'

Lorraine was almost afraid to meet his eye. 'Well, yes, that's a big part of it. I didn't exactly have a good induction into motherhood back then, so I've been worried that I'd be a crap mother now.'

He folded his arms around her and her heart soared. 'Oh, Lori. You'll make a fantastic mother. Don't let some loser from the past ruin the rest of your life. We're a team now, and I'd never betray you like he did.'

'I know, Barry. And I love you for it. God, I'm exhausted from all these confessions!'

'Well, I don't know about you,' said Barry, standing up from his chair. 'But I could do with a glass of wine. Is there still that half bottle of white in the fridge?'

'I think so,' said Lorraine, her stomach lurching even at the thought of alcohol. 'But I won't, if you don't mind.'

'Are you sure? Can I not tempt you with even a small one?' Barry placed two wine glasses on the table and sat down with the half-empty bottle of white in his hand.

'Best not. I, em, don't want to risk being sick again.' She was dying to do the test and see his reaction but one thing at a time.

As if reading her mind, he took a long sip of his wine and looked at her with tears in his eyes. 'Lorraine, I love you more than you'll ever know. This doesn't change anything between us. You didn't even know me back then. Yes, you probably should have shared this with me before now, but I do understand why you didn't.'

'Oh, Barry,' she said, rushing over and throwing her arms around him. 'I love you too. I love you so much. I've been wanting to tell you this for such a long time but I've only just got the courage to do it now.'

He hugged her back, placing feather kisses on her head. 'And why now, Lorraine? How come you were able to tell me now when you'd been so frightened to do it beforehand?'

This was it. She had the perfect opportunity. 'I'll show you why.' Much to Barry's surprise, she hopped up from the chair and rushed out to the hall to grab her handbag from where it was hung on the banister. 'This is why, Barry. I thought you needed to know before we got on with the rest of our lives.'

Barry stared at the pregnancy test that his wife was holding in front of his eyes. 'Oh, my God! So you're ... you're ... are you ...?'

'Well I don't know for sure yet,' she said, grinning at the look of shock on her husband's face. 'I was waiting to do the test with you. But judging from all the symptoms I've been having and I'm also late with my period, I reckon there's a fairly good chance that the answer to that is yes!'

Barry rushed over to her and lifted her up, twirling her around and around in his arms. 'Well, what are we waiting for then? Let's go and see what the rest of our lives have in store!'

'Oh, God, if I had to wait another day with this test burning a hole in my bag, I'd have gone mad!' Lorraine had never felt happier as she ripped open the first of the tests and headed into the little downstairs toilet.

'Don't you want to read the instructions first?' said Barry, unfolding the piece of paper from the box.

'I've read them a hundred times,' giggled Lorraine from the other side of the door.

What on earth had she been so worried about? She should have had faith in her husband. They were a great team and she should have confided in him long before now. Still, everything was back on track, thank God. She placed the saturated test on the windowsill as she washed her hands. Three minutes. In three minutes' time, they'd know their fate. Everything was falling into place now and all she needed was to be able to tell her husband that he was going to be a daddy. And although she was technically already a mother, this time she was really going to be somebody's mammy!

CHAPTER 33

Maggie woke with a start. It took her a moment to realise where she was. The bedclothes were damp from her sweat and she felt even worse than she had when she'd got into bed earlier. Glancing at the clock, she couldn't believe it was already almost six. She'd been asleep for hours. She'd kill Dan for not waking her. What a waste of a day.

If she didn't get up now, she'd never sleep tonight and she was doing a shift at the bakery in the morning. Pulling herself up into a sitting position, she swung her legs out the side of the bed and felt around for her slippers. When she'd found them, she stood up and was shocked to realise how weak she felt. Her legs felt like jelly and she had to support herself by holding on to the wall as she pulled on her robe and headed towards the stairs. Sure, she'd eaten barely anything all day – it was no wonder she was feeling weak.

Just as she was about to head down the stairs, she stopped dead. She could hear voices coming from the kitchen. Oh, God! She didn't feel a bit like entertaining visitors and she certainly didn't look the part. She took a couple of steps down and strained her ears to try to make out who was there.

'I couldn't be happier, Dan. Honestly, I feel on top of the world. I can't wait to tell Maggie.'

Marco! She should have known. He often popped in on a Sunday evening, hoping to cadge the end of the roast beef to make a sandwich. She was always berating him for his eating habits. Most of his meals consisted of meat, eggs or cheese bundled in between two slices of bread! She wondered what he was so upbeat about this evening. Probably Claude-related, she guessed.

'And I didn't even have to persuade him,' Marco was saying. 'Well, not too much! He was really keen on the idea himself, thank God.'

'Well I'm sure Maggie will be delighted, Marco,' Dan was saying. 'But you'll have to wait until tomorrow to tell her. She's not been feeling well again and she's sleeping.'

'Oh, listen to me yapping on about myself. The main reason I came down was to see how she is. Is she no better?' Marco sounded concerned and Maggie felt bad for lurking on the stairs.

'She's worse today, actually. I really think she needs to be checked out. She's beginning to scare me.'

'Well, you should definitely persuade her to see a doctor,' said Marco. 'I'll leave her in peace for now and drop in tomorrow.'

'There's no need to go, Marco,' Maggie said, coming down the stairs as Marco and Dan came out of the kitchen. 'I'm up now – we may as well stick the kettle on.'

'Maggie! You shouldn't be up. You look awful.' Dan rushed to her side and tried to lead her back up the stairs.

'Oh, thanks for that, Dan. Kick a girl when she's down, why don't you? And I don't need a minder nor do I need to go back to bed. I feel much better after that rest.'

'Sorry,' said Dan, letting go of her arm. 'But I just want to look after you. I don't feel like I've been doing enough of that lately.'

Maggie smiled at her husband. 'Dan, you're the best husband I could ever wish for. Stop putting yourself down. You look after your little family just perfectly.'

'I, em, I'll head off, guys,' Marco said. 'I'll leave you two to it.'

'Don't be silly, Marco,' said Maggie, leading the way back into the kitchen. 'Come on back in and tell me what this good news is all about.'

Marco glanced at Dan. 'Is that okay with you, Dan?'

Dan grinned. 'The lady has spoken. Far be it from me to put a stop to her gallop! You two go and sit down and I'll make the tea.'

'Right then, so tell me what you're so excited about, Marco.'

Marco didn't need to be asked twice and sat back down at the kitchen table. 'Oh, Maggie, it's Claude. He's staying. Can you believe it? He's staying here in Ireland.'

Maggie wasn't sure what to say to that. From what Rita had told her, Claude may well be just using Marco, but she simply couldn't bring herself to tell him.

'Mags, did you hear me? Claude is staying here in Ireland after all.'

'Well that's good, Marco, isn't it? Is he not going back over to New York at all?'

'He'll have to go back over at some stage to pack up his stuff and sort things out with the landlord, but he's not in any hurry. He was due to go back on Wednesday, but that's not going to happen now.' Marco was beaming and Maggie realised she'd never seen him so happy.

'Here we go,' said Dan, placing cups of tea on the table. He pulled up a chair himself and watched his wife closely. 'So how are you feeling now, Maggie? You look as though you have a little bit more colour in your cheeks.'

'I'm a lot better for that rest, Dan, thanks. A few more good rests like that and I'll be the picture of health again in no time.' She knew it was going to take more than a few good rests, but now wasn't the time to mention that.

'So, anyway,' said Marco, who was obviously bursting to continue his story. 'Claude is going to stay with his parents for the moment until he gets some steady income. It means he won't have to worry about rent or food or anything.'

Maggie was thankful for that much. If he'd been moving in with Marco, she would have had to have said something straight away. She just didn't trust Claude after her conversation with Rita. It was clear that he had an agenda, though she wasn't sure what it was yet. Was he using Marco just to get a juicy story about the lost ticket? Or was he looking for an excuse to justify moving back to Ireland and Marco was just the stepping stone in the bigger picture? Whatever it was, she didn't like it and she'd have to say something to Marco at some stage.

'So where does his family live?' asked Dan, dunking a ginger nut into his tea.

'Somewhere over off the Navan Road, so it's not too far away. Apparently, it's a pretty big house. I think his parents aren't short of a bob or two!'

'And are you going to meet his parents?' asked Maggie, loosening her dressing gown. She made a mental note to check the timer on the central heating. It was far too hot in the house.

Marco looked pensive. 'He hasn't mentioned it yet, but I'm hoping he'll introduce me soon. If *my* parents lived over here, I'd have no problem introducing *him*. I think he's just a bit shy about these things.'

Dan nodded his head understandingly. 'I'm sure he'll— Maggie, are you okay?'

Maggie was rubbing her right shoulder and looking distracted. 'I'm fine, Dan. Stop your worrying, will you. I think I just slept funny on my arm. It'll be grand in a few minutes. Go on, Marco.'

'Well,' said Marco, delighted with his audience. 'You know this business idea I was telling you about, Maggie? Well I'm more determined than ever now to get it off the ground. It would be lovely for Claude to know that there's a job there for him if he can't get anything else. I swear, I'm going to tear this street apart looking for that bloody ticket!'

'But you can't centre everything you do on Claude,' said Dan, looking worried. 'I'm not saying it won't work out and I'm not trying to put a dampener on your plans, but you need to be sure it's what you want to do for you first.'

'I know you're just looking out for me, Dan, but I swear, I couldn't think of anything I'd rather do with the money. You know how much fashion means to me. To actually have my own shop and the opportunity to sell my own designs would be more than I've ever dreamed I could achieve.'

The doorbell sounded, causing them all to jump. 'What now?' sighed Dan, getting up to answer it.

Maggie sighed inwardly too. Usually delighted to have a house full of visitors, this evening she just wanted to curl up on the sofa and watch a bit of *Downton Abbey*, which had become the highlight of her Sunday night.

'Hiya, Mags,' said Lorraine, arriving into the kitchen. 'Marco! I'm glad you're here too – it'll save me going in next door to you to tell you the news too.'

Dan was looking stressed. 'Lorraine, Maggie hasn't been feeling great so maybe we should all leave her to get a bit of rest.'

'*Dan*! I've told you, I'm all right. Don't mind him, Lorraine. Sit yourself down and tell me the news.'

'Right,' said Lorraine, not having to be asked twice. 'But, firstly, I just want to say that I'm on a mission now to find that bloody lotto ticket. It is more relevant now than ever.'

'Ha! That's exactly what I've just been saying,' said Marco. 'You're not the only one with news, you know!'

'Really?' Lorraine looked a bit put out. 'So go on, you tell me your news first.'

'No, you first,' smiled Marco, leaning back in his chair and folding his arms.

'Okay so. Well, you know how I was going to have a chat with Barry?' She waited until all three of them nodded. 'We finally managed to have a good heart to heart this afternoon – all cards on the table. No more secrets and no more lies.'

'Oh, that's brilliant,' said Marco. 'Isn't it, Maggie? Maggie, are you listening?'

Maggie had been listening but she wasn't hearing anything properly. Pain had gripped her again, making her feel light-headed and sick. The words just sounded muddled up.

'Maggie,' said Dan, jumping up to go to her side. 'You look like you're going to keel over. What's up?'

Maggie began to stand up, holding on to the table for support. She felt as though she was going to throw up. *Oh, God, please don't let me do it at the table. Give me the dignity to make it to the bathroom in time.*

'Ma, I'm starving,' said Stephanie, appearing in the kitchen. 'Are you making tea? Can we have— Jesus, what's wrong with Ma?'

'*Maggie*,' shouted Lorraine, joining Dan at her friend's side. 'Let's get you sitting back down.'

'I'm just … I need to …' They were the last words that came out of Maggie's mouth before she felt herself slide to the floor. She felt as though there was a rope around her body, and someone was pulling it tighter and tighter. She couldn't resist it any longer. She didn't have the strength. She was aware of mumbles in the background. Someone was putting something under her head and someone was checking in her mouth. She was aware of the panic surrounding her, but she just wanted to sleep. She'd be okay after a good rest.

Her mother used to always say that the world seemed different when you were exhausted. She used to say that the best tonic for any ailment was a good sleep. She suddenly felt like a little girl again, as her mother stroked her hair.

'*Sleep now, Maggie. You give so much of yourself to everyone else, now is the time for you to rest. You'll be fine. I'll look after you. I've missed you so much, sweetheart. It will be great to have you back again …*'

CHAPTER 34

Monday, 19th September

Marco sat on the old grey wall outside the Mater Hospital and gulped in deep lungfuls of the cold night air. He hated hospitals – especially A&E, where he'd spent a good part of the night. He'd never been able to stomach the sight or smell of vomit, and he'd balked at the guy who'd come in drunk and proceeded to throw up all over the place. He just didn't know how the nurses put up with it. They deserved medals for all they had to deal with.

It was only 5 a.m. and still dark, but there were already people scurrying about, either starting their day or finishing their night. He watched a couple wander lazily down the road, holding hands and giggling about something. He envied their carefree state and how they seemed so unaware of the awfulness of some of the situations inside those hospital doors.

What a shock last night had been. Maggie of all people! She'd always been the strong one on the street. She'd been the one they all looked up to and went to with their problems. She never complained about anything, and maybe they'd all been wrong to just assume she never had anything to complain about!

Poor Maggie. And poor Dan and Stephanie! They'd been out of their mind with worry when Maggie had collapsed. After the ambulance had arrived, the paramedics had worked on her for a couple of minutes before whisking her off to the hospital with Dan by her side. Marco had followed in a taxi with Lorraine and Stephanie. Lorraine had been going to take them in her little car but Marco had thought she was in too much shock to drive.

Everyone had been scared about what was going to happen to Maggie. Stephanie had sobbed the whole way to the hospital, fearing the worst, and Lorraine hadn't been much better. He'd felt very emotional himself, but had tried to keep it together for the two girls.

When they'd arrived, Dan had been pacing up and down in A&E, and Maggie had been in a resuscitation room. Stephanie had run to her dad and Marco hadn't been able to stop the tears at the sight of them sobbing their hearts out. Nothing like this had ever happened to him before. Even though his parents lived abroad, he was lucky that they were fit and healthy. He'd never been touched by any sort of tragedy, ever.

Maggie was now stable but still very weak. They'd been doing a number of tests on her to find out what was wrong. It seemed from initial findings that it wasn't, as they'd feared, a heart attack, but they were still waiting on more news. At least she was alive – thank God for that. When he'd arrived at the hospital and saw Dan's tear-stained face, he'd feared the worst.

Lorraine had been very quiet after they'd arrived at the

hospital. He'd assumed that she was feeling guilty, as he was, about rattling on to Maggie about their own stuff and not realising that she needed some attention herself. Marco felt awful about that. Dan had warned him that Maggie hadn't been feeling well but had he listened? He'd been so keen to tell his friend his fantastic news that he hadn't really cared whether she'd been up to it or not.

Lorraine had stuck around for a few hours but bailed at midnight, claiming she wasn't feeling well and didn't want to pass her germs around to anyone. Marco had eyed her suspiciously when she'd said that. I mean, they were in a hospital, for God's sake. It was hardly a germ-free environment. But it did make him wonder what she'd been going to tell them when she'd arrived at Maggie's earlier. She'd been bursting with news but hadn't had the chance to share it before Maggie had collapsed. Still, they'd no doubt find out as the day went on.

Marco wondered if Claude was asleep. He'd been really lovely earlier when Marco had rung him. He'd insisted on Marco staying at the hospital, telling him not to worry about their date. They could see each other any time now that Claude wasn't going back to New York. It was very early but Claude had said he could text him any time. He'd give him a try.

Hi, Claude. You're probably sleeping but I've just come outside for a breath of fresh air and thought I'd try you. It's so depressing here. Maggie is doing okay but we still don't know the full story. I wish you were here with me. M xx

He pressed 'send' and stuck the phone back in his pocket. Claude was a deep sleeper, so it was unlikely he'd respond. It was hard to believe it was only yesterday evening when they'd brought Maggie in. The time was dragging and he felt like he'd been here for days. It seemed like a ridiculous thing to think, but he missed Claude. This time yesterday morning they'd been in bed together, snuggled up in the warmth of the duvet, oblivious to what was about to happen. Suddenly, a vibration from his phone made him jump. He pulled it out of his pocket expectantly, knowing it could only be one person texting him at this time of the morning.

Hiya, Marco. Glad Maggie is doing well. Can you turn on to DM on Twitter? This texting is so slow. X

Marco's heart warmed at the sight of the text from his gorgeous boyfriend. He loved saying that to himself – *boyfriend*! It felt so good to have somebody who'd be there for him no matter what, especially at a time like this. He tapped on the Twitter icon and it immediately filled the screen.

@Marcofashion1: I'm here, Claude.

@ClaudeRIP: This is so much better. My phone is so bloody slow with texts. What did we ever do before Twitter!

@Marcofashion1: I know what you mean. Did I wake you with my text? Sorry if I did. I was just dying to talk to you.

@ClaudeRIP: I had the phone by my bed. I wouldn't have told you to get in touch if I didn't mean it. How are you doing?

@Marcofashion1: I'm okay, Claude. It's just awful to think of Maggie lying there so sick.

@ClaudeRIP: Have you seen her yet or has Dan even seen her?

@Marcofashion1: They let Dan and Steph in for a short time, but she was very drowsy. They wouldn't let me or Lorraine in, but I was almost glad, to be honest.

@ClaudeRIP:Why? Didn't you want to see her?

@Marcofashion1: Not like that, Claude. I couldn't bear to see her with tubes and wires and whatever. I just wanted to be near in case, you know.

@ClaudeRIP:Well, I'm sure Dan appreciates it and so will Maggie when she's on the mend.

@Marcofashion1:Thanks, Claude. I'd better get back in to them. I'll catch up with you a bit later.

@ClaudeRIP: Okay. Keep in touch. I'm sure you'll want to sleep for some of the day but if you feel like it, I could come over later.

@Marcofashion1:That would be great. I'll give you a buzz when I'm home later. Sleep well. xx

Marco felt much more relaxed and positive as he placed the phone back in his pocket. Maggie was going to be all right – he just knew it. She'd be sitting up in the bed later, telling them all about her experience and they'd all ooh and ahh at her story.

He felt buoyed up at the prospect of seeing Claude. He knew he shouldn't be thinking of enjoying himself while his friend was lying so sick in a hospital bed, but he just couldn't help himself. He couldn't imagine what his life would be like without Claude. He was giving up a lot to come back to Ireland and be with him, and it made Marco feel very special and loved.

He thought idly about Claude's Twitter name and made a

mental note to remind him to change it. It wouldn't seem right to continue using the company's name. Marco never really liked it anyway. I mean, who'd call their company a name that shortened to RIP? It was a disaster waiting to happen!

His mood became more sombre again as he headed back in to the hospital. He was exhausted, but he really didn't want to leave Dan and Stephanie. But at least Steph had managed a couple of hours' sleep on the uncomfortable plastic chairs. He and Dan hadn't been able to sleep a wink. He'd check and see how Maggie was doing and then see what Dan's plan was. They were all going to need to get home at some stage and have a shower and change at the very least. And none of them would be much good to Maggie if they didn't get some sleep.

Just as he turned the corner in the corridor, he saw Dan talking to a nurse and rubbing his forehead. Oh, God. Please don't let it be bad news. He looked as though he was crying and Stephanie was fast asleep on a chair beside him. The nurse rubbed his shoulder soothingly and he flopped down onto the chair beside Steph. Marco was rooted to the spot as he saw Dan put his face into his two hands. It was obvious from the rise and fall of his shoulders that he was sobbing and Marco wanted to turn around and run away. This couldn't be happening. Not to Maggie. Not to his lovely, generous, beautiful friend who'd been his rock throughout his life.

He rushed over to Dan and kneeled down on the floor beside him. He put his two arms around him. 'Oh, Dan, what's happened? Is it bad news?'

Dan looked up, tears streaming down his face. 'No, Marco. She's okay. It looks like she's going to be all right. It's gallstones! Bloody gallstones! She might have to have an operation but, other than that, she's going to be all right!

She's even beginning to moan now about all the wires and monitors attached to her.'

'Oh, Jesus, that's brilliant,' said Marco, standing up and pulling a chair over to sit beside him. 'When I saw you, I thought ... I thought ...'

'Sorry, Marco. It's just been such an emotional night. They were worried that she wasn't responding well and had barely been awake, so when the nurse told me it was looking good, I was so relieved.' He started crying again and this time Marco joined in.

'Are they going to let you in to see her?' sniffled Marco, blowing his nose. 'You must be dying to talk to her.'

'They're just in with her at the moment but I should be able to go in then. I'm not sure they'll let you in though. Not at the moment anyway.'

'Don't worry about me, Dan. I'm just delighted she's improving. So what's your plan then? Are you going to come home after you've seen her? I could order us a taxi?'

'I wouldn't want to leave yet, Marco. I'd prefer to be here for another while. You go, I'll be fine.'

'I don't want to leave you, Dan. And you'll really need to get some rest. You know when Maggie is properly awake she'll have you worn out from talking, so you'd want to have plenty of energy for that!'

Dan smiled. 'Oh you've no idea how I'm looking forward to hearing her rattle on about this and that. It will be music to my ears! But why don't you order a taxi and take Steph home. I'd be happier if I knew she was getting some sleep. It's been a very traumatic night for her.'

Marco was glad he had an excuse to leave. Now that he knew Maggie was going to be okay, all he wanted to do was curl up into his bed and sleep. 'No problem, Dan. I'll call one now.'

'I'll just wake her up so she can peep in at her mam before she goes. And thanks, Marco. You've been brilliant. You're a real friend and we're very lucky to have you.'

Tears pricked Marco's eyes at Dan's kind words. 'It's no problem. Sure Maggie is like a mother to me. I couldn't bear it if anything happened to her.'

'Well, she'd give you a slap if she heard you saying that,' giggled Dan. 'She'd remind you that she's like a big sister, not a mother!'

'Ha! Too true! Now I'll go and ring that taxi and leave you to talk to Stephanie.' Marco walked back out towards the front door of the hospital to make the call. Thank God things were improving. The past few hours had made him realise just how much Maggie really meant to him.

Sleep had never seemed so enticing. He'd go home and have a few hours before getting back up to face the day. He was due back in work today, but he'd ring in and tell his boss what had happened. She'd be sympathetic and tell him to have the day off – she was good like that. She'd always been a fair and generous boss, but he couldn't wait for the day when he had nobody to report to and he'd be the one in charge. And that time would be sooner rather than later if they could just find that damn ticket!

Marco couldn't wait to sit down with Claude later. He was bursting with ideas and plans and they really hadn't had time to discuss it all properly. One thing was for sure, the future was certainly looking rosy. He was possibly going to realise his dream to start his own fashion business and he had somebody he loved to be by his side through it all. Life didn't get any better than that!

CHAPTER 35

It was only 7 a.m. but Lorraine couldn't sleep. She'd been at the hospital until midnight with the others but had felt really sick and had to leave. She knew Marco hadn't been too happy about it. He seemed to think she was making excuses to get out of there. He hated hospitals and probably felt that he should have been the one to leave. When she'd asked if he'd wanted to share a taxi home, he'd sniffed loudly and said that he thought that at least *one* of Maggie's friends should be there for her. She knew he was stressed about Maggie so she hadn't said anything to him, but she'd have a word later.

She rolled over in the bed and spooned into her husband's back. It was so good to have him back again. Not that he'd gone anywhere, but he may as well have, the way he'd been so distant of late. Their conversation had been tough but she was so thankful they'd finally got everything out in the open. Barry had been amazing. He'd been upset and shocked, but he'd been quick to reassure her that it didn't change a thing and that he still loved her.

She'd been dying to tell Maggie and Marco about what had transpired. As soon as Barry had headed up for a shower, she'd hot-footed it down to Maggie's. She'd wanted to get back quickly before Barry came back down so she'd rushed in, ready to spill her news, without a thought for anyone else. That's why she was feeling guilty about what happened to Maggie. She wasn't stupid enough to think it was her fault, but she'd been so caught up in the whole Barry saga recently that she hadn't realised anything was amiss with Maggie. And then she goes over and witters on to her about the ticket and news, when clearly Maggie wasn't in any fit state to listen! God, she'd got such a fright when Maggie had keeled over like that. It had been terrifying to see her lying there, completely lifeless. They'd all felt so helpless.

Thank God she was doing okay. Marco, despite being annoyed with her, had sent her a text a couple of hours ago to tell her that Maggie was awake and giving out about the bed. She was a fighter and Lorraine knew she'd be back on her feet soon. She'd play things by ear over the next few days and see if Maggie was well enough to hear her news. She'd be careful this time though. She wouldn't barge in and demand that everyone listens to her. She'd learned her lesson yesterday. She'd listen to her friend first and gauge whether she was in form to hear the news from the outside world.

'What's up, Lori?' said Barry, turning to face her and rubbing his eyes in an effort to wake up properly. 'Can't you sleep? Are you still feeling sick?'

'I'm fine, Barry. I'm just thinking about Maggie, that's all. And I don't feel a bit sick this morning. I could murder some scrambled eggs or something.'

'Right, I'll get cracking in the kitchen so.' He made a feeble attempt to drag himself out of bed but Lorraine pulled him back.

'Not at this early hour, you won't! Let's just stay here and chat for a while and if we don't go back to sleep, how about we both go down and cook some breakfast in an hour or so?'

'Sounds good to me,' he said, snuggling back down under the duvet. 'Come here and give me a cuddle. It's been too long since we've been close like this.'

'I know,' said Lorraine, revelling in her husband's attentions. 'I've missed you so much, Barry. Let's look on today as a brand new start. I know it's a cliché, but it's the first day of the rest of our lives.'

'Definitely. I wish I didn't have to go to work though.'

'I wish you didn't either, but you don't have to be in until twelve and I want to go up to the hospital anyway.'

'Has there been any further word on Maggie?' asked Barry, his face almost touching hers.

'Yes! Marco's been in touch. Gallstones are what caused the collapse. Apparently the pain was so bad and she hadn't been eating so her body just gave in. Thank God it wasn't a heart attack. I couldn't bear it if … if …' She almost choked on the words as the events of last night caught up with her.

Barry was quick to pull her to him. 'Shhhh, Lori. She's going to be fine. Maggie is a strong woman. She'll come back fighting, I know it.'

'Let's hope so,' said Lorraine, wiping her tears on the duvet. 'What would we all do without her? I realised last night how close we are. She's like a big sister to me.'

'Well, I'm sure the two of you will be sitting at her kitchen table before long, gossiping about all sorts. And you still have to tell her about us. Did you even get to tell Marco yet?'

'I didn't think it was right to talk about my news under the circumstances. There'll be plenty of time for that.'

'Of course there will.' Barry looked pensive. 'And I don't want to seem callous or anything, but—'

'But what?' Lorraine looked slightly alarmed.

'We should really push things a bit more about this ticket business, Lorraine. We need to find it – now more than ever.'

'I know we do, Barry. But it doesn't seem right talking about it while Maggie is in hospital. And we certainly don't want to be stressing her out about anything.'

'Of course I don't mean straight away or anything,' said Barry, reassuringly. 'I just mean that as soon as Maggie is well, we'll need to try to get to the bottom of things. That two hundred thousand euro never seemed more enticing!'

Lorraine thought of how she'd suspected her husband and felt ashamed. The money would certainly come in handy all right and would bring them both peace of mind. 'We'll definitely push the issue as soon as Maggie is out of hospital.'

'And what about Majella?' asked Barry, stroking his wife's hair. 'Is she still the chief suspect?'

'I suppose you could say that. She's due home tomorrow and we'd planned to have a meeting to try to get her to own up. The others are convinced she's taken the ticket, especially Marco.'

'And you're not?'

'Not entirely ... I don't know. Something about it just doesn't ring true. Why would she go off on a luxury weekend if she's taken the ticket? She knows we're all gunning for the person who has it, so why would she flaunt that in our faces and make us suspect her?'

'You have a point,' said Barry, trying to untangle his legs from the mess of the duvet. 'Let's just see what happens over the next few days. But, for now, I'm wide awake and those scrambled eggs are just shouting at me from the kitchen.'

Lorraine laughed, glad to have the old Barry back again.

'Well go on and answer them then! You can get them to call me when they're cooked!'

'Ooooh, very clever! I'll give you that one but you're on clean-up!' He searched under the duvet with his hands until he found the soft flesh at the top of her leg and proceeded to tickle her.

'Stop, stop,' giggled Lorraine. 'Go on and get started on breakfast. I'll be down in a minute.'

Barry did as he was told and hopped up out of the bed, pulling half the bedclothes with him. Lorraine watched as he awkwardly pulled a pair of socks onto his whiter than white feet and grabbed his navy towelling robe from the back of the bedroom door. Barry wasn't by any means athletic in frame. He was skinny and bony and his shoulders always seemed to hunch over. But she didn't want anyone else. She loved every protruding bone in his body!

Despite her worry over Maggie, she felt strangely elated. She never realised that the burden of her secret had been weighing so heavily on her shoulders. She felt so much lighter for finally sharing it with Barry. Now there were no secrets between them. She didn't have to worry about her past coming back to haunt her. She didn't have to be scared of Barry finding out. She'd told him every little detail of what had happened all those years ago and, in fairness to him, he'd taken it very well. Now she was ready to move on with her life.

All that remained now was for them to talk to Marco about it. She didn't talk to him much about being his mother but it was necessary in this case. She needed Barry and him to continue the relationship they already had. She didn't want Barry to look on him any differently because he was her son. She didn't want Marco to feel awkward that Barry knew about it. As soon as they had a chance, she was going to take Barry with her and sit down with Marco and talk to him – and tell him that he was going to have a new baby brother or sister!

'Claude! I wasn't expecting you. Come on in, come in.' It was only ten in the morning and Marco had been sitting at his kitchen counter, sipping a cup of tea. He'd been thinking of ringing Claude but hadn't wanted to disturb him too early. And now, here he was like his fairy godmother, at the front door.

'I know I should have rung first, Marco. But I just wanted to see you. I know you've had a tough night so I thought you could do with a boost.' Mimi was yapping frantically, circling Claude's legs in a frenzy, and Marco almost felt like doing the same!

He embraced his visitor in a hug and held on to him tightly. 'Oh, you've no idea how good it is to see you, Claude. I've been home for a few hours now but couldn't sleep a wink.'

'So has there been any more news?' asked Claude, hugging Marco back.

'Not since I tweeted you earlier. I took Stephanie home in a taxi with me, but Dan is still there. God love him, he'll be exhausted if he doesn't come home and get some rest.' Finally releasing his hold on Claude, Marco led the way into his kitchen and filled the kettle with water.

Claude parked himself on a kitchen stool. 'I suppose you'll want to go back up and see her again today? Or will she be allowed visitors?'

'I'm not sure what the protocol is, to be honest, but, yes, I definitely want to go and see her if I can. Even if they make me sit outside the room – at least she'll know I'm there.'

'You're very good to her, Marco. You two are very close, aren't you?'

'We are,' nodded Marco, placing the two mugs of tea on the table. 'Since my folks emigrated to Spain, Maggie has been like a mother to me.'

Claude nodded. 'I suppose I'm getting a sense of the street you raved on about now. I can see how you all pull together at a time of crisis. It's lovely really.'

'Well, thank God for that, Claude. It's a pity it's taken something like this for you to see it, but now maybe you'll realise that I wasn't exaggerating about Enda's. And just wait until everyone else hears about Maggie. They'll all be down to the hospital in a shot to see how she is.'

'So she won't be short of visitors then, will she?'

Marco nodded. 'Maggie is probably the most popular and loved person on the street. Everyone is going to be shocked when they hear what's happened. We're like family to her.'

'I wonder will it make whoever stole that ticket come forward,' said Claude, watching Marco carefully. 'I mean, if everyone is so close, surely whoever took it will feel awful about it under the circumstances.'

'You might have a point there,' said Marco, leaning his elbows on the counter. 'It will be interesting to see what Majella has to say tomorrow.'

'I'd love to be a fly on the wall when you have that conversation! I'd love to hear her admit it was her.'

Marco rubbed his eyes. 'Let's hope she will. After my conversation with her the other day, I'm convinced she's got the ticket. She's a decent person really, so hopefully she'll do what's right.'

'You look shattered, Marco. Should I just go and leave you to go back to bed?'

'Are you joking? If I was going back to bed, you'd be coming with me! But seriously, I *am* knackered but I'd prefer to get through the day and sleep later on tonight.'

'Well, then, how about you get yourself organised and we go out for a few hours. We can grab some lunch somewhere and go and see a movie or something.'

'Oh, I'd love to, Claude, but I'll need to check in with Dan first. I'd hate to abandon him and Stephanie.'

'Well why don't you make a few phonecalls? I'm in no hurry so I can just watch Jeremy Kyle or something while you're organising yourself.'

'Right,' said Marco, jumping up from the stool. 'You go and make yourself comfortable and I'll check in with Dan. I'll have to have a shower though so I might be a while.'

'Take your time, Marco. This little lady will keep me company.' He indicated Mimi, who had settled herself comfortably on Claude's shoe. She'd really taken to him and vice versa. It warmed Marco's heart to see the two of them get on so well.

Marco smiled as Claude took his little cockapoo in his arms, rubbing her lovingly before heading into the sitting room. He shouldn't feel happy, under the circumstances. He should feel sad and upset that his lovely friend was lying in a hospital bed. But he couldn't help it. His new-found relationship with Claude was giving him a feeling like champagne bubbles in his stomach. It was such a wonderful feeling to love someone and have them love you back. He made sure that Claude was out of the way before closing his eyes, blessing himself and offering up a little prayer that he could stay this happy forever.

CHAPTER 36

'Hiya, Rita. I just thought I'd pop in to see if you've heard the news?' It was eleven o'clock and Marco had just been about to leave with Claude when he'd realised that Rita probably didn't know anything about Maggie. He'd asked Claude to hang on for just another few minutes while he slipped down to tell her.

Rita, who was looking frazzled and exhausted in a grubby tracksuit, just stared at Marco. She opened her mouth to say something but no words came out.

'Rita, are you all right? What's wrong?'

'I, em, what news are you talking about, Marco? I haven't heard any news.' Her lip wobbled and she looked as though she might cry, which completely confused Marco.

'Well, for someone who hasn't heard any news, you look pretty upset.'

Rita sighed and opened the door further so Marco could follow her into the kitchen. 'Just tell me, Marco. What is it?'

'Didn't you hear all the commotion last night?' asked Marco, sitting himself down at the kitchen table. He was careful to sit on the edge of the chair, avoiding what looked like dried Weetabix stuck to the seat.

'I didn't hear a thing. I was feeling knackered and fed up so I went to bed early with the two boys. What commotion?'

'The ambulance! Half the street was out to see what was going on.' Marco loved drawing out stories, but Rita didn't look in the mood to humour him.

'Jesus, why? What's happened?'

'Maggie collapsed,' said Marco, delivering the news in the 'ta da' style that only Marco can. 'She just dropped down on the floor right in front of us, Rita. It was awful.'

'Oh, my God,' said Rita, covering her mouth with her hand. 'Is she okay? What's wrong with her?'

'Rita, she's fine. Well maybe not completely fine but it's not as bad as we first thought. She has gallstones. Apparently they've been bothering her for a while and she didn't say anything. She might need an operation but she's going to be okay.'

Rita was still in shock. 'She was only here with me yesterday morning. She said she wasn't feeling well and I wanted to get Dan for her but she insisted she'd be all right. I knew I shouldn't have listened to her – she looked awful!'

She started to cry and Marco quickly went to her and put his arm around her. 'Rita, it's not your fault. You know what Maggie is like. She's her own woman. If she said she didn't want Dan coming over here and fussing, well you could hardly go against her, could you?'

'But she almost collapsed here in the kitchen,' sobbed Rita. 'Maybe if I'd gone and got help at that time, she wouldn't have ended up in such a state.'

'Don't be silly,' said Marco, squatting on his hunkers beside Rita and squeezing her hand. 'Even if you'd gone for Dan, she wouldn't have gone to the hospital at that stage. And she's doing well now, so stop your worrying.'

Rita hiccupped and blew her nose. 'Do you think ... do

you think …' She paused, as if deciding if she should ask the question. 'Do you think stress could have contributed to the illness? I mean, with the ticket and everything and … and any other stuff.'

'I really don't know much about medical stuff, so I couldn't say if it was a factor. The whole ticket debacle has been stressful for everyone.'

'So she didn't talk to you about anything yesterday, did she? I mean, I'm assuming you two didn't have a chance to have a proper chat about things before … you know.'

'Well, when I went down to her yesterday evening, she'd been feeling sick but said she was a lot better. I wanted to tell her my news about me and Claude. He's staying here in Ireland, you know. I wanted her to be the first to know.'

'Oh!' Rita went pale. 'And what did she say about that?'

Marco was a bit put out that Rita didn't seem more delighted for him. 'She was happy about it, of course. But then Lorraine came in and that's when it happened. She just took a funny turn and before we knew it, she was on the floor, out cold.'

'God, it must have been terrifying. And was Stephanie there?'

'She was, poor thing. She must have sobbed solidly for an hour afterwards. I took her home in the early hours of this morning but I've just checked on her now and she's getting organised to go back in. Poor Dan is still at the hospital.'

'Well, God love them all. I'll say a prayer for her. Are you going back in yourself today?'

'I'm off out for a few hours with Claude, but he needs to finish work on the documentary later, so I'll probably go in and see her then.'

'So the documentary – has he told you what's in it yet?'

Marco looked at Rita quizzically. She really was acting

very strange today. 'Well, we know what's in it, Rita, don't we? He'll be editing the bits of footage from here together with some pieces they did elsewhere. Hopefully he's going to make Enda's look like an idealistic place to live!'

Rita stood up suddenly, signalling the end of the conversation. 'Right, well I'd better let you go off then. Just do me a favour, talk to Maggie, will you?'

She'd already headed out towards the door and Marco followed, feeling a little confused. 'Of course I'll talk to her. Are you okay, Rita?'

'No, I mean talk to her properly. Ask her to tell you what we discussed.'

'What do you mean?' asked Marco, alarmed at what Rita said. 'What did you discuss?'

'I have to go,' she said, giving Marco a gentle push out the door. 'Just tell her I told you to ask.'

The door closed, leaving Marco standing there, completely at a loss as to what Rita was going on about. Well, he wasn't going to worry about that now. She'd been acting really strange and he suspected maybe she'd taken some sleeping tablets. If she hadn't heard a thing when the ambulance had come, she must have been in a pretty deep sleep. She probably didn't even really know what she was talking about herself. For now, he had a day with his boyfriend to look forward to, and nothing was going to put a stop to his fun!

'I'm so sorry, Dan. I should have told you. I feel awful that you had to get a fright like that.' Maggie was feeling very fragile, hooked up to various monitors, but she felt stupid for not sharing her doctor's concerns with her husband.

'Maggie, don't let's worry about that now,' soothed Dan, gently rubbing her hand. 'The most important thing is you're going to be okay.'

'I know, but ... but ... what if ... what if ...? I could have been on my own and you or Stephanie could have come home to ... to ...'

'Shhhh now, Maggie. Don't go upsetting yourself. There's absolutely no point in talking about the "what ifs". You're here now and you're going to get the best possible treatment. You'll be home before you know it.'

Maggie raised a weak hand to rub away the tears from her eyes. 'I've been so scared, Dan. I knew the doctor was concerned about my symptoms, so I couldn't help thinking the worst.'

'Shhhhhh, now. Come on, don't be thinking about that now.' Dan rubbed her arm comfortingly.

'I was going to tell you, honestly I was. But with everything else going on in the street, I just kept putting it off. Oh, Dan ...' She burst into sobs and Dan was quick to scoop her gently into his arms.

'I ... I ... was full sure I had cancer or something,' she continued between sobs. 'With the nausea, the dizziness, the pain ... I really thought I was a gonner.'

'Well, thank God it's nothing like that, Maggie. Gallstones are common enough and very treatable. You'll be back to yourself before you know it. And even if you have to have your gallbladder removed, they can do it by keyhole surgery now, so it's really not a big deal.'

'Don't mind me, Dan, I'm just tired and emotional. I feel bad for keeping you all in the dark.'

Dan shook his head. 'It's me who should feel guilty for not taking better care of you.'

Maggie looked at her husband and was touched by the concern on his face. How could she have been so foolish as to ignore something like this? 'Dan, don't ever think you don't take good care of me. I couldn't wish for a better husband. I've no doubt if you'd known there was something amiss, you'd have dragged me down to the hospital before I could blink.'

Dan smiled at his wife. 'That's true. I only wish I'd had the opportunity before all of this.'

'Well, it's getting sorted now and I'm already feeling a lot better so let's look ahead rather than back.'

'Deal!' said Dan, squeezing Maggie's hand and bending over to place a gentle kiss on her cheek. 'Having said that, I was thinking last night about all the goings on in Enda's this past couple of weeks. I'm sure the stress of that hasn't helped you either.'

'Well it has been a bit stressful, I suppose. Between the missing ticket and all that's been going on with Lorraine and Barry, there certainly hasn't been a dull moment.'

Dan shook his head and looked sternly at his wife. 'You take on too much, Mags. Really you do. Barry and Lorraine are big enough and bold enough to sort out their own problems – you shouldn't let yourself get so involved.'

'I can't help it, Dan. It's just my nature. Lorraine is my best friend and you know I'd do anything for my friends.'

'I know, love, but from now on, you've got to start putting yourself first. No more stressing over other people's problems, okay?'

'I'll do my best,' Maggie said, thinking of the whole ticket business and already planning their next move. Now that she knew she didn't have any huge health worries, she was beginning to think about what that money would mean to them.

'And you talk to me about anything that's worrying you or stressing you out from now on,' continued Dan, still watching her carefully.

'Well, now that you mention it, we've really got to get this whole ticket business sorted. I know I'm in here and I know you're going to say it's not important in the scheme of things, but it *is*, Dan. It's important that we find out where the ticket is – that money could help us all in so many ways.'

'Maggie, Maggie, Maggie,' said Dan, looking exasperated. 'Money isn't everything. Your health is what's important now. We can deal with the ticket thing when you're fit and well.'

'I knew you'd say that,' grinned Maggie. 'I know you're right to a certain extent but that would be all well and good if it just involved you and me. There are the others to think about too.'

'Well, let *them* think about it, Maggie. There's nothing you can do from in here. I'll have a word with Marco later and see if he can follow up on things.'

'Marco!' said Maggie suddenly. 'Jesus, I completely forgot about him.'

Dan looked puzzled. 'What are you talking about?'

'Remember my chat with Rita? What with not feeling well and everything, I never got to tell him about Claude. I can't believe it went right out of my head.'

'Maggie, for God's sake! Will you stop stressing yourself out over other people's problems? I feel like I'm talking to the wall!'

'Ah, Dan, don't be like that. You know Marco needs to know about Claude's plans before he starts getting in too deep.'

Dan was quick to answer. 'I agree, Maggie, but I'll have a word with him when I'm chatting to him about the ticket. I'll tell him what Rita said.'

'No, Dan. It would be better coming from me. You know what you're like – you'd only give him snippets of the story. I need to tell him everything she told me so that he can have a clear picture of what that man is really like.'

'Well, I suppose there's no telling you otherwise, is there? I'm sure Marco will be in to see you later. Just make sure you don't get yourself all wound up. Tell him what Rita told you and then leave it to him to sort out, okay?'

'Okay, boss,' smiled Maggie. 'I'll behave myself. Now get yourself off home and get some rest. I'm knackered myself and wouldn't mind a nap.'

'Well, I wouldn't say no to a bit of shuteye, to be honest. Stephanie is coming up with a bag for you. Is there anything else I can bring up later?'

'Just yourself, love. That's all I want.' Maggie put her hand over her husband's, then smiled cheekily. 'But if you want to stick in a bit of washing while you're home, that would be great. There's a pile up on the landing I hadn't got around to sorting.'

'Your wish is my command, Maggie. I'll just go and see if I can see someone to ask them for an update before I go.'

Maggie felt tears in her eyes as Dan bent over to kiss her gently on the forehead. 'Thanks, Dan.'

'What for?' asked Dan, sweeping a stray red curl back behind Maggie's ear.

She grabbed his hand and held it to her lips. 'For just being you, Dan. Thank you for being wonderful, beautiful, caring you!'

CHAPTER 37

Lorraine kissed her husband – a long and passionate kiss. 'See you later, Barry. I'll pick up a DVD this afternoon and we can order a Chinese when you're home.'

'Bye, love,' said Barry, hugging Lorraine tightly. 'I should be in before eight but I'll give you a buzz during the day.'

Lorraine pulled her dressing gown tightly around herself as she stood at the door and watched Barry head off to work. She'd never take their relationship for granted again.

If the past couple of weeks had taught her anything, it was to be honest. If only she'd told Barry about Marco before. If only she'd asked him what was troubling him. If only … she had so many regrets about how she'd handled things but, thankfully, it had all worked out in the end. She and Barry were back on track again, they had no more secrets and the best bit of all was they were going to have a baby.

Closing the front door and heading back upstairs, she thought of Maggie lying in a hospital bed and felt a bit guilty for her happiness. She'd had a text from Dan only an hour ago and it seemed that Maggie was doing well and in good spirits so that was a good thing at least. She'd have a quick shower and head on in to see her.

Buoyed up with the thoughts of a good heart to heart with her friend, she had herself showered and dressed in ten minutes. Pulling her hair back into a ponytail, she applied a light brushing of mineral foundation and a touch of lip-gloss. That would do her. She hardly needed to get glammed up to go to a hospital. She reckoned no matter how bad she looked, she probably couldn't look worse than most of the people in there!

It was a glorious day, so she decided to walk. She'd always been active but not so much of late so she decided to take the longer route in to town. It would probably take her half an hour, but after feeling so sick over the previous few days she felt she could do with the fresh air. Thankfully, she was feeling fine again today but she stuck a plastic bag into her handbag, just in case! But she needn't have worried. All thoughts of being sick left her as she strolled out onto the quays and headed towards the city. As she passed the National Museum, she thought about how lucky they were to live in such a central area with easy access to fantastic amenities. She hadn't been to the museum herself in years but she'd definitely be visiting more when the baby came along. It was never too early to give them a good education.

The hospital was buzzing when she arrived. It must have been dinner time because the smell of cabbage was overwhelming, as was the rattle of plates and cutlery. Lorraine was praying they'd let her in. They'd become very strict about visitors in the hospitals with all these superbugs flying about. She'd brought up a bag with a few bits in so that if they tried to stop her, she'd say she was bringing in some stuff to her friend.

Maggie was in a different room to the one she'd been in the previous night, but Dan's precise directions led her right to the door. She hovered outside for a moment, worried about what she might see. She was so used to Maggie being the life and soul of the street. She was everyone's rock and Lorraine couldn't bear the thought of seeing her looking fragile and sick. She took a deep breath and pushed the door.

'Ah, Lorraine, howareya. Brilliant timing! Steph came up a half hour ago but is already gone to the coffee shop. You know young people – they just can't hack it in places like this!'

Lorraine breathed a sigh of relief when she saw Maggie looking, not exactly healthy, but much brighter than she'd expected. 'Maggie, oh God, we were so worried. How are you feeling now?' She launched herself at her friend and hugged her tightly.

'Steady on,' laughed Maggie. 'I may be on the mend but I'm not sure body-surfing me is the way to go!'

'Jesus, sorry, Mags. I'm just so happy to see you looking bright and sitting up. I expected … you know … I don't know what I expected actually, but it wasn't this.'

'Well, if you'd come in an hour or two ago, it might have been different. I had all sorts of stuff attached to me. But they seem to be happy with my progress so they've removed some of it.'

'That's brilliant, Maggie,' said Lorraine, pulling up a stool to sit beside the bed. 'And how's the pain?'

'I know it sounds mad, but I'm actually feeling better than I have in weeks. They have me on this thing' – she pointed to a drip attached to her left arm – 'and not only has it taken the pain away but it's giving me the greatest buzz I've had in ages!'

Lorraine giggled at her friend. 'Good for you, Maggie! Seriously, though, I'm so relieved to see you looking better.

We got such a shock last night – we didn't know what to think.'

'It must have been awful for you all,' said Maggie. 'I had the easiest part to play! Once I was out cold, I knew nothing about what was going on!'

'You're unbelievable, Maggie. Always thinking of other people. And I'm so sorry I had to leave last night. I felt really guilty leaving the others, but I really wasn't feeling well.'

'Were you not, Lorraine? What was up with you? Come to think of it, you were coming over to tell us something last night before the incident, weren't you?'

'I was, Maggie, but that's not important now.'

'Ah, go on out of that, Lorraine McGrath. Sure saying that to me is like dangling sweets in front of a baby! Come on! Tell me, what's the news? If I remember correctly, you said you had a heart to heart with Barry?'

'Well …' Lorraine said, slowly. 'I did have a heart to heart with him and I told him *everything*!'

'Oh, my God,' said Maggie, her eyes out on stalks. 'Did you really? Did you tell him about Marco? What did he say?'

'He was surprisingly okay with it. Can you believe that? All my worrying was for nothing. If only I'd told him years ago!'

'Well, he knows now, and that's the most important thing. He must have been a bit shocked though.'

Lorraine nodded. 'He was shocked, surprised, hurt – but as I filled him in on the whole story, he said he just felt sorry for all I'd been through.'

'Well, fair play to him for that. He could have been very upset with you for keeping something like that to yourself. He's gone way up in my estimation.'

'Why? Had your estimation of him gone down or

something, Maggie?' Lorraine felt concerned. She hated the thought that her friends might think anything but good things about her husband. Things were good again and she didn't want anything to burst her happy bubble.

'Well, if I'm honest, I haven't thought very good things about him recently.' Maggie watched her friend carefully. 'From what you've been telling me, he wasn't behaving very well. Did you manage to get to the bottom of that?'

Lorraine smiled. 'You won't believe this, Maggie, but it all came about from him overhearing one of our conversations. He came in one day when you and I were talking about Marco and from what he heard, he thought I was having an affair and you were persuading me to tell him!'

'Oh, Jesus Christ Almighty!' said Maggie, her eyes opening wide. 'I don't believe it! Oh, now I just feel sorry for him. Can you imagine what he must have thought if he overheard half of what we were saying? The poor fella.'

'That's exactly what I thought when I heard,' said Lorraine, relieved that Maggie understood his dilemma. She'd forgiven her husband for his behaviour and she needed her friends to do the same. 'The past few weeks were just one big misunderstanding. Thank God it's all sorted now.'

'Well, thank God for that is right.' Maggie's smile faded again and she looked thoughtful.

'Are you okay, Maggie? Do you need me to get someone?' Lorraine felt panicked when she saw the look on her friend's face.

'No, no, I'm okay, Lorraine. It's just that I was talking to Rita on Saturday and there's probably something you should know.'

Lorraine felt suddenly anxious. She'd learned by now that life never seemed to run entirely smoothly for her and she almost expected something to happen to put a dint in her happiness. 'What is it? Come on, tell me. Is it something bad?'

Maggie looked at her and opened her mouth to speak, then seemed to think better of it.

'Come on, Maggie. You need to practise what you preach. If there's something I need to know, you have to tell me. No more secrets. Is it something about Barry?'

'Ah, no, it's nothing like that. It's just … it's just the ticket thing. Rita and I are convinced it's Majella. I know Marco was dead sure about it, but I had my doubts at first.'

'Oh,' said Lorraine, feeling relieved that Maggie hadn't something more sinister to tell her. 'I can't say I'm entirely convinced myself, to be honest, but it will be interesting to see what happens when Majella comes home tomorrow.'

'It certainly will. Well, since it looks like I'll be stuck in here for a while yet, I'll have to leave it up to you lot to try and sort it out. Try to get a meeting organised again and see if you can suss Majella out.'

'We'll look after it, Maggie. You just concentrate on getting better. We all want to get to the bottom of the mystery and get our hands on that ticket, so I can assure you we'll be doing all we can.'

'Good girl,' said Maggie. 'Maybe when I come out of this place, I'll be in the money and can think of heading off somewhere nice and warm to recuperate. Wouldn't that be lovely?'

'Oh, God, a holiday – yes, that would be perfect. Although …' Lorraine paused for effect. 'I'm not entirely sure I'd be up to the travelling.'

Maggie shot her a quizzical look. 'And why wouldn't you be? Don't tell me you've got some secret medical condition too! What are we like?'

'Well, it's a condition all right, Maggie. But a good one! Barry and I are expecting our first baby. Well, his first … our first together … you know what I mean!'

'Oh, Lorraine, that's brilliant news. How fabulous. And what does Barry think? Is he thrilled?'

'He's over the moon, Maggie. We both are. I know I was nervous and unsure about the whole baby thing but I honestly couldn't be happier. We're going to be a proper little family. It just feels … I don't know … right, I suppose!'

'How did you manage to slip past me then?' A stern-looking nurse had just come in and had her hands on hips, glaring at Lorraine. 'Maggie isn't really up to visitors at the moment.'

'I'm fine, nurse,' said Maggie, jumping to Lorraine's defence. 'And she was only bringing me up some stuff I needed.' She indicated the Tesco bag on the floor.

'All right then,' said the nurse, her face softening a little. 'But I think you should get some more rest now, Maggie. The doctor will be around to see you again shortly.'

Lorraine stood up. 'Sorry about that, nurse, I won't keep her any longer.' She turned to Maggie. 'I'm delighted you seem to be on the mend. Let me know if there's anything you need and I'll be up again tomorrow.'

'Bye, love,' said Maggie, putting her arms around Lorraine, who'd bent down to kiss her. 'And I'm delighted for you, really I am. I can't wait to get out of here and start shopping for baby stuff with you.'

'Ah, it's a bit early for that, but there'll be nothing stopping us from talking babies! I can't wait for you to impart your wisdom on me!'

'Well, you get in some of those jam biscuits I like and I'll be down for a chat as soon as I get out of here.'

The nurse, who was checking Maggie's blood pressure, cleared her throat loudly, leaving Lorraine in no doubt that she should be gone.

'Right, I'm definitely going this time. Look after yourself, Maggie.' Lorraine gave the nurse a sickeningly sweet smile before heading out the door with a spring in her step.

Maggie was glad she hadn't told Lorraine that Claude had her private conversation on tape with a view to using it in a documentary. God, she still couldn't believe that Claude had been so manipulative. She'd really thought he was into Marco. Maybe he was – but he had a funny way of showing it! But whatever about keeping it from Lorraine, there was no doubt Marco needed to know.

She dreaded telling him. It was such a pity she hadn't found out about Claude's plans earlier – maybe she could have warned Marco before he'd fallen head over heels for this guy. Well, she'd put it right now, no matter how it hurt him. In the long run, it would be better for him to know.

She'd told Dan that she wouldn't stress herself out about anyone else's problems, but she just couldn't help it. He knew she was going to talk to Marco about Claude and not get involved in anything else, but she still couldn't help worrying about the ticket. Something just didn't feel right.

The truth was, she wasn't sure it *was* Majella who'd taken it. She'd been trying to piece together the events of that night when she'd put the slip of paper with the numbers out on the table and asked who was going to do the numbers next. She'd tried to remember who might have taken it. She'd tried very hard to picture somebody actually taking the slip and saying they'd do it. But all she could remember was feeling dizzy and praying to God that she wouldn't keel over. She'd only sipped on a Diet Coke all night and even at that, she'd felt very close to throwing it up. The trouble was, the night had been a blur and no matter how hard she tried, she just couldn't remember anything.

She tried to turn in the bed but the drip attached to her arm made it difficult. Despite putting on a show for her family and friends, she felt very vulnerable. She hated being so helpless and wasn't used to not being in control.

But Maggie was a firm believer in fate. Sometimes life dealt you a hand that seemed unfair or one you didn't think you could cope with. Maggie's mother had instilled in her the belief that everything happened for a reason. She'd seen her mother yesterday – but thankfully she'd only come to visit, not to take her away. She now had a chance to grasp life with both hands. How many people got a second chance like that? When she was well again and out of here, she'd make sure that not a single moment was ever wasted. Her life was good, but she was going to make damn sure that, from now on, it would be amazing!

CHAPTER 38

At six o'clock exactly, Marco strolled through the front door of the hospital, hands in pockets and humming to himself. He'd had such a fabulous day with Claude that nothing could stop him from smiling, not even visiting Maggie in hospital.

Of course, he'd be completely devastated if Maggie was really sick but thankfully, gallstones were fixable. Lorraine had reported that she'd seen her earlier and she was in great form. And that wasn't all that Lorraine had told him!

Fancy her telling Barry about him being her son after all this time. It didn't bother Marco one bit that people knew, but he respected Lorraine's feelings on the subject. He'd never really thought of Lorraine as his mother. Yes, biologically, she was the one who gave birth to him, but that was where the nurturing ended. His *real* parents were his grandparents who'd brought him up. He'd had a brilliant upbringing and didn't have any bad feelings at all towards Lorraine. He loved her as a sister and, thankfully, they'd grown to be friends.

Thank God Barry had taken it all so well. Marco liked him – Barry could be a bit offhand at times, but he looked after Lorraine well and they were perfectly matched. He'd been acting very strange lately and that had worried Marco, too, but Lorraine had filled him in on their chat and it looked like it had all been a huge misunderstanding.

Just outside Maggie's ward, Marco rolled up the sleeves of his red and grey checked shirt before dispensing some of the hospital disinfectant into his hands. He was paranoid about hospitals and always worried he'd take home some disease or other if he wasn't careful!

'Maggie, thank God!' he said, making a beeline to hug his friend. Dan, who was sitting on an uncomfortable-looking chair at her side, looked tired and strained.

'Well, you're a sight for sore eyes,' said Maggie, hugging him back. 'I thought you'd never get here to rescue me from my nagging husband.'

'Ah, Mags, I'm only trying to look after you – you know that.' Dan looked hurt.

'I'm only joking, you big eejit!' Maggie gave him a playful slap. 'Sure, I'd be lost without you.'

Marco shuffled uncomfortably. 'Should I maybe go and get a coffee and let you two have a bit more time together? I probably should have said I was coming, but I didn't think.'

'Don't be silly, Marco,' said Dan, getting up off the chair. 'Sit yourself down there. I'll go and have a coffee myself and you two can have a natter.'

Marco sat down gratefully. 'Well, if you're sure?'

'Of course. But remember, Maggie – no stressing yourself out over stuff. I'll be back in twenty minutes or so.'

'He means well but he's driving me insane!' said Maggie, after her husband left the room. 'He won't let me mention the lotto ticket or Lorraine's stuff with Barry or anything that he thinks will stress me out!'

Marco laughed. 'But he's probably right, Mags. You do

worry over everyone else's problems. You should really be concentrating on getting yourself well again.'

'I know, Marco, but the best medicine for me is a good old natter. You know how I love hearing all the news.'

'I know, Maggie. Well, the news is all good with me so Dan shouldn't have a problem with me updating you.'

'Go on, what's happened now?' Maggie's face looked serious all of a sudden and Marco wondered if maybe Dan was right and he shouldn't be bothering her about stuff.

'It's nothing really … just me and Claude … and how things are going so well …'

Maggie shifted in the bed and reached for a glass of water on the locker. Marco grabbed it and handed it to her. She looked distracted. 'Are you okay? Are you in pain or something? Should I get the doctor?'

'No, I'm fine, Marco. Tell me about you and Claude.'

Marco watched her carefully. 'Are you sure? I wouldn't want to bore you with the details if—'

'Just bloody well *tell me*, Marco!'

Marco was hurt by Maggie's uncharacteristic outburst. 'Maggie, what's wrong? Is there something up? Have I done something to upset you?' He was shocked at Maggie's fury.

'Sorry, Marco. I didn't mean to shout at you but I can't keep it in any longer. I really need to tell you.'

'Tell me what, Maggie?' Marco was alarmed. Maybe she was a lot more ill than she was making out. Oh, God, he prayed it wasn't too serious.

'Claude is a fraud!'

Marco was completely thrown by Maggie's statement and began to giggle uncontrollably. 'What's this? Poetry hour?'

Maggie's face was serious. 'Marco, you need to listen to me. Claude is not what he's pretending to be.'

'What? What do you mean?' Marco began to realise that Maggie wasn't messing about. 'What are you saying, Maggie?'

'Oh, Marco, I hate to be the one to tell you, but I want you to hear the full facts. Dan was going to tell you so that I wouldn't get het up about it all and I wouldn't worry, but I told him that—'

'*Maggie*! Just tell me, for feck's sake!'

'All right, Marco. I'll tell you exactly what happened and I'll leave you to draw your own conclusions.' Maggie began with what Lorraine had told her, then her visit to Rita the previous morning. She proceeded to tell him every last bit of their conversation, being careful not to leave anything out.

Marco sat there, speechless. He couldn't believe what he was hearing. He kept hoping there'd be an explanation at the end of it, but it seemed that the only explanation was that Claude had been using him. He was gutted. He felt as though somebody had punched him in the stomach.

'Are you okay?' asked Maggie, kindly, placing her hand over Marco's. 'You've gone very pale. Oh, God, maybe I shouldn't have told you.'

Marco opened his mouth to say something but no words came out. Instead, his eyes filled with tears and one by one, they began to spill out. He couldn't help himself.

'Jesus, Marco, I'm so sorry.' Maggie reached over and pulled a clump of tissues out of the box on her locker and handed them to her friend. 'Say something, will you?'

Marco gulped for air and wiped his eyes with the tissues. 'Oh, Maggie, I knew it was too good to be true. I just can't believe it.'

'Marco, you need to talk to him. I'm just telling you what

Rita told me but you'll need to find out exactly what his plan is. Maybe we have it all wrong.'

'Do you *really* think we have it wrong, Maggie?' asked Marco, blowing his nose. 'Does it sound like we got the wrong end of the stick?'

'Well, it doesn't, no. But it's probably still worth talking to him.'

'And to think I was delighted that he was showing such an interest in what was going on in my life! He always said he wasn't interested in money, so I was chuffed that he was showing such an interest in the lotto win and the lost ticket. So all this time, he was just doing research for this … this *programme.'*

'Now, Marco, you don't know that yet. Don't go jumping to any conclusions.'

But Marco was jumping ten steps ahead and wasn't listening. 'I wonder when this idea of his began to form. Maybe he was never into me at all. Maybe his intention all along was to get a juicy bit of gossip from me that he could use to make us all look like fools!'

'Marco, Marco, stop it!' Maggie looked alarmed. 'You and Claude had formed a bond long before the lotto was won, so you can't say he'd been planning this for ages. But for whatever reason, Claude is now putting together a documentary that will show us all in a terrible light rather than the lovely documentary that we thought was being made.'

Marco was trying to make sense of it all but Maggie's words were just whirring around in his head, until suddenly he slapped his hand down on the bed. 'He was the one, Maggie. He was the one who put the thought in my head.'

'You've lost me now,' said Maggie, taking a sip of her water.

'Remember on that first night when I met him in the Westbury? Well, he was the one who suggested that somebody had robbed the ticket rather than it being lost. I told him at the time that it was ridiculous and I wouldn't even consider it, but I did. I came straight over to you and told you.'

'Yes,' said Maggie, nodding her head. 'And I went over to Lorraine the next morning and told her! It looks like your man may have purposefully set the cat amongst the pigeons!'

'I can't believe it, Maggie. I've been such a fool. Imagine me thinking that he was madly in love with me. Imagine me believing that I could be so blissfully happy with him. Imagine me believing in fairytales!'

'Ah, Marco, it may not be as bad as you—'

'No, Maggie! Don't sympathise with me. I'm not going to cry another tear over that ... that ratbag! How dare he play with my feelings like that. And how dare he lie to us all the way he has!'

'So what are you going to do? Will you talk to him?'

Marco's lip trembled again and his previous angry state began to melt into one of hurt. 'I honestly don't know. But one thing is for sure, it's the end of us. No matter what he says, I can't get over the fact that he used me for information when I was clearly so into him. I wonder if he felt anything for me at all.'

'Marco, I think you need to sleep on it,' said Maggie, kindly. 'You're probably reading too much into it. Talk to him and see what he says. And, for what it's worth, I've seen how he looks at you. And it's definitely not the look of a man who feels nothing.'

'Thanks, Maggie. You're very good to say that. Well, regardless of whether he felt or feels something for me, I can't get past the fact that he's putting a documentary together that's going to make us a laughing stock. I want nothing more to do with him. I love Enda's and my friends far too much to ignore what he's doing.'

'This is all looking very serious,' said Dan, appearing back at the door of the room. 'So what are you two talking about?'

Maggie shot her husband a warning look and despite his upset, Marco couldn't help feeling amused. 'I've just been filling Marco in on my conversation with Rita yesterday. He's a bit upset about it.'

'Oh, yes,' said Dan, awkwardly. 'Terrible business, that.'

Marco stood up. 'It is, Dan. It's an awful mess. I'm just sorry that I brought that ... that ... pig into our lives.'

'Ah, Marco,' said Maggie. 'Don't go off like that. Stay for another while and let's talk it through.'

'Maggie, you have other things to worry about so let me handle Claude.' Marco bent to kiss her. 'And you did the right thing in telling me. It would have been awful if things had gone any further and if I'd *really* fallen for him!'

Maggie looked concerned. 'Well, as I said, sleep on it and don't do anything rash.'

Marco was at the door. 'You look after yourself, Maggie, or at least let your husband look after you. I'll be back up tomorrow at some stage.'

His head was in a spin as he walked out the main door of the hospital. He still couldn't believe that his lovely Claude had turned out to be such a horrible person. How could he have treated him like that? How could he have lied just to get a good story? Marco had never been intimate with someone the way he'd been with Claude and tears stung his eyes again as he thought of the lovely moments they'd shared.

He zipped his beige leather jacket higher up around his
chin and stuck his hands in his pockets and he walked in the
direction of home. And all this business about coming home
to Ireland. He'd probably planned to come home anyway
and it had suited his plan to pretend Marco had been the
reason. All of a sudden, Marco was exhausted. All he wanted
to do was curl up in his bed with Mimi at his feet and sleep.
Maggie was right. He needed to sleep on it. He'd turn his
phone off and lock his door. If Claude tried to see him
or speak to him tonight, he'd have a hard job. Marco was
turning the tables and this time, *he* was in charge. *He'd* decide
if and when he'd talk to Claude. He wouldn't let his guard
down ever, ever again.

CHAPTER 39

Tuesday, 20th September

'Okay, okay, keep your knickers on!' Marco pulled his robe tightly around him as he rushed downstairs. It was only nine o'clock but he'd been woken up by a loud banging on the door. He disarmed the alarm and pulled back the chain before turning the key. 'Jesus, give me a chance to—'

'Hello, Marco. You wouldn't answer your phone so I had to come.'

'C– Claude. I wasn't ... I didn't ... what are you doing here?'

'Well aren't you going to let me in?'

Marco reluctantly held open the door. He'd turned his phone off at around midnight, having refused to answer it or return any of the text messages Claude had sent. He'd been so upset by Maggie's revelations that he'd tossed and turned most of the night before falling into a fitful sleep.

'So what's up, Marco?' Claude followed Marco into the little kitchen. 'Is it Maggie? I've been worried sick about you – I know how close you two are. She's not ...?'

Marco plonked himself down on a stool and looked at the man he'd thought he'd been in love with. 'Maggie's fine. She's going to be in there for a while yet, but she's doing well.'

'Well, that's good,' said Claude, sitting down beside him. 'But why the bloody hell have you not answered any of my calls? I thought we were going to see each other last night. I rang you a million times and left loads of messages.'

Marco leaned his elbows on the table and put his head in his hands. He wished he hadn't opened the door now. He wished he was more prepared. If he'd known he was going to see Claude this morning, he'd have planned what he was going to say to him. He'd never been much good at ad-libbing.

'*Marco*! Talk to me. What's wrong?'

Marco took his hands down from his face and looked Claude in the eye. He wanted to cry. He wanted to be told it had all been a misunderstanding. He wanted Claude to put his arms around him and make it all okay. But despite all that, he was angry. How dare Claude trample on his feelings like that? How bloody dare he? So instead of tears, he fixed him with a cold, steely look that made Claude visibly squirm. 'I know what you're doing here, Claude. I know about your plans.'

Claude looked confused. 'What I'm doing here? I'm here to see why you wouldn't answer my calls. What plans?'

'Don't come the innocent with me and try and twist things around,' spat Marco, banging his fist on the counter in a very un-Marco-like fashion. 'I mean, I know what you're up to.'

'Marco, what's got into you? I honestly haven't got a clue what you're talking about.' Marco noted that Claude did look taken aback but he wasn't going to be fooled.

'I know about your little *arrangement* with Rita! I know about your secret meetings and I know how you've been using me!' Marco felt his voice wobble but he was determined to hold it together.

'Ah, Marco, no – you've got it all wrong.' Mimi, who'd been sleeping in her basket at the back door, woke up with the raised voices and began yapping at their feet. Claude bent down to pet her. 'You're such a cutie, Mimi, aren't you? And your daddy must have washed you today – look how clean and shiny you are.'

Marco could feel his blood boil. Claude was obviously playing for time. 'Have I, Claude? Have I got it all wrong? Are you telling me it isn't true – that you didn't have secret meetings with Rita about a different documentary entirely?'

'Well, I'm not saying I didn't meet up with her, but … it's just—'

'That's all I needed to know, Claude. I just needed to hear it from your own lips.'

'Marco, no, I'm telling you, you're not seeing the full picture.'

'Well, paint it for me then,' Marco said, standing up and pacing up and down the room, much to Mimi's delight. The little cockapoo seemed to think it was a game and was gleefully weaving herself back and forth around Marco's feet.

Claude sighed and looked dejected. 'You've got to understand, Marco, that RIP is my employer. If they tell me to do something, I've damn well got to do it or they'll make me pay!'

'That's a load of bullshit, Claude, and you know it! Aren't you leaving the job? Are you telling me that they *made* you do it?'

'Well, no, not exactly … well, sort of …'

'For feck's sake, Claude! Can't you even answer a straight question? Well, maybe then you can confirm or deny this!

Rita said that you approached her and asked her if she'd be interested in giving her story about the missing lotto ticket. She said that you wanted a "warts and all" piece, telling how St Enda's Terrace was falling apart because of the lotto win and how the previously friendly street was turning into a nightmare, with everyone blaming each other on losing or robbing the ticket!' Marco could feel his face getting redder and redder and his voice getting higher and higher with every word. Even Mimi had retreated to her basket, obviously realising that the game wasn't so much fun after all.

Claude fidgeted with the buttons on his jacket which he still hadn't taken off and wouldn't meet Marco's eye.

'So it's true then?' asked Marco, almost reaching hysterical proportions. 'It's true that you've been conning us into thinking you were making a nice documentary?'

'I'm sorry, Marco. I'm really, really sorry. Yes, I did interview Rita for a new documentary about the missing ticket but—'

'Right! That's all I need to know.' Marco opened the kitchen door and gestured for Claude to leave. 'You're not welcome here, Claude. And I suspect you won't be welcome anywhere on the street when word gets out about what you've been doing.'

'Marco, don't be like that. Just give me a chance to—'

'*For fuck's sake, just go!*'

Claude hopped down from the stool and his face was red and strained. But as he walked down the hall to the front door, he turned to Marco. 'You know, I'm glad this came out, Marco, because it's made you show your true colours.'

'*Me* show *my* true colours? Jesus Christ, don't make me laugh!'

'It's true,' spat Claude, his look of bewilderment replaced

with one of anger. 'I thought you were such a lovely, generous guy. I thought you were mild-mannered and loving, and always saw the good in people. But look at you now, jumping to conclusions and not even bothering to hear my side of things. I'm well out of this sham of a relationship!'

'You've just taken the words out of my mouth, Claude. I'm so glad I've realised what you're like, and I'm so happy things didn't go any further with us.'

'Well, that makes two of us!' Claude continued to the front door. 'You're nothing but a fake – somebody who pretends to be the nice guy when really the demon is just lurking beneath the surface. Good riddance *Mark* Gallagher!'

'Oh, now you're just being childish! And you're still trying to make me believe that Claude is your *real* name? Are you still pretending that your parents christened you with a name like that? I bet it's Bob or Joe or Frank, or something!' Marco knew he was sounding silly but things were so far gone now that he didn't care. He hated the name he'd been christened with and he'd reinvented himself as Marco from a very early age.

'Believe what you want, *Mark*! I'm beyond caring. And to think I was giving up so much for you. I'm so bloody glad this has all come out now.' He went to open the front door but Marco put a hand out to stop him.

'Before you go, Claude, I just want you to know that you were never going to be any more than an experiment for me really. I don't do relationships and I was quite interested to see how it felt.'

Claude's face crumpled a little. 'Marco, you don't mean that.'

'Oh, I do. But one good thing has come out of it all – it's confirmed to me why I don't do the whole relationship thing.

It's just not for me. So go on, off you go. And don't bother coming back.' He pulled the door open wide, leaving Claude in no doubt that the conversation was over.

Claude opened his mouth to say something, but no words came out. He stood rooted to the spot for a moment before pushing past Marco and out the door. He strode down the path without a backward glance before Marco slammed the door shut.

Alone in the hall, Marco's resolve crumbled and the tears finally came. He rushed up the stairs and threw himself on his bed, sobbing into his pillow. How would he ever get over this? Life would never be the same again. He'd loved Claude so much. They'd only known each other a short time but he'd really fallen for him. He cursed the day he'd first come across him and bloody RIP Productions. It was unbelievable to think how quickly things could change. Only yesterday he'd been deliriously happy, feeling fulfilled and in love, and today his life was falling apart. Shite, shite, *shite*!

Marco blinked in the glaring sun as he emerged from the house. After Claude had left, he'd spent a good hour wallowing in self-pity. He'd snotted and snivelled and had almost thrown Mimi halfway across the room when she'd proceeded to jump on the bed and lick the stream coming from his nose.

He'd only managed to cop on to himself when he'd received a text from Maggie, worried that she'd upset him. When he'd thought of his friend in hospital and how *she* was worrying about *him*, he'd got himself up and into the shower and had been determined to pull himself together.

It was almost midday and he'd decided to venture out with

Mimi. The fresh air would clear his head. He hadn't been able to reduce the red puffiness around his eyes and the sun wasn't helping either, but he was determined not to cry another tear for Claude.

He was about to turn right from his gate and head out of the estate when he looked up into the little cul-de-sac and noticed Majella's car parked in her driveway. So, she was back! Well, he'd go for his walk and have a think about what he was going to say because one thing was for sure, he was going to make sure she paid for the upset she'd caused.

As he walked, his emotions were whirring around and around in his head and he felt so angry he was fit to burst! How *dare* Claude treat him like that – how bloody *dare* he! How *dare* Majella take that ticket and wave it in their faces by going off on a luxury few days when all hell was breaking out on Enda's! Bloody bitch! And why should she be allowed sit in her house, no doubt with her feet up, drinking coffee, painting her nails, watching daytime telly? He stopped suddenly. Why should she indeed! Well maybe it was about time he hit her with a bit of reality.

Turning around, he began to stride purposefully towards Majella's house. In contrast to Marco's anger, Mimi was snoring peacefully in his arms, oblivious to what was about to unfold. He took the driveway in a few long steps and banged with his fists on the door, ignoring the doorbell and knocker.

'Jesus, Marco, are you trying to bang the door down or something?' said Majella, opening the door in a white towelling robe.

Marco was momentarily shocked to see his neighbour looking tired and haggard, considering she'd just had a few days of pampering, but he pushed past her nonetheless. 'Never mind that. I think we need to have a little chat.'

'Jesus, Marco. Who's rattled your cage? What's up with you?'

'I'm not going to pussyfoot around, Majella. It's you, isn't it? And think carefully before you answer because we've all talked about it and come to the same conclusion.'

Majella stared at him in confusion. 'It's me what, Marco? What conclusion? Come on in and have a cup of tea and stop talking in riddles.'

Marco followed her into the kitchen but wasn't backing down. 'Don't pretend you don't know what I'm talking about. You have the ticket, haven't you? You've taken the lotto ticket. Well, just so that you know, there's a solicitor involved now, so you'll just get yourself into a whole load of trouble if you try to claim the money for yourself.'

'Have you gone completely mental?' asked Majella, plonking herself down on a stool at the counter. 'Of course I haven't bloody well got the ticket! What on earth makes you think that I have?'

'Stop trying to deny it!' Marco refused to sit down, deciding he'd feel more in control if he stood. 'You're the only one who hasn't bothered to ask about the ticket when everyone else has been hysterical about it. I spent a good hour in your house last week and not once did you ask about the ticket or if there were any developments.'

'Oh, for God's sake, Marco. That doesn't mean anything. Maybe I had a lot more on my mind.'

'One million euro, Majella! Surely something like that would take prime position in your mind, no matter what else was going on! You don't just forget about winning an amount of money like that.' Mimi had woken up with all the shouting and Marco opened the back door to let her outside.

Majella's face turned red and she looked close to tears.

Marco took it to be a sign of guilt. 'And then there's your little luxury weekend too,' he continued. 'I thought you were as strapped for cash as the rest of us. How on earth could you afford something like that unless you were rolling in it?'

'Get out, Marco! Get *the fuck* out of my house!'

Marco was a little taken aback at the ferocity of Majella's words.

'Did you hear me? Fuck off back to your little group of gossips and if you come near me again, I'm calling the police!'

'Well, there's no need for that sort of—'

'*Fuck off!*'

'Right, right, I'm going,' said Marco, rushing to the back door where Mimi was watching the exchange and scooping her up in his arms. 'You haven't heard the end of this, though. I'll be talking to the others later and we'll be deciding how to handle things.'

Majella didn't say another word but shooed Marco out the front door.

Marco was completely taken by surprise by her outburst. 'You know, this is not looking good for—' But it was too late. Majella had slammed the door in his face, leaving him standing with his mouth open on the doorstep.

That had been way too weird. He hadn't known what to expect because he hadn't really thought the whole thing out, but somehow he'd thought Majella would have broken down and sobbed her confession to him. He'd expected that she'd have produced the ticket and apologised profusely for her indiscretion. They would have all been cross with her, but would have celebrated having the ticket in their hands at last.

He wandered back to his house in a daze. His anger had somehow dissipated and he was feeling unsure about everything. Would Majella have got so upset and angry if he'd been right? Oh, God, imagine he'd accused her like that and she was innocent. As he turned the key in the door, he thought about Claude. He'd never really given him a chance to explain himself this morning either. What if he was wrong about him, too? Well, he obviously wasn't completely wrong because Claude himself had admitted to part of it at least. Maybe he'd talk to him and give him a chance to explain. But not yet. He had other priorities. He'd let things settle down over the next few days and then maybe he'd contact Claude and they could meet up for a chat over the weekend.

It was only lunchtime and so much had already happened. He was looking forward to going back to work tomorrow. He'd rung in sick yesterday and today because of Maggie but he was really pining for a bit of normality away from what was turning into a nightmare of a street! He opened the back door and went outside with Mimi. Sitting down heavily on a white plastic chair, he breathed in the smell of lavender from the garden and immediately felt a little calmer. He'd always believed in positive thinking, so he was going to try to turn things around. With a bit of luck, by the end of the week they'd have the ticket back and maybe he and Claude would have sorted a few things out. He wouldn't be rushing to take him back or anything, but maybe when they both had a few days to calm down, they could talk to each other like adults. Ah, yes, things weren't looking so bad after all!

CHAPTER 40

Dan looked in the mirror as he washed his hands in the little downstairs toilet. He barely recognised himself. He seemed to have acquired a number of new grey hairs in just the past few days. That was the trouble with having such jet-black hair – every single grey one stood out like a sore thumb. His face was pale and his eyes were red and bloodshot, showing the strain of recent events.

He wished Marco would hurry up. He had Lorraine and Rita waiting in the kitchen but he didn't want to get started until they were all there. He'd texted them all soon after coming back from the hospital an hour ago and asked them to come around for a meeting. Majella had shocked him by texting that they could all go to hell! What on earth was that all about?

He felt almost sick with anxiety. What would they all say? How would they react? It seemed to be one drama after the other at the moment, and he'd briefly toyed with the idea of not saying anything for a while, but it needed to be said. He was drying his hands just as the doorbell rang.

'Come in,' said Dan, opening the door wide for Marco. 'The others are already here, so I won't keep you all long.'

'Thanks, Dan. Sorry I'm late but I fell asleep out in the garden and didn't see the text until I woke up.'

'Don't worry about it.' Dan paused before entering the kitchen. 'I'm sure it was an awful shock to you to hear about Claude yesterday. If there's anything I can do?' He rubbed Marco's shoulder awkwardly. He was never one for the grand gestures – Maggie was the one to offer the big bear hugs and always knew the right words to say. Dan was already feeling the pressure of the big shoes he had to fill while his wife was in hospital.

Rita and Lorraine were already sitting drinking tea at the kitchen table and Marco gratefully sat and poured himself a cup from the old blue Denby teapot. 'So what's this all about, Dan? Is Maggie okay?'

Dan was quick to nod his head. 'Maggie is doing great. All the indications are good. I've just been on the phone to her and I'm heading in to her in a bit. I … I just needed to talk to you all first.'

'So, go on then,' said Rita, checking her watch. 'I don't want to leave Stephanie with the boys for too long.'

'She'll be fine, Rita. She's been dying to start babysitting, so it will be a good test for her and if there's a problem, she knows we're only a few steps away.' Dan had wanted to make sure they could all be there to hear what he had to say so he'd sent Stephanie around to Rita's to allow her to come over. It was a pity Majella wasn't there, but he couldn't worry about her now.

'What's this all about, Dan?' asked Lorraine, shifting uncomfortably on her chair. 'I want to get back to Barry soon too. He's working a late shift so I want us to have a bit of time together before he goes in. I want to take full advantage of these few days off work.'

'Right,' said Dan, sitting himself down at the top of the table. 'I called you all here to talk about the missing ticket.'

'That bloody ticket,' said Rita, shaking her head. 'Will we ever get to the bottom of it?'

'Well … I have a confession to make,' said Marco, looking down at the table.

'Jesus,' said Lorraine. 'What confession?'

Rita's jaw dropped open. '*You?*'

Dan was confused for a moment before realisation dawned. 'Ladies, ladies, Marco doesn't have the ticket because—'

'For feck's sake! Of course I don't have the ticket. What I was going to tell you is that I've had a bit of a run in with Majella this morning about it. I sort of went down there accusing her of taking it!'

'*Marco!*' Lorraine glared at him. 'We agreed to approach it carefully. Oh, God, what did she say?'

Marco looked mortified. 'Well she wasn't too happy about it.'

'But did she admit to anything?' asked Rita, her eyes out on stalks.

'Well, no, but she did get very angry. She used some choice language and practically threw me out of the house!'

Rita clasped her hands together. 'Well, that's a bloody guilty woman for sure! So what are we going to do about her?'

'Hold on, everyone.' Dan held up his hand to stop the conversation going any further. 'I didn't know about Marco's confrontation with Majella so it's not why I called you here. Although it does explain the text I got from her just a little while ago.'

Rita and Lorraine gasped when Dan showed them the text but Marco didn't seem surprised. 'I'm telling you,' he said. 'She was like a woman possessed when I asked her about the ticket. I almost had to cover Mimi's ears!'

Dan looked at them all and took a deep breath. 'Marco, you might have some apologies to make.'

'What do you mean?' Marco shot Dan a look of alarm.

Dan put his hand in his pocket and took something out. He slapped it down on the table and waited for a reaction.

'Jesus Christ,' said Lorraine. 'Is it … is that …?'

Rita looked completely shocked. 'Fuck me!'

'Oh, my God,' said Marco, turning pale. 'Dan?'

Dan picked up the ticket and held it up for them to inspect. 'It was me. Guys, I'm so sorry. It was me all along.'

'I … I don't know what to say,' said Lorraine, close to tears. 'Why, Dan? Why did you take it?'

'You fuckin' bastard, Dan,' spat Rita. 'What did you think you were doing? How dare you rob our winnings like that! And to think I was jealous of you and Maggie, of your relationship, of how much everyone seemed to love you. I always imagined it must be brilliant to have a husband that everyone liked so much. How bloody *dare* you!' She put her head into her hands and began to sob.

Dan looked shocked by her outburst. 'Rita, I'm really, really sorry. I … I just didn't think. Lorraine, Marco, I want you to know I never meant to hurt anyone. It was just … it was just …'

'Let's all calm down for a minute,' said Marco, who looked as though he was also close to tears. 'Dan, I'm in shock here. This is so unlike you. Why don't you tell us what happened.'

'Well, there isn't much to tell really,' said Dan, his voice quivering. 'If you remember, I joined you all in the pub that night after the bingo. Maggie had put the slip of paper with the numbers on the table and everyone had thrown in their money. Nobody seemed to want to take charge of doing the numbers, so I picked it up and stuck it into my pocket before we left. I played the numbers the next day and the rest is history.'

Lorraine looked like she'd seen a ghost. 'Come on, Dan. You can do better than that. Why did you take it? Why did you pretend you knew nothing about it? God, you were even there on the night when we saw the numbers being called out! How come you didn't say something then? Did you immediately decide to try to keep all the money for yourself?'

'Yes,' said Rita, tears still spilling down her face. 'And more importantly, did *Maggie* know about this? Was it a conspiracy between the two of you?'

'Absolutely not!' said Dan, slapping his hand on the table. 'Maggie knew absolutely nothing about it. This was all my doing. She never knew I took the ticket to play the numbers and she certainly didn't know I'd been hiding it.'

'But, Dan, why?' asked Marco. 'Was it for the money? Did you really think it was worth deceiving all your friends to get your hands on the extra share of the winnings? Was two hundred thousand euro not good enough for you?'

Dan ran his hand through his mess of black hair and shook his head. 'I wish I could give you all a proper explanation, but I honestly can't. I don't know why I did it. I think it was partly because I thought that money would change us all. Maybe I thought we'd be better off without it.'

'Oh, for fuck's sake!' Rita was off ranting again. 'You can't expect us to believe that! You're saying that you took it out of the goodness of your heart because you thought we wouldn't be able to handle the money? That's the most ridiculous thing I ever heard in my life.'

'I'm inclined to agree with Rita,' Lorraine said, staring at Dan in disbelief. 'And even if it's true, you can't go around making judgements like that. That money belongs to all five of us – what gave you the right to decide we shouldn't have it?'

'I really don't know what else to say,' said Dan, not meeting their eyes. 'For now, why don't one of you take the ticket and put it into safe-keeping until we have a chance to cash it.'

'*We*? Until *we* have a chance to cash it?' Rita looked at him incredulously. 'After what you've done, do you really think you're entitled to a share of the money?'

'I know you're upset, Rita,' chimed in Marco. 'But no matter what he's done, he's still entitled to a share of the money. Well, at the very least, Maggie is. What's she going to think when she hears about all this?'

'I've rung her already,' said Dan. 'I'd been thinking about it all morning and as soon as I decided to tell you all, I rang her first. I was afraid that one of you would ring her or go down to her as soon as you heard. I wanted her to hear it from me first.'

'Ah, poor Maggie,' Lorraine said, shaking her head. 'How did she take it?'

Dan shifted uncomfortably in his chair. 'She was shocked, of course, but you know Maggie – always ready to give everyone the benefit of the doubt.' He looked pointedly at Rita.

Rita sniffed. 'Well if it's true and Maggie didn't know anything about it, then I feel sorry for her. She must feel awful to be married to a lying, scheming scumbag!'

'*Rita!*' Marco looked shocked. He'd really had his fill of

feisty women today. 'That's a bit harsh. Let's just concentrate on the fact that we have the ticket and we're all going to get our share of the money. If it's okay with everyone, I'll take the ticket home and lock it away until we decide when we're going to collect the winnings and who's going to go in.'

Dan shot Marco a grateful look. 'Listen, I know you're all as mad as hell and I know I deserve it, and I know I don't have the right to ask you, but, for Maggie's sake, can we deal with this when she's better? And you can say what you want about me, you can decide never to speak to me again, but please, please don't make Maggie suffer for this.'

'Of course we won't, Dan,' said Lorraine, rubbing his arm awkwardly. 'We'd never take it out on Maggie. And, look, the main thing is, we have the ticket now. We have all the time in the world for explanations at a later stage.'

'Right, I'm off,' said Rita, standing up suddenly. 'I'm not ready to do the gushy sympathy yet! I'm happy for you to hold on to the ticket, Marco. At least it will be in safe hands this time.'

Lorraine stood up too and wrapped her cardigan around her tightly. 'That's fine by me, too, Marco. Just make sure you put it somewhere safe.'

'I ... I really am so, so sorry, guys.' Dan followed all three of them out to the door. 'If it means anything, which it probably doesn't, I never would have tried to claim that money for myself. I ... I think I just panicked at the thought of us all being rich all of a sudden.'

Rita didn't stay around to hear any more but just stormed off out the door and towards her own house. Lorraine, still looking shocked, just nodded at Dan and headed off too. Marco paused before leaving. 'I want to be angry at you, too, Dan. I want to scream and shout at you and tell you what a mess you've made of everything. But, somehow, I believe you. I honestly believe you didn't do anything out of malice or bad intention. Let's leave it there for now and we'll talk about it again. For the moment, I have some bridges to mend!'

'Oh, God, I'm so sorry, Marco. I wish I'd told you before you accused Majella. No wonder the poor thing was so upset. Tell her I'm sorry, will you?'

'Dan, I have my own apologies to make without having to make yours too. I'll leave that to you! Right, I'm off. Tell Maggie I'll be in later.'

Dan closed the door and breathed a sigh of relief. Thank God that was over. It had been horrible. He'd hated seeing his friends' faces as he admitted to taking the ticket. He hoped that in time they might even be able to forgive him. But, if not, he'd just have to live with it. The main thing was that they didn't take any of this out on Maggie. His wife was his main priority and he'd do anything to protect her. Maggie was his life and he'd honestly thought he'd been about to lose her when she'd collapsed. Thankfully, they'd been given another chance and now with the lotto money, he'd make sure she wanted for nothing. He'd deal with the people of Enda's at a later stage but, for now, things were beginning to look up.

Maggie tossed restlessly in the lumpy hospital bed. She hadn't been able to eat her dinner after Dan's phone call and now she was failing miserably in her attempts to get to sleep. God, she couldn't have been more shocked when Dan told her about the ticket. She still couldn't take it in. He'd said that he couldn't really explain why he'd done it, which just seemed a bit odd. She was definitely missing something.

He'd be talking to the others around about now, and Maggie wondered how it was going. They'd be all as mad as hell. She could just picture the scene. Poor Dan! She should be angry but, for some reason, she just felt sorry for him. She hoped they weren't giving him too much of a hard time. They'd be entitled to really, but it was so out of character for Dan to have done something like that, even if his intentions were good. Hopefully, they'd concentrate on the fact that they had the ticket back at last and could plan to collect the winnings.

But something was niggling at the back of Maggie's mind. Something just didn't feel right. Again, she was trying to remember back to that night in the pub, but it was still all a blur. She did remember Dan coming to the pub because he'd had to hold on to her as they'd walked home. She'd been so dizzy that it had been an effort to put one foot in front of the other. It was possible that he had just grabbed up the slip of paper and the money before they'd left. But the whole idea of him hiding the ticket just didn't sit right with her. She'd have a chat with him when he came up in the afternoon and see if she could get to the bottom of it. For the moment, she needed to sleep. There was so much going on in her head that she felt worn out. She closed her eyes and offered up a prayer to her ma that everything would work out in the end.

CHAPTER 41

'It just doesn't ring true, Lorraine. I can't explain it, but I just don't think Dan is telling the truth.' Maggie was sitting up in the bed, chatting to Lorraine who'd just arrived. Dan had come in an hour before but had retreated to the coffee shop to let the two friends have a chat.

'But he has to be, Maggie. Hasn't he got the ticket and everything? What other explanation could there be?'

Maggie sighed. 'I honestly don't know. My head is spinning from thinking about it all.'

Lorraine looked concerned. 'Maggie, you'd want to mind yourself. There's no point in you worrying about things while you're in here. We all want you to get better so you need to do as the doctors say and stay away from stressful situations.'

'That's all very well and good, Lorraine, but I'm not exactly going looking for them, am I? The stressful situations seem to have been following me around lately!'

'Well, all the more reason to use this as an opportunity to rest. There'll be plenty of time to worry about everything else when you're home.'

'I know, I know. I'll get stuck into these magazines and

try not to think too much about it. You're a good friend, Lorraine. And I'm truly sorry for the whole ticket mess.'

'It's not your fault, Maggie. And Dan was very clear in explaining that you had nothing to do with it. It will all blow over in time anyway. At least he did the right thing in the end.'

'That's true,' said Maggie, nodding her head. 'But that's what makes this all seem so surreal. Dan is a good and decent man. He's always done the right thing. I still find it hard to believe he'd do something like this.'

'Well, look on the bright side,' said Lorraine, picking at the grapes on Maggie's bedside locker. 'At least we have the ticket now and very soon we'll all be two hundred thousand euro richer! Isn't that worth celebrating, rather than us wallowing?'

'That's true, Lorraine, that's true.' Maggie knew she should just stop trying to work out the hows and whys of the situation, but she just couldn't. She just wished that the cloud of fuzziness from that night would clear and give her some sort of clue about what really happened. She knew her husband inside out and, one thing was for sure, Dan wasn't telling the truth!

'What do you want now?' Majella asked, opening the door to Marco. 'Haven't you said enough for one day?'

Marco couldn't blame her for being snotty with him. 'I know you're annoyed with me, Majella, but please let me come in to explain.'

'I don't want to talk any more about it, Marco. There's enough shit going on in my own life without you adding to it. How dare you treat me the way you did today. So, no, you can't come in.'

She tried to close the door but Marco stuck his foot in to stop it. 'Please, Majella. I only want to apologise. There's been a development with the missing ticket and I'm sure you'll want to hear about it.'

Majella sighed and opened the door for Marco to come in. 'I wouldn't be too sure. I'm sick of talk about that damn ticket. There are more important things in life.'

'I know, I know,' Marco said, putting on his best sympathetic voice. 'But you have to admit, a lotto win is a pretty big thing too.'

Majella didn't offer tea or a drink but instead just stood and faced Marco in the kitchen. 'So what is it then? And make it quick.'

'I ... I just want to apologise for my appalling behaviour earlier. I was upset and angry about something else and I suppose I took it out on you.'

'So go on then, what's happened?' Majella sat down on a stool and indicated for Marco to do the same. 'What's caused this change of heart? You were so adamant earlier – or do you still think I took the ticket?'

Marco sat down, glad that at least she was talking to him. 'I know you didn't take the ticket, Majella. The culprit came forward today. I only wish he'd done it before I came shouting the odds to you!'

Majella's eyes widened. 'No way! Go on then – who was it?'

'It was Dan,' said Marco, shaking his head. 'Maggie's Dan. Can you believe it?'

'Dan O'Leary? No way! He's the last person I would have suspected. So go on, what happened?'

'Well, he called us all over to the house a while ago and said he had something to tell us.'

'Oh, that's right,' said Majella. 'I was rude to him, too. I'd just had the argument with you and I was in a foul mood. And I haven't forgiven you for that either, Marco. But go on for now.'

Well, at least she wasn't screaming at him like earlier. He relayed the events of the meeting to her and enjoyed how she hung on his every word.

'Well, thank God the ticket has turned up – but Dan? I still can't take it in. He's such a lovely guy. It just doesn't seem right.'

'I honestly thought you'd be a lot angrier,' said Marco, watching his neighbour carefully. 'I thought you'd be gunning for whoever took the ticket, especially since we ended up pinning the blame on you.'

Majella got up and went into the little kitchen. She filled the kettle with water as Marco watched and waited for her to say something. 'I used to place a lot of importance on money, Marco, but things have changed. Cuppa?'

'I'd love one, thanks.' Marco noticed the pained expression on Majella's face as she busied herself with the cups, waiting for the water to boil. 'So what's changed then?'

She popped teabags into the cups and poured in the freshly boiled water. She didn't speak until she'd brought the cups over to the counter and had sat back down beside Marco. 'A number of things have happened, Marco. And none of them good. Did you know that Chris had been made redundant from his job?'

Marco's jaw dropped. How could he not have known that about his neighbour? 'Jesus, Majella. I'm so sorry to hear about that. I had no idea.'

'Of course you didn't,' she said, generously. 'We decided not to tell anybody. Chris is proud, you know. It all happened so quickly – there was the threat there, but isn't there a threat in every place of employment at the moment with this bloody recession? We never actually thought he'd be let go. But one day a couple of months ago, they just called him in and told him the news. He was devastated.'

'I can imagine,' said Marco, patting her hand. 'But I still see him going out to work in a suit every day.'

'He's working in a DIY shop over in Swords. He's not one to sit and wallow, and he just got out there looking for anything he could get. It only pays a quarter of what he was earning in the insurance company, but we have to be thankful for small mercies.'

'Jesus! I don't know what to say. And there was me, coming over here this morning, ranting and raving. I'm so, so sorry, Majella.'

'It's okay, Marco. I suppose I can understand how it looked. But I've had so much on my mind that I didn't have the time or energy to think about the lost ticket. Yes, I was as annoyed and upset as any of you at first because that money would do an awful lot for us. And I probably would have continued to be annoyed about it if … if …'

Marco was alarmed when he saw a tear trickle down Majella's face. He grabbed a tissue from the box on the counter and wiped it gently away. 'If what, Majella?'

She took the tissue from Marco's hand and blew her nose. 'If I hadn't lost the baby!'

'What?' Marco was alarmed at this sudden turn of events. He was still taking in the fact that Chris had been made redundant, but now this!

'I was pregnant, Marco. Chris and I hadn't planned to have children for another year or two, but it just happened. And when it did, we were over the moon. It was the best news ever. There'd been so much doom and gloom from a financial point of view and then Chris had lost his job. A baby just seemed to be a gift from God.'

Marco got up off his stool and put his arms around Majella. In truth, he didn't know what to say to her. How awful.

'Everything seemed to be going well,' she continued, blowing her nose again. 'Until a few days ago. I started to bleed and went into the hospital to have it checked. They did a scan and told me that the baby was there, but they couldn't detect a heartbeat. I would have been almost three months gone. They sent me home to wait and, sure enough, I miscarried that night.'

'Oh, God, Majella. I don't know what to say.'

'I just crumbled, Marco. We'd got so used to the idea of becoming a little family that I just couldn't cope – I still can't.'

Marco shook his head. 'Here we were, all in a flap about the missing ticket when you were going through the most awful ordeal. So how are you now? And the spa weekend – did that help?'

'There was no spa weekend, Marco. There's always so much activity on this street – always someone calling to the door, and I really didn't feel like facing anyone. My mam suggested we go over and stay with her for a few days so she could look after me while Chris was in work.'

'Oh, God, and there we were thinking you were off having a good time.' Marco felt tears spilling down his own cheeks as he got up off his stool and wrapped his arms around his neighbour. 'There must be nothing worse than losing a baby.'

Majella wiped her eyes. 'That's for sure. Physically I'm still not great but that will get better – emotionally, I don't know whether I'll ever recover.'

'Well, we're all here for you, Majella. And I know it seems

cold talking about it, but the money should ease any financial pressures you have.'

'It will,' said Majella, nodding. 'And I'm sure we'll appreciate it in time. It's just hard to think positively about anything at the moment.'

'Oh, God,' said Marco, suddenly. 'I've just realised you probably don't know about Maggie.'

'What about Maggie? Jesus, don't say there's been more drama!'

'Now, I'll say firstly that she's okay and getting better but Maggie collapsed and was taken away by ambulance the other night.'

'What? Is she in hospital? What happened?'

'Yes, she's in the Mater but, as I said, she's up and about and already giving the nurses earache, so don't you be worried about her. She needs an operation on her gallbladder but apparently it can be done by keyhole surgery so she won't be too laid up. She'll be home soon enough so you can catch up with her then.'

'Well, we certainly can't say that Enda's is a boring place to live! For feck's sake! What else could possibly happen? And how about you, Marco? Any dramas to report?'

Marco opened his mouth and was about to launch into the whole Claude saga, but thought better of it. Majella didn't need to hear him wittering on about trivial stuff when she had so much going on in her own life. 'Not a thing, Majella. I'm just plodding on as usual – nothing to report at all.'

'Well, I'm glad someone is having a smooth run of things. Now, I don't want to be rude, but I've a million things to do here. Chris had to go straight in to work as soon as we were back this morning, and I've a ton of washing to do.'

Marco took his cue and stood up. 'I really am sorry, Majella

– for what you've been through and for how I treated you this morning. I should never have taken my bad mood out on you and I should never have jumped to conclusions.'

'It's okay, Marco,' said Majella, opening the front door. 'I think when bad things happen to us, it makes us more philosophical. I don't think I'll ever stress about the little things any more.'

'That's a good lesson to learn, but a hard way to learn it.' Marco put his two arms around Majella's neck and hugged her tightly. 'Come down to me any time you want a chat, okay? Don't bottle things up.'

'Thanks, Marco. I appreciate that. And the same goes for you. I really enjoy chatting to you and, just so you know, I wouldn't want to live anywhere except Enda's.'

Marco walked back down to his house with his head in a spin. God, he'd come away from Majella's with a lot more information than he'd bargained for. He'd thought he was going to shock her with revelations about the ticket, but all that had paled into insignificance when he'd heard what had been going on for her and Chris. God love her. God love them both. What a terrible few months they'd had.

If there was one thing he'd taken from their conversation, it was not to stress about the small, unimportant things. It had made him feel much more philosophical about Claude. He'd contact him at the weekend and see if he wanted to meet up. He wasn't ready to forgive him yet, and he didn't even know if Claude had any feelings for him at all, but he wanted to give him the chance to explain. He opened his front door and was met by an over-excited Mimi. He scooped her up in his arms and cuddled her. With all the madness, thank God for the uncomplicated love of his little cockapoo!

'It was me! Jesus Christ Almighty, Lorraine. It was bloody well me!'

Lorraine looked at her friend in shock. Maybe she was dreaming. They'd been chatting away when Maggie had started to nod off, so Lorraine had just sat beside her bed in affable silence. 'Maggie, are you okay? I think you were just having a dream.'

Maggie looked at her friend. 'No, Lorraine. I wasn't asleep, I've been thinking about what Dan said and trying to remember back to that night. I mean, it was me who took the ticket!'

'Now you're not making sense,' said Lorraine, alarmed that Maggie was getting so excited. 'Of course you didn't take the ticket.'

'Well not intentionally, I didn't. But it was me who took the slip home that night and me who did the numbers the next morning. I only have a fuzzy memory of it but that's what happened.'

'Jesus! Are you saying that Dan lied?' Lorraine was confused at the sudden turn of events and not at all sure that Maggie knew what she was talking about.

'That's exactly what I'm saying, Lorraine. Oh, God, I can't believe I haven't been able to think of it before now. But that night when we were in the pub after the bingo and the slip and the money were on the table, nobody seemed to want to take responsibility for it.'

'That's what Dan said, Maggie. But he said he took them and played the numbers.'

'He didn't,' said Maggie, her voice getting higher with every sentence. 'I remember now that I noticed a barman hovering, waiting to take the empties. I was afraid he'd snatch up the money, too, so I stuck the slip and the money into my cardigan pocket. Then shortly after, I thought I was going to be sick and everything just became a blur.'

'Are you serious, Maggie? Were you really the one to take the slip or are you just trying to protect Dan?' Lorraine was finding it hard to believe Maggie's story. It had been difficult enough to swallow the fact that Dan had taken the ticket, but now she didn't know what to believe.

'More like *he's* trying to protect *me*, Lorraine. I can't believe I forgot, but when I went down to the shop for milk the next morning, I found the slip in my pocket with the money so I played the numbers. I'd still had that bloody pain and I half thought I was going to faint on the way home.'

'Oh, my God,' said Lorraine, realising Maggie was telling the truth. 'That's unbelievable. So you reckon the ticket has been in your pocket all along?'

'That cardigan has been lying on a chair in my bedroom for weeks. The label says 'hand wash only', so I kept meaning to wash it. Dan must have picked it up because I asked him to put in some washing last night.'

'Jesus! He must have found the ticket and decided to take the blame himself. Did he not even ask you for an explanation?'

'Not a bit,' Maggie said, tears beginning to pour down her face. 'He just rang me and confessed it was him. He said he wanted me to know before he told you lot.'

'Amazing,' said Lorraine, shaking her head. 'There's not many who'd do something like that. He must love you so much, Maggie.'

'What's going on in here then?' said Dan, appearing at the door of the ward. 'Why are you crying, Maggie?'

Maggie looked at her husband through her tears. 'Dan, I think we need to call a meeting!'

CHAPTER 42

'So let me get this right,' said Marco. 'Maggie, you were the one who played the numbers and forgot all about it. Then Dan found the ticket in your pocket when he went to wash your cardigan and because he didn't want the blame to fall on you, he pretended it had been him all along.'

'That's about it, Marco.' Maggie looked at her husband, who was squirming in his chair. She'd insisted that he ring the others and get them to come up to the hospital as soon as possible, so that they could clear up this whole sorry mess. He'd been dead against it. He'd felt that it would be better to leave things as they were, with only Lorraine knowing the truth, but she'd been adamant.

Rita didn't look entirely convinced. 'But how come you didn't remember, Maggie? It seems unbelievable that with all the talk about the ticket, you just happened to forget such a huge thing.'

'I know it sounds unbelievable,' said Maggie, nodding her head in agreement. 'And I'd probably be suspicious if I were you. But I swear to you, I really didn't remember. I'd been feeling so sick around that time that everything was a bit of a blur. I have to admit that something has always niggled me about that night, but I honestly didn't imagine that it was the fact that I actually had the ticket myself!'

'Well, I believe you, Maggie,' said Majella, who'd been listening quietly to the story. 'I don't think for a minute that either you or Dan would ever set out to fool us or deceive us. I think we should all just thank God that the ticket has turned up and stop looking for explanations.'

'Here, here,' said Marco, clapping his hands. 'Surely the important thing is that the money will be ours now that we have the ticket. We'll all be two hundred thousand euro richer. Imagine what that money can do for us all.'

'You're right,' agreed Rita. 'It will be amazing. I can't even begin to imagine the peace of mind it will give me, knowing I won't have to scrape every penny together just to feed my children. It's bloody fantastic!'

'Are you okay, Maggie? You've gone very pale.' Lorraine jumped up from her chair and went to her friend. 'All this has probably been too much for you. We should really have waited until you were home and well before we had any discussions about it.'

'No, no, I'm fine, Lorraine. I'm just thinking of all the trouble I've caused. But I didn't mean to, honestly I didn't.' She began to cry, softly first and then, to everyone's alarm, big loud sobs came out. She couldn't help it. It was like a release of pressure. The fate of that bloody ticket had been playing on all their minds since the win, and now at last they could put it to rest.

'Ah don't cry, Maggie,' said Marco, grabbing her hand. 'Nobody blames you for it. We know you didn't mean to deceive us. Come on now – everything is going to be all right.'

'And I'm sorry for misleading you all too,' chimed in Dan, who'd been sitting quietly throughout the exchange.

'But when I found the ticket, I honestly didn't know what to do.'

'Out of curiosity,' said Rita, watching Dan carefully. 'Did it never cross your mind when you found the ticket that maybe Maggie *had* been hiding it from us all?'

'*Rita!*' said Majella, crossly. There's absolutely no need for that.'

'No, it's okay, Majella. I know where she's coming from. And the answer is no, not for a minute did I ever think Maggie had taken the ticket. I knew straight away that it had somehow been forgotten. Maggie doesn't have a dishonest or bad bone in her body and she'd never have done something like that.'

'Thanks, love. That means a lot.' Maggie blew her nose and for about the hundredth time today thanked her lucky stars for the gift that was her husband.

'And I'm sorry for how I reacted this morning,' said Rita, quietly. 'I said some awful things to you, Dan. It was only because I was so shocked and because I respect and admire the both of you so much.'

Dan stood up and Maggie noticed how there were tears glistening in his eyes. 'Right, from here on in, let's all stop being sorry! Life is good. My Maggie is going to be okay and we can all finally get our share of the money that's due to us. It's going to make a big difference to us all so let's be grateful for what we have.'

'Group hug,' said Marco, standing up and waiting for everyone to follow.

'Good idea!' said Lorraine and Majella in unison.

Rita, not one for open displays of emotion, shifted awkwardly on her chair. 'Well, I agree with everything you're saying but there's no need for—'

Marco wasn't having any of it and swept her up off the chair. They all moved over to the bed where they could include Maggie in the group hug.

'Hey, watch the patient,' she shouted, her head buried in a sea of bodies. But she was delighted. She'd always felt things would work out in the end. She'd never lost faith in Enda's and she never would. There was something special about it. Her mother had seen it and Maggie saw it too.

What did I tell you, Maggie. Never lose the faith!

'Thanks, Ma,' whispered Maggie, under her breath. 'Thanks for everything!'

CHAPTER 43

Wednesday, 21st September

Marco was carefully folding the shirts that had come in from a new designer that morning when the bell on the door tinkled, indicating a customer. He preferred to be kept busy as the day just dragged otherwise. The shop had been relatively quiet all morning so he was more than ready for some customers.

'Good morning! So what can I do for— oh, Felicity, hello. I didn't expect to see you today!' Marco looked in shock at his regular Friday customer and couldn't believe his eyes. Her usual sleek, bobbed auburn hair was frizzy from the rain and her face that was always perfectly made-up was bare. She looked about twenty years older.

'Come on, Marco, I haven't got time for pleasantries. I need you to come with me.'

He looked at his customer quizzically. She'd always fascinated him, but he'd never put her down as being loopy. 'What are you talking about, Felicity. I'm working. Where do you want me to go?'

Felicity looked panicked. 'Look, I'll explain on the way, but I need you to lock up the shop and get into the car with me.

I've parked up on the kerb outside and if you don't come with me now, I'll get towed away.'

'I'll tell you what,' said Marco, convinced that she was losing it. 'You go and find a parking spot for your car and I'll stick the kettle—'

'Marco! I'm not joking around here! My son is on the 15.45 flight to New York and his father and I are gutted. He won't listen to us but he might change his mind for you!'

Alarm bells started to ring in Marco's head, but he still couldn't quite figure out what Felicity was talking about. 'Felicity, I'm not sure … what … did you say? New York? Today? Jesus, you don't mean, you're not saying—'

'Yes, Marco, that's *exactly* what I'm saying! *Claude is my son.* I only put the pieces together last night. He always keeps his personal business very quiet. I knew he was seeing someone over here, but he didn't give much away. He was so upset yesterday that I finally got it out of him. When he told me your name and where you worked, I couldn't believe it.'

But Marco had tuned out of what she was saying and was looking at his watch. 'The 15.45 you say? And he's definitely going back to New York?'

'That's what I've been trying to tell you,' said Felicity, throwing her hands up in the air. 'He said that you were the reason he'd decided to stay in Ireland and now that you didn't want him, he may as well go back.'

'Oh, for fuck's sake – sorry, Felicity. The bloody fool. Why didn't he just come and talk to me before making such a big decision?'

'Well, if you get a move on, you can ask him yourself. I reckon we'll make it to the airport in half an hour from here. I'll drop you off at departures and with a bit of luck, you'll catch him before he goes through the gate.'

Marco was in a fluster. 'But surely we can ring him. I can—'

'His phone is off, Marco. The only option we have is to go ... *now!*'

Marco didn't need to think about it any more. 'Right, what are we waiting for then?' He grabbed his coat and switched off the lights. He turned the sign to 'closed' and after quickly setting the alarm, he hopped into the passenger seat of Felicity's BMW.

'So what makes you think he'll talk to me now?' asked Marco, as they negotiated the one-way streets around St Stephen's Green. 'We did have a pretty nasty row – maybe he won't want to see me at all.'

'Marco, he loves you, plain and simple. Claude was never really one to talk openly about his relationships – I don't know whether he thought we'd be shocked or something – but he really opened up last night. He sobbed his heart out and told me that you were the love of his life.'

Marco drew a breath when he heard those words. *The love of his life?* God, that was a big statement. It gave him a tingle to hear it but there were still a lot of unanswered questions. He pondered over her words for a few minutes. 'Did he tell you what happened, Felicity? Did he tell you he'd used me just to get information for his job?'

'Well, I don't know the ins and outs of it,' she said, dashing through an amber light on O'Connell Street and clutching the wheel in frustration as she came up against yet another red. 'But he did say that there'd been a huge misunderstanding.'

'But he even admitted to some stuff. How could it have been a misunderstanding if— Jesus, Felicity, watch out will you!' Marco was stamping his right foot on the floor as though he was controlling the brakes. Felicity was like a woman possessed, zooming through the streets and beeping pedestrians out of the way.

'Relax, Marco, will you. You want me to get you there in time, don't you?'

'Yes, but—'

'Well, let me do the driving! All I know is that Claude was asked by his producer to make a new documentary about the missing lotto ticket, which he disagreed with. But he felt he couldn't say no because he was looking for a reference from them. So he went ahead and did as they asked—'

'You see, that's what I was talking about. Why the bloody hell did he *have* to do it? Wasn't he going to leave the job anyway? All that upset for a reference.' Marco was furious and began to wonder if he should be bothering with the airport at all.

'Well, if you'd let me finish,' said Felicity, swinging left onto Gardiner Street, 'I was going to say that he went ahead and got some footage but destroyed the tapes afterwards!'

Marco paled. 'So he … he *destroyed* the tapes? Oh, God! That's what he was trying to tell me and I wouldn't listen. I'm such a bloody eejit. Why did I not just listen to him?'

'Well, if we get there on time, you'll have your chance.'

'*If* we do,' sighed Marco, eyeing a group of kids coming towards them. It would be just his luck if they got car-jacked or something. Luckily the lights changed to green and they were off again.

'So tell me, Marco. Do you feel as strongly about Claude as he does about you? I mean, I want him to stay here more than anything else in the world, but I also want him to be happy. It broke my heart to see him so hurt.'

Marco looked at Felicity and saw the concern and love for her son on her face. It was strange to be in this situation with her. She'd always been so guarded about her personal life and now it seemed he was part of it! 'Felicity, I'm so sorry for the upset I've caused. But honestly, I really do ... you know ...'

'You do what, Marco?' Felicity glanced at him.

Marco reddened at having to say the words. 'I love him. I really do. And I'm just praying to God that I get the chance to tell him.'

'Well, thank God for that,' said Felicity, smiling. 'And look, there's hardly any traffic here so fingers crossed we'll catch him.'

They drove in silence and Marco looked out the window at the familiar landmarks. He'd spent many happy Sundays around there, drinking in Quinn's pub before a match in Croke Park. With a bit of luck, he'd be able to bring Claude with him the next time.

He was relieved when they finally took the exit for the airport because although it was only 12.50 p.m., it was likely Claude would go through the gate early to have a look in the shops. And the only way he'd get through the gate to talk to him would be if he had a ticket. 'Come on, Felicity, put the foot down.'

'Almost there, Marco. It'll be all right.'

'I really hope so,' Marco said, holding on to the edge of his seat as Felicity swung around the bend. 'Do you think he's planning on going back for good?'

'Well, that's what he said last night. We'd been so happy the other day when he told us he was staying in Ireland. We were getting our boy back. He's an only child, you know, and it broke our hearts when he went off to America.'

'I can imagine,' said Marco, patting Felicity's knee awkwardly. 'Right, here we go, fingers crossed I'm not too late.' The new Terminal 2 building seemed to rise out of the ground like a spaceship as Felicity pulled up outside.

'Best of luck, Marco. I'll go and park and come in. If he's

already gone through, I'll even pay for a ticket so you can go through yourself and bring him back!'

'Thanks, Felicity,' he said, jumping out of the car. 'And thanks for all you've done. You're a very special mother indeed.'

Marco ran inside and looked around. He searched the sea of people to see if he could see Claude's face, but there was no sign of him. He ran to a screen and checked the details. The flight seemed to be on schedule so the likelihood was that he was gone through. Fuck it, fuck it, fuck it!

He did a quick sprint around the circuit of the departures area but to no avail. Felicity had offered to buy him a ticket so that he could go through to the gates, but was that taking things a step too far? She'd probably pay a fortune for a last-minute flight and there were no guarantees that Claude would even want to talk to him!

He leaned one shoulder on a wall to catch his breath and consider what his next move should be. His head was still in a spin and he wished he could think straight. All he knew was that he wanted to see Claude at that moment more than anything else in the world.

'*Marco*! What on earth are you doing here?'

Marco swung around and there he was, emerging from the gents, pushing a trolley of luggage in front of him. Claude! He could scarcely believe his luck.

'Claude, oh, Claude.' He was completely lost for words so he just grabbed him and hugged him tightly.

Claude didn't return the hug but instead pulled away. 'Why are you here, Marco? And how did you know where I was?'

Marco was shaking and very close to tears. 'It's a long story, but I've come for you. Oh, Claude, I'm so sorry about our argument. I really am. I know now that you weren't trying to use me. I know about you destroying those tapes.'

'My mother!' Claude shook his head and looked around, as though expecting Felicity to be peeping around the corner.

'Yes, it was your mother and I'll be forever grateful to her for coming to get me.'

Claude didn't seem convinced. 'But Marco, what do you want from me? What's changed? I always knew I'd done nothing wrong but I'm going back to New York because you didn't trust me. And not only that, but you didn't even give me a chance to explain.'

Marco was panicking now. What if Claude had his mind made up? What if he couldn't get him to stay? 'I know and I'm sorry, Claude. I did jump to conclusions. But there was a lot of other stuff going on as well with the ticket and Maggie and everything. And I probably wouldn't have taken it all so badly if I wasn't … if I wasn't—'

'Go on then, if you weren't what?' Claude's stare was still cold.

Marco looked down at the floor. 'If I wasn't so in love with you. There, I've said it.' He looked up and met Claude's eye. 'Claude, I'm completely in love with you. I probably was even before I met you in real life. You and me – we just fit. I can't really explain it, but we just feel right.'

Now it was Claude's turn to look at the floor. It seemed as if he was going to say something and then thought better of it. Marco began to cry softly. 'Well, say something, will you? I've just thrown my heart out on a plate in front of you and you're giving me the silent treatment. If you don't feel the same, just tell me now. I can take—'

Claude gave him his answer by pulling him into his arms and placing his lips on his. He kissed him long and hard, holding his face lovingly in his hands. Marco had to fight for breath when Claude eventually pulled away.

'Well, they do say actions speak louder than words,' Claude said, winking. 'Now, let's get out of here before I change my mind again!'

'Oh, Claude, I really am sorry about ... about everything,' said Marco, hardly believing that things were beginning to work out. 'I promise I'm going to make you happy. You won't regret your decision for even one moment.'

'Just make sure I don't,' Claude said, putting his arm around Marco as they pushed the trolley of luggage towards the exit.

Just then, Felicity appeared through the doors, puffing and panting and looking like she'd been dragged through a hedge backwards! 'Oh, he found you, love,' she said, grabbing her son and hugging him tightly. 'So am I taking you home?'

'You certainly are, Mam. And have you room for one more for dinner?'

'Always,' said Felicity, beaming, as she grabbed the trolley and led the way out of the airport towards the car park.

'And for the record,' said Claude, stopping suddenly and turning to Marco. 'I'm completely and totally in love with you, too. I was definitely going to New York, but I think I would have come back. I couldn't have stayed away – I love you far too much.'

A lump in Marco's throat stopped him from replying but instead he took Claude's hand as they followed Felicity outside. The rain that had been pelting down all day suddenly stopped and the clouds parted.

'Look, a rainbow!' said Claude, pointing up to the sky. 'My life has suddenly become full of colour!'

Marco squeezed his hand. 'And I think I've just found the pot of gold at the end!'

THE END

ACKNOWLEDGEMENTS

I keep expecting somebody to wake me up and tell me that the last year has just been a dream. Honestly, how did it happen that I'm already writing my acknowledgments for Book Two? I still haven't got over the shock (good shock, of course!) of seeing *Any Dream Will Do* in the shops and now *The Terrace* is joining it on the shelves. It really is a dream come true and I have so many people to thank for making it happen.

Now you'll have to excuse me while I go into mush mode for a moment. It doesn't happen very often, but I think it's necessary on this occasion. I've been married to my husband, Paddy, for eighteen years and it's just not enough to say he's one in a million. He irons, cooks, cleans, shops (and no ladies, you're not having him!) but the most important thing is he's my rock. When I'm running around like a headless chicken, bemoaning the fact that I can't split myself in two or magic up a third hand, he'll sit me down, make me a cup of tea and listen to my grumbles. Somehow the world always seems brighter when I see it through his eyes. Also, he's six foot five which means it's absolutely vital I keep my wardrobe full of the highest heels possible – just so he doesn't feel odd! So thank you for it all, Paddy, and I love you loads.

Those of you who know me, or follow me on Twitter, will know how much I talk about my four children. Because of them, my life is hectic, exciting, manic, fabulous, crazy, unpredictable and the best life I could ask for. They make me mad, then make me laugh. They make me stressed, then bring me a cup of tea. At times, they break my heart but, without a doubt, they show me what pure love is. If I was sitting in a room, chatting to you all now, I'd be bringing out the photo album but for now, just imagine the most beautiful children – Eoin, Roisin, Enya and Conor – and let me tell you how much I love them.

I've dedicated this book to my parents, Paddy and Aileen Chaney, because, without their love and support, I wouldn't be where I am now. I grew up in the happiest house imaginable and they always taught me to follow my dreams. They instilled in me the belief that the world is my oyster and that I should always believe in myself.

Mam and Dad, thanks for forty-three years of unconditional love and I love you very much. Also, I apologise for anything of a sexual nature in this book that no parent should have to read from their children!

I want to thank my brother, Gerry Chaney, and his wife, Denyse, for all their support. Having grown up with just one brother and no sisters, I feel very lucky for Gerry to have become one of my best friends and Denyse to be the sister I never had. I also want to thank my lovely in-laws for their continued support, especially my wonderful mother-in-law, Mary.

I owe a huge thanks to my lovely agent, Sheila Crowley, from Curtis Brown Books, who believed in me from the beginning and never had any doubt that she'd see my books on the shelves some day. Thank you, Sheila, for your continued support and friendship. Thank you to my fabulous editor, Ciara Doorley from Hachette Ireland, who I'm convinced has a secret magic wand which she uses to add sparkle to my books. Thanks to Joanna for her endless patience and eternal smile, Ruth for putting up with me in the car for hours on end and telling people I'm wonderful, and to Breda, Margaret, Jim and the rest of the brilliant team at Hachette Ireland.

When I'm writing, I tend to go into my own little world and sometimes forget about friends. Thanks to my ever-patient friends, Bernie and Dermot Winston, Lorraine Hamm, Angie Pierce and Sinead Webb, for understanding that I haven't completely abandoned them and for being ready with a glass of wine when I finally come up for air. Thanks to Vanessa O'Loughlin for always being at the other end of the phone for advice and support. Huge thanks to two of my newest and best friends, Niamh O'Connor and Mel Sherratt, for allowing me to bend their ears constantly with plot ideas, and for being there to talk me around when I hit a wall.

Did I mention Twitter yet? No? Well I couldn't let this opportunity go by without talking about my favourite virtual room. Rarely a day goes by without me paying a visit to the Twitterverse. When I take a tea break now, I don't go watching recorded episodes of *Corrie* like I used to, I hop on to Twitter to see who's around. I've made so many friends there, a lot of whom I can now call 'real-life' friends. A special mention has to go to the girlies – Jane, Barbara, Hazel G, Hazel L,

Eleanor, Denise, Debbie, Ruth and any I've forgotten to mention – for keeping me sane with breakfasts in Avoca. A book will come of those breakfasts yet! Also a special thanks to my writing hero, Marian Keyes, a new tweeter, who makes me howl with laughter every day.

Thanks to Jim Sheridan for his help and advice and for the endless laughs on Twitter. Thanks to Judy Cronin who helped me with some research for *Any Dream Will Do* and apologies for omitting her name in those acknowledgments. Thanks to Eleanor O'Reilly in the National Lottery headquarters for her help and to Sandra in my local Eurospar in Ballyowen Castle in Lucan. Thanks to Grace Lombard for her help and advice and for delivering it with tea and cake!

That brings me nicely on to my neighbours. Firstly, I have to say, *The Terrace* is completely fictional and none of the characters are based on anybody I know in real life. Having said that, the idea of such a close-knit neighbourhood is probably born from living on such a wonderful street. My neighbours are also my friends and we really look out for each other. I'd like to thank each and every one of them for their friendship and I hope we'll all still be going out partying when we're on our Zimmer frames!

Thanks to all the school mammies and daddies who stand with my children when I arrive at the school late, having fallen asleep with my head on the keyboard and for collecting them when I've run out of diesel on the motorway!

And lastly to you, my dear readers, thank you, thank you, thank you! I'm grateful beyond words that you've taken the time to buy and read my books. Without you, this dream wouldn't be possible and I just wish I could thank each and every one of you personally. If you do want to chat to me, you can find me on Twitter at @mduffywriter or you can email me via www.mariaduffy.ie. I love to hear from readers so don't be shy! I hope I can continue to make you smile with my books and I wish you all the best that life can bring.

Maria x